"Set in a time made thick with societal Vetsch's *Millstone of Doubt* weaves a class the new. An artfully told story that will have you wondering at the outcome until the final pages are read."

—Ruth Logan Herne, *USA Today* best-selling author

"I've been eagerly awaiting *Millstone of Doubt* ever since I read the first book in this series. This novel proved every bit as riveting, with characters I'd already come to know and love. A diverse cast offers endless wit and fascinating, well-rounded perspectives, and intrigues that are layered and textured. It's the perfect combination for a fully satisfying mystery. I can't wait to read the next one!"

—Jocelyn Green, Christy Award–winning author of *Drawn by the Current*

"*Millstone of Doubt* is a romantic Regency mystery, beautifully threaded with God's grace. I am sure fans of the first book in this series will revel in the deepening relationship between Daniel Swann and Juliette Thorndike."

—Alissa Baxter, author of *The Viscount's Lady Novelist*

"*Millstone of Doubt* captivated me from the first sentence and kept me guessing the entire novel. Suspense and intrigue held me on the edge of my seat, suspecting various red herring characters of their part in the murder. I laughed over Lady Juliette's predicaments as the elegant but feisty heroine developed her craft spying for the crown. The dashing and intelligent Bow Street runner, Daniel Swann, comes to life as the hero with his hidden insecurities and quirks.

Millstone of Doubt weaves an artful blend of the opulent splendor of the aristocracy and the grit and sweat of the working classes, and the underlying current of tension between the two sustains throughout the story. Erica Vetsch is the master of all things Regency. Her keen eye for historical detail, rhetoric, and knowledge of people and customs place readers inside a delightful era of history."

—Lorri Dudley, author of *The Duke's Refuge* and the Leeward Islands series

Millstone
of Doubt

THORNDIKE & SWANN

REGENCY MYSTERIES

Millstone *of Doubt*

ERICA VETSCH

KREGEL
PUBLICATIONS

Millstone of Doubt
© 2022 by Erica Vetsch

Published by Kregel Publications, a division of Kregel Inc., 2450 Oak Industrial Dr. NE, Grand Rapids, MI 49505. www.kregel.com.

Published in association with the Books & Such Literary Management, 52 Mission Circle, Suite 122, PMB 170, Santa Rosa, CA 95409-5370, www.books andsuch.com.

The persons and events portrayed in this work are the creations of the author, and any resemblance to persons living or dead is purely coincidental.

Library of Congress Cataloging-in-Publication Data
Names: Vetsch, Erica, author.
Title: Millstone of doubt / Erica Vetsch.
Description: Grand Rapids, MI : Kregel Publications, [2022] | Series: Thorndike & Swann regency mysteries
Identifiers: LCCN 2022017622 (print) | LCCN 2022017623 (ebook) | ISBN 9780825447143 (paperback) | ISBN 9780825469145 (kindle edition) | ISBN 9780825477614 (epub)
Subjects: LCGFT: Mystery fiction. | Novels.
Classification: LCC PS3622.E886 M55 2022 (print) | LCC PS3622.E886 (ebook) | DDC 813/.6--dc23
LC record available at https://lccn.loc.gov/2022017622
LC ebook record available at https://lccn.loc.gov/2022017623

ISBN 978-0-8254-4714-3, print
ISBN 978-0-8254-7761-4, epub
ISBN 978-0-8254-6914-5, Kindle

Printed in the United States of America
22 23 24 25 26 27 28 29 30 31 / 5 4 3 2 1

To Julie Klassen and Michelle Griep. You are both shining examples of what friendship should be.

To all the members of the Inspirational Regency Readers group on Facebook. You are so appreciated!

And to Peter, always, with my love.

Chapter 1

Thorndike House
London
March 1, 1816

THE PROBLEM WITH CONCEALING A weapon beneath a day dress at a social gathering became all too apparent to Lady Juliette Thorndike the moment she sat beside the Dowager Duchess of Haverly. Juliette had only worn the pistol because, following her abduction last month, Uncle Bertie had insisted she never again go anywhere unarmed. Though she couldn't think of a single reason she would need a weapon at a small party hosted in her parents' home, she had decided to humor him. And now here she was, less than a half hour into that party, and the strap holding the pistol against her thigh had shifted and loosened, the gun parting company with her leg.

At least she hadn't been standing when the defection occurred, but now what?

A flutter of panic arrested her breathing. She imagined herself rising, the gun clattering to the floor, and the entire guest list for the Venetian breakfast gasping in horror. The dowager would first stare and then glare, and Uncle Bertie would roll his eyes and issue a statement forthwith that she was an embarrassment and completely untrainable. As her primary instructor in the art of spy craft—as well as the possessor of a dry, sharp wit—he would not let such a faux pas pass without censure.

Not to mention what her parents might say. The Earl and Countess of Thorndike had tailored the guest list especially to bring certain people into countenance with one another, to gauge reactions and elicit information without the subjects being aware they were under study by several agents of the Crown. If Juliette caused a ruction, today's mission would be disrupted.

Juliette gripped her fingers in her lap. She couldn't exactly hike her skirts and apprehend the fugitive weapon. How was she to rectify the situation?

"It's a lovely party. Though with your mother as hostess, I would expect no less." The dowager sipped her tea. "Do you think Duke Heinrich von Lowe will remain in England for the rest of the Season? It has been pleasant having him at these social functions. He lends such a continental flair to the gatherings."

Juliette nodded, barely taking in the dowager's words while inching her hand alongside her leg, hoping to pin the pistol with her palm. At least the firearm was encased in a holster. Her only prayer was that she wouldn't accidentally fire the gun, piercing either herself or the velvet upholstery of her mother's settee. But the satin of her dress worked against her, sliding and slipping, failing to give purchase.

Twenty-five guests filled the drawing room of her parents' London townhouse, nibbling hors d'oeuvres and chatting. Midday sun slanted through the tall windows, and on one of the sofas, Juliette's mother held court with the guest of honor, Duke Heinrich von Lowe of Brandenburg.

Her mother was exquisite, her black hair coiffed in the latest style and her dress as fashionable as tomorrow. Crystals glittered along the neckline of her blue gown, catching the light and winking. She leaned in to hear something the duke said and then she laughed, causing heads to turn.

The duke's military dress, complete with sash and medals, made him noticeable in the group, as did his carefully parted blond hair. Juliette had met him only last month at her debut ball, but they had attended several functions together, and she had found him courteous and interesting. He was a favorite of hostesses throughout the *ton* and had accepted many invitations.

His gaze met hers, and he inclined his head. He'd paid considerable attention to her recently, and the look in his eyes now was intent and ardent. Her throat closed a fraction, and she looked away. His interest flattered but she didn't take it seriously. They barely knew each other, and rumor had it he would return to Germany soon. And hadn't she promised herself that during this, her first Season out in London society, she would not succumb to the attentions of any man? She wished only to reacquaint herself with her parents and find her way in her post-boarding-school life.

Not to mention assimilating everything she'd learned about her family and her history over the last few weeks and embarking on this new journey as a fledgling agent for the Crown.

Praying her face did not give away her discomfiture—both at the duke's interest and at the fact she still had not secured the infernal pistol—she walked her fingers along her leg. To her horror, she brushed the butt of the gun, inching it toward the edge of the settee. She stiffened, yanking her hand back for fear of sending it over.

But might that be the best course of action? The settee rested atop a thick Axminster carpet. If she could ease the gun over the edge, perhaps she could cough to cover the thump it would make and then kick it under the sofa to retrieve later.

The dowager prattled on, oblivious to Juliette's plight. "I am ready for this chilly weather to break. I'm anticipating a trip to the seashore to visit my daughter, the Countess of Rothwell, this spring, and I hate to travel in the cold. It's bad enough coming down from Oxfordshire for the Season in the dead of winter, but to have the frost linger this far into the spring is unbearable."

The dowager was one of those ladies who was quite content to have observers rather than participants in any conversation she held. Juliette smothered a smile and nodded, which was all the encouragement the dowager needed to continue.

Juliette's fingers approached the butt of the gun again through her pale-pink gown. She drew in a breath and pushed.

She let out a cough she hoped would disguise the impact. But rather than thudding to the floor, the weapon didn't budge. A tug pulled along the back of her thigh. She was sitting on the strap she had used to bind the holster to her leg.

Botheration. She couldn't move it up, and she couldn't move it down. At least she no longer needed to worry about the gun crashing to the floor before she was ready, but then again, she had no way of stopping it from doing so when she was forced to rise. She shoved again, just to make sure she couldn't move the thing without being obvious, but she bumped the dowager's elbow slightly.

"What are you doing?" The dowager pinned her with a stare. "You're jerking as if you've contracted Saint Vitus' dance. Sit still, child."

Juliette stopped wriggling, the pistol just inches from where she could secure it. "I am sorry." Her words were forced through a clenched-teeth smile. Uncle Bertie glanced her way, and she wanted to melt into the floor. He missed nothing, and somehow she knew he was aware of her exact predicament. He raised his brows in a mocking query, a smile touching his lips, and she glared at him. He was enjoying her discomfiture altogether too much.

Mr. Pultney, the family butler, unwittingly came to her rescue by appearing at the drawing room door. "Breakfast is served."

The guests deposited their small plates on the nearest flat surfaces and drifted toward the hall. Juliette remained seated even when the Duke of Haverly came over to assist his mother to her feet.

"Lady Juliette, you're looking quite fetching today." The duke, handsome and well-built, smoothed his long hair back into the queue at his nape.

Juliette always felt safer when the Duke of Haverly was about. He was not only capable and intelligent, but he was now the director of the agency, her parents' and Bertie's supervisor. And he had a lovely wife, Charlotte, who was also at the party and with whom he was clearly besotted.

"Are you enjoying your debut Season?" he asked.

"Yes, Your Grace, especially since my parents were able to rejoin me here in London."

The dowager adjusted the lace at her cuffs and leaned on her cane. "So unfortunate they had to be away when you arrived home from finishing school. Still, there it is. Noblesse oblige. When the needs of the estate call, one must go." She looked down at Juliette, her gray curls clustered beside her cheeks. "Aren't you coming?"

"Please, go ahead. I'll just be a moment."

The dowager sniffed. "Waiting for someone special to escort you? Of course you are. Come, Marcus." She put her hand through her son's arm, a calculating gleam in her eyes. "These girls today. So canny."

Heat charged into Juliette's cheeks as the duke, leading his mother away, glanced over his shoulder. The dowager thought she was setting her cap for someone in particular? Looking for an escort?

As if she would. This was her year of freedom, of enjoying herself and not worrying about flirting with men or finding a husband. And at the moment, her only concern was getting a gun out of her skirts.

The moment both Haverly backs were turned, Juliette raised her leg, dislodged the strap holding the holster, and let it fall to the carpet with a soft thump.

"Lady Juliette."

Her chin jerked up. Duke Heinrich.

Frantically searching with her slipper, she found the pistol and slid it across the carpet, nudging it beneath the settee, hoping her hem hid the movement. She barely avoided puffing her cheeks out in a huge sigh as she disguised the weapon.

"Duke Heinrich, I hope you are enjoying yourself?"

"Very much. Your mother has given permission for me to take you into the dining room." Duke Heinrich offered his hand.

Behind him, near the door, Juliette's parents, the Earl and Countess of Thorndike, waited arm in arm, clearly as besotted as the Duke of Haverly and his wife, though they had been married years longer. A warmth that held a hint of longing surrounded Juliette's heart.

Juliette took the duke's hand, rising and smoothing her skirts. She felt behind her with her foot once more to ensure the gun was out of sight, then rested her fingers on his arm. "Thank you, sir."

As they entered the hall, a footman opened the front door, allowing a brisk breeze to scurry into the room. Juliette turned, and her breath caught.

Don't be ridiculous. You knew he was invited today. And for pity's sake, don't blush. He'll think you a silly chit.

Though she scolded herself, she felt a thrill race along her collarbones. Ever since they had worked together last month, first at odds and then so closely in the matter of the stolen artwork, Mr. Daniel Swann had never been far from her thoughts.

Which was absurd. He was a detective and a colleague, but she was a lady of the *ton*. There were expectations she must fulfill. Not that she was a snob. Of course not. It was just that while their professional lives might intersect, their personal lives lay far apart.

None of which kept her from acknowledging that Daniel Swann was a fine-looking man. He dressed very well in clothes a dandy would envy, while keen intelligence shone from his eyes, intriguing and unsettling her.

He had played a significant role in rescuing her from kidnappers too. Brave and daring. She would not be human if such heroism didn't attract her attention.

Duke Heinrich paused to greet the detective. "Herr Swann, you are joining us today?"

Juliette couldn't tell if the duke was pleased or surprised or both. It was unusual to have someone of Daniel's stripe as an invited guest at a society gathering, but then again, her parents were known for bringing eclectic groups together.

"Or is it that there is something amiss? A crime perhaps?" The duke smiled as if jesting, but questions lingered in his pale-blue eyes.

"Your Grace." Daniel nodded. "Lady Juliette." He bowed, handing his cloak and hat to the footman. "I have been invited by the earl and countess. A thank-you, I believe, for services rendered."

"Well deserved." The duke's hand tightened over Juliette's on his arm. "Not only at the return of all that stolen artwork, but when those men kidnapped Lady Juliette . . ." He shook his head. "You were most brave in recovering her, and I thank you sincerely."

Daniel's eyes darted from the duke to Juliette, and his brows came down. Juliette flushed. Did Daniel, too, hear the proprietary tone in the duke's voice?

Agatha Montgomery, Juliette's best friend, hurried toward them from the dining room. "Jules, I've been hoping for a moment alone with you—" She skidded to a halt, blinking. "I beg your pardon. I didn't realize you were busy." Shifting her weight, she twisted her fingers together, biting her lip.

Juliette could not ignore her imploring look. Clearly she had something of import to share, though with Agatha, everything was important and nothing trivial. At least it would give Juliette an excuse to escape Duke Heinrich's attentions for a moment—and Daniel's presence too—until she could compose herself properly.

"Gentlemen, if you will excuse us?" She stepped back. "Agatha, perhaps we can move into the salon?"

As she linked arms with her friend, Uncle Bertie appeared in the dining room doorway. He jerked his chin toward Daniel and beckoned. "Ah, good, you're here. Juliette, are you coming?"

"Please, go in without us. I need a word with Agatha." *And an opportunity to retrieve my pistol before it is discovered.*

Agatha all but bolted into the drawing room, spinning on her toes to face Juliette. "You'll never guess."

"What is it?" Juliette sneaked a glance at the settee, noting that the tip of the holster protruded from beneath the edge.

"Alonzo proposed. He actually proposed." Agatha bounced, clapping her hands, color riding her cheeks and happiness sparkling from her eyes. "I'm getting married."

Juliette dropped to the settee, her mouth agape. "What? When?" The couple had barely known each other a month. Was that long enough to know if you wanted to marry someone?

"He asked Father's permission. Alonzo told me Father jested about someone finally taking me off his hands, but I think he's very pleased. A viscount, heir to an earldom. For me. Can you believe it?"

Juliette pulled herself together, knowing that her misgivings and startlement would rub the bloom off the moment for Agatha. She leapt up and grabbed her friend's hands, squeezing them before drawing her into a hug. "Congratulations. I had no idea it was becoming so serious between the two of you. You two haven't known each other very long. Are you in love with him?"

Love wasn't strictly necessary for marriages these days—especially ones as advantageous as this one would be, making Agatha a viscountess and eventually a countess. But Juliette and Agatha had spent long hours after lamps were extinguished, lying in their dormitory beds and declaring they would never marry for less than true love.

Agatha's blush deepened, and she ducked her chin. "I do. I love him very much, and he says he loves me."

Juliette squeezed Agatha's upper arms. "That's all that matters, then. Have you chosen a date?"

"Oh, goodness no. Since we *have* known each other such a short time, Father has insisted upon a longish betrothal, perhaps waiting until autumn or even Christmastime to wed. Alonzo would like us to be married at his family's country estate since his grandfather is frail and cannot travel. Doesn't that sound lovely? A church wedding at a country estate?" Agatha's eyes took on a far-off look, as if she could see herself in nuptial finery with her groom at her side.

"Lovely indeed." Juliette was so distracted by news of the engagement she forgot herself, reached down, retrieved her pistol, and wrapped the strap around the holster absentmindedly.

"What is that?" Agatha asked.

Juliette glanced down, mortification washing over her. She barely resisted tossing the gun away from herself. "I believe it is a little jest planted by Uncle Bertie. He has hinted that if I am going to be kidnapped with any frequency, perhaps he should stash weapons about the house. Do not worry—it isn't loaded." She silently begged God's forgiveness for the lie. The gun certainly *was* loaded. "Let's go into the dining room before someone comes in search of us. I cannot wait for you to announce your news."

"Your uncle has a peculiar sense of humor. As to the announcement, that will happen tomorrow night at the party. Father wants to tell everyone himself." Agatha's brows fell. "He was supposed to be here this afternoon though. He went to the Hammersmith Mill, but he was coming here straight after, and he's late. Again. Why must his work always take precedence over other things? Me in particular? He'll probably arrive late to my wedding."

"I'm sure he'll come soon. You know how men can be, losing track of time when they're working." Juliette took the pistol with her to the dining room. Passing a potted fern on a plinth in the hall, she tucked the gun into the fronds for retrieval later.

Uncle Bertie would not count that she had fulfilled her task of remaining armed at all times, but sometimes one had to improvise.

Daniel found himself seated too close to the outspoken Jasper Finch and much too far away from Lady Juliette at the Venetian breakfast. Though breakfast was a bit of a misnomer. It was the middle of the afternoon. Why couldn't his hosts just say they'd invited him for luncheon, like normal people?

"The Luddites were right to be afraid those machines would be problematic. Look at what's happening to our factories and industries." Jasper Finch punctuated every word with his fork, poking the air. "Jobs gone, people thrown out of work by this automation and mechanization. First it was the textile industry, and now it's milling. Mark my words—this new trend will bring about an economic crisis. The common man will not stand for being thrown out of work."

"Why don't they find other work to do?" a man opposite asked.

"Other work? If you've spent your entire life, from boyhood apprenticeship to adulthood, learning and perfecting your trade, what else are you supposed to do with your skills when your employer tells you

you're no longer wanted? There are weavers and embroiderers and millers and rope makers and sail makers and more being shoved out of their way of life in droves, without so much as a fare-thee-well."

Poke, poke, poke with the silver tines.

"But it's progress," the same guest said. "That has to be good for the country, does it not?"

"Progress? To impoverish thousands in order to make a few men rich? I think you and I differ on what should be classified as progress."

Finch droned on, but Daniel allowed his mind to turn to other things.

First to Lady Juliette. She looked lovely as always, her dark hair and eyes shining. Composed, a smile on her heart-shaped face as she listened to Duke Heinrich von Lowe, who bent to whisper something to her.

An odd feeling twisted in Daniel's gut as he acknowledged how well they looked together. The duke was masculine, handsome, and courteous—and, as much as Daniel wanted to dislike him, friendly as well. Several times, he and the duke had met early in the day to ride in Hyde Park. Only a few weeks ago the duke had purchased a horse Daniel had been hired to sell, and lately the duke enjoyed taking the animal for brisk gallops in the deserted park at dawn. After the rides, he invited Daniel to his lodgings for breakfast and conversation.

Yes, as much as Daniel wanted to dislike the duke for his obvious interest in Lady Juliette, he couldn't.

The man was his friend.

Shrugging off those conflicting thoughts, he turned to the other item preying upon his mind.

He'd received a summons to the lawyers' office. An appointment set for the following week, no doubt to wrap up the guardianship. His twenty-fifth birthday loomed, three weeks away, at which time his mysterious patron would no longer support him. An anxious feeling in his chest warred with elation at the thought of finally being free. No more obligation to do as his patron expected. No more errands and tasks handed down through the offices of Coles, Franks & Moody by a faceless, nameless entity who expected total obedience in exchange for his financial and influential aid.

But also no more power moving in the shadows for Daniel's benefit. No more quarterly allowance, no more fine clothing appearing from merchants on a regular basis. Daniel would have to survive on his wits and his salary from the Bow Street Magistrate's Court.

A niggle of doubt burrowed into his chest. What if, after all his chafing against the restraints of his guardianship, he found he could not make a success of his life without it? What if, without the weight of his unknown patron moving behind the scenes, Sir Michael Biddle, Daniel's supervisor, found a way to terminate his employment at Bow Street and he was forced to find another way to support himself?

Rubbish. Stop cowering. You have a tidy sum laid by after all the reward money pressed upon you when you returned that stolen artwork. And you're not without skills and education. And you do *have another job, even if you have no idea what it entails or if you'll be a success at it. Nor what being an agent for the Crown pays. You failed to discuss the matter when you were recruited.*

He looked down the table to where Sir Bertrand Thorndike conversed with the Duchess of Haverly. The duchess's husband, Marcus Haverly, was Daniel's new part-time employer, though they had yet to set terms and expectations. He had supposed his invitation to this luncheon was in part to acquaint him with the new tasks he'd be asked to undertake.

"Don't you agree?" Finch waved his fork near Daniel's face, and he jerked.

"Your pardon?"

"I say, you *were* woolgathering, weren't you? I asked if you agreed. Mill owners are the latest ogres of the workforce, automating their mills to the point where honest men cannot make a living." The budding anarchist leaned back, dropping his fork to his plate with a clatter that drew the attention of the rest of the party. "I had hoped to encounter one such mill owner here and confront him. Where is the *good . . .*" He trod heavily on the word, coating it with sarcasm. "Mr. Montgomery? Was he afraid to face me?"

Lord Thorndike raised his brows, his expression bemused. "I am interested in your views, Mr. Finch, and I had hoped to bring you and Garfield Montgomery together to discuss your differences, but perhaps we can save that for later, when the ladies have retired to the conservatory? I'm sure the gentlemen will find the conversation most stimulating once we are alone." He signaled the footmen to begin clearing plates for the next course. "Are you aware that you are seated beside one of London's finest? Mr. Daniel Swann of the Bow Street Magistrate's Court. Mr. Swann is an investigator."

Finch jerked as if someone had kicked him in the knee beneath the damask tablecloth. He raised his serviette and dabbed his lips. "A runner? Here?" The incredulity in his voice did Daniel no service. "Whatever for?"

From the looks of those around the table, most of the guests wondered the same thing. Brows raised or lowered according to their dispositions, Daniel supposed. He could almost feel the drawing aside of skirts.

The Dowager Duchess of Haverly, seated near the Countess of Thorndike, sniffed—and her sniff could be heard across the channel. "I knew you had quite an eclectic taste in guests at your events, Lady Thorndike, but really, a rabble-rouser and a policeman? What's next? Blacksmiths and stevedores?"

"We've never had a blacksmith to luncheon before, have we, my dear?" the earl asked his wife. "Poets, artists, policemen, thespians, and activists, but no blacksmiths. I shall have to make inquiries. I should think a stevedore or blacksmith would have an interesting perspective to share."

The dowager gaped like a trout before snapping her jaws shut. A gleam of mischief lit the earl's eyes, knowing he'd provoked the old bird.

Lady Juliette didn't seem to be abashed, smiling from one parent to another. The earl and countess were known as broad-minded and unconcerned about class distinctions. Perhaps their work behind the scenes of society led them to see the world differently.

The earl bent a benevolent smile on his daughter.

A twinge of loss plucked at Daniel. Lady Juliette had an enviable relationship with her parents, something he had never known. His own father was a mystery his mother had refused to divulge.

He casually looked toward the angled screen in the corner, separating the formal dining room from the servants' area. His mother was the housekeeper in this very home. They hadn't spoken in more than a dozen years, and Daniel didn't know if they ever would. After all, she had gotten rid of him at the earliest opportunity and gone on with her life as if he had never existed. And he had forged his own way without her help. They were strangers to each other.

"I have to agree with the dowager. It is most unusual to have such . . . ordinary people at a society luncheon." Viscount Coatsworth smoothed his hand down his waistcoat. "It seems the policeman turns up at many of these functions. Almost as if he wishes he were one of us."

Heat built along Daniel's collar. He'd managed to get crossways with the viscount upon their first meeting, and clearly Coatsworth had not forgotten. He never missed an opportunity to put Daniel in his place.

"You never answered my question, Swann." Finch spoke into the silence. "Do you agree that sometimes violence is necessary when all other avenues have been exhausted?" He looked squarely at Daniel, a challenge in his eyes. "Since you're a policeman, you must be used to violence. You don't carry a truncheon just for appearance's sake."

Daniel clenched his fists on his thighs out of sight, wishing he had never come, or at least hadn't arrived until much later, after the rest had gone. The Duke of Haverly's stare was particularly intense. What if Daniel answered in a way the duke didn't approve? Would he terminate his offer of employment?

What could he do but speak honestly?

"When violence erupts, I often question whether all other avenues have truly been exhausted. Violence rarely brings about the results we desire, instead escalating and harming and further dividing the factions and sides until the original objective is lost in the fury that has built into an explosion." He picked up his goblet. "I will not say it is never necessary, such as in the defense of one's person or to protect someone else, but to use violence as a means to bring about social change, especially violence that results in the injury or death of innocent people, is often weak and cowardly."

Finch scowled, but Daniel paid him little mind. Lady Juliette had her head tilted, as if considering what he'd said. They had been involved in more than one escapade that had a touch of violence, not the least of which had been her kidnapping by spies last month.

The earl changed the conversation, and after what Daniel considered much too long a time spent over a meal, they pushed back their chairs and rose.

"If you ladies will join me," Countess Thorndike said, "I would love to show you some of the new plantings in the conservatory, and the gardener has created bouquets for each of you to take when you depart. Gentlemen, we'll rejoin you shortly." She led the way, and the ladies followed like bright birds.

At the door, Miss Agatha Montgomery paused, her face troubled. She returned for a whispered conversation with Lord Thorndike, and he eventually nodded and beckoned to Daniel, who had risen with the rest of the gentlemen when the ladies did and now stood with his hands on the back of his chair.

"Mr. Swann, Miss Montgomery is quite concerned that her father has failed to appear at today's party. If I have the carriage sent round, would you accompany the lady to her father's place of business? With a proper chaperone, of course."

"Of course, milord." Daniel bowed to Miss Montgomery. With her red hair piled high, she was nearly as tall as him.

"Lady Juliette will accompany you as well." The earl nodded to his daughter.

"I'll go." Viscount Coatsworth approached. "There's no need for the Bow Street runner."

Daniel gritted his teeth. It seemed beyond Coatsworth's ability to pass by an opportunity to cut him down to size. He turned to the earl to await his decision.

"Perhaps you should all go. It's a pleasant day, and I have no doubt you young people will have a more enjoyable time in the carriage than sitting in the house listening to your elders discuss things in which you have little interest."

"Thank you, Father. Perhaps we will return in time to bid our guests farewell," Lady Juliette said.

How did she feel about being part of the excursion? Would she rather stay with the German duke? And if the viscount was willing to accompany the ladies, why did the earl want Daniel to go?

"If not, your mother and I will make your excuses. That's settled, then. Miss Montgomery is certain he's at the mill in Hammersmith. At least that was where he was headed before he was supposed to come here. I would suggest you start there." Thorndike opened his watch. "The party here will go for another hour at least, but perhaps two. And I would like to speak to Montgomery, so even if it's later, ask him to call round."

"Yes, milord." Daniel inclined his head to the earl.

Coatsworth said nothing to Daniel, behaving as if he were invisible while they waited for the ladies to prepare for the short journey. When they assembled in front of the house, the carriage was brought round and Coatsworth took charge. "Lady Juliette, sit with Miss Montgomery and me on this side. We'll let the servants sit opposite."

Servant?

The maid in her white cap and woolen shawl was already aboard, and Miss Montgomery took the bench across from her, facing the rear of the carriage.

Lady Juliette tugged on her gloves, then took the viscount's hand to allow him to assist her. Daniel resisted the urge to swat him away and do the job himself. He might not be a titled gentleman, but he was no tramp either. Coatsworth snubbed him as if afraid his company would tarnish the group.

"Thank you, but no," Juliette said. "I don't enjoy sitting backward in a carriage. I'll sit beside Miss Brown. You take the place beside Agatha. Mr. Swann can share our bench." She sent an apologetic look Daniel's way, and he relaxed his fists.

When they were all seated, Daniel had no complaints. He was quite close to Lady Juliette, so close he could smell her perfume. Her gown flowed and whispered in that mysterious way ladies' clothes had that never failed to catch a man's attention. Even now a fold of the silky cloth lay on his knee, and he resisted the urge to touch it.

Opposite, the viscount's mouth puckered as if he'd licked up a spoonful of vinegar, and he studiously avoided acknowledging Daniel's existence. Coatsworth patted Miss Montgomery's hands gripped together in her lap.

Hmm, very familiar. There must be something brewing between them of a serious nature for him to be so bold.

"I don't know if I am worried or vexed. It is like Father to be late to every function, but not to fail to appear entirely." Miss Montgomery gnawed her lip. "He can be most exasperating at times." Her voice had a tinge of fondness, but her eyes held the tightness of anxiety.

"I'm sure he's fine. Just caught up in something at the mill. You said he is overseeing extensive renovations." Lady Juliette smoothed her skirt off Daniel's trouser leg, putting her hand between their limbs as if guarding her leg from brushing his.

Did she think his company odious? In their several encounters, she'd never treated him anything but cordially—or at least civilly. But perhaps Coatsworth's attitude had rubbed off? Did she see herself as superior to others the way the viscount did?

Again he wished himself away from these feelings of inadequacy and doubt, of not being quite good enough to be in the company of those who considered themselves his "betters." In the detectives' room at Bow Street Magistrate's Court, he was among his peers, respected and accepted though having the least experience. It was where he fit best, not the dining rooms, salons, or carriages of the beau monde. Perhaps he *was* inferior to the gentry because he would rather share a costermonger's meat pie with his partner, Ed Beck, than consommé with the peerage.

They left the more densely packed part of the city and headed into the open countryside. Hammersmith was less than ten miles from Berkley Square, and the road was good.

When they reached the village that bordered the Thames, they turned a bit south toward the river and pulled to a stop several houses up the lane from the mill. Daniel noted sounds of splashing water in the distance as he wrenched the carriage door open and leapt to the cobbles, eager to escape the confines of the closed space and get out first so as to be the one who helped the ladies.

The smell of the river mingled with the smell of grain, and even from this distance the thumping and bumping of machinery said the mill was in production. The narrow lane between the houses, which led down to the mill, was currently blocked by a wagon piled high with sacks of grain. That explained why the driver hadn't stopped closer to the mill before decanting his passengers.

The mill stood sentinel above the houses, a stone tower with a hefty presence to it. Like a mother hen with chicks gathered near, the dwellings huddled around the base of the mill. How long had it stood here, grinding grain into flour, feeding England one wagonload at a time? A hundred years? Two?

And if what the anarchist Jasper Finch said was true, it was due for an overhaul and refitting to bring it into this modern age.

Lady Juliette emerged from the carriage and took Daniel's waiting hand, her shoe peeping from beneath her skirts to find the iron step. A buzz of bees' wings under his skin began the moment her fingers made contact with his, and he took a fortifying breath. She was so proper and beautiful, yet beneath the facade, he also knew her to be brave and determined. A heady combination.

The instant her foot hit the cobbles, a flash of light, followed by a *whump*, rocketed down the narrow lane, and the world exploded.

Chapter 2

DANIEL OPENED HIS EYES, HIS head throbbing. His body felt pulped, as if he'd been trampled by a herd of Highland cattle. Something bit into his cheek as he lay sprawled on the cobbles, and he tasted the coppery tang of blood.

Sprawled on the cobbles? Why was he on the ground? Had he fallen? His thoughts scattered and fragmented, refusing to organize.

He blinked hard, wincing against the throbbing inside his skull. Had someone hit him?

Drawing in his arms and planting his palms on the rough stones, he pushed himself away from the ground, pausing on hands and knees to ease the dizziness swirling behind his eyes. To his left, a horse lay on its side, kicking and struggling, tangled in the harness like a fly in a web. The animal's mouth was open, but no sound came out—or at least no sound that could be heard above the ringing in Daniel's head. He straightened to his knees and pressed his palms to his temples.

What happened? He tried to draw a deep breath, but dust and smoke choked him, and he gagged, coughing, doing an agony to his head. He staggered to his feet. Rocks and rubble littered the small courtyard.

A man stumbled by, eyes wide, face streaked with blood and dirt. His head and shoulders were covered with white powder.

Daniel turned a slow circle, unsure of where he was, until his eyes lit on the carriage with the Earl of Thorndike's crest on the black door.

The mill. The trip to find Mr. Montgomery . . .

Lady Juliette! What had become of her? He swung wildly, looking one direction and then another, but he couldn't see her anywhere. She had been emerging from the carriage when whatever had happened . . . happened.

The carriage had slid several yards, dragging the horses backward and to the ground. One would never trot again, and the other continued to thrash. The driver was nowhere to be seen, but the tiger, a youngster of thirteen or fourteen summers, bent at the head of the struggling horse, trying to calm him. As Daniel moved toward the vehicle, the door opened and the viscount's head and shoulders emerged. His hat was gone, and his cape wrapped around his shoulders as if trying to strangle him.

His eyes were wild. He mouthed something to Daniel, beckoning him before disappearing within once more. Or had he spoken aloud? Daniel's ears still rang so loudly he heard nothing else. It was as if someone had locked him in a glass room with a banshee. He could see the world around him, but nothing else penetrated his shrieking prison.

He glanced toward the end of the street. Yellow flames licked through the gaping doorway of the mill. Every window was an empty eye socket, no glass to be seen. Rock dust filled the air, and men ran past him from the center of the town toward the burning building, buffeting him in their haste.

Daniel reached the carriage and peered inside. The maid and Miss Montgomery bent over Lady Juliette, who lay on the floor. She must have been knocked back when the mill . . .

Exploded?

That must have been what happened. A mill explosion.

He'd heard of such things, but he'd never been close enough to one to become collateral damage.

Coatsworth sagged into the corner of the coach once more, his limbs lax, staring. Miss Montgomery's carefully arranged hair now lay in auburn tangles on her neck and cheeks, but she gave all her attention to Lady Juliette.

"Is she injured?" Daniel asked, startled to find he couldn't even hear his own voice. When Miss Montgomery gave him no heed, he had to assume her ears were ringing as well. He touched her sleeve.

At that moment Lady Juliette jerked, her body stiffening as she came to herself. Her legs stirred, and Daniel realized that far more of her shapely limbs showed than was proper. And something poked beneath her petticoat, affixed to her leg just above the knee. Was that a pistol in a holster? He had no notion what a woman's underpinnings looked like, but he was certain weaponry wasn't standard issue. He reached in and tugged her hem down.

The maid blinked, and her mobcap tumbled off her head. She had a red mark on her cheek that would soon blossom into a bruise. They must have been tossed about like pebbles in a jar when the blast hit.

Though Miss Montgomery tried to prevent her, Lady Juliette sat upright. Her pelisse tangled about her arms, and she eased aside the cloth, as if she wasn't quite sure of her movements.

"Lady Juliette, are you injured?" Daniel asked. He couldn't gauge how loudly he was talking, but it must have been quite loud, for with a pop, his ears began to work, and the last word all but echoed in the confined space.

With the inrush of sound, he began to understand the chaos going on around them. The horse's screams, shouting, the crackle of fire, boots on cobbles . . . somewhere a woman or child sobbing.

Lady Juliette pushed her hair out of her eyes and edged toward the door.

He reached for her waist to draw her out of the carriage. She put her hands on his shoulders, and he easily lifted her and set her feet on the ground. Keeping hold of her, he bent to look into her eyes. Was she steady enough to stand alone?

Her hands gripped his shoulders, and his spanned her waist. As she inhaled, he felt the movement of her ribs. Heat rushed into his ears, and his heart tripped. He had never held a woman in such a way. He wanted to draw her close, to put his arms properly around her and protect her, to usher her to safety away from the pandemonium going on around them.

Brazen thoughts for a mere officer of the court to think about the daughter of an earl.

"Thank you." Her voice sounded quavery, but she stepped back. He let her go, staying close lest she succumb to faintness. With shaking fingers, she loosened her bonnet strings and retrieved her bonnet from where it trailed down her back. Looking around her at the tumult, she let the now-battered straw millinery fall to the street.

"Are you injured?" he asked again. He could see no damage, but he must make certain.

"I do not believe so. Merely shaken." She gulped in a breath and coughed. Dust sifted from the air, landing on her dark hair and the shoulders of her pelisse. "What happened?" She looked up at him properly for the first time, and her face went pale as milk. She blinked and swayed, and he gripped her again.

"Blood." The word strangled its way out of her throat. She wavered so much he feared she would collapse, but as he bent to pick her up and place her back in the carriage, she planted her palms on his chest and pushed. "You're bleeding." She stared at his mouth, gripping the doorframe of the carriage.

He touched the corner of his lips, and his fingers came away red. He must have cut himself when he fell. Using his cuff, he swiped at the blood. Lady Juliette could not stand the sight of blood, as he remembered from her encounter with ruffians in a London alley mere weeks ago.

"Little harm has been done. I am well, I assure you." He'd suffered worse wounds shaving.

She nodded, but she averted his gaze. Once more he swiped at the trickle. Was he making it better or worse? He had no time right now for her squeamishness, and yet he didn't want to leave her to faint on the cobbles.

Miss Montgomery and the viscount descended from the carriage.

The viscount kept his arm around Miss Montgomery's waist as they tried to take in what had happened.

"There appears to have been an explosion at the mill." Daniel hated saying such in front of Miss Montgomery, but it was impossible to miss. More men hurried past them toward the stone structure. Smoke tendrils filled the air. "If neither of you are hurt, I must go help. There may yet be men to save." Daniel gripped the viscount's arm. "See to the ladies."

He unclasped his cloak and swirled it around Lady Juliette's shoulders. "Look after that for me." He wouldn't want to be encumbered by the garment if he was sifting through wreckage or fighting a fire, and she needed to be kept warm.

Daniel felt the back of the waistband of his trousers, reassured to feel his truncheon still there under his coat. As an officer of the Bow Street Magistrate's Court, he must step into the crisis and lend aid.

Miss Montgomery broke free from the viscount and clutched Daniel's arm. "My father! You must save my father. He was in there. Let me come with you." Her eyes were like burning holes in her pale face, and fear etched her features. He hoped she wasn't going to have a fit of hysterics, though he wouldn't blame her.

Daniel shook his head. "No, it will not be safe for you. Stay, and if I'm able, I'll bring him to you." He caught the viscount's eye and jerked his head. "Keep her here. And help the tiger with the horses."

The viscount's mouth set in a sour line, as if he was not in favor of taking orders from a mere peace officer, but Daniel ignored his pettiness. With a last glance at Lady Juliette, he joined others hurrying toward the mill. He still felt sore and light-headed, but he had a job to do.

The closer he moved to the mill, the worse the destruction. Tongues of masonry and splintered wood clogged the narrow lane, and split shingles lay like scattered playing cards on the cobbles. Broken barrel staves hung slack around a spilled pile of dried beans, and rubble crunched beneath his boots. Buildings around the mill had taken the brunt of the blast, with windows broken, thatch and roofing blown off, and belongings strewing the street.

Two men passed them heading away from the mill, carrying an injured man on a door between them, carefully picking their way along. The wounded man groaned with each shift of his weight. At least he had survived the initial blast. As they passed a low stone wall, one of the men brushed against it, and it gave way, stones tumbling down. The man had to skip out of the way, juggling his hold on the door and nearly spilling the patient.

How many other walls were ready to give way after the shaking they'd taken? Would there be another explosion? What had caused this one?

Several lines had formed, men passing buckets of water from the river up the bank to the mill. Daniel had expected more fire, but they seemed to be making good headway already. Heat and steam rose each time a gout of water cascaded through an open door or window to douse the flames. At first glance it appeared the entire mill hadn't yet been engulfed. Perhaps they stood a chance of saving the structure.

A dwelling next to the mill had not fared as well. There must have been a candle or lantern burning, or perhaps that was where the fire had started? A blaze gusted from every window and door, and the thatched roof smoldered, ready to ignite. The bucket brigade hurried to quell the flames, not so much to save that building but to prevent the fire from spreading further.

Daniel headed to the right, away from the fire since plenty of men were already there helping. Here on the side away from the flames, the air was cooler, and they were more likely to find survivors. A handful of others were busy pulling aside splintered wood and broken stone, climbing over a glacier tongue of detritus spilling through an opening where once had hung wooden doors large enough to drive a wagon through. Those doors had been blown flat and now lay a good twenty yards from the mill, half leaning against a blacksmith's shop.

"Here, you, lend me aid." A burly man in a dirty leather apron—the blacksmith himself?—waved Daniel over to the wreckage-filled doorway. "There's someone here."

A hand, the same chalky color as the dust coating everything, lay under a pile of broken wood. Daniel and the big man tossed aside splintered planks.

"He's most likely dead, but be careful, just in case," Daniel cautioned.

"Agreed." The stranger lifted the end of a beam that must be all of a foot square as if it were mere kindling, letting it fall to the side with a thump that sent flour and rock dust swirling into the air.

The buried man stirred, his fingers clenching and grasping.

"He's alive." Daniel shoved away a broken toolbox and a bucket that would never hold water again, revealing the man's head and shoulders. "Sir? Sir, can you hear me?"

There was no more movement, but when Daniel felt the man's neck, his pulse beat there. "Can you find something to carry him on?" he asked his co-rescuer. "Where is the nearest physician?"

"On the high street. This here is the mill manager, Mr. Coombe. A good man." The stranger brushed his hands down his apron. "I'll find some men to carry him."

Daniel eased the mill manager over so as not to cause further damage, but he wanted to get the man's face out of the dirt and ensure he could breathe. A nasty cut adorned his forehead, and his arm lay at an odd angle.

"Do you think it safe to go inside? The structure won't fall, will it?"

Daniel turned from where he knelt. Viscount Coatsworth stood, eyeing the upper floors uncertainly.

"What are you doing here? What about the ladies?"

"Duke von Lowe arrived. And Agatha was beside herself, insisting she be allowed to come down here and search for her father. I told her I would come instead. I left the women with the duke, and here I am. Do you think he's in there? And if so, where?" The viscount surveyed the area with a grimace, dusting his hands together as if to get off dirt—though he had yet to touch anything.

Heinrich? Why had he come? Had Thorndike or Haverly sent him? Or was it Juliette who had drawn him here?

The blacksmith returned with three men, and they carefully loaded Mr. Coombe onto a blanket and carried him away, navigating the treacherous terrain as a team.

Daniel turned back toward the warehouse attached to the mill. "This way. If there's anyone left inside, they'll most likely be in this part of the building." Had the blast weakened the stone walls? Jarred the roof loose? Was another explosion imminent? Daniel shoved those thoughts aside. Despite the potential danger, if there was a chance of saving a life, he must act. And he had promised Miss Montgomery he would locate her father.

The viscount followed, his knuckles white and his movements stiff, as if ready to bolt at the first sign of trouble.

Climbing the pile of wreckage half filling the doorway, Daniel winced as splinters dug into his skin. Slipping and grasping, and then sliding and bracing, he made it onto the warehouse floor. Inside, the center of the room was clear. The broken bits had been forced to the perimeter and away from the main part of the mill. Here, grain heaped along the walls, with tatters of burlap embedded in the piles, bags burst and thrown about like pillows tossed by an angry giant. Gaping sacks of flour lay everywhere, and the air let in through the broken windows swirled the dust up and out.

Smoke hung in ribbons in the air, and the shouts of the men fighting the blazes in the other part of the mill echoed through the room. A door on the river side of the warehouse had also been blown open. Perhaps someone else had been hurled outside like the manager. They should check before venturing into the hallway connecting the warehouse to the mill.

"What do you think happened?" the viscount asked between coughing spates. "What caused this?"

Daniel didn't want to speculate, but with his recent conversation with Mr. Finch on his mind, he suspected something sinister.

"This way." Lifting his lapel to cover his mouth and nose, Daniel made his way under a sagging beam toward the side of the warehouse that faced the river. Outside, a landing and a set of stairs hugged the side of the building, leading to a walkway over the waterwheel and the mill race that had been built to force water over the giant paddles. The wheel turned, but off balance, wobbling as if it had become disconnected from the shaft. Daniel gripped the railing, dizziness overtaking him as he looked down on the moving water.

Get hold of yourself, man. It won't do for you to lose your head and need rescuing too. He steadied himself, refusing to show weakness in front of the viscount.

The walkway twisted around a corner and, though flat, felt as if it gained in elevation as the ground fell away beneath the supports. When Daniel navigated the water-splashed planks to the bend, his heart rate increased. He had no head for heights. On this side of the building, though the glass had been blown from the windows, no flames appeared. The villagers must be winning against the fire.

At the far end of the walkway, where it terminated against the stone wall, a man lay on his back, head and feet dangling, close to over-balancing and tipping into the river. As Daniel approached, the man stirred.

"Have a care. Don't fall into the water." Daniel touched his shoulder. "Easy . . . let me help you." He put his hand under the man's elbow and assisted him. "Slowly until you see if you're injured."

"What happened?" Grimaces accompanied every movement.

"There was an explosion. Part of the mill is on fire, and you must have been knocked unconscious by the blast. Were you out here working on the wheel?"

The man blinked. "An explosion?" He put his hand to his head. "Working on the wheel? Of course I wasn't working on the wheel. I'm not a warehouseman." He tried to straighten his waistcoat, which was too fine to belong to a laborer. "I'm an accountant. A man of numbers."

Daniel studied the open window above them. "Then Someone was looking out for you, sir. You could have been blown into the water quite easily." He pointed to the foaming water pouring off the water-wheel. "Let us get you to a less precarious spot."

"You said it was an explosion?" The man groaned. "Mr. Montgomery was afraid of this, but I never thought they would do it. I thought it was all talk. Threats, nothing more." The man remained rooted to the walkway, swaying slightly, squinting as if the sunlight reflecting off the water was too bright for his eyes.

Daniel's attention sharpened. "Threats? Was someone threatening to do something like this?"

Nodding—and then wincing as if he regretted it—he spoke over the sound of the water rushing below. "Luddites. Anarchists. There was a message nailed to the door last week, and there have been others, letters. Mr. Montgomery was bringing in new methods, new machinery, which would increase the production of the mill while reducing the workforce needed to operate it." Despite his lurching condition, the man paused to puff out his chest a bit and smooth his hair. "At my suggestion, of course. Mr. Montgomery relies upon me heavily for advice and direction in his business affairs."

"What did the note say? Do you know who left it?" Daniel kept hold of the man's elbow, but his detective's curiosity took hold.

The man gripped the handrail and limped along the walkway. "I don't know who wrote it, only that it promised retribution if we let workers go. It could have been anyone who works here or any of a dozen groups of rabble-rousers who are against progress."

A hot coal of anger burned hard in Daniel's gut. His initial hunch was confirmed. Violence to get attention. With no thought of the damage done to people and possessions. There would be no flour milled at this site for a long time, if ever again. Every man employed here was now without work. Every family who needed flour would have to find another source.

"Come. We'll sort it out when we stand on firm ground." Daniel handed the man up the steps to where Coatsworth waited and followed them both through the warehouse out into the street.

When they finally stood in the lane, Daniel asked, "Your name, sir?" He might prove a useful source of information as the investigation began.

"Mr. Earnshaw. Hubert Earnshaw. I am Mr. Montgomery's accountant, both personal and business." He didn't seem to realize he had already told Daniel his occupation. "I had an appointment with Mr. Montgomery. The hallway from the milling floor was blocked by a cart that had overturned, and men were shoveling spilled flour. The air was thick with dust. I had to go around through the warehouse to enter from that direction. Mr. Coombe was there, carrying a toolbox . . . which is odd, because he doesn't usually do manual labor. He's the mill manager."

"Mr. Earnshaw, where are the offices located? I need to find Montgomery."

"The hallway to the left." He pointed into the warehouse. "His office overlooks the race and wheel, though how he can stand the noise is beyond me. He says he likes the sight of the moving water."

"Right. I'll go back. Mr. Earnshaw, head that direction, and you'll find people who can help you." Daniel pointed up the lane toward where the Thorndike carriage sat at the far end. He caught sight of his cloak, still draped around Lady Juliette. She was bent over someone lying on the ground, and the red sash indicated the man next to her was Duke von Lowe.

Daniel shoved down the uncomfortable feeling in his chest at seeing them together and entered the warehouse once more.

Coatsworth, to his credit, followed Daniel back into the building, and this time they went deeper into the structure, entering the passage that must lead to the offices. At the far end of the stone hallway, shadows moved through the smoke and steam, pouring water on hot spots. Soot streaked the walls of the passageway. The machines and inner workings of the mill must have been destroyed, but perhaps the structure could be saved.

Montgomery would have a long task ahead of him to rebuild.

Two bodies lay in the hallway, strewn atop a pile of half-burned flour sacks that had spilled from a cart. This must be where they had been shoveling the flour Earnshaw mentioned. Daniel checked both men but found no sign of life. The blast must have sucked all the air out of the hallway and tossed them hard against the stone wall. He shook his head at the viscount and checked the office door opposite.

The top half of the door had once contained a glass window, but that opening now gaped. The rest of the door looked as if a sneeze would disintegrate it.

A blizzard of paper—some with charred edges—lay in drifts over every surface, and in the center of the room, sprawled like an abandoned rag doll, lay Mr. Montgomery.

Daniel rattled the door handle, surprised when the door remained firm. It was sturdier than he had thought. He reached through the broken glass to open it from the inside, but nothing happened. Feeling lower, he tried to locate the key, but only the keyhole met his fingertips.

"Stand back," he said to the viscount, who peered over Daniel's shoulder before shouting "Garfield!" upon seeing Mr. Montgomery on the floor.

Daniel shoved him away, stepped back a pace, and raised his boot, kicking hard at the latch. Thankfully, the door splintered, rocketing open and thudding against the wall before listing on its hinges.

Coatsworth nearly ran Daniel over getting to Montgomery's side.

"Garfield." He dropped to his knees and took the man's hand, leaning over to press his ear to his chest.

"Is he alive?" Daniel squatted and touched Montgomery's neck. Nothing. He brushed aside some debris, and his hand stilled.

A perfectly round hole perforated Mr. Garfield Montgomery's forehead.

He had not been pulped by the explosion.

He had been shot.

———⁂———

Juliette eased her head to the side, trying to unknot her neck. She hadn't been knocked unconscious by the blast, but she had been toppled onto her back, landing at an awkward angle in the bottom of the carriage and hitting her head on the far door. And she'd been stunned for a moment or two.

Just as well she'd been wearing her bonnet, which cushioned her head—though that bonnet would never see a walk in Hyde Park again. Still, better a hat crushed than her skull.

Surreptitiously, she felt along her thigh for her pistol. At least this time she'd fastened the holster securely. Not even being tossed about in an explosion had dislodged it.

"Do you think he was in there?" Agatha's hand shook as she brushed a red ringlet off her cheek. "Do you think Alonzo and Mr. Swann will find him?"

"Let us move away." Duke Heinrich made shepherding motions up the lane. "The smoke and dust are very bad."

Heinrich's arrival had shocked Juliette nearly as much as the blast. His excuse, that he was concerned about her well-being, puzzled her. Why had he thought she needed his aid when she was in the safe company of Daniel, Agatha, and Alonzo? Should she be flattered or concerned that he had followed them? His proprietary air bordered on smothering.

"We cannot leave. Mr. Swann said he would bring my father here." Agatha gripped the handle of the carriage door as if she expected the duke to haul her away bodily. "I must be here when they return."

At the far end of the street, the roof on the house beside the mill burst into flames, sending tongues of fire high into the air, black smoke billowing. Those who had been fighting the blaze were forced to back away.

Please, God, let everyone have escaped. Juliette bit her lip. Was Mr. Swann safe? Was he, too, trying to combat the fire? Or was he somewhere inside the mill, searching for survivors?

"Surely there is some way we can help? We cannot merely stand here as spectators." Juliette stepped aside as two men, with a third man's arms draped over their shoulders, slowly made their way up the street. The third man's head hung low, and he did little to help them, covered in dust and soot . . . and blood.

Her stomach roiled. *Why? Why did You give me this weakness, God? It's not rational. How can I help people if my knees turn to water and my thoughts become sparkling pinwheels every time I see blood?*

She shifted restlessly. "Agatha, if we just stand here and wait, it will seem interminable. Let us lend aid. Drag the seat cushions out of the carriage. Heinrich"—she abandoned formality—"find us buckets of water and blankets. Knock on doors and get sheets or tablecloths to use as bandages." Though at the moment, how she would bind wounds without fainting was beyond her. However, she must try.

She motioned to the approaching men. "Lay him here. Let us see if we can help him."

Agatha handed her the bench cushion from the carriage, and Juliette laid it on the cobbles. The men eased the injured man to the ground. Without a word, they turned and went back toward the mill.

The wounded man groaned, sweat on his brow making putty of the dust clinging to him.

"Sir, where are you hurt?" Juliette tried not to look at the cut on his forehead, filthy and still bleeding. She took her handkerchief from her pocket and laid it over the wound.

"Ribs, mostly." The words ground from between clenched teeth.

Agatha edged closer. "Were you in the mill? Have you seen my father, Mr. Montgomery?"

Juliette removed Mr. Swann's cloak, then her pelisse, and folded the pelisse to place under the man's head. She put the cloak on again as cold air bit through her day dress.

"Wasn't in the mill. In the lane. Bringing grain. Got thrown into the side of a building."

Juliette had no idea how to treat injuries, but surely making the man comfortable came near the top of the list. "Sir, what can we do for you?"

"I don't suppose you'd have any gin, would you?" He smiled through clenched teeth. "I could use a draught."

"I am sorry I have no spirits, but someone has gone to fetch water. We'll wash your wounds and bandage you." Again she averted her gaze. It wasn't seemly for unmarried women to act as nurses, but what could they do? It was every hand to the work in a crisis.

Heinrich reappeared carrying an ewer and holding a stack of toweling under his arm. "The inn up the street has become something of a hospital. Perhaps we should transfer this gentleman up there." He set the pitcher down and handed the towels to Agatha.

"You go. I must stay with the carriage and wait for my father." Agatha's mouth set in a stubborn line.

"By rights I should escort you both back to your homes. Your sensibilities must be affronted at such chaos. At least let me take you to the inn." The duke motioned to the tiger, who had tears streaming down his face, making him seem even younger than he was. "Stay with the carriage, and tell whoever comes where I've taken the ladies. And watch my horse. Do not allow him to be stolen." He pointed to his mount, a shining bay with white stockings, snorting and pulling at the reins tethering him to the rear carriage wheel.

The youngster nodded, his signature striped vest hanging open, the buttons torn off. He had witnessed both carriage horses, which he'd helped care for each day in the stable mews behind the Thorndike townhouse, killed. One by the blast, and the second by a merciful bullet when it was discovered he could not be saved.

And worse yet, the coachman had been so forcefully ejected from his driver's seat that he had flown completely over the carriage and landed on the cobbles, dying instantly. Alonzo and Heinrich had carried him out of the road and covered him, but it seemed wrong to leave him here alone.

"Heinrich, the boy should come with us. We cannot leave him alone. He's just a child. Help us get this man to the inn, and then you can return here. Direct any wounded you encounter so they may find help as well. When Mr. Swann and the viscount come with Mr. Montgomery, you can inform them of our whereabouts. Now, Agatha, bring those supplies and help me." Juliette made her voice as forceful as she could, calm and authoritative so Agatha wouldn't argue.

Agatha, well used to Juliette taking the lead, paused, assessed her options, and nodded. She picked up the ewer and towels. "You will send them to us immediately when they arrive, won't you?" she asked the duke.

"Yes, Fräulein." Heinrich nodded. He did not appear in favor of Juliette's dictates, but he went along for now.

Juliette knelt beside the injured man. "I am sorry to move you again, sir, but we will get you off these cobbles and into a bed."

"Let me find another man to help. You cannot possibly carry him, and the boy will be of little use." Heinrich frowned.

Juliette motioned for Agatha, Miss Brown, and the tiger to go ahead of her, and Heinrich stopped a man on the street for help.

"The inn is in the next lane, on the left." Heinrich's voice came from behind her.

The narrow passage, with its cantilevered upper stories, was clogged with people. Juliette, keeping Mr. Swann's cloak gathered around her, wended her way toward the door beneath the sign that said "The Bell & Rose"—a more gentle and genteel name than the building suggested.

Stepping into the taproom, the odors of ale, smoke, and cooked meat assaulted Juliette. Stools and benches had been pushed aside, and several injured townsfolk lay on the tables. Men, women, and—to Juliette's horror—a child.

Her stomach lurched, her head whirled, and her knees turned to aspic. The child had a cut on her arm, and blood dripped down her hand. A woman struggled with the frantic youngster, trying to get her to hold still long enough to have the injury wrapped.

"You there, help or get out. We've no time for gawkers." A red-faced woman in a mobcap and stained apron shoved past Juliette, her arms full of blankets. "Bit soon for the gentry to come gawping."

"We've come to assist." Agatha stepped forward. "How may we help?"

Heinrich and his helper brought the wounded man through the doorway. "Where should we deposit this gentleman?"

"Anywhere you find room. I'm not a hospital, and I shouldn't have to take in these people." The woman's eyes blazed. "I didn't invite any of you in here."

"Now, Hazel, calm down. This is the logical place." A man straightened from a crouch, wiping his hands on a towel. "Far enough from the blast to have escaped damage but close enough and large enough to treat the wounded. I explained all of this." Instruments stuck up from the front pocket of his apron. He reached into a bag and pulled out a brown glass bottle, uncorked it, and patted his apron. "Where is that spoon?"

"You're the doctor. It in't my job to find your equipment when you can't lay a hand to it." The woman dropped the blankets on a bench and jammed her hands on her ample hips. "I should just walk out and leave you to the place. It's falling down around me anyway. I could kill me old man, if he weren't already dead, leaving me with this millstone strapped around me neck."

Heinrich lowered the injured man to lean against the wall beside the door, nodded to the fellow who had helped him, and brushed his hands along his thighs.

"Lady Juliette, I must insist we leave. This is no place for you. The wounded are receiving help enough." Heinrich glared at a man who sat propped in a corner. He held a jug, lifting it by the thumbhole handle to swig from it. Some of the contents dripped into his filthy beard, and he swiped at it with the back of his hand. All the while, he never took his leering gaze from Juliette.

A shiver skittered up her spine.

"We cannot leave the area until Mr. Montgomery arrives." Juliette kept her voice low. "And we can lend a hand here while we wait. The men will be back soon, and I won't rest easily until I know they are unharmed."

"Is it Mr. Montgomery you wait for, or is it someone else?" Heinrich's eyes narrowed.

Heat built under Juliette's collarbones, and she was thankful for her dark Welsh complexion, which hid blushes. Whatever did he mean, and what business was it of his?

"Don't tell me you are jealous?" Agatha nudged the duke. "Juliette would never allow her head to be turned by a . . . detective. She's a lady. The daughter of an earl." She looked to Juliette for confirmation of her declaration.

Juliette swallowed her embarrassment and lifted her chin. "I'm not allowing my head to be turned by anyone. This is neither the time nor the place to speak of such silly subjects when there are people in need." She motioned to the maid. "Frannie, look in the kitchen and see about making tea. A lot of tea. And you, what's your name?" she asked the tiger who lingered on the doorstep. She felt bad that she didn't know it already.

"Paul, milady." He whipped off his tricorn and tugged his forelock.

"Paul, find a bucket and the closest well. We're going to need plenty of hot water. Then locate the firing or coal store and make certain we do not run short. Can you do that?"

"Yes, milady." He swiped at his nose, the tear tracks still plain on his face.

"What should I do?" Agatha pushed up the sleeves of her pelisse. Worry tugged at her expression, but her lips were set in a determined line.

"If you can bear to help the doctor . . ." Juliette's voice trailed off, and she knew herself a coward, giving Agatha a duty she could not stomach herself. "I'll go help in the kitchen or perhaps make bandages . . ."

Agatha squeezed her arm. "Do not worry. I understand."

Heinrich moved to bar Juliette's way. "I cannot leave you here. This is unseemly." He eyed the poorly dressed, injured, and shocked people crowded into the taproom. "What would your parents say?"

"They would tell me to do what I know is right. Return to the carriage and wait for Viscount Coatsworth and Mr. Swann to bring Mr. Montgomery. You must look after your horse and the body of our coachman." She flipped the edges of Mr. Swann's cloak back over her shoulders. "There is work to do, and we must do it."

The duke muttered in German as he turned away, but he stopped and came back, taking her hand in his. "Please do not think ill of me.

Or that I have overstepped with my comments. I merely wish to see to your safety."

She relented and gave him a smile. "I know. But these are extreme times, and we cannot stand on protocol. I will be safe enough here."

Juliette entered the kitchen of the inn and reconsidered ever staying at a coaching inn again. Dirty dishes, dust, mud tracked through the back door . . . disgusting. Frannie pushed the swee over the small fire in the fireplace and hung the kettle from the iron rod. Her hands were streaked with soot from even that small task.

"It's a shambles, milady. I don't know where to start."

At least in here Juliette didn't have to face any blood. But she had less of an idea where to start than her maid. The fire smoked as the chimney failed to draw properly.

"Hot water and bandages. I've sent Paul for fresh water and to scare up some fuel for the fire. Where can we obtain material for bandages?"

"Bedsheets would be simplest, though I don't know that you could find a clean one within these walls."

"See if you can find a linen press. I'll keep the fire going and try to clear some space to work."

Daniel's long cloak hampered her movements, but she was loath to lay it aside. The kitchen had not one clean square inch on which to set anything, and the cloak did warm her. She located a large tub beside the back door and dragged it inside to fill with dirty dishes and cookware.

The noise she made stacking crockery masked other sounds, and only at the last moment did she sense she was not alone.

"What a tasty morsel to find in the kitchen." Before she could turn, a man's hand clamped over her mouth, stifling her scream. Filthy hair scrubbed the side of her face as he pressed his beard against her skin.

Shock and fear gave way to anger and training. Blessing Uncle Bertie for his instruction, she rammed her elbow backward into the man's doughy middle. As the air left his lungs, she stomped as hard as she could on his foot, using the small wooden heel of her shoe to inflict the most pain. His grip loosened, and she whirled in his grasp to thrust the heel of her hand sharply up against the base of his nose. When he staggered back, she hiked her skirt and kicked him . . . in that place Uncle Bertie had guaranteed would take the fight out of any man. She made good contact, and the man howled, his nose gushing blood.

The edges of the room closed around her in blackness, and she fought against it, backing toward the door to the rear courtyard.

Don't faint . . . don't faint . . . don't . . .

Her assailant stumbled backward toward the taproom door, colliding with another man. Juliette braced herself to run but then recognized the doctor.

"What are you doing in here, Boggs?" The physician scowled, looking from the nosebleed to Juliette's disheveled appearance.

She gulped and tried to smooth her hair and her nerves.

Swiftly assessing the situation, the doctor shoved Boggs into the taproom. "Get out of here before I box your ears. Which wouldn't be difficult, seeing as a mere slip of a girl has already half finished the endeavor."

When Boggs had gone, the doctor took a couple of steps toward Juliette but then stopped. "Are you injured, miss? Did he harm you?"

Juliette swayed, gripping the table edge. "Sir, your hands."

The man's hands were red with blood. He glanced at them, and with a shrug wiped them on his apron. Juliette closed her eyes against the tide of dizziness. She raged at her weakness even as she fought it.

"If you are unharmed, I will return to my patients, but perhaps you should sit down. Not everyone is equipped to fight rascals and stitch wounds in the same day."

Frannie edged past the doctor, folded cloth clutched to her chest. On her heels came the tiger, a bucket of water sloshing against his leg in his haste.

"Just what we need. You, look after the lady here, and you, boy, bring that water into the taproom."

By the time Juliette's head cleared, Frannie had set to work with a will, making tea, clearing clutter, and creating a clean space on the table. Juliette gained a new appreciation for the work the servants in her parents' houses had to do.

"Milady, these were in a cupboard upstairs. Will they do?" Frannie held up a pair of wrinkled linen sheets, yellowed with age. "They're dusty, but they're all I could find."

"Give them a good shake outside and see about cutting them into bandages. Well done finding that much in this disaster."

When the girl ducked out into the stable yard, Juliette took a moment to lift her skirt and remove the pistol from the holster strapped to her thigh, mentally thanking Uncle Bertie for insisting she always be armed. She slipped the gun into her dress pocket, feeling the unaccustomed drag of its weight. She might need it should Boggs or another like him return.

She sorted out a knife from an assortment in a box on a shelf, giving it a practiced flip. It landed with a quiver, the point sunk into the top of the scarred and battered table. That should do for tearing sheets into bandages.

"Lady Juliette?" Duke Heinrich's shocked pale-blue eyes stared at the knife, still vibrating in the scarred tabletop. "This is no place for you. I am taking you and Miss Montgomery to your townhouse. I have procured the coach belonging to this . . . inn." He swallowed, grimacing at the chaos and filth. "I really must insist. It is not safe for you here."

Dust and dirt streaked his military uniform and dulled the medals on his chest. His jaw set, he stood with legs braced, erect and stiff, as was his wont, and this time his expression brooked no argument.

"Come, Lady Juliette." He held out his hand. "It is dangerous for you here."

She had a better idea than he of the dangers lurking in this inn, but she must refuse. Before she formed the words to restate her argument against being removed, a wail from the taproom grabbed her attention. Her heart shot into her throat as she recognized the voice. Thrusting her hand into her pocket to cover the pistol, she ran past the duke, bumping him out of the way in her haste but not stopping to apologize. Agatha might be in danger.

"What is it?"

Viscount Coatsworth caught Agatha as she fainted, and a sinking feeling invaded Juliette's middle.

Daniel Swann stood silhouetted in the doorway. His broad shoulders blocked out much of the light, and when he stepped inside, sweeping his hat from his head, his clothes and face were streaked with soot and dust.

His eyes met Juliette's, and he gave a small shake of his head.

How she came to stand before him, she didn't know, but she looked up into his face. "Daniel? What happened?"

"Not yet. We must get Miss Montgomery out of here." The grim set of his mouth told her the news was bad.

"That is what I have been trying to do." Heinrich helped the viscount lower Agatha onto a high-backed bench along the wall. "What you should have done from the outset, Herr Swann, instead of leaving them in the street."

Daniel's mouth tightened at his chastisement, and Juliette whirled on Heinrich. "That is unfair. Lives were in danger, and he had to go help."

"Don't." Daniel placed his hand on her arm, then glanced down at the pistol in her hand. His brows rose, and she tucked the gun back into her pocket, highly aware of his touch and chiding herself for it.

Neither the time nor the place, remember? She must tend to Agatha.

Her friend showed no sign of coming out of her faint even as the viscount chafed her hands. If only the Dowager Duchess of Haverly were here, she would have sal volatile to shove under Agatha's nose. A proper dowager would never be without her smelling salts.

Daniel took Juliette's elbow and drew her outside into the street.

Heinrich came too, brows down in contrition. "I am sorry, Daniel." He inclined his head. "I should not have upbraided you. You did what you had to do. But we should take the ladies out of here with all haste."

"Where is Mr. Montgomery? Is he wounded?" Juliette asked.

"He's dead." Daniel jammed his hands into his pockets, his shoulders hunched. "When we came through the door without him, Miss Montgomery took one look and swooned. We hadn't even told her. I don't know what she's going to do when she learns the truth."

"So he *was* in the mill." Juliette huddled in the folds of Daniel's cloak. "I had hoped he was elsewhere when it blew." Poor Agatha.

"It wouldn't have mattered if the mill had still been whole."

"Why?"

"He didn't die in the blast. He was murdered."

Chapter 3

DANIEL TROTTED UP THE SHORT set of steps into the Bow Street Magistrate's Court and headed for the detectives' room. His cloak lay over his arm, and he pitched it at the hook behind his desk as he passed. A glimpse of his reflection in the mirror over the fireplace made him wince. Tunneling his fingers through his hair, he tried to restore some order to his dark curls. His clothes were filthy, but that couldn't be helped.

Now to beard the lion in his den.

"What happened to you? You been crawling through the dustbins?" Owen Wilkinson, one of the office boys, stood with his hands on his hips, an insolent grin twisting his lips. "You look like you got dragged under a curricle the length of Rotten Row."

"Very nearly." Daniel brushed at his lapels and scowled at the state of his boots. "Is Sir Michael in his office?"

"He is. Just sent me to fetch some tea."

"Good. While you're at it, please get me a cup of coffee. You can leave it on my desk."

It was certainly part of the duties of an office boy to fetch tea and coffee, so Daniel didn't feel bad asking, but Owen always put on such a martyred air, as if he was vastly underutilized as an office boy. He had proven helpful on Daniel's last case, but he still carried a chip on his narrow shoulder and thinly veiled his contempt for Daniel.

Bracing himself to face another man who always seemed to doubt his capabilities, Daniel headed down the hall to Sir Michael Biddle's office. As the supervisor in charge of the court detectives, Sir Michael was Daniel's guv'nor.

"Come in," his voice responded to Daniel's knock on the door casing. He didn't look up from his writing when Daniel entered. "I hope you let the tea steep long enough. Last time it was the strength of day-old dishwater."

"Sir Michael."

The man raised his head. "Oh, what do you want?"

Pleasant as always.

Daniel forced himself not to frown. "I have a new case."

"Did it involve rolling in a pigsty?" Sir Michael sat back, his leather chair creaking. "What is the meaning of your coming into my office in such a condition?"

Deep breath. Don't respond in kind. Don't give him reason to dismiss you.

"Sir, there's been a murder. I was nearby when it happened, and I would like to take the case."

He outlined the basic facts that he knew of what had happened to Mr. Montgomery, which, when laid end to end, made for a very short string.

"Shot, you say? How do you know he wasn't wounded by some flying bit of metal or stone? This could be an unfortunate industrial accident." Sir Michael steepled his fingers, bracing his elbows on the arms of his chair.

As if Daniel could not recognize a bullet hole.

He took a calming breath. "I arranged for the body to be sent to Rosebreen. When he's completed his examination, I'll confirm the cause of death. Until then, it might be best to let everyone assume the blast killed Mr. Montgomery."

"Just so. No reason to have everyone jumping when there's nothing to jump at. I don't suppose you have suspects to attach to your hypothesis of murder?"

"There has been some unrest at the flour mill because of progressive improvements Mr. Montgomery was making. They had at least one threat. It's possible that Luddite types were at work here, attempting to force Mr. Montgomery to leave things at the mill the way they have been for centuries. Perhaps Montgomery would not be persuaded. Perhaps they found a permanent way to stop him."

"That's a lot of supposition. Especially since you don't know it was a murder just yet. Was anyone else wounded or killed?"

"Yes to both. And the mill will be inoperable for some time. If Montgomery was murdered, the explosion could have been set off to cover up the fact. The fireball and concussive blast knocked people over from a hundred yards away. Structural damage, fire, and broken glass and masonry for a city block. If the explosion was deliberate, the perpetrator must have assumed everything would be destroyed to such an extent that the death of Mr. Montgomery would be assumed to be due to the blast."

Daniel fisted his hands behind his back. "I want to investigate both the murder and the explosion. The damage to property is considerable, and there are several deaths, not just Montgomery's. The mill manager was found buried in the rubble. I don't know if he will survive."

"The mill is in Hammersmith, you say?"

"Yes."

"That's outside our jurisdiction."

"You send detectives from Land's End to John O'Groats when the need arises. Hammersmith's magistrate and night watchmen are hardly equipped to investigate something of this nature."

"If it is anarchists as you suspect, the Home Office should investigate." Sir Michael picked up his quill and studied the hardened tip.

"If I can tie it to the work of anarchists, we can turn it over to the Home Office, but they won't want to wade in until it's confirmed."

And I can always ask the Duke of Haverly what the Home Office would like to do.

From what Daniel had been able to discern, the Duke of Haverly practically *was* the Home Office.

A tap at the door, and Owen entered carrying a tea tray.

Daniel waited while the office boy fussed with pouring and milk and sugar and the like. It was as if he was deliberately taking his time, hoping they would say something that his ever-gathering ears could capture.

"Enough." Sir Michael waved him away. "Swann, are you sure you want to take on a case at the moment? When you're so near the end of your tenure here?"

Daniel tensed. "Am I? Near the end?"

Sir Michael smirked. "I believe the understanding we have had with each other these past two years is coming to an end. Certain restrictions and limitations will be lifted? Certain support withdrawn?"

Aware of Owen slowly retreating, Daniel waited, forcing himself to relax. When the door finally closed behind him, he said, "Sir Michael, I will not know the extent of the support or lack of it until I meet with my solicitors. I have worked hard to earn my place here, and I am a good detective. A detective who is asking to investigate a murder and industrial sabotage. If you could send word to the Hammersmith magistrate offering my services, I believe he will be amenable to accepting our assistance."

Sir Michael assessed him with a steady gaze, and Daniel refused to flinch. If he was going to be fired, he could do nothing about it, but he would not grovel.

"Very well. There are no detectives free at the moment to assist you. You'll have to make do with Owen as your second man. If you want the job, that's the best I can do."

Owen. Pity Ed Beck, Daniel's customary partner, was on a case in Yorkshire. Now he'd have to drag a reluctant office boy along with him.

Still, it was his case now. He'd show Sir Michael his competence.

———— ❦ ————

"Poor Agatha. What state was she in when you left her?" Mother shuffled and dealt the whist cards, practicing to keep her fingers nimble.

"Devastated. We got her back to the house, and a physician was called. He gave her something that sent her to sleep. Otherwise I would not have felt comfortable leaving her at all." Juliette sat at the table in the War Room on the top floor of her parents' townhouse.

All traces of the previous case involving art theft and hidden codes had been removed, and the blackboard and corkboards were clear. The majority of the space was now taken up by training materials to teach agility and balance and strength. Uncle Bertie practiced his balance by standing on two small blocks while wielding a sword. He mimicked thrusts, parries, and ripostes while staying up on the wooden plinths.

Father belied his breeding and all instruction in proper deportment by lounging in a wingback chair with one leg thrown casually over the arm. He pinched the bridge of his nose. "Swann was certain Garfield had been murdered?"

Juliette nodded. "He said Mr. Montgomery had been shot. Viscount Coatsworth was with him when they found the body, and he confirmed it. They both felt Agatha had to be told the whole truth from the beginning."

"Is there any chance it was not a bullet but something in the explosion that . . ." Her mother trailed off with a small wave of her hand.

"Unlikely." Uncle Bertie lowered his sword and hopped off the blocks. He reached for a towel and then shook first one leg, then the other, as if to work out the fatigue his exercise had created. "I imagine our Mr. Swann has seen his fair share of bullet holes. The question is who did it, and why?"

"Exactly." Juliette tapped the table lightly with her fist. "Whoever did this should answer for his actions. Murder, not just of Mr. Montgomery but also other workers at the mill. Where should we start with our investigation?"

"*Our* investigation? Jules-girl, there are proper authorities to look into something like this." Father straightened. "Most likely the magistrate in Hammersmith will request the aid of Bow Street, especially considering a detective was on the scene at the time. This is a matter for the police and court system, not a matter of national security."

"But, Father, we should look into it ourselves, shouldn't we? Agatha is my best friend, Mr. Montgomery was your friend, and this could be the work of anarchists." Juliette gripped her hands together atop the table. "Industrial espionage and anarchy fall under the mantle of the Home Office, do they not?"

"To a certain extent, but we do not choose our assignments. We are directed by our superiors through proper channels. We cannot jump into a case merely because we know some of those affected. We could run afoul of another operation without intending to, things of which we are not aware. The espionage trade is one of compartmentalization, not knowing something until you need to know. At any rate, your mother and I will not be available for some time. We've been given another assignment." He looked to his wife with a smile, then gave an apologetic one to Juliette.

Juliette looked from one parent to the other. "Is it something I can help with?"

"I'm afraid not, darling." Mother stacked the whist cards, butting them together and returning them to the box that held tokens, fish counters, and more cards. "We're heading to France on a diplomatic mission for the Prince Regent." She gave the words *diplomatic mission* extra emphasis, by which Juliette inferred a dual purpose for the trip. "We cannot divulge anything further, but suffice it to say what we learned on the Selby case last month will aid us in our objective."

Juliette's heart sank. "You're leaving? How long will you be gone?" She had just been reunited with her parents after years away at school, only to return to England to find them missing. Restored now, they faced the prospect of being separated again?

"Difficult to say," her father answered. "We will, of course, be as efficient as possible, but these envoys can take time. We'll be liaising with the new regime and trying to take their measure while peace is being established. And we'll have some other work to do behind the scenes." Father rose and went to stand behind Mother's chair, his hands resting lightly on her shoulders. "It is good that your mother prepared well for this upcoming Season with the dressmaker and tailor. Otherwise we would not be properly equipped for appearing in French society. Melisande is always considered au courant when it comes to sartorial splendor." He smiled proudly.

Bereft, Juliette blinked. "Am I to accompany you?"

Mother leaned across the table and squeezed Juliette's hand. "I am sorry, darling, but no. You are to remain here with Bertie, continue your training, and represent the family at the various functions to which we've been invited. I know you're disappointed. We are too. But duty before personal desire." She released Juliette's hand.

Juliette sat back, twisting the gold and garnet ring on her finger, wanting to protest that it wasn't fair. When would it be her turn to be first in her parents' lives? How many sacrifices must she make for this birthright they had passed on to her? Her parents were government agents, but did that mean the Crown owned them body and soul? And if so, did the Crown own her now too?

Every which way she turned, she was confronted and thwarted. Not only were her parents abandoning her once again, but they would be no help in investigating what had happened to Mr. Montgomery and the mill.

Bertie propped his hip on the edge of the table, hooking the towel around his neck and holding on to the ends. "You will not be bored while they are abroad. You have much still to learn and many social engagements to attend. The dowager can step in as your chaperone once more, I've no doubt."

Juliette glared at Bertie, who laughed. He well knew her thoughts on the dowager's overbearing and strict rules for debutantes. Still, she had been able to evade the woman's draconian ways and help with the last caper. She would find a way to investigate this new one.

"And don't get any notions about poking into the Montgomery case." Her uncle tilted his head, the lamplight gleaming off his black hair. "I recognize that expression, young lady. As your father said, Montgomery's death is a matter for the authorities. If you go nosing around, you're likely to land yourself in a vat of trouble, and you might even blow your cover. If there is anything to concern us in the case,

Swann will let us know. Until then you should focus your attention on your training and your debut Season. Keeping up the appearance of a marriageable debutante is essential."

Juliette crossed her arms, feeling mutinous. She might be green when it came to being a spy, but she knew better than to tromp around an investigation like a cart horse in a rose garden. And as to appearing as a marriageable debutante . . . it was beyond time she made it clear she had no intention of marrying anytime soon. Her ambition was first, to become reacquainted with her parents after so many years abroad at boarding school, and second, to learn her new trade as an agent for the Crown. There would be plenty of time to think of marriage once she had completed those goals.

Though at the rate at which she was moving toward those two things, she might very well be an old maid before either was accomplished.

She shot Uncle Bertie a glare so he would know how displeased she was with him. He merely grinned.

"Speaking of being a marriageable debutante"—Father helped Mother with her chair—"there has been some speculation concerning you, Juliette."

His words jerked her attention from the silent sparring with Uncle Bertie. "What?"

"It appears that the preference one Duke Heinrich von Lowe has shown toward you has not gone unnoticed. The Dowager Duchess of Haverly asked if the duke has made his intentions known."

"A German duke. Not bad." Bertie did up the buttons of his open waistcoat and adjusted his watch chain to hang perfectly. "You could be quite an asset to us if you lived in Germany. There's always so much intrigue and backstabbing—sometimes literally—amongst the Visigoths. Having an agent in the upper echelons of German society might prove useful. You could do worse than marry Heinrich."

"An asset?" Was that what she was considered now? What about what she wanted? How far did they expect her loyalty to the Crown to extend? To marry a man she barely knew, move to a foreign country, and continue to spy on those around her? She scowled at Bertie.

"Anyway, it's manners to wait to be asked before one starts planning a wedding."

"Bertie, stop quizzing her," Mother said. "Juliette, darling, you are under no pressure to marry anyone, much less a foreign duke, merely to provide intelligence and information. If your heart lies with the duke, then we will support you. If not, I'm certain you will find a way to hand him his congé gracefully. Has he made an approach to you?"

"He has not asked me to marry him, certainly, though he did inquire as to whether I might be interested in traveling to Germany to see his home and meet his family. With you and Father as well," she added.

"It sounds as if he is working up to the pivotal question." Father grinned. "As your mother says, we will not bring any pressure to bear upon you. You are free to do as you wish as relates to the duke. However, I must reiterate, you should not interfere with the investigation into Mr. Montgomery's death. Bertie's correct in saying it is a matter for the police. Your help on the last case was invaluable, but you are not as yet a fully trained agent. The death of Mr. Montgomery is sad, and certainly the culprit must be brought to answer, but a simple murder does not fall under our auspices. Mr. Swann and his associates will learn the truth, and justice will prevail."

"Your task is to support Agatha through her grief and to continue your tutelage with Bertie in our absence." Mother placed the card box on a shelf near the door. "We will write to you while we are away, and I'll bring you some new dresses and accessories from France."

Her parents linked arms and left the War Room to prepare for dinner, and Bertie tossed aside the towel and shrugged into his coat.

"Well done managing not to let the entire world know you were carrying a pistol today at the luncheon. Though I thought for a time you had blown the gaff. Came untied, did it?"

Drat the man.

"Tomorrow we'll work on your self-defense. It's one thing to carry a weapon and another altogether to know how to use it. Or to protect yourself when you cannot reach your weapon. You never know when you'll need to dispatch an attacker, and you've barely begun that side of your training. You have to keep a cool head under pressure and remember what you've been taught. That comes with repetition."

She would not mention that she had been forced to defend herself against the odious Boggs earlier that very day.

"Your parents are headed to France, and I've been given the task of investigating our congenial Mr. Finch. Hopefully, he is more talk than action. You can dodge or accept the attentions of the German and continue your training." Bertie looked satisfied with his tidy summing-up of their roles.

Juliette retreated to her bedroom. As she prepared for dinner, tilting her head as her maid pinned her brown curls up, Juliette stared at her reflection in the lamp-lit mirror. But instead of her own image there, she saw Agatha's. The grief-stricken eyes, the pale face, the bewildered slackness to her mouth.

What would Juliette want if it had been her father killed? She would want justice. She would want help. She would want anyone who could aid her to get to work.

She could not refuse. She owed Agatha so much.

Chapter 4

THE DAY AFTER THE MILL explosion, Daniel approached the coroner's office. He was more at ease than he had been the first time he had visited, but he couldn't say he looked forward to the experience. The cold yellow brick and plain boxlike exterior seemed so fitting for the tasks undertaken within. His last excursion to this place had been to witness the autopsy of an art dealer who had gotten himself stabbed to death by a traitorous spy who had ransacked his gallery to hide his real crimes. This time, however, Daniel must learn more about the death of a man he'd actually met while he was alive.

Owen Wilkinson sauntered at Daniel's heels, hands thrust into his trouser pockets, acting as if he hadn't a care in the world. A touch of anticipation feathered across Daniel's skin. Owen needed taking down a peg or two. The experience ahead of him might be just the thing.

The same insouciant clerk from before sat at the desk inside the door, but this time he shrugged and jerked his thumb to the hallway behind him. "Been waiting for you."

Daniel didn't answer, giving a nod as he passed through the front office. Owen kept up, and once in the tiled hallway, asked, "Why are we here? I thought we were going to the hospital to see the mill manager and then out to Hammersmith."

Clamping his teeth, Daniel let the insolent tone drift by. "Wilkinson, you are the probationary officer here. It is not your place to question my itinerary or methods." It galled him to know Sir Michael had promoted the little beast from office boy to potential magistrate's investigator. And that he had assigned Wilkinson to Daniel to train.

More galling was that he suspected Sir Michael of forcing Daniel to groom his own replacement. The meeting with his solicitors loomed, and doubts gripped Daniel's middle as he once again wondered what the future held.

What if the final wrapping up of his guardianship meant Sir Michael could remove him from Bow Street? Daniel had some funds laid by, money that would see him through the next little while, but he loved his job. And the men he worked with . . . for the most part. If he lost his job, he would lose the identity he had built for himself.

He had, by turns, been the son of an unwed servant, the general dogsbody on a country estate performing every task from bootboy to stable groom to gardener's helper, and an outcast at a posh boarding school where his love of books was ridiculed and his only acceptance was found in his athletic ability. His years at university had been lonely ones, not fitting in with the wealthy sons of influential families who studied alongside him. It wasn't until he met Edward Beck, a Bow Street Magistrate's investigator, that he found himself drawn to an occupation that had become more than a job. It had become an avocation. A calling.

Had God called him to be a Bow Street runner? Daniel didn't know. He didn't feel the job was any kind of sacrifice, yet it seemed to him that the God preachers talked about mostly called people to do things that were hard, that cost them something in the doing. Certainly not something they enjoyed or might have a talent for. *That* God seemed as remote and unknowable as Daniel's erstwhile father or his mysterious patron.

"Are we going in or not?" Owen asked, jarring Daniel out of his thoughts.

He chided himself for woolgathering in the early stages of the case. How long had he been standing in the tiled hallway? "Of course we are. This way." He strode to the far end, where the coroner's office was located.

He went through the open doorway into the cluttered room. "Dr. Rosebreen?" He held out his hand to the small man behind the messy desk. "Mr. Swann, from Bow Street. We met last month on the Selby case?"

The doctor, whose head was wreathed in cigar smoke, rose, shaking Daniel's hand and then shrugging out of his coat. "Yes, of course. And you solved that case quite tidily, as I understand. I can only hope you do the same for the current one. Mr. Foster has prepared the body. Shall we begin?" He rounded the desk, dropping his coat onto a chair piled with papers and books.

Owen stood in the doorway, eyes round as shillings. The walls of the office were covered with shelves, and on the shelves stood specimen jars and preserved biological samples beyond Daniel's ability—or desire—to identify. Owen seemed particularly fixated on a container holding a fetal pig suspended in clear liquid. The office boy . . . no, the probationary investigator . . . swallowed, his face so pale his freckles stood out like pepper flakes.

Satisfaction lodged beneath Daniel's breastbone. If Owen was unsettled by a pig in a jar, he was going to be stunned by what came next.

They followed Dr. Rosebreen into the cold tiled room where Mr. Montgomery lay on a slatted wooden table. Mr. Foster, Rosebreen's assistant, set a metal bucket on the concrete floor with a clank.

Daniel steeled himself as Rosebreen donned his indescribable apron and reached for the sheet. Moving to the side so as not to block Owen's view, Daniel crossed his arms and braced his feet apart.

The room smelled of vinegar and lavender buds and death. The lavender buds were used as a natural disinfectant and to mask other smells, but the odors of death and decay still hovered.

"There is no need for a complete autopsy, as the cause of death is clear." Rosebreen whisked back the sheet halfway to reveal the pale, unclothed torso of Mr. Montgomery.

Regret colored Daniel's thoughts. He had known Mr. Montgomery. Had returned his treasured stolen painting to him, been rewarded by him, been scolded and doubted by him, and had taken the brunt of his loud displeasure. Daniel had witnessed his delight in his daughter, his fine house, and the artwork he collected with what bordered on obsession.

Now he lay here on this table, a corpse with no dignity, his life taken by a miscreant who remained at large.

A familiar burning began in Daniel's gut. The desire to find justice for someone who could not seek it for himself. To level the scales once more.

"The marks on the body can be accounted for by the explosion. His hair and clothes were singed, and the small cuts were made by flying glass." Dr. Rosebreen bent over the corpse, his eyeglasses perched dangerously near the tip of his nose.

Mr. Foster, at his rolling writing desk, dipped his quill in the inkwell and took dictation. He was nearly as wide as the desk was tall, and his moustache seemed to have grown bushier in the month since Daniel's first meeting of the assistant.

"There was a fire after the blast," Daniel offered.

"Yes, I can imagine. I've seen the victims of an industrial explosion before. I was called in to help when a group of malcontents torched a warehouse down at the docks. They intended to destroy imported fabric of the East India Company, a protest against putting English weavers out of work, but the fire spread to nearby naval stores, including a black powder magazine. The damage to bodies was much more severe than this. Some were never recovered."

"When was that, doctor?" Daniel asked.

"Oh, you would have been a lad at the time. Aught three?" The doctor picked up a metal probe. "Time to go fishing for that bullet. I only hope I can get it without having to remove the top of the skull."

Daniel looked over his shoulder to see how Owen was faring. Was he ready to "flash the hash"? Or to perhaps subside into a faint like a sheltered miss?

Far from it apparently. Owen stepped forward. "Can I have a better look?" He bent over the bullet hole in Montgomery's forehead.

"Of course." Rosebreen seemed pleased. "The problem with probing for a bullet inside the brain cavity is . . ."

He went on, but Daniel didn't hear. His gorge rose, and he fought it down. Taking calming breaths through his nose, he swallowed extra saliva again and again as clammy waves rippled down his body and sweat broke out on his skin. Here he had been sure Owen would get his comeuppance for being arrogant and perhaps disgrace himself at the sight of a dead body, but instead Daniel was the one fighting black spots crowding his vision.

"Ah, there it is." The doctor held aloft the lead ball, examining it in the light from the windows high on the opposite wall. "Small, which explains why it didn't create an exit hole."

He reached for a bowl and dropped the ball into it with a *plink*, sloshing in a bit of water and rolling it around.

Daniel forced himself to concentrate, to ask an intelligent question. "How large a gun?"

"No blunderbuss, that's for certain." Owen examined the bullet. "A gambler's sleeve gun? Or a muff gun?"

"A muff gun? Do you think some lady shot him?" Daniel scoffed, grateful for the distraction.

"You don't have to be a lady to fire a muff gun." It was Owen's turn to scoff.

"Well, I see no black powder around the wound, which means the shot was not taken close to him. I believe we can rule out suicide." The doctor retrieved the bullet from the bowl and polished it with the edge of his apron.

"How much skill would such a shot take? And how far must one be from his target to make the shot and leave no powder marks?" Daniel narrowed his eyes. Were they looking for a marksman, or had someone merely gotten lucky?

Owen scratched the hair over his ear. "Little gun like that isn't very accurate, but it doesn't throw a lot of powder either."

"And you know this because . . ."

"Been filing reports at the office for the better part of four years now. I read 'em before I file 'em. This in't the first muff gun killing in London, you know." The defiant gleam in his eyes chafed Daniel. Young pup.

"The boy's correct. I'd say your killer could have stood within six feet. Or if he is adept with a small pistol, he could have been as far away as twenty. Twenty-five if he was quite lucky."

"Couldn't have stood that far away as the office isn't that big. He might have been in the passageway. How long had Montgomery been dead when the blast occurred?" Daniel tried to imagine how it all happened, but he knew it was too soon. He would have to talk to people who were inside the mill that day to piece together Mr. Montgomery's last hours.

Rosebreen shook his head. "Impossible to say. The gunshot killed him. There was very little blood around the wound. You say you found him on his back?"

"Yes."

"Then gravity would have pooled the blood inside the head. The glass cuts didn't bleed much either, and the rest of the fluids settled along his back and legs. The body wasn't moved until I came for it." The doctor wiped his hands on his apron and tugged at the strings. "That's all I can tell you. He was dead before the explosion, but for how long I cannot say." He shrugged and lit another cigar. "The dead can only tell us so much. The secrets you seek are hidden among the living."

"Aren't they always?"

"I'll prepare the body for burial. I understand the sexton will be retrieving it in a few hours." Rosebreen studied the glowing end of his cigar.

Daniel uncrossed his arms. "Owen, wait here and get a copy of Mr. Foster's report, and then take the bullet and the report back to Bow Street."

Owen scowled. "Where will you be?"

"Making inquiries."

He would go to the mill first, then the Hammersmith magistrate's office. Tomorrow was Sunday, but on Monday he would need to speak with Miss Montgomery, a task he dreaded. Perhaps he would enlist some help.

Monday morning, Juliette descended the stairs from her bedchamber, Daniel Swann's card in her hand. Mr. Pultney had informed her of his arrival, and she had hastily changed into a new gown and checked her appearance in her dressing table mirror. All the while she had mocked herself for caring what Daniel Swann might think of her.

Uncle Bertie would have chided her as well, being cloistered in her room at this time of day, but with the departure of her parents this morning for their mission to France, she had been overtaken with a malaise of the spirit that left her listless and dissatisfied with life. It chafed to find she was not as flexible and willing to change her ideas and desires as she had once thought. All she had hoped after years away at boarding school was to return to her family and to be with them, to know them.

But from the moment of her arrival on home soil just over a month ago, it had been one crisis and revelation after another, all preventing her from experiencing her debut Season in the bosom of her family as she had wished. With her parents on the Continent for an indeterminate amount of time, she was left to wait and fill the hours.

And mope.

The arrival of Mr. Swann was a welcome reprieve from her thoughts. He had been left cooling his heels by the front door.

"I apologize. You should have been shown to the drawing room." She stopped on the bottom step, her hand on the newel post.

"I haven't time. I understand Miss Montgomery is receiving mourning guests this afternoon. I hoped to see her before they arrive and that you would accompany me. I have questions Miss Montgomery may find difficult or troubling to answer, and if you are there, you can lend her support."

Juliette nodded. "Of course. I planned to attend the reception, but I can go with you now. Let me inform Mrs. Dunstan and gather my maid to come along."

At mention of the housekeeper, Daniel flinched, and his mouth grew hard. Why did he seem to have such dislike for the woman? Juliette found her to be pleasant and efficient, a trusted confidant of her mother's. But the few times she had seen Daniel and Mrs. Dunstan together, he was stiff and formal, she kept her head bowed, and the pair of them avoided looking at each other. So odd, because he treated no other staff with such cold indifference.

"Is Sir Bertrand at home?" the detective asked.

"He is not. I expect him for dinner, but you know my uncle. His plans are quite . . . fluid." At least Daniel now knew the secrets her family held, their other lives behind the front. He had recently joined the ranks of employees of the Crown, so she didn't have to guard every word she said as she did with others. "We will be home before he returns, I'm sure."

Juliette tried not to let her relief show. If Uncle Bertie were home, he might forbid her to go to Agatha while Daniel questioned her. He had been quite firm that Juliette was to stay out of the investigation. But Bertie could not fault her if she was going at the behest of the detective and merely to support her friend through a terrible time, could he?

Bundled and bonneted, her maid in tow, Juliette nodded to the jarvey, Mr. Cadogan, before stepping into the carriage. He tipped his hat and gave her a cheeky grin. "Good day, milady."

"How are Sprite and Lola today, Mr. Cadogan?"

"Fine and fit, milady. Thank you for asking." He beamed at his horses, his pride and joy.

As she settled inside the cab, arranging her skirts, she said to Daniel, "Mr. Cadogan might be the only carriage for hire in all of London, as often as I seem to encounter him."

"He haunts Bow Street and Drury Lane, so he's frequently to hand when a detective needs a conveyance. I think he enjoys being on the periphery of law enforcement."

Juliette leaned back as the carriage jerked into motion. "So many different people in London, and each with their own story, their own hopes, dreams, struggles. Does he secretly wish he was a detective, or does he just like knowing what's going on so he can gossip with his fellow drivers?"

Daniel shrugged. "Could be either or both. Cab drivers are easy to discount, almost as if they're not real people, just around for the convenience of those who can afford to hire a carriage. Lots of occupations are like that."

The way he spoke, as if from experience, sharpened Juliette's attention. "Surely you don't find people overlook you, a Bow Street detective?"

"No, but I haven't always been a detective, have I?" He turned to look out the window, and Juliette, though curious, knew she would be prying if she asked him to explain further.

Daniel's long legs took up much of the room, and Juliette slid her heels back to create space. Her maid sat quietly in the corner, smoothing the lace trim on her cap. Another occupation that was easy to overlook.

Time to change the subject. "Will you have many questions for Agatha? I cannot imagine she will know anything of import. Her father treated her as a pet more than a person. Showing her off and certainly proud of her, but not including her in any serious discussions of his business or his personal matters."

"A few questions about his routine and relationships, but I am hoping to draw out more, something that will point me in a clear direction. Often people don't realize the significance of a bit of information until someone else points it out."

"How does one go about apprehending a murderer? Mr. Montgomery was murdered, was he not? You are certain?" Poor Agatha. Death was difficult enough, but to have someone you love killed on purpose?

"We are certain. The coroner found evidence that the wound was not self-inflicted. No, someone shot him. As to finding that someone, every case is different, but there are some commonalities. Who had a reason to wish Montgomery dead? Who also had both the ability and the chance to carry out the deed? If you have not those three things in one suspect, you do not have your killer. Motive, means, and opportunity." His eyes were bright and his face lively, as if he truly enjoyed the art of detection.

He leaned forward. "As to motives, there are three basic reasons. Power, money, and . . ." He looked away, red creeping up his neck above his cravat.

"And?"

Daniel cleared his throat. "Suffice it to say there is a third, and it has to do with men and women, and we'll leave it at that."

It was Juliette's turn to feel the heat rushing to her cheeks. She understood his meaning, but it was improper for such things to be discussed between unmarried individuals.

"Surely you can discount that as a motive in this case." Mr. Montgomery must have been in his fifties and a widower for many years. "I would think power and money more likely."

"You might be surprised. In any case, a detective never draws conclusions before he's begun his investigation. Once the pieces are assembled, he may formulate theories and lines of inquiry, but until he has gathered the basics of what happened, he must keep his mind open to all possibilities."

This sounded very much like one of her uncle Bertie's lectures. "Are you quoting someone?"

He smiled, and her heart kicked a bit sideways. He really was a handsome man.

"I am, actually. My mentor, Mr. Beck. Ed is a great teacher, and I've learned much from him. I wish he were here on this case with me, but he's been called away to Yorkshire to investigate a missing woman."

"I didn't realize your duties took you all over the country. I thought you worked exclusively for the Bow Street Magistrate's Court." The carriage rocked gently toward Eaton Square.

"Primarily, but any principality can call us in for help. Our reputation is growing throughout the country, and more and more often we're asked to assist on tough cases."

Which meant he could be called away at a moment's notice, like her parents. Like she herself could be once she completed her training.

A black wreath hung on the Montgomery front door, and straw had been spread in the street to dampen the sounds of traffic going by.

A footman granted them entrance, and before he could inquire of his mistress whether she was home to callers, Agatha flew out of the drawing room in a cloud of black silk and into Juliette's embrace.

"Oh, you came. I heard your voice, and I was so thankful. It's been awful here alone. And I'm dreading this afternoon's reception. I know it is something I must do, but I hate it." Her voice was thick with tears and grief, and Juliette squeezed her tightly.

"I'm so sorry I couldn't come. My parents were in such a flurry of packing and preparing to leave for France that I couldn't get away. I will not ask such a banal question as how you are feeling. I will only say how very sorry I am and offer any help I can." She turned Agatha, keeping her arm about Agatha's waist. "Let us go into the salon. You could use a bracing cup of tea." Juliette hugged her dear friend to her side and led her toward the drawing room.

Before they got there, Juliette remembered Daniel and the reason for their visit. "Agatha, Mr. Swann is here too. He needs to ask some questions about your father—if you are feeling up to it."

Agatha stiffened, glancing over her shoulder. "Of course. I know it is necessary, but I cannot imagine that I know anything that will assist him. And there are callers coming soon. Can this not wait until another day?"

Daniel stepped forward. "My apologies, Miss Montgomery, but the matter cannot be put off. Delay could mean allowing the person who killed your father to escape justice."

Her shoulders drooped, and she groped for her handkerchief. "Very well."

He followed them into the drawing room, where the staff had pulled the drapes and lit several candelabras and lamps. Juliette led Agatha to the settee and indicated that Daniel should take the chair adjacent. The footman waited for their cloaks, and as Juliette handed hers over, she noted the long table prepared with food and drink for the coming guests.

"I'll pour you some tea, Agatha," Juliette said. "I assume you would prefer coffee, Mr. Swann?"

His eyes met hers, part surprise, part gratitude. "If you will, thank you."

A flicker of satisfaction burned beneath her stays at remembering his preference for the bitter brew.

Daniel had his notebook on his knee, his pencil in hand. "I do apologize if these questions distress you, Miss Montgomery, but I must ask them. Can you think of anyone who would want to harm your father? Had he mentioned any trouble at the mill or in his personal life?"

Agatha shook her head, touching her handkerchief to her nose. "No. But he would not have told me in any case. He felt business was too much for a woman's *so-called* weaker mind, and he would not have wished to burden me." She blinked, looking to Juliette as she accepted the cup of tea with milk and sugar but then placed it on the table next to her.

"Did he ever speak of unrest among his workers, particularly at the mill?"

"Do you think one of his own employees killed him?" Agatha paled. "Alonzo said it must be the work of anarchists. You should speak to that odious Mr. Finch, who was so outspoken at the Thorndike luncheon."

"We are looking into that, of course, but it would be unwise not to explore other lines of inquiry."

Agatha nodded, throttling her handkerchief. "I don't know what I can tell you that may be of help. By teaching me nothing of his business, my father has merely left me unequipped to inherit them. What am I to do?"

Juliette handed Daniel his coffee and sat beside Agatha. "You are not to worry about that just yet. Your priority is to see to the funeral arrangements and to grieve. You have your father's men of business to assist you, and you must rely upon them, at least for the next little while."

"She also has me." Lord Alonzo Darby, Viscount Coatsworth, stood in the drawing room doorway, removing his gloves one finger at a time. "You may lean upon me, my dear." He nodded to Juliette and glared at Daniel as he tossed his outer garments to the footman. With long, commanding strides he closed the distance and went to one knee before Agatha, taking her hands in his. "I will help you navigate these unfamiliar waters."

Agatha closed her eyes, nodding slightly, biting her bottom lip. "I do not know what I should do without you. You have been such a rock."

Juliette slid down the settee, making room for Alonzo to sit beside Agatha. Realizing she would not be able to see Agatha's face from her new position, she rose and took the chair opposite. A twinge of something . . . jealousy perhaps? . . . bit her, but she tamped it down. It was right that Agatha's fiancé should have preeminence in her thoughts. She and Juliette had been closer than sisters for a long time, but that they were growing up and developing other, closer relationships was to be expected.

She only wished she liked the viscount better, though her only true complaint was in how he treated Daniel Swann and others he felt were not of his station. In his care of Agatha, he could not be faulted.

"Why are you here?" Alonzo asked the detective, his voice sharp. He retained Agatha's hand, rubbing his thumb along her wrist. "Can you not see she is distraught?"

"There are questions only she can answer, and they are urgent."

Daniel's tone was without inflection, but something in it caught Juliette. Did it bother him, Lord Darby's pompous attitude to someone he considered his inferior? Or did it amuse him? It certainly didn't seem to discomfit him.

"I am here, gentlemen. Grieving, yes, but capable of speaking for myself," Agatha said with a bit of spark.

Juliette winked at her, applauding the edge to her words. "Agatha, was your father behaving any differently over the past few days?" If she was here to support and help, she might as well ask the questions on her own mind.

Daniel's attention swung from Lord Darby to Juliette, his brows rising.

"You know how he was, one moment shouting, the next laughing. He was excited about a new painting coming up for auction soon. When he returned home from the mill the evening before the . . . that day, he was irritable, but about what, I could not say. He was often irritable when he returned from his places of business, never certain they were being managed as well as he would like."

"Garfield had too many diverse investments and businesses," Lord Darby said. "I advised him in this, but he refused my counsel." As if such a thing were beyond his comprehension, he shook his head. "I told him if he could not trust his very competent managers to oversee his properties, then he should sell, consolidate, and manage one company himself to his own satisfaction."

He turned to look into Agatha's eyes. "That will be my advice to you as well, my dear, when you are up to discussing such things. I offered to help him sell the less profitable holdings, and I shall extend that same offer to you. I am yours to command." He raised her hand to his lips, brushing her knuckles with a kiss.

Juliette stared at the painting over the mantel. Her parents were openly affectionate with each other, but such a display from the viscount to Agatha set up a discomfort . . . and if she were honest . . . a bit of envy. What would it be like to be cherished and championed by a man so much that he did not care who knew about his affection?

A fleeting image of Duke Heinrich shot through her mind, but the thought of him kissing her hand . . . or her lips . . . did nothing to move her. He was a nice man, but he sparked no romantic thoughts in her. Most couples married for expediency, necessity, or to follow their families' wishes, not for love. Was she wrong to want to hold out for something more?

The footman entered. "Mrs. Fairchild has arrived, ma'am."

"Mrs. Fairchild?" Agatha looked at Lord Darby, who shook his head. "Perhaps she was an acquaintance of my mother's long ago? Please show her in." Agatha straightened her back and composed her face into serene, if still grief-tinged, lines. Her fiancé let go her hand, though it seemed with reluctance.

A slender woman with pale-yellow hair and Wedgwood-blue eyes swept into the room. She wore black from head to toe, and she clutched a black lace handkerchief. Arrestingly beautiful, she looked ethereal and elegant, though she must be all of forty. Both Daniel and Lord Darby shot to their feet.

"Dear Miss Montgomery—may I call you Agatha? I am prostrate with grief." She held out her hand.

Agatha clasped the woman's fingers but dropped her hand quickly. "Mrs. Fairchild. So nice of you to call." A puzzled crease appeared between her brows as she sized up the newcomer.

"I had to come." She pressed her hand to her chest. "My poor, dear Garfield." Two perfect tears tumbled over her lower lashes. "However will I go on? Ours was a once-in-a-lifetime love."

Juliette smothered a gasp. Love? Who was this woman? Agatha clearly hadn't known her, not by name nor by sight. Had her father really kept something so momentous from his own daughter?

Then again, her parents had kept even bigger secrets from her for her entire life. Perhaps all parents were deceptive, keeping their children in the dark about the most important parts of their lives.

Agatha's eyes narrowed. "Really, Mrs. Fairchild? My father did not mention having great affection for you. In point of fact, he never mentioned you at all."

"My dear, he wished to wait until you were settled back in England before introducing us. He knew how important your debut Season was, and he wanted no distractions. We were willing to put aside our happiness until he found *someone* to wed you." Mrs. Fairchild delicately dabbed at her cheeks with her handkerchief, managing to look like a porcelain doll in spite of being "distraught."

Juliette winced. Found someone to wed Agatha? As if it were an arduous task not undertaken lightly? Agatha hadn't needed any machinations by her father. She had found a match, the heir to an earldom, by being her own lovely self.

Mrs. Fairchild sighed. "He did not wish to upset you upon your arrival by revealing our attachment. And now it is too late." Again, she dabbed at perfect tears. How was it that she could cry so prettily? Even her eyes stayed clear. "Introduce me to the gentlemen, dear." She trained her eyes on first Lord Darby and then Daniel.

Agatha made the men known to her guest, giving Alonzo his full title and calling Daniel merely Mr. Swann, not mentioning his occupation. "And this is my friend Lady Juliette, daughter of the Earl and Countess of Thorndike."

"A pleasure." Mrs. Fairchild nodded. "I wish we had met under more felicitous circumstances."

Mrs. Fairchild, belying her diminutive stature, reigned over the conversation. She attached herself to Lord Darby, barely letting anyone else get a word in edgeways.

Juliette watched for Daniel's reaction, and with satisfaction she noted his lowered brows and careful study. Did he think her beautiful? Was he affected by her charms though she was nearly old enough to be his mother?

Juliette struck down the thought as unworthy. She might feel antipathy toward the woman, but the fault was in her own heart. Everyone dealt with grief differently, and if Mrs. Fairchild had really loved Mr. Montgomery and anticipated marriage, she must be truly bereaved.

"Have you had time to consider your options, my dear—what you will do with your inheritance? I would be happy to guide you. I have been widowed and have walked this path before. Of course, you are not widowed, but many of the issues of inheritance and what to do with your father's assets will be the same. I know Garfield would want me to assist you."

Agatha looked to the viscount, then said, "Thank you for your offer, but I have all the aid I need at the moment."

A tiny arrow formed between the widow's brows, and she leaned over and patted Agatha's hand. Agatha flinched. "I feel I would be remiss if I failed to warn you that some will approach you only out of a desire to get their hands on your money. You're very wealthy now, and some of a predatory nature will try to take advantage of you. Perhaps you would allow me to, ah, scrutinize those who would seek to advise you?"

"Mrs. Fairchild." The viscount removed the widow's hand, taking possession of Agatha's himself. "While we appreciate your interest, Miss Montgomery is well looked after." He lifted their clasped fingers. "I am an experienced man of business, and she has several capable managers, solicitors, and accountants who will help her. For the time being, she should be allowed to focus on her grieving."

Juliette had never admired the viscount more.

Agatha's lips trembled, and her eyes grew bright with unshed tears. "Thank you, Alonzo."

The widow, as if taking the measure of things, sat upright and gave a tremulous smile. "Of course. I did not mean to intrude, only to help. It is in my nature to want to help. Garfield often said it was one of my many lovely traits."

Though Juliette had not known Garfield Montgomery well, she couldn't imagine him saying such a thing. The thought of him, all bluster and bravado, tenderly wooing a lady sent a giggle through Juliette. She tried to cover it with a cough, but her eyes met Daniel's, and she knew she had failed to fool *him*, at least. His lips twitched, and he looked away. Was he imagining the same thing?

"I'm so sorry." She sipped her tea. "A tickle in my throat."

More guests arrived, and Agatha was able to escape the direct attentions of Mrs. Fairchild. Voices were low, faces somber, as condolences were expressed. Agatha, with Alonzo for support, greeted people by the drawing room door. The servants brought fresh pots of tea and coffee and saw to the refreshment table.

"Mingle and listen, if you will." Daniel's whisper brushed the tendrils of hair over her ear, sending a shiver down her spine. "I shall do the same. Don't let on that I'm from Bow Street. It isn't common knowledge that Montgomery was murdered, though I suspect news will leak soon."

She nodded and moved away.

One man entered with a bandaged head and bruised cheek. "Miss Montgomery, my name is Hubert Earnshaw, and I was your father's accountant. I am so sorry for your loss. Garfield Montgomery was a great man, and he was my friend."

"Thank you. I've seen you with my father. Were you at the mill when it . . ."

"Yes, miss. I had an appointment with him that day. The blast nearly knocked me into the river. I was fortunate to land on the walkway over the waterwheel instead of being blown into the water." He touched his bandage. "I wish I had not been late for our meeting. Perhaps if someone else had been there, the killer would have stayed his hand. It will be my lifelong regret."

So the fact of murder was indeed out.

Agatha nodded, but the viscount scowled, patting Agatha's hand in the crook of his elbow. Perhaps he thought it bad form for the accountant to bring up the murder at such a time.

Juliette tried to be observant without appearing so, as Uncle Bertie had taught her. Most of the guests were business associates of Mr. Montgomery. There were a few women in attendance, and snippets of their conversations caught her ears.

"I heard the manager is near death at St. Bart's. Head injury. Poor chap. He'd probably be better off to have died in the blast than to linger like he is."

"Wonder what she will do now? Sell everything? She'd be sitting on a tidy sum. I wouldn't mind buying the distillery or the woolen mill. And didn't he invest in a copper mine down near Truro?"

"I think the gristmill can be rebuilt. The stone walls are intact. If she doesn't wish to rebuild, she can sell the property. Someone will buy it. Especially if the wheel and mechanisms are still functional. Hammersmith is the perfect site for a gristmill."

"What about his artwork? If the daughter decides to sell it all, the prices will go down quickly. Too much available all at once."

Juliette circulated, finally coming to stand beside Daniel, who had secured himself a place near the windows.

"It seems everyone here knows what Agatha should do. They all have opinions, but none of them seem to agree."

"Everyone is an expert at someone else's business. What do you make of Mrs. Fairchild?" Daniel put his coffee cup on a passing tray.

"She's beautiful. I had no idea Mr. Montgomery was interested in any woman. Nor did Agatha. How awful for her to learn he was keeping such a secret from his own daughter."

"If they were on the cusp of marriage, as she intimated, why wasn't she a guest at your debut ball? I combed through the guest list repeatedly when that painting was . . . *stolen*." He slanted a knowing glance at her. "She was not included on the roll. Her intended throws a ball for his daughter and her best friend, and she doesn't attend? They would not have needed to let on they were anything more than friends if that was his wish on such a big night for Agatha, but for her not to have been invited?" He shrugged. "I shall never understand the upper classes."

Did he include her in his generalizations? It hurt to think he might. That he saw such a yawning gap between his own circumstances and hers.

"I wish Agatha's father had treated her as an adult with a good mind and kind heart. Now he will not have the chance. He should have told her about Mrs. Fairchild."

A murmur went through the room as a man and woman in somber clothes entered. They looked unremarkable to Juliette, but others clearly knew more than she.

"Who is that?"

Juliette shook her head. "I've no idea."

"Carlyle," said a man behind her. "He's a nerve showing up here."

Daniel's attention sharpened, as did Juliette's. "Why would you say that, sir?" Daniel asked.

"They were noted rivals. Carlyle has a mill of his own on the river, just a mile above Montgomery's, and they often competed for the same farmers' grain. There were rumors, and I, of course, could not substantiate them, but . . ." He bent forward, his eyes alight, clearly enjoying the gossip. "They accused each other of all sorts of skulduggery. Sabotage, pinching customers and workers, and"—his voice lowered further—"I heard customers weren't all Montgomery stole from Carlyle. I heard he cast his eye toward Carlyle's wife."

It was a day of revelations into the romantic life of Garfield Montgomery. If this rumor was to be believed, he was something of a Lothario. It staggered the mind.

Juliette studied Mrs. Carlyle with interest. Brown hair, blue eyes, sharp features, shapely of figure, and considerably younger than her husband, who was portly with gray peppering his dark hair. She was nothing like the ethereal widow who had staked a claim on the deceased.

What had Mrs. Fairchild thought of the rumors? Had she known?

Had Mr. Carlyle killed Mr. Montgomery in a fit of rage over being made a cuckold by his wife and his rival? Was it something as pedestrian as that? Not money, not power, but that other motive?

Again her thoughts went to Agatha. If she came to know all that people were saying about her father, it would break her heart.

Daniel took her elbow and guided her toward the door. "I'm never going to finish my interview with Miss Montgomery in the midst of all these people. I must go to Hammersmith. Perhaps I can return today, but it will be very late. If you get an opportunity, would you ask her a few questions for me once the guests leave? I will have Cadogan remain outside for whenever you're ready to go."

"How will you get to Hammersmith if you leave the carriage here?" They passed into the foyer.

"I will rent a horse from the nearest livery."

He was an excellent rider. She had seen him take the biggest fences without fear. She wished she were going with him rather than staying in the somber drawing room, but Agatha needed her. Juliette had been next door to neglectful in the opening weeks of their first Season, and now, in the face of her friend's bereavement, Juliette must attend her.

"What questions should I ask Agatha? And when will I see you again to give you her answers?" She prayed she didn't sound too eager.

"Ask her if her father owned a gun. Or if he mentioned trouble at the mill over his proposed renovations. Ask if he received any strange letters or visitors here at the house."

"I will. Should I ask about his relationships with women?"

"I do not want to distress her overly. The rumor about Mrs. Carlyle is, thus far, unsubstantiated. She may very well be innocent, and to have it spread would damage her reputation. Find out what you can, but quietly. If you do not hear from me in the next day or so, you can always send a note to the Bow Street office with your findings." He motioned to the footman beside the door. "My hat and cloak, if you please."

When his belongings arrived, he swirled his cape around his shoulders with a practiced maneuver Juliette found quite graceful, then settled his hat atop his dark hair. "Good day, Lady Juliette."

When he had gone, she squared her shoulders and turned back to the reception. She had her mission, however small. And surely Uncle Bertie wouldn't think her interfering? She was helping one friend while supporting another in her grief. There was no harm in that, was there?

Chapter 5

DANIEL LEFT THE MONTGOMERY HOUSE and, after a quick word with Cadogan, headed toward the nearest livery stable. His rented horse made up for his lack of beauty by having bags of stamina. The gelding pulled like one of those new steam engines, had a mouth like cast iron, and a trot that could jolt a man's teeth out of his head, but his canter was smooth and steady.

Which gave Daniel time to assess what he'd learned thus far. Mr. Montgomery had a business rival who might have had a reason to dislike him personally. The widowed Mrs. Fairchild claimed a romantic relationship, while rumors surfaced that another woman might have been Montgomery's quarry. His holdings were diverse and plentiful, and he had a considerable amount of wealth as a result, which could lead to professional jealousy, or perhaps he had crossed someone in his business dealings. He kept his daughter ignorant of most of his doings, and he had ill prepared her as his inheritor, which left her vulnerable to predatory businessmen.

Any of these bits of information could lead to the killer, but they could also lead to nothing—which was often the way early in a criminal investigation. Sifting through the noise to get to the truth.

An eerie feeling swept over him as he pulled his horse to a trot and then a walk on the high street of Hammersmith. Though just over seventy-two hours had passed since the explosion, much cleanup had taken place. The streets were mostly clear, though sunlight still glinted off broken glass here and there. He passed the lane leading to the inn that had served as an infirmary, but he didn't turn in. He would check with the local doctor later to see if he had any information.

At the bottom of the street, a crowd gathered around the mill. Daniel frowned. Were these the employees, working to get the mill operational again? Had someone given the all clear already?

Dropping from the saddle, he drew the reins over his mount's head. Perhaps he should stable him. He had thought to tie him near the mill, but with so many men crowded around, he decided not to risk it. He would find a livery.

His horse taken care of, he returned to the lane. The closer he strode to the mill, the more uneasy he grew. These men were not working. They appeared to be waiting, but for what? Nearly twenty in all, wearing rough clothes and heavy boots.

A man climbed atop a barrel and held up his hands, but he wore nice clothing, a fancy waistcoat with a watch chain, and a white cravat intricately tied.

"Men, thank you for coming. This"—he swept his arm toward the damaged mill—"should serve as a warning to those who think they can rise to success by treading on the backs of their own workers."

A cheer and raised fists from the crowd. One man carried a pitchfork, and he pounded the handle on the cobbles.

"Montgomery was warned. He was told not to bring in that new equipment from American mills. Yet you stood right here not a month ago while the crates were unloaded from the barge." The spokesman pointed toward the river. "He's lucky you didn't tip them in the drink right then, bringing in these modern machines and doing men out of their livelihoods. You've spent your whole lives as millers, learning the trade, keeping the traditions alive, and for what? So a rich man who never bent his back to a shovel or a grain sack could rip your way of life from your grasp?"

A rabble-rouser with nothing better to do than foment trouble.

Daniel had heard enough. He drew his truncheon from his belt and looped the strap around his wrist. "Gentlemen, you need to disperse."

He raised the truncheon for all to see. "I am an investigator of the Bow Street Magistrate's Court. This area is under investigation, and you cannot congregate here."

"You have no authority here. This is Hammersmith, not London." The shout had come from the back.

Aware that he was one man against twenty-odd, Daniel held his ground. He must show no fear, no weakness, else they would pounce. They could not be allowed to do further damage to the mill, nor could he allow them to compromise any evidence that may remain. Men in mobs could be driven to do things no man alone would contemplate.

"You know nothing of these men's troubles," the spokesman shouted. "They've no work now, no livelihoods or ways to care for their wives and children and old mothers. And who's to blame? Montgomery!"

Another cheer of agreement.

"If such is the case, then he paid a hefty price." Daniel threaded his way through the men until he stood beside the barrel the spokesman perched upon. "He was murdered, and the man who killed him is walking free. There is nothing to be gained by demonstrating now."

With Rosebreen's confirmation of cause of death, there was no longer any reason to keep the truth hidden. He gauged the response to his declaration. No one seemed shocked at the pronouncement of murder. Either they had already heard, or they had suspected from the start.

The rabble-rouser shook his head. "This mill will be rebuilt either by the Montgomery family or by a new owner, and woe to the rebuilder who insists upon changing the way these men have milled flour here for a thousand years."

"You keep saying *these men*. Are you not a miller by trade?" Daniel asked, stepping back until he felt the stone wall behind him. He eyed the crowd. He did not want one of these men to get behind him.

"I've come to help them. Woodrow Trotter's my name, and I fight for the laborer."

The men murmured agreement and stepped forward, crowding Daniel. Pray he didn't have to reach for the pistol in the waistband at the back of his trousers.

"You, sir, stir up trouble where there was none, and you inflame and agitate rather than help. I ask you men again, disperse. Or if you wish to gather, you must do it elsewhere. This is a crime area, under investigation by the authority of your local magistrate and in cooperation with the officers of Bow Street. Those who choose not to leave the area will be arrested for trespassing."

Though how he would arrest twenty men, he didn't know. But he wouldn't go quietly. He must preserve what evidence remained, and he must stand for the rule of law.

"What is all this?" An elderly, gentle voice cut through the tension. "If you men desire to congregate, I wish you would do so in my church. The doors are always open for worship and prayer." A white-haired vicar made his way to Daniel's side. "I know you are fearful, gentlemen, and you are looking for someone to blame, but a dead man and a detective from the city are poor choices. We will survive this mishap, we will come to the aid of those in need, and we will do so without agitation from outsiders. We have always taken care of our own in this village, and now will be no exception. If you have needs while the mill is rebuilt, make them known at the church. That is one of the reasons the church exists."

His face became stern, and he stared at Trotter. "Sir, I do not know you, but you are surplus to requirements. I suggest you take your radical ideas elsewhere and leave the good men of Hammersmith alone."

Though nearly a foot shorter than Daniel, the vicar's words had a strong effect upon his listeners. They trickled away in twos and threes, heads bent, shuffling up the street until only a handful remained. Even Trotter climbed from his perch, and with a huff, straightened his cravat, tugged on the bottom of his waistcoat, and stalked away with his nose in the air.

A large man with a red face and impressive whiskers stood his ground, legs braced, a wheel spoke in his beefy hands.

"George, you were told to go," the preacher reminded him.

"Go? Where? I got no job now." He waved the wooden spoke at the mill. "How can I go home to my little 'uns and say I have no bread for 'em and no money to get any?"

"And you believe shouting in the street will change that?"

"It's better than getting drunk down the pub."

"Marginally, I suppose, but both are futile. If you turn your energies to helping this young man find out who killed your employer, you will be that much closer to the mill being repaired and reopened."

Lowering his truncheon, Daniel asked, "Sir, you were employed here?"

"Worked here since I was a lad."

"Excellent. I have questions."

"Don't help him, George," one of his companions said. "He works for the enemy, the toffs who lord it over us. Look at his clothes. He's a toff himself. I bet I could feed my youngsters for a month on what that cloak cost."

It was true, but that Daniel possessed such fine clothes was not of his doing. He followed the orders of the faceless patron who had controlled his life for the last thirteen years, lived where he supplied, wore the clothes he chose.

"Gentlemen, you don't really care about my clothes. You care about my ability to find a murderer, and you care about feeding your families. If you want this mill repaired and to have your jobs back, the fastest course is to give me aid."

"He speaks wise words, which you would do well to heed. Stop blustering and do what you know is right." The vicar nodded and walked away.

Daniel mentally called down God's blessing upon the man for defusing the volatile situation with sensible words.

"What questions you got?" the man called George asked. He tossed the broken wheel spoke to the ground, where it clattered against the cobbles and came to rest in a pile of rubbish.

"Were you working here on the day of the blast?"

"Aye. We were." He indicated his two companions.

"Where were you when the explosion happened?" Daniel reached into his coat pocket for his notebook and pencil.

"I was up there." He pointed to the top floor. "Mr. Coombe, the manager, sent me up to check the pulleys on the lift belts. Something was sticking, he thought, and he wanted me to knock it loose."

"And you gentlemen?"

"Below. Where the grinding stones are. We were milling fine flour and were nearly done. An order for some coarse was next up, so we were going to make the changes to the speed of the stones and replace the screens."

"And you weren't injured?"

"Not unless you count being scared out of my boots," George said. "The whole place shook. I thought the end had come."

The other two nodded.

"Did you see anything before the blast? Hear anything? Did you hear the gunshot that killed Montgomery?"

George shook his big head. "You ever been inside a working mill? You cannot hear your own self screaming half the time. That's why we have hand signals for the machinery areas and heavy doors between the mill and the offices and warehouse. Some of the men stuff cotton in their ears, it's so loud."

Daniel frowned. "Those doors were open. Do you think they were blown wide by the blast?"

The oldest of the three scratched his stubbly whiskers. He had gnarled hands with enormous knuckles that spoke of a lifetime of hard labor. "You'd have to ask someone who was on the main floor. Mr. Coombe would know."

Mr. Coombe was insensible in a hospital bed at St. Bart's and could very well never regain consciousness.

Daniel asked several more questions, but he felt he'd gotten all he could from the workers. As he turned away, George put his beefy hand on Daniel's arm.

"What?"

"Earlier in the day, I nipped into the warehouse to . . . well, I like a drink about halfway through the shift. Sort of picks me up, you know?" He had the large nose and cracked blood vessels of the drink addict. "Not a lot, just a sip. And I was looking for an out-of-the-way place."

"What did you see?"

"It in't what I saw, but what I heard. There was a row going on in the guv'nor's office. A real donnybrook."

"Who was it? And what was the argument about?"

"I recognized Mr. Montgomery's voice. His is even louder than mine. But I didn't recognize the other fellow's."

"And the fight?"

"I was trying not to get caught, you see, so I was hurrying to find a corner out of sight, and I went past the office quick-like."

"I understand." Daniel wished the man would hurry the story. He was supposed to meet with the engineer and examine the crime scene again. The man would be here any moment.

"The other man, whoever he was, said, 'We'll decide this on the village green. I demand satisfaction.'"

"He was challenging Montgomery to a duel?"

"That's what it sounded like to me. Only well-heeled gents mess about with duels. Working men would have settled it right there in the office, fist to fist." He raised his own fist, the size and shape of a mace, and his companions nodded.

"And when was this?"

He shrugged. "Morning, but not early. The mill was in full voice, so you can't hear the church bells to tell the time. It was before the noon meal."

"I see." Daniel jotted down George's words. The man in question might have been Mr. Carlyle if the gossip at Agatha's was to be believed. He would have to pay Carlyle a visit.

"Did you see the man leave?"

"No. Mr. Coombe came into the warehouse, and I ducked out and went around to the mill doors. Got back to work so no one would miss me."

"And you saw nothing more suspicious?"

"No. 'Twas a normal day. Do you think whoever it was in the office didn't wait for the duel and just killed Mr. Montgomery? Just shot him right there?"

"It's too soon to draw any conclusions. I will need your full names and addresses in case I think of anything else to ask you—or you're called upon to testify at a trial."

As they were giving the information, a smartly dressed man with precise movements came up the lane, tilting his head back to look at the top of the mill, then slowly perusing the walls, windows, and doors. He had a cane tucked under his arm and a jaunty angle to his hat.

The structural engineer.

Daniel nodded to the mill workers and approached the man. "Sir, I believe we have an appointment."

"Ah, you must be the detective. Isaiah Hoffman, at your service." He flicked his fingers, and a card appeared. A small smile played about his lips. "Shall we begin? I do not want to be behind my time."

"Daniel Swann, Bow Street." Daniel took the card and tucked it into his pocket.

"She's had a bit of a shake, hasn't she?" Hoffman used his cane tip to poke at the stone wall. Dust came off but no mortar. "The building seems to have withstood it quite well. I have seen far worse."

"Is it safe to go inside?"

"Do not rush. A thorough assessment will take time." He pursed his lips. "I viewed the building plans before I arrived. I have them all up here." He tapped the side of his head under his hat brim. "My firm designed both the addition of the warehouse some years ago and the new plans for expansion and modernization. Do you know where the worst of the damage was done?"

"The main mill floor, from what I understand. That's where the fire was."

"Then I believe we should enter through the warehouse and work our way across." He tucked his cane back under his arm and strode to their right. "This way, young man."

As if measuring a line, Mr. Hoffman paced off the distance with even, identical steps until he turned at the corner of the building and stopped before the warehouse doors. Wood and metal and a quantity of flour spilled from the opening. He studied the debris. "This appears to be mostly the contents of the warehouse itself. Barrel staves, cooper's rings, sacking and inventory. These beams, however, are troubling." His lips twitched, and his eyes narrowed. "Unless . . ."

He bent to study one of the thick chunks of wood. "Ah yes." Straightening, he smiled. "These are not structural. Or at least not yet. Not a single peg or nail hole, mortise or tenon. These are the supports the firm recommended for the renovation, and clearly Mr. Montgomery purchased them and had them delivered in advance of the work. They must have been leaning against the wall near the door when the explosion occurred."

Daniel nodded. "This is where we found the manager, Mr. Coombe. Half-buried and pinned."

Stepping carefully, Mr. Hoffman made his way into the warehouse. Dust hung in the air, and the smell of water, smoke, and flour clung to everything. Light filtered in from open windows high up in the walls under the eaves.

"I was up the street when the explosion happened, and it knocked me to the ground even at that distance." Daniel pointed toward the hall where the offices lay. "I cannot imagine what it felt like to be in the building."

Mr. Hoffman pressed his hand against a support column, giving it a brief shake. Dust cascaded down, but the wooden post stood firm. "The stone walls were both an asset and a liability. They contained the blast, but they also condensed and directed the force both upward and through these halls. It isn't unusual for roofs to be blown completely off in cases like this. However, it appears the explosion did no damage to the roof supports here in the warehouse. By the time the impact got here, it had already diminished. This area will not need much in the way of repairs."

"I had a feeling the damage could have been much worse. Do you think the blast was set off as a warning of more to come?"

Hoffman paused. "You are thinking this was deliberate sabotage?"

Daniel shrugged. "It's possible. There were threats. At least one anonymous letter promised trouble if Montgomery went ahead with the proposed renovations."

"Interesting." Hoffman's bright-blue eyes were like pinpoints, and Daniel could almost see the gears turning in his head as he took in the new information.

"Let's look in the owner's office, Mr. Hoffman. That's where the murder took place."

"Are you counting the deaths here to be murder before you know if the blast was intentional?" The engineer's head turned a quarter of the way around, his brows rising symmetrically.

"It's possible the blast was accidental, but Mr. Montgomery did not die in the explosion. He was already dead, shot to death in his office sometime before."

Hoffman tapped his chin. "That is most disturbing. Let us proceed."

The smoke smell increased as they moved toward Montgomery's office. Soot caked the walls of the stone hallway, and debris littered the floor.

Daniel indicated two places on the floor. "Two men were killed here. I understand they were cleaning up a flour spill. The impact threw them into the wall. Here are the shovels and the cart they were using." He lifted the broken handle of one shovel and tossed it onto the pile.

"Was it breezy that day?" Hoffman asked.

Daniel thought back. "I do not believe so. There was a chill in the air but no wind."

Again Hoffman pursed his lips as if in deep thought. He poked at the ceiling with his cane. "There is surface damage to the wood but nothing structural. The fire must have burned out quickly." He clasped his cane behind his back with both hands, rocking on his toes as he studied the scene.

"Yes, they were able to subdue the flames before the entire building caught. I was amazed at how quickly they organized bucket lines to bring water up from the river." The door to Montgomery's office stood open now, the shattered glass panel crunching under Daniel's boots. The area where Montgomery's body had lain was the only clear space. Every other surface was showered with papers and documents and ash. "The fire flashed through here quickly. Some of the papers burned, but others look untouched."

"That is the nature of paper. A single sheet will be gone in seconds, but a stack can burn for hours or even smolder and douse itself." Hoffman shoved through the pages on the floor with the tip of his cane. "Again, I do not see any structural damage here. Cosmetic only." His gaze sharpened again. "Was the window open, or did someone open it afterward?"

The river side of the office had two windows. One was shattered completely with the sash in the closed position, but the other sash was raised. Again, no glass in the frames. "I didn't open it, and no one lingered in here long enough to do so. Not with the danger of fire or another explosion lurking."

"I would suspect thieves and looters, but what would be the point? The place is open to the wind now." The engineer shrugged. "One would not need to enter by an open window. One could dance through the doors."

"For the past three nights, two watchmen have been on duty to keep the curious or nefarious away. Trusted men hired for the purpose. If there are any clues here, I don't want them wandering off in the hands of a thief." Daniel squatted and leafed through brittle sheets of paper. Orders, it appeared, filled and delivered. Neat rows of columns. He would put Owen on gathering and organizing the charred pages. The office boy would be thrilled.

"You may wish to secure this, however. It appears to be the mill's strongbox." Wood and metal scraped on the floor as Hoffman dragged a well-strapped cube from beneath a counter. Once painted red, with metal strips crossing it in squares, a large lock hung from the hasp.

"How soon will you be able to determine the extent of the damage and whether it is feasible to rebuild?"

"It will take a few days to finish my examination, and then you shall have my report. Or rather Miss Montgomery shall have it, since she is paying for my services. At first glance, it appears the structure is still sound, but I've yet to see the main working parts where the fire burned the longest. I will err on the side of caution when it comes to my recommendations, I assure you."

"Do you have any theories as to the cause of the explosion? Was it deliberate or an accident?"

"I cannot say until I've made a thorough examination. I prefer to complete my work before positing theories. I am no expert in arson or explosives, merely architecture. I do know someone a bit unorthodox but brilliant I can call in as an expert."

"Are there such people as experts in arson and explosives?" Daniel asked.

"Arsonists and bombers come to mind." Hoffman's lips twitched, and Daniel appreciated his wry humor. "However, the young man I have in mind is a scientist."

"While you are looking things over, keep your eye out for the murder weapon. We're looking for a small gun, not unlike a ladies' muff gun or a gambler's sleeve pistol."

"If I find such a thing here, I shall inform you immediately."

Daniel rode back to London balancing the strongbox on his lap. His horse did not care for this maneuver and let him know it all the way. By the time he returned the horse to the livery and toted the box up the steps and into the Bow Street offices, he was tired and irritable.

Owen sat at Daniel's desk—where he had no right to be—his back to the room, swinging gently from side to side. He drummed his fingers on the chair arms, eyes raised to the ceiling, seemingly oblivious to Daniel's arrival.

Thomas Fyfe and Matthias Tollivar, two of his fellow detectives, sat at their desks, bent over the inevitable paperwork that came along with working at Bow Street. When they looked up, Daniel tucked the box under his arm and raised one finger to his lips to indicate his desire for quiet. They nodded, grinning like fiends.

Daniel eased silently across the detectives' room, calling upon his recent training with Sir Bertrand Thorndike on covert movements, careful not to alert Owen to his presence. When he stood across the desk from Owen's back, he raised the strongbox in both hands and let go, dropping it flat onto the desk with a bang that shot Owen out of the chair as from a catapult. The boy's yell ricocheted around the room, melding with the hoots of laughter from Fyfe and Tollivar.

Owen staggered against the wall, his hand to his narrow chest, eyes wide as cartwheels. "What'd you do that for?"

"Why are you sitting at my desk?" Daniel yanked at the frog closure of his cloak and swirled the garment off. He hung it with his hat on the peg behind his desk and rolled the chair close. "I may have to drag you around with me over the next few days, but that doesn't mean you're a fully trained detective with a right to sit in this room."

He knew he sounded petty and gruff, but he was cranky. He wanted Ed back, steady Eddie, who always knew which avenue of an investigation to pursue, who never said a cross word, and who pulled his weight.

Owen scowled, folding his arms. "The guv told me to wait for you to return. I brought back the report and the bullet like you said, and I've run all over London the past few days gathering information for you, but Sir Michael isn't best pleased that you went to Hammersmith without me today. You're supposed to be training me, not having me run your errands." He shot a defiant look at Daniel that rasped his nerves.

"Part of your training is to do all those little things that receive no glory or notice but are essential to solving cases. And I have another one for you. The engineer has given permission to enter the warehouse and offices at the mill. I want you to go there with a wagon and boxes and pack up all of Mr. Montgomery's papers. Bring them back here, commandeer one of the interview rooms, and begin sorting them."

Owen's brows crashed down. "Sort them how? And why am I always stuck with paperwork? Why can't I question a suspect or a witness or something?"

Daniel counted slowly in his head, praying for patience. "Details matter in a murder investigation. You are nowhere near ready to question suspects, even if we had any. As to the office papers, bring in our consulting accountant. I want to know where the mill stood financially and if that played any role in Montgomery's murder."

A youngster of about ten summers bounded into the room, his head nearly dwarfed in an enormous cap. "Letter for Mr. Swann." He held aloft a folded paper with a red wax seal.

"Here." Daniel waved the child over, fishing in his pocket for some pennies.

Checking the seal, his heart raced. Coles, Franks & Moody, solicitors. Was this the missive he'd been waiting for, to wind up the patronage once and for all?

He broke the seal and read quickly, his heart sinking. Instead of his long-sought emancipation, this was another directive from his guardian. Another "favor" asked, to which Daniel could not yet say no.

He could not wait for the scheduled appointment to wind up his guardianship.

Chapter 6

JULIETTE HAD NEVER BEEN TO a funeral before. The Thorndikes had little extended family, and her grandparents had passed away before she was born. Uncle Bertie had instructed her that it was rare for women to attend funerals, and under no circumstances was she to show any emotion. A stoic appearance was required for all in the congregation.

The service at St. George's in Hanover Square was fittingly somber. Agatha's face was veiled in black, her dress seeming to absorb all color. There were some distant cousins of the Montgomery family present, but Agatha was the principal mourner. Because their engagement was not yet public, Lord Darby did not sit beside her, instead finding a place a few rows back. All alone, Agatha appeared fragile, and Juliette's heart ached for her friend. At the same time, she was proud of her for adhering to the expectation that she would remain composed.

Juliette sat with Uncle Bertie on the aisle, where they had an excellent view of the catafalque and black-draped coffin. Agatha had insisted upon white flowers everywhere, and the heady scent mixed with grief nearly choked Juliette.

Bertie shifted his long legs, straightening the seams on his black trousers. He looked as elegant and stylish as ever. And his dark eyes never stayed still for long.

Juliette tried to concentrate on the sermon, but she was distracted. For the first time in her life she had carried a weapon into church.

Though this time the pistol was securely strapped to her leg with no chance of coming unstuck, she was acutely aware of it. What did God think of her bringing such a thing into a house of worship?

The reverend droned on, and her mind wandered to her parents. Were they safe in France? Were they obtaining the information they sought? Were they attending parties and meeting people who would be good contacts for the future?

Did they miss her at all?

As they rose for the recessional, Juliette bent to pick up her reticule and prayer book. From the corner of her eye, she spied Jasper Finch, the man who had been so outspoken about laborers' rights at the Venetian breakfast.

Why was he here? He had been so cutting in his opinion of men like Mr. Montgomery, it seemed odd he would attend the man's funeral. His opinions about violence as a solution came back to her, and she shuddered.

Organ music rose to fill the barrel-vaulted space, and Bertie bent to her ear. "Now we must endure the interminable luncheon."

The guests exited row by row, and as the widow Mrs. Fairchild passed, she was supported by a younger man. She trembled and held her handkerchief to her face, but she maintained her composure. Even in her grief she was startlingly beautiful.

Who was the man with her? A relative? Or had she sought to replace Mr. Montgomery so quickly?

Juliette shoved away that thought as unworthy.

Bertie offered Juliette his arm when it was their turn, and they made their way up the stone-flagged aisle. Near the back, taking up several rows, sat stalwart, rough-hewn men in common clothes, some with bandages and splints. Mill employees, casualties of the explosion. On the opposite side, Agatha's staff members clustered together, some stoic, some with damp eyes.

It seemed almost a crime that the sun was so bright and the temperatures warm. They stepped out onto the columned porch as the coffin was loaded into the back of the hearse for the trip to the cemetery. A small group of men would accompany the body to the burial on the south side of the river, but women were not expected to attend.

Only a handful of people had been invited to the luncheon back at the Montgomery house, and Juliette was surprised that Daniel Swann was among the guests. Was he here as Agatha's friend or in his capacity as a detective? Juliette had not been able to give him Agatha's answers to his questions posed after yesterday's reception at the Montgomery residence. Perhaps they would have a few moments alone to confer. If not, she had the answers on a slip of paper in her reticule.

She didn't miss the scowl on Lord Darby's face at sight of the detective. Why must those two always rub each other the wrong way? It couldn't be jealousy, for Agatha had no interest in Daniel. It must be snobbery. Darby considered Daniel beneath him, and he liked to draw attention to the fact.

In her own home, Agatha relaxed her grip on emotions, occasionally dabbing at her eyes with her handkerchief as she accepted condolences.

The Widow Fairchild was another case altogether. She threw off societal strictures and mourned in every direction. "I do not know what I shall do now. My poor Garfield. I'm absolutely prostrate with grief." She said this each time she encountered a new person and again when they were seated around the luncheon table. "We were to be married, you know."

Juliette was sorry Agatha had extended an invitation, though she could hardly escape it considering the pressure Mrs. Fairchild had put upon her.

Mr. Earnshaw, still sporting his white bandages and bruises, sat across and a few chairs down from Juliette. "He was a good man of business, very knowledgeable and forthright. I never knew him to hesitate to make a decision he thought was right. And he took good care of his workers. Every Christmas he gave out gifts. Never missed a one."

Duke Heinrich, at Juliette's right hand, leaned over and whispered, "Have you noticed that a dead man never did anything but kindness in life? He might have been the biggest villain the world has ever seen, but once he is dead, we must not speak ill."

"What good would it do besides distressing Agatha, who loved him, bombastic nature and all? Mr. Montgomery was a fine father and a smart businessman. He could be sharp of tongue and quick to anger, but he was also generous and caring, especially toward Agatha."

Heinrich leaned back. "I would not have you think ill of me. I was not speaking of Herr Montgomery in particular, but only in generalities."

She smiled, and he relaxed. "No harm done."

Returning her smile, he touched her arm. She looked up and caught Daniel's stare. Something flashed between them, and she was acutely aware of Heinrich's hand on her sleeve.

"Have you given some thought to my invitation to visit my homeland?"

She broke her stare with the detective and blinked at Heinrich. Truthfully, she hadn't given the notion a minute's reflection in the past several days. Too much had happened to draw her mind away.

"It is most generous of you—and kind. My parents are away at the moment. At the behest of the Regent, they are part of a diplomatic contingency to France to settle postwar issues not sorted by the Congress of Vienna. Perhaps we can discuss it once they return."

The reprieve relieved her. She very much liked Heinrich, but the ardent look in his eyes made her uneasy. Agreeing to travel to Germany to meet his family would deliver a strong message as to her receptiveness should he propose marriage, a message she wasn't certain she wished to send.

Again she was aware of Daniel's eyes on her, and she picked up her fork and gave her attention to her food.

"It is too bad that Mr. Montgomery had such an argument with Mr. Coombe just before he died." Mr. Earnshaw took up his glass and drank deeply as all attention focused his way. "Not that they didn't argue frequently. Mr. Montgomery liked to tell his manager how to manage the mill, and Mr. Coombe had his own ideas." The accountant half smiled at the memory. "They were at loggerheads on at least a weekly basis."

"They argued that morning?" Daniel asked. "Do you know the cause?"

"I do not, though I can surmise. It was probably about the renovations Mr. Montgomery had ordered. Mr. Coombe was in favor of the changes, but not the timing. Many of the mill's customers are emptying their grain bins and planting now. The excess grain is being brought to the mill to be ground, and Mr. Coombe wished to finish the orders before stopping to tear out the old machinery and install the new. He thought mid-May or even June a better time so everything could be renovated and ready for harvest this fall. Mr. Montgomery was not one to wait upon an idea, and he wanted the changes made as soon as possible."

"What time did they have this argument?" Daniel reached into his coat and withdrew the small notebook he never seemed to be without.

Awareness rippled around the table, a reminder that a detective sat amongst them and he was in search of a killer. Some showed disapproval, some keen interest. Juliette looked to Agatha, at the foot of the table, and at her father's empty chair at the other end.

"Perhaps this is not the best time to discuss such matters," Uncle Bertie interjected smoothly. "We must consider Miss Montgomery's feelings."

"I agree. It's uncouth at best." Lord Darby frowned at Daniel. "I don't understand why you are here. You're a policeman." He said the word as if it tasted bad.

Daniel tucked his pencil into his notebook, red creeping up from his collar.

"He is here at my invitation," Agatha said, her voice steady. "He did my father a great service only weeks ago, and my father thought highly of him. He did return a treasured painting that had been stolen, after all."

"And," Duke Heinrich said, "he captured a killer and rescued an entire cache of stolen artwork worth many thousands of pounds. The newspapers called it a nearly impossible feat." He raised his glass and nodded toward Daniel.

Juliette carefully avoided looking at Uncle Bertie, whom she had helped to steal most of the artwork, and at Daniel, who had not only suspected them but at one point had tried to arrest them. Thankfully, no one else here knew how the true events unfolded.

The luncheon concluded with no more being said about either Daniel's presence or the argument between Mr. Montgomery and Mr. Coombe.

Was Mr. Coombe now a suspect? Did the mill manager shoot his employer over something as trivial as a schedule for renovations? Had anyone investigated this line of inquiry?

Guests rose and began to depart, once again expressing their condolences and sorrow at Agatha's loss but also looking relieved to escape the grieving household. Amongst the departures, Juliette managed to pass by Daniel close enough to slip the paper with Agatha's responses into his pocket, as well as a few deductions of her own. She surreptitiously tapped his elbow as she went by but didn't look at or acknowledge him.

Mr. Earnshaw bent over Agatha's hand. "I am sorry for bringing up anything unpleasant. I should not have spoken about your father and Mr. Coombe in such a manner. They had their differences, but each had great respect for the other. I was most blessed to work for your father, and I hope that in the coming days I may be of service to you as well. When you are ready to go over your father's financial papers, I will be happy to review them with you."

"Thank you, sir. You are most kind. I'm sure I will be in contact with you soon." Agatha sounded daunted at the prospect of going through her father's records.

"I'll walk you out," Daniel said to the accountant.

"I'll take my leave as well." Uncle Bertie clasped Agatha's hand. "Juliette may remain with you if you feel that would be beneficial. I'll send my carriage round for her later."

"Thank you, Sir Bertrand. You are most kind." Agatha's face was pale, and she looked ready to wilt.

"Come, Coatsworth." Uncle Bertie motioned for Lord Darby to leave with him.

Though the young man frowned, he took his leave of Agatha. "I regret I shall not see you on the morrow. I've been summoned to Kent to attend my grandfather. He is declining, as you know, and has requested my presence. When I return to London, I will speak with you."

Agatha nodded, her large eyes speaking volumes.

When the door shut on the last of them, Agatha went into the drawing room and collapsed onto a chair. "What an awful day."

"You were very brave, a credit to your father." Juliette joined her, slipping her feet out of her shoes and tucking her legs up on the settee, grateful to relax. Agatha must have felt the same, for she, too, took off her shoes, wriggling her toes in her black stockings.

"I feel as if I'm walking about in a cloud of cotton wool. Fuzzy of thought, fuzzy of perception. All the faces blurred together. I don't think I heard a thing the preacher said, nor most of the guests."

"Surely some stood out." Juliette thought of Alonzo Darby.

"The Widow Fairchild." Agatha pulled a face. "What was my father thinking? She's beautiful, yes, but awful too. One would think the entire day was about her and that no one else mattered. A week ago I'd never met her, and now she's acting as if she was set to move in next month."

"She was certainly dramatic. Who was that with her today? He was quite attentive."

"A Mr. Donaldson, she said, but she gave no other information. Perhaps she's already moved on from my father to a new conquest?" Agatha put her hand over her eyes. "I can but hope."

The housekeeper carried in a tray. "I thought you might like some tea, ma'am."

Agatha stiffened and dropped her hand. "Thank you."

When she had gone, Juliette asked, "What is it?"

"Before, when my father was alive and master of the house, the staff all called me *miss*. Now they call me *ma'am*. Each time serves as a reminder that I am now mistress of this house. Juliette, what am I going to do? I know nothing of business or money matters. How can I possibly see to my father's affairs? Ha, affairs. I didn't even know he was on the verge of proposing to a woman I had never met. What else don't I know? What other shocks lurk around corners?" She sagged back into her chair.

The door opened a few inches. "Ma'am?"

Mr. Mifflin, the aged and proper secretary to Mr. Montgomery, edged into the room. He carried a small strongbox on his palms, like a magus offering a gift.

"What is it?" Agatha sounded as if she couldn't bear to be bothered by one more trivial question.

"Ma'am, it's gone. All of it." His voice cracked.

"What's gone?" Juliette asked.

"All the household money. I went to pay the hearse driver, and when I looked, there wasn't so much as a shilling left. The box is empty." He set it on a side table, opened the lid, and tipped it up to show nothing inside. "There was more than a hundred pounds in here this morning. I fear one of the guests must have stolen the money."

Agatha's bleak eyes met Juliette's. "I guess one more surprise lurked today after all."

The day after the funeral, Daniel set out from London with Owen in tow. Carlyle's mill was located in the hamlet of Wattleford Hill, some three miles upstream from Montgomery's mill in Hammersmith. Nearly identical in design, his mill rose in stone and wood high above the houses clustered at its base.

As Daniel approached, this time in Cadogan's cab, the thumping sounds of a mill at work overcame the rattle and clatter of the horses' hooves. A bready, woodsy, watery smell surrounded him. He realized he was tense, anticipating another explosion, and he forced himself to relax.

"So we finally have a suspect?" Owen tugged on his jacket sleeves, which were inches too short. Clearly it was the best he had, and was cleaned and pressed, but he'd outgrown it some time ago.

"Possibly. Let us say he is a person of interest." Daniel cautioned himself not to get ahead of the investigation.

"But this fellow argued with the victim. He challenged him to a duel, which means he was ready to shoot him."

"We have the word of one mill employee, who admits the mill was terribly loud and that he was hurrying by the office in order to find a quiet place to drink alcohol during the workday. He's hardly a stellar witness, and what he heard—or thought he heard—could be completely different from what was actually said."

Not to mention Earnshaw's report that Mr. Coombe had argued with Montgomery that morning. Montgomery could be pugnacious, but had he quarreled with two different men in quick succession?

"Still, it's better than sifting through charred office paper looking for who knows what. Seems like every case you get, you stick me with the paper." Owen crossed his arms and narrowed his eyes. "I like being out and about and talking to people better."

"You take the jobs that come your way. Nobody gets to do only the things they like all the time."

And didn't Daniel know it. The most recent missive from his solicitors sat like a boulder in his mind. He'd been ordered to do some odd things from time to time at the behest of his mysterious patron, but this was by far the most demanding. What wouldn't he give to have been asked to ride a horse for sale, or deliver a young man safely to school, or guard a payroll from bank to business—all things he'd been asked to do in the past. This latest demand was ludicrous. Not only was it occurring squarely in the middle of a murder investigation, but the duty would take him into an area in which he was completely out of his depth.

It will be over by tomorrow, and with only days to go until your twenty-fifth birthday, you will never have to submit to these "requests" again. Just do as you're told and keep your mouth shut for a few more days.

The cab halted, and Daniel cautioned Owen. "You're here to observe, nothing more. I'll ask the questions. We'll talk about what we hear later, when we're alone."

Mouth set mutinously, Owen nodded. "What if I think of a question you haven't asked?"

"Then we'll come back to it another time." Daniel yanked open the door and climbed out. That Owen would think of a question Daniel, the more experienced officer, wouldn't was ridiculous.

They entered the mill through the warehouse, dodging workers stacking sacks and rolling barrels marked *Wheat* and *Rye*. Every door and window stood open, and a young boy operated a fan by running on a treadmill, sending clouds of dust out of the warehouse, where it dissipated on the breeze.

Daniel didn't remember seeing such a contraption at Montgomery's mill, but he hadn't been into the mill proper. Perhaps their fanning system was located there?

He stopped a worker with a hand on his arm. He had to shout to be heard. "Mr. Carlyle's office?"

The man jerked his thumb back out the warehouse doors. "Up the street. On the left."

So Carlyle didn't have his office in the gristmill. At least they could get away from this infernal noise. As they returned to the sunshine, Owen smacked at his clothes. Even in such a short time, they were coated with flour dust. "Dunno how they stand it. The noise and the dust and the hard labor," he said as they made their way up the hill away from the river.

The buildings on the high street were stair-stepped, each beginning a few feet lower than the one farther along. An apothecary, a print-shop, a bakery, and finally, the offices of Carlyle Mill.

Daniel stopped in surprise halfway across the outer office. A young lady sat behind a tall desk, her head bent over a ledger. She had light-brown hair and an ink smudge on her cheek. Her lashes fanned upward to reveal green eyes.

He jerked off his hat and elbowed Owen to do the same.

"Good morning, gentlemen."

"Good morning." Owen blurted out the greeting before Daniel could form the words. "We're detectives from London. Here to see Mr. Carlyle, if you please."

Daniel wanted to roll his eyes. The young jackanapes was trying to impress the lady, but he sounded pompous to Daniel's ears.

The green eyes widened. "Detectives? Is Mr. Carlyle in trouble?"

Stepping in front of Owen to remind him to keep his mouth shut, Daniel shook his head. "No. We have a few questions regarding the death of someone he knew. Would you inform him we are here, please?" Daniel withdrew his card and placed it on the slanted desktop.

She took it, read the name, and leaned to the side. "Do you also have a card, sir?"

Owen patted his pockets, adopting a frown. "I must have left them in my other coat. My apologies. Owen Wilkinson is my name. And what would yours be?"

"Miss Carlyle."

"Miss?" he asked.

"That's correct. My father owns the mill." She waved in the direction of the river as she slid off her tall stool. She wore black sleeve protectors up to her elbows, and she had a pencil stuck into her updrawn hair. "I'll see if he wishes to receive callers."

Not if he was in the office, not if he had time, but if he wanted to see them.

She disappeared through a frosted-glass door, and the minute she was out of sight, Owen let out a low whistle.

"Control yourself. You act as if you had never seen a pretty woman before."

"Never one prettier than that."

"Remember the part about you being seen but not heard?" Daniel shook his head, and this time he did roll his eyes. "Left your card in your 'other jacket.' You're lucky I didn't knock that nonsense into a cocked hat in front of the lady."

Owen shrugged and jammed his hands into his trouser pockets. "I'll have a card someday, when I *am* a detective."

Miss Carlyle returned. "This way, gentlemen."

She led them into a well-appointed but unostentatious office, where Carlyle sat behind a dark-wood desk. The top was scarred and ink stained, with ledgers and papers arranged on it. Clearly a working-man's room.

"You may go, Abigail."

"Yes, sir." She closed the door gently, and her shadow disappeared from the glass.

Carlyle held Daniel's card. "Bow Street, eh? I suppose this is about the Montgomery matter? Didn't I see you at his place when my wife and I called on his daughter?"

"You did, sir." Daniel handed Owen his notebook and pencil. "May we sit?"

"Fine, though I don't know what I can tell you." He tossed the card onto his desk. "I knew Montgomery for years, didn't like him, often competed against him for business. I don't know anyone who would have wanted to kill him, unless it was one of his own soon-to-be-out-of-work employees. There was trouble over some of his modern ideas, streamlining his methods to reduce the number of men he needed to run his mill."

Owen started to sit in the chair before the desk, and Daniel cleared his throat. The office boy looked up, and Daniel indicated the chair along the wall.

Seated, Daniel crossed his legs and swung his foot. "Everyone seems to be talking about the updates at the mill in Hammersmith. Was it such a radical idea? Doesn't every industry make improvement to aid production and efficiency?"

"Of course, but gradually, most times. The changes Montgomery was making would gut the mill, completely altering the structure and layout. He hoped to cut his workforce in half. He planned to start within the fortnight, so half the men making their living at his mill might soon be headed to the poorhouse. Men who have worked there since they were lads, men whose fathers and grandfathers worked that mill long before Montgomery got his hands on it. He's only been in the milling business for three years. He was proposing to change generations of history and those men's entire way of life."

"How long have you been in the milling business?"

"I was born to it. There's been a Carlyle in charge of this mill since Good Queen Bess sat on the throne, and I plan to survive the current addled monarch and his pompous son." He leaned back, as if satisfied he could accomplish his plans.

"You and Montgomery were business rivals?"

"Of course."

"Is it true that you had planned to purchase the mill in Hammersmith once upon a time and were outbid by Montgomery?" It was a stab in the dark, but it made sense. If the mill had been for sale that recently, Carlyle would most likely have wanted to purchase it.

The man's face darkened. "I was outbid. By an interloper from the city who didn't know a bee from a bull's foot about milling. Throwing around bags of money and acting like a lord. The only smart thing he did was hire Abel Coombe to run the place, and where do you suppose he found him?" He poked his chest with his thumb. "Here. At my mill. He stole him from me."

"Did that make you angry?"

Carlyle's gaze sharpened, and he didn't answer for a long moment. "Of course it did. But that was three years ago. I've moved on, replaced Coombe with another manager, and gotten back to the business of grinding grain. I lost out on the mill and had my manager pinched, and I thought the best course of action would be to mind my own affairs and ignore what was happening downriver."

Sensible, but Daniel wondered what else lurked behind that pragmatic exterior. "Sir, if that was your intention, to ignore Montgomery and his mill, why were you in his office in Hammersmith on the morning of the explosion?"

Eyes shifting from Daniel to Owen and then to the clock on the wall, Carlyle finally said, "It was a private matter."

"There is no privacy in a murder investigation, sir."

The corners of the miller's mouth went down, and his eyes grew hard. But he said nothing.

"If I told you I had a witness who would testify that he heard the two of you arguing in Garfield Montgomery's office, and that you challenged him to a duel, he would be lying?"

Again, nothing. But a flicker of concern flashed across Carlyle's face. Dueling was illegal, though rarely prosecuted.

"What would cause a man to challenge another to a duel? Dueling is often more a matter of pride than of honor, regardless of the participants' claims. And what wounds a man's pride most?" Daniel uncrossed his legs and leaned forward. "Could it be that you suspected Montgomery of not minding *his* own business? Could it be that you suspected him of having an affair . . . with your wife?" He said it baldly and forcefully, waiting for a reaction.

With stony features, Carlyle slowly rose. Daniel followed suit, balancing on the balls of his feet, body tense.

"Gentlemen, our interview is finished. I want you to leave now."

"Sir, there is a murder to solve. Would you prefer we take you into custody and continue our interview at Newgate?"

"You've no grounds to arrest me."

"You were overheard shouting at the victim in his office and challenging him to a duel mere hours before he was found murdered. I believe I have grounds." Daniel put his hand on the knob of his truncheon at his belt. "If I feel you are lying, or avoiding my questions, I can take custody of you and bring you before a magistrate to answer. Then the matter would be out in open court for all to hear. If you wish the situation to remain private, I suggest you return to your seat and tell us what happened."

He doubted Carlyle was accustomed to being spoken to in such a manner, especially in his own office. They faced each other across the desk as the clock ticked.

Finally, Carlyle's shoulders lowered, and he returned to his chair. Daniel did likewise, adjusting his coat and crossing his legs. "Start from the beginning."

Carlyle glanced at Owen, then turned back to Daniel. "You are certain this will go no further?"

"I make no promises, but if the issue can be concealed, I will do it."

"Very well. I suppose that is the most I may expect from the police." He said the word *police* as if it were coated in vinegar and mud.

"About Montgomery?" Daniel asked.

"It's no secret I loathed him. His business practices were legal but not honorable. I mentioned he stole my mill manager right at the start. He also took other workers, offering them better wages and housing in Hammersmith than I could afford here. He cut prices to draw away my customers. He had many businesses, but I have just the one. He could afford to take a loss at his mill for a time if it meant driving me out and making a bigger profit in the end. His intention was to force me to sell . . . to him."

His knuckles whitened on the blotter. "And if that weren't enough, he made advances toward my wife." The accusation was studded with bitterness.

"Advances that were returned?" Daniel asked softly.

Carlyle stared at the ceiling, taking deep breaths. "I've no proof, only suspicions. She is lying to me. Never where she says she will be or with whom. I confronted her a few days ago, but she refused to answer. And when I accused Montgomery in his office, he denied it. That's when I challenged him to the duel."

"Why challenge him to a duel if he denied the charge?"

"What else was he going to say? And he laughed at me." His chin came down. "Told me I was a fool. That if my wife was cheating on her vows, it wasn't with him. The liar."

"So you shot him." Not a question.

The miller jerked as if he were the one shot. "Of course not. I told you, I challenged him. Why would I murder him in his office when I was prepared to fire at him honorably the following morning? Anyway, there were men everywhere in the mill. If you have a witness who heard us arguing, would he not have heard a gunshot?"

Daniel spread his hands. "He heard the shouts as he passed the door, and he did not linger in the passageway. We visited your own mill on the way here, and when it is in full production, you well know one can barely hear a cannon's report from the next room. It's possible you decided you may not survive a duel and decided to finish Montgomery then and there. You certainly had motive enough. Having your wife's affections purloined by the man who sought your professional and personal ruin." He removed his truncheon and tapped it in his palm as if deep in thought.

Owen, in a savvy move, stood and came into Daniel's view, twisting a pair of darbies in his hands as if ready to clap them on Carlyle and drag him away.

"No. That wasn't the way of it at all. If you don't believe me, ask Freddie Marsh. He'll tell you. I left Montgomery's and went straight to his place of business. He agreed to be my second at the duel, and we went to talk to the barber. The barber would act as the medical. Why would I go to that trouble if I knew Montgomery was dead? I was with Marsh and the barber when the mill exploded. I didn't know Montgomery had been shot until the next day. I thought he died in the blast."

Or you could have been establishing an alibi.

"When you heard the mill had exploded, what was your first thought?"

Carlyle studied his hands in his lap. "My thoughts do me no credit, but I was glad. I didn't know Montgomery had died, not right away, but I was glad his business was damaged. I hoped it was beyond repair and that he would now leave me and my wife alone."

"Did you have any suspicions as to how the mill exploded?"

Carlyle shrugged. "My first thought was that it was his workers, angry about the changes and destroying the mill to punish Montgomery. Which is bold, since Luddite laws are harsh. You can be executed for malicious damage to industrial machinery. Then I thought anarchists might be behind it. There have been rumbles, workers striking around the country, roused by anarchists who come into town and get men stirred up. Or it could have been an accident. Mill accidents are not unheard of."

Daniel tapped his chin. He would have to check Carlyle's alibi, this Freddie Marsh and the barber, but he would put Owen on that. If they verified the man's story, he might have to cross Carlyle off his short list of suspects.

But he would reserve judgment. Carlyle might be telling the truth, but it was unlikely to be the entire truth. In his experience, people lied when questioned by the police.

For now, he must return to London and dress for tonight's task.

Chapter 7

JULIETTE HELD THE ADMITTANCE VOUCHER to the most exclusive social club in all of London, possibly the world.

Almack's.

"Are you ready?" Uncle Bertie asked as he swung open the carriage door.

She nodded.

For such a prestigious destination, the building was nothing to boast about. Plain brick with few adornments, a small entrance, on a narrow street off St. James's Square.

"The dowager will meet us in the ballroom." Uncle Bertie handed his cloak and hat to the liveried servant, who looked Bertie's attire up and down and gave a nod of assent. It amused Juliette that there were such strict gatekeepers with the power to turn away anyone they deemed improperly dressed.

Juliette showed her ticket to the attendant, who invited her to take the staircase up to the second floor. "Enjoy your evening, milady."

This was supposed to be a momentous occasion, her first time at Almack's, arranged by her mother. Her mother, who was not present . . . again. The work in France was important, Juliette knew, but it still irked her. She hoped the objective was worth the sacrifices they were all making.

Bertie took her elbow on the stairs. "You are clear about your mission?"

"Yes." She hadn't forgotten the reason she was here.

"Observe. And do not ask questions that could arouse suspicion. If he's on the dance floor, ask the dowager to introduce you. If he stays in the card room all night, I'll watch him there."

Her first truly social event since the Venetian breakfast, and she was right back to work looking for criminals. The life of a spy that she had willingly decided to enter was now taking shape in tangible ways. One was never away from one's post. There was never a time when she was not gathering information, looking for subtle behavioral cues or connections that might mean something. Even a debut at Almack's became cover for clandestine pursuits.

The target of the evening was Lord Robert Sewell, third son of an earl and an official in Customs and Excise who may have taken bribes to look the other way on importing infractions. Their task was to watch, listen, and observe with whom he made contact, as they had information that the bribe money might be paid tonight.

The ballroom was not as large as Juliette had imagined, but it was beautifully appointed and well lit. Large windows, delicate trim work, and a smooth, shining dance floor that must take ages to wax and polish. Beneath a small balcony where musicians set up their instruments sat a trio of women on a small dais—a selection of the famous patronesses of Almack's. Dragons every one.

Juliette laced her fingers at her waist, her garnet ring pinching beneath her white gloves. What if they didn't think her up to the mark?

She was properly dressed in a white gown, no jewelry bar the small ring she never took off, and her hair pinned and curled in the latest fashion for a debutante. They couldn't cavil at her appearance.

Nor her pedigree. She was the daughter of an earl of long-standing ancestry and land ownership. Parliamentarians, benefactors, friends of kings and princes.

So why was she so nervous?

Because they had given the squint to attendees of equal and better measure. Even the Duke of Wellington, hero of Waterloo and savior of Britain, had been turned away from Almack's doors because he was not dressed in accordance with their rules.

The dowager duchess accepted a kiss on the hand from Uncle Bertie and a kiss on the cheek from Juliette.

"Thank you for stepping in for my sister-in-law once again. Juliette and I are most grateful."

"Of course, though I am surprised. Tristan and Melisande gone off again? And this time to France? How can they hope to successfully launch a daughter into society from the Continent? All this gadding about cannot be good for a person's constitution. One should remain settled in the civilized and structured culture of England." The dowager spoke as the voice of authority on every subject.

"When one is asked by the Regent, one cannot say no. I wish they were here, but I understand why they had to go." Juliette tucked her ticket into her reticule. And she did understand. She just didn't like it.

"Let us get your introduction over with, then see about finding you a partner. The first set will begin soon, and you cannot find a husband sitting on the sidelines."

Juliette stifled the desire to set the dowager straight on her misapprehension that the sole aim of every debutante was to snare a husband as quickly as possible. Her Grace would never believe it. And in most cases, she was correct. Girls rushed to the altar with the first man of suitable pedigree and fortune who showed a glimmer of interest. Juliette had other plans. She would take her time. Finding someone suitable took on grave new depths considering her family heritage and secret life.

As they waited their turn to greet the patronesses, Juliette surveyed the quickly filling room. It had all the makings of a crush. Uncle Bertie had disappeared into the card rooms and soon would be donning his persona as a sot. Thankfully, while he was quite adept at pretending to be foxed, he never actually became drunk.

As she and the dowager neared the front of the presentation line, Juliette's nerves did a reel. She hadn't been this nervous since making her curtsey before the Queen.

"May I present Lady Juliette Thorndike, daughter of the Earl and Countess of Thorndike." The dowager nudged Juliette. "Lady Juliette, Princess Esterhazy, Lady Jersey, and Lady Sefton."

The three eyed her as she curtseyed, flicking their fans and communicating with one another through glances.

At last one of them spoke. "Welcome to Almack's, Lady Juliette. I hope you have an enjoyable time."

"Thank you." She and the dowager turned away, and she caught a sigh coming from the dowager that matched her own. Had even she been nervous about braving the patronesses?

"Is there anyone in particular you would like as a partner this evening?"

Startled that the dowager would ask her preference—something she had never done before—Juliette hesitated. Should she ask to dance with Robert Sewell?

"Very well. If you've no objections, Duke Heinrich von Lowe has asked for the quadrille. That is second on the card." The dowager led Juliette to a settee between two tall urns of flowers and settled herself. "Give me your reticule. I'll look after it. Sit with me, and we'll see what eventuates for the first."

"Is the duke here? I didn't see him." She scanned the crowd before taking a seat.

"Everyone is here, my dear. It's Wednesday night in London. Where else would anyone who *is* anyone be?" The dowager flicked open her fan and stirred a breeze that moved the gray curls clustered around her cheeks. "Even my son and daughter-in-law have come out of their library for the evening. It's hard enough to get Charlotte's nose out of a book, but Marcus encourages her in the pursuit. No good will come of it, though neither will heed my advice. It's just not the done thing to be a bluestocking, and yet Charlotte persists." She shrugged, as if she could not be held responsible for whatever dire events befell the duchess for being so reckless as to read books.

Her son approached, accompanied by a younger man. "Mother, Lady Juliette, may I present Mr. Adam Stevenson. He's requested both an introduction and permission to ask Lady Juliette for the first dance." Marcus Haverly was as suave and handsome as ever, his hair still unfashionably long, giving him a rakish, piratical air. "Stevenson, my mother, the dowager, and her charge for the evening, Lady Juliette Thorndike."

The young man, who must be at least twenty, though he looked younger, reddened, bowed, and stammered. "Hon . . . honored."

Juliette took his offered hand and tried to encourage him with a smile, but that seemed to fluster him more. He looked everywhere but at her face, and his was so ruddy he appeared near bursting into flames. The first dance was a four in hand, and if he didn't compose himself, it would be disastrous.

The musicians began, and the dancers took their places in the lines. Mr. Stevenson bore a look of utter concentration that did not bode well for her. If he must think so hard about the steps . . .

But when the movement started, it was Juliette who felt chagrin. He was precise and light on his feet, elegant in every movement, far distant from his awkwardness of earlier. As she loved to dance and knew herself to be quite good at it, she gave herself over to the pleasure of the moment, mirroring his movements, taking his fingers when required, keeping her steps fluid and graceful, as she had been taught.

When they reached the end of the line and turned to promenade, her eyes met Daniel Swann's. The surprise was like an impact to her knees, and she stumbled to a halt, causing a gentleman to bump into her.

Gathering her wits, she resumed the movement, but she couldn't regain her grace. Why was Daniel at Almack's? Was there another crime to investigate? But he was dressed in fine gentleman's attire, identical to the other male guests. Did that mean he was here to dance and socialize? A policeman? Smelling salts would be required if his occupation became widely known.

Her thoughts swirled and bounced on the subject of Daniel. Then she saw the girl.

An odd feeling whipped through Juliette, hollow but sharp.

The young lady had her hand on Daniel's arm, and he bent with a smile to listen to something she said. Juliette turned to watch them as she and Stevenson marched around the corner, and she nearly collided with another couple.

Get your wits about you, girl. You're making a cake of yourself. Purposefully, she focused on her partner, trying to put the image out of her head. Whatever Daniel Swann was doing was no concern of hers. She wasn't here to observe him. Robert Sewell was her target. Listen, observe, report.

And don't make a spectacle of yourself in the process.

At last the set ended, and she was returned to the dowager with a bow. At the dowager's side sat Duke Heinrich, who rose at Juliette's approach.

"Thank y-y-you for the favor of d-d-dancing with me, Lady J-J-Juliette," Mr. Stevenson stammered. He turned on his heel, and Juliette wanted to call him back to apologize for her inattention, but he was gone in the crowd.

"You are looking most lovely this evening, Lady Juliette. Putting the other ladies here to shame." Heinrich took her hands, his eyes warm as he bent over her knuckles. "I am to have the pleasure of your company for the next, yes?" He tucked her hand into the crook of his elbow and put his hand over her fingers there. Very proprietary.

A group of women to their right clustered together talking, and when another joined them, her voice carried to those around.

"You won't believe it, girls. I tell you, it reminds me of the night that soldier Evan Eldridge paraded in here like he belonged. I don't care if he was made an earl. It wasn't right then, and it isn't right now. That man doesn't even have an ill-gotten peerage behind him. He's"—the woman lowered her voice—"a detective. A policeman. At Almack's."

"I'm surprised the doorman allowed him entrance. Or that the patronesses allowed him to stay."

"He must have had a voucher to be admitted."

"Oh, he did. Signed by whom, I don't know, but there it is. I was here when he arrived, and believe me, the doorman scrutinized that card, trying to find a flaw. In the end, he had no choice."

"Who is that he's with?"

"That's Anne Victon, the daughter of Thomas Victon, from Yorkshire, who owns all those textile mills. She had her debut a month ago, and I heard hardly anyone attended. And she's received almost no invitations to anything else, all because of her father. His money is so new it's practically shiny, and he's splashing it all around and making a rodomont of himself."

The woman leaned in closer. "He's hired that Lady Cathcart to chaperone his daughter, and we all know she'll take on anyone with enough blunt to pay for her services. Word is she's supposed to find a titled gentleman to marry his daughter. Who would want him for a relative when he's so crass? Do you suppose he had to pay for someone to dance with her? Is that why the Bow Street runner is here? Because he's poor and needs the money? He's handsome, I'll give you that, but he has absolutely nothing else to recommend him."

"Perhaps it's the Prince Regent at work again. He's the one who got the Eldridge man admitted. He is a man of odd whims."

"It *would* take an act of the prince himself to get a common policeman a voucher to Almack's. I don't know who is more addlebrained, the King or his son."

"Shh, that's scandalous talk. And it isn't any worse having a policeman admitted as having the daughter of a *tradesman*. I don't care how rich her father is."

Juliette had heard enough. The poor girl. She made a mental note to add Anne Victon to any guest list she had a part in drawing up. Her parents would definitely approve.

"Shall we go and greet Mr. Swann?" she asked Heinrich. At least the duke wasn't caught up in the pettiness of some people. He had always treated Daniel as a friend.

"Of course." Heinrich bent a knowing gaze on her. He had heard the gossip too.

As they passed the doorway of the card room on the way, she spied Uncle Bertie leaning against the mantel, watching a table of four men. He looked up, gave her a wink and a nod toward the players, and went back to work.

He had found Robert Sewell. As soon as a chair opened at the table, he would no doubt take it and glean the information they were after. Juliette could relax.

At least until they made the half circuit of the room and fetched up beside Daniel and his partner.

"Good evening, Herr Swann. It is good to see you here." Heinrich shook his hand, speaking a bit louder than necessary.

Juliette could have hugged him for his open acceptance of Daniel.

"And who is this charming young Fräulein?"

The girl, who looked to be a couple of years younger than Juliette's nineteen, blushed prettily as Heinrich took her hand.

"Your Grace, meet Miss Anne Victon of Leeds. Miss Victon, this is Duke Heinrich von Lowe of Brandenburg, and Lady Juliette Thorndike." Daniel's blue eyes flicked to hers.

They did make a nice couple, Anne in her delicate muslin and Daniel in his formal coat and breeches.

"How do you do, Miss Victon? It's a pleasure to meet you. Are you enjoying your debut Season?" Juliette put herself out to be kind. Something about Anne Victon reminded her of a cautious deer edging from the forest.

"Yes," she said without conviction. "I've never been to London before. It's so much bigger and busier than Leeds."

"I felt the same way. It's all a far cry from my family home in Pensax or boarding school in the mountains outside Geneva. Your dress is charming. I love that shade of blue. It reminds me of a piece of sea glass I found once." Juliette tried to put the girl at ease. "Have you danced yet tonight?"

A shadow crossed Miss Victon's face, and her hand tightened on Daniel's arm. "No. Not yet."

"You are in for a treat. Mr. Swann is an excellent partner." Juliette harked back to the one dance she had shared with the detective, at the ball thrown by the Ash Valley Hunt Club. The same night she'd learned the truth of his upbringing and the unfortunate circumstances of his birth. She could scarcely imagine what the gossips in the room would have to say if they knew he was baseborn, the illegitimate son of a domestic servant.

Heinrich leaned in and whispered to Juliette. "Help me do both of them the favor, yes?"

She nodded, unsure of what he was asking.

"I know I am promised to Lady Juliette for the next dance, but I wonder if she would mind if I postponed the pleasure. Miss Victon, would you share the next with me? And Herr Swann, you would partner Lady Juliette?"

Light dawned. By dancing with such an illustrious guest as the foreign duke, Miss Victon's stock would rise. As would Daniel's if someone of Juliette's social standing partnered him.

Either that or her stock would fall, but she didn't care about such things anyway. If the silly gaggle of gossips wanted to pass around faradiddles, that was not her concern.

"You wouldn't mind?" Miss Victon asked Daniel. "I would not want to slight you, and I seem to have trouble knowing what is proper here in London and what isn't."

"I have the same trouble." Daniel smiled wryly. "I'll share you for one dance. I know the duke well, and he will take care of you. Your chaperone, Lady Cathcart, will not mind. She's sure to think you've done better for yourself. It's Lady Juliette who will have to settle, should she agree with the exchange."

The music began, and Juliette put her hand in his offered one. A tingle went from her fingertips to her chest as his clasp tightened.

Dancing with Juliette was every bit as intoxicating as Daniel remembered. Their one other dance, at the Ash Valley Hunt Club Ball, had ended abruptly with an intrusion of work that led to their racing back to London in the dead of night.

Pray no work interfered tonight, because he never wanted this dance to end.

Each time she circled him, he inhaled the scent of roses. Her white dress of some shiny, slippery material shimmered and whispered, in that way women's clothes had of mesmerizing unsuspecting males.

He did not mind being a willing victim for this evening. Mostly because he knew his patronage would end with the coming of his twenty-fifth birthday. There would be no more missives from the solicitors with orders to do this or that. There would be no more tasks such as partnering a girl to her first night at Almack's.

No more invitations to society events that would bring him into Lady Juliette's sphere. If they encountered each other in the future, it would be in their roles as agents in training, but he could not see how their paths would intertwine much once their instruction was completed. He would continue his work as a detective—the Lord and Sir Michael willing—occasionally bringing information to the Duke of Haverly, and she would continue as an aristocrat, attending parties and social events and marrying advantageously, gathering her own information that might prove useful to the Crown.

Their lives would lie far apart, and he would be unable to bridge the gap.

Heinrich went down the row with Miss Victon's fingers on his sleeve, smiling boldly, as if he couldn't be more pleased with his partner. It had been clear from the start that the duke and Juliette had deliberately brought Miss Victon and himself into their social circle tonight. Juliette was kind, drawing more words from Anne in a few moments than Daniel had been able to elicit since meeting her an hour before. And the duke proposing a partner switch was certainly drawing looks and whispers. Heinrich was a good man.

Which caused a ball of jealousy to sit in Daniel's gut like an anvil. Heinrich had the status, money, and position to pursue Juliette right to the altar. He was clearly fond of her, perhaps more than fond. Her parents would approve such a match, wouldn't they?

How did Juliette feel about the German duke?

Her hand rested on Daniel's arm as they promenaded down the long side of the ballroom, and her dark eyes reflected the candlelight. He admired the way her hair curved back from her brow, teasing little curls at her temples. Daniel had reason to know how soft her hair was, how it felt against his cheek. The memory buzzed under his skin like bees' wings.

They parted and turned to join the appropriate lines, and Daniel found himself beside Duke Heinrich. The duke was due to leave for his homeland in a few weeks. Would he be taking a new bride with him?

"Am I so unpleasant to partner?" Juliette asked as the steps brought them close once more. "You look entirely too grumpy for my peace of mind."

Realizing he was scowling, Daniel smoothed his expression. "I apologize. My thoughts took me to an unpleasant place."

"Is it the investigation? Are you any nearer a solution?"

They separated, and he had to wait for the next movement before he could answer. "We are following leads. I questioned one likely suspect who had a strong motive, and we are confirming his alibi."

"Agatha is overwhelmed with it all. I hope you are able to solve the case quickly to give her mind a small measure of ease. Did the answers to her questions help? I'm sorry I had to pass them to you on paper. I would like to have discussed them with you."

"The fact that her father did own a gun turned out not to be significant. It was of too large a caliber to be the murder weapon." He kept his voice low, for such a conversation would no doubt get him thrown out of the place if it were overheard. Bad enough they had been forced to allow a policeman inside. Having him discuss unsavory work elements would be too much. "What does Agatha intend to do? Sell everything and live on the proceeds, or try to find a manager to help her?"

"I should think that Viscount Coatsworth may have some influence on her decisions. They were planning to announce their betrothal in a few days. The death of Mr. Montgomery has delayed that celebration." Juliette looked past his shoulder. "The viscount is here tonight. His trip to his grandfather's estate must have been very short. Or perhaps he hasn't gone yet? He told Agatha he would see her upon his return. I don't know how long they will have to delay their wedding, with Agatha in full mourning."

Daniel kept his expression neutral, but he grimaced inwardly. Coatsworth always managed to abrade him. Even his compliments to Daniel, rare as they were, resembled hornets. There was always a sting in the tail.

"An admirable job," Coatsworth had said when Daniel returned Montgomery's stolen painting. "For one of such plebian origins."

Daniel had contemplated landing the supercilious viscount a plebian facer.

Coatsworth stood alone near the doorway into the refreshment room, a stark look on his face. Actually, more ashen than stark. Staring into an unseen distance and paying no attention to those around him.

Perhaps he grieved the loss of his future father-in-law more than anyone suspected. But if that were the case, why would he be present at a social event like this?

Returning his attention to his partner, Daniel pushed aside the present and gave himself over to a pleasant daydream, one in which he was a peer with every right to court Lady Juliette. It was nonsense but harmless enough. He knew his place in the world, and he was content with it.

Most of the time.

When the music came to an end, Lady Juliette sank into a graceful curtsey, and he bowed from the waist, offering his hand to steady her as she rose.

For a long moment they stood still, and he looked into those dark, beautiful eyes, thickly lashed. He wanted to memorize every aspect of her face . . . until he realized he already had. The straight, narrow nose that tipped up ever so slightly at the end, the full lips, the curve of her cheek, the way the light shone off her brown curls. She had left a lasting impression upon him.

A man cleared his throat, and they both turned away.

"Here they are." Heinrich beamed down on Miss Victon. "And they seem to have fared as well as we."

"Thank you for the dance, Your Grace." She blushed, her voice barely above a whisper. "You are a very fine partner, and I appreciate that you have tried to make my first ball at Almack's so pleasant."

Daniel was proud of her. Miss Victon was shy, and most likely painfully aware that her father's abrasive nature and newfound wealth put people off. She was smart too. Quick to pick up on the kindness of Heinrich and Juliette.

"The next dance is a waltz, and as debutantes, Anne and I are excluded." Juliette flicked open her fan. "I propose that we make our way to the refreshment room for some punch and cake. The gentlemen may accompany us, or they may partake in the waltz, there being no strictures on which dances men are allowed to do." She quirked her eyebrow in a way that was familiar to Daniel and said louder than words that she didn't agree with the discrepancy in standards.

"I've no desire to waltz at the moment. I say we make it a foursome for punch and cake." Daniel offered his arm to Anne. "Shall we report back to your chaperone first for permission?"

"That would be proper, would it not?" Anne nodded, then turned to Juliette. "My father hired Lady Cathcart to be my chaperone for events like this to which he and Mother are not invited. She's really not very good at it, for she seems not to care what I do when we go out."

"Which is not the case for Lady Juliette's personal dragon, the Dowager Duchess of Haverly. She minds to the smallest degree everything Juliette does." Heinrich smiled. "We shall make our intentions known to the dowager and receive her permission to enter the refreshment room. Perhaps we shall bribe her with promises of cake." He held out his arm, and Juliette took it.

Daniel stomped hard on his envy. "Shall we meet in a few minutes?"

Daniel led Anne back to her duenna, and all the way, she chattered about how nice Duke Heinrich was, and how kind of him to dance with her, and people were actually smiling at them. Anne was like a different creature from the mouselike girl who had emerged from the carriage.

Lady Cathcart leaned over to whisper into the ear of one of the many women in this particular corner of the ballroom, and the two broke into laughter. Several of the older ladies eyed Daniel as he waited for a break in the conversation, and under their glares, Anne seemed to shrink into herself again.

Daniel bowed and asked permission to take Miss Victon into the next room.

"I don't know what your father was thinking, child, to send you here to Almack's and to hire this man to see you weren't left on the sidelines. Still, he's paying me good money to be here. Go, have your refreshments. Don't get into any trouble. Or if you do, don't tell me about it."

The women let out peals of laughter.

"Oh, I don't know, Almina. Perhaps the child has unplumbed depths. She did manage a dance with a duke, after all. Both of these two reaching above their stations." A woman with brassy yellow curls clustered about her seamed face narrowed her eyes and pointed with her fan. "You'd do well to remember your place."

Daniel touched Anne's hand. The odor of strong drink hovered around the women, and more than one cheek was too flushed, more than one eye too bright, for them to be entirely sober. A drunk man was bad enough, but in Daniel's eyes, there was something terribly wrong about a drunk woman, particularly one claiming to be a lady.

"Let's go meet the duke and Lady Juliette. We don't want them to think we're not coming." He stood erect, looking down his nose at the cluster of women. If this was the nobility, give him squalor any day.

Anne gave him a tremulous smile and nodded.

Once in the refreshment room, Anne relaxed again. Daniel and Heinrich fetched punch and cake for the ladies. Daniel eyed his pastry, poking it with his fork. This might be the vaunted Almack's, but he'd purchased penny cakes from costermongers that looked better. The high-in-the-instep patronesses clearly didn't wish to spend the bawbees on quality food.

The duke was kindness itself, asking Miss Victon questions about her home and answering with stories of his own. And all without sounding pompous. How did someone who owned several castles, a title, and more money than a man could spend in two lifetimes manage to be humble and self-deprecating?

It made him difficult to dislike.

With Anne and Heinrich in a lively conversation, Daniel turned to Juliette. "Did I see Sir Bertrand in the game room?"

"Yes. He is a wonderful dancer, but he prefers cards to quadrilles." She took a dainty bite of a pink-frosted cake, her tongue darting out to lick a crumb on her lip.

Daniel's collar tightened.

"The Sewell affair?" He kept his voice low.

She studied him, as if unsure whether to confirm or deny. They were both new to the espionage game, working clandestinely for both the Home and Foreign Offices when called upon to do so, and they had been drilled not to ask too many questions, not to share information unless told to do so, and never to divulge the particulars of a case to someone not immediately involved.

"Never mind. I shouldn't have asked." He sipped his punch, regretting putting her in such an awkward position as to have to refuse him.

"There's the viscount. I should speak to him." Juliette set down her fork and pushed back her chair. Daniel rose to pull it out, and Heinrich stood, brows raised.

"I'll just be a moment," she told the duke. "I see someone with whom I wish to speak."

Without asking, Daniel went with her. He had a few questions he'd like to ask Lord Darby. Thus far there had been no sign of who had stolen the household money belonging to Agatha Montgomery, but perhaps Lord Darby would have some ideas. He was more familiar with the staff and guests who had been in the house at the time of the theft. It seemed a minor crime compared to the murder and the destruction of the mill, but it fell under Daniel's purview, as he had been present just before the theft was discovered.

"Good evening, Lord Darby." Juliette touched his arm. "I did not expect you to be here tonight. I thought you would be in Kent. You were to visit your grandfather, were you not?"

Coatsworth looked at her as if he didn't quite understand her questions. He appeared to be dazed, his eyes staring but not seeing.

"Alonzo? Did you visit your grandfather, or did something alter your plans?"

He shook his head. "I came back this afternoon." The words were all but mumbled, unlike the outspoken viscount.

"Is something wrong?" Juliette asked. "Is it Agatha?"

"Agatha?" He focused. "No, she's fine. I mean, she is as fine as she can be under the circumstances."

"And you? Are you all right? You seem a bit distracted. Would you like to sit down? We've a table with plenty of room."

Coatsworth seemed to notice Daniel for the first time, and he recoiled, as if he'd encountered a Nile viper. "No, thank you." His glare was as frosty as the North Sea in January. "I will not sit at a table with this man. Not ever." He turned sharply and plunged from the room.

Daniel crossed one arm, propped the other elbow upon it, and tapped his lips with his fist, sighing. "Was it something I said?"

Juliette, who had scowled at the viscount's rudeness, laughed, her displeasure softening into humor. "It must have been."

Sir Bertrand entered, sighted Juliette, and came over. "Was that Lord Darby hurrying away like his coattails were on fire?"

"It was he," Daniel confirmed. "We were so rude as to invite him to sit with us."

"He seems quite out of sorts. I think love has addled his brain," Juliette offered.

"That seems to be the universal effect of romance." Sir Bertrand shrugged. "It is why I avoid entanglements of the heart. I need my wits about me. Are you having a pleasant evening, Juliette?"

"I am. And you?"

"Profitable. I believe someone from the River Police will be paying a call to Customs and Excise at the London docks tomorrow, which will tidy up the situation completely. You, Lady Juliette, are now free of any other work but to enjoy yourself tonight." He nodded at Daniel. "I came looking for you, however. Mrs. Fairchild is in the gaming room, and she's playing at one of the high-stakes tables. She's with that Donaldson gentleman who accompanied her to the Montgomery service."

"Is she winning?" Daniel hid his distaste. The woman was far too emotional for his liking, always seeking to be the center of attention. "And why is she in the card room when she is better suited for the ballroom?"

"That's the odd thing. She's not winning. But Donaldson is, and quite handsomely. I have been watching their table, and I think they're working in tandem while the other two players are paying the price."

Daniel weighed his options. Was this really a matter for the police? Not under normal circumstances. If people were silly enough to wager over a game of chance, they must take whatever results came their way.

But if the tables were tilted in someone's favor unfairly, that was another kettle of fish.

"Do you know how they're doing it? Marked cards, or illegal dealing, or signaling?"

"I heard quite a bit of table talk, but they were all doing it. I suspect Donaldson is the acute mind and Mrs. Fairchild is the distraction. She is displaying her . . . er . . . wares rather boldly."

He would have to step in, he supposed. "If you'll escort Lady Juliette back to the duke's table, I'll wander into the card room and see what eventuates."

"Oh, no," Juliette protested. "I want to see what she does. There is something quite off about Mrs. Fairchild, especially her supposed relationship with Mr. Montgomery, how that sort of sprang out of the blue once he was no longer here to refute her claims. I received a note from Agatha this afternoon. Mrs. Fairchild stopped by her house again, and according to Agatha's report, she intimated that if Agatha was loyal to her father's memory, she would not be stingy when it came to giving out little presents to those who also loved him. I cannot tell if Agatha is being overly dramatic or if something unsavory is going on. I only know I do not care for the woman."

"Do you have any idea where her friend Donaldson was on the morning of Montgomery's murder?" Sir Bertrand asked, his hand to his chin. "That might be worth looking into as well."

Daniel remembered one of the first lessons he'd learned when he was a green detective at Bow Street. Everyone was a suspect until they weren't. Until he cleared Mrs. Fairchild and Mr. Donaldson, they were suspects, though he could think of no reason why either of them would want Mr. Montgomery dead. The Widow Fairchild stood to gain much more if she had wed Garfield Montgomery, if her claims of a near-betrothal were to be believed. However, if Daniel could prove they were cheating at the gaming tables, it would give him some leverage when it came to questioning them about their movements around the time of Montgomery's murder.

With Juliette on his arm, Daniel strolled into the card room. Smoke hung near the ceiling, testament to the many cigars consumed during the evening. At the far end, a pair of waiters poured and delivered drinks to the tables.

A few women were present, but only Mrs. Fairchild sat at a gaming table. The others sat or stood around the room, as if bored. Perhaps waiting for a partner to finish his hand and return to the ballroom?

Sir Bertrand followed, but at a distance, and he separated from them to stand in the second doorway. It was a maneuver right out of the Bow Street training. Bar all forms of escape.

Talk buzzed, and the tink of fish counters hitting bowls and cards being snapped down covered their approach to the targeted table. A few paces away, Daniel removed Juliette's arm from his and moved into Mrs. Fairchild's view.

She shrugged and laid her cards facedown, a pouting expression on her pretty face as she waved for Mr. Donaldson to rake the counters toward himself. "That's three hands in a row. Why won't you show mercy on a poor widow woman?" She put her hand to her throat and batted her eyelids. The neckline of her dress was daring, to put it mildly. Daniel returned his gaze to her face, his mouth firming. She had dropped the persona of grieving woman, at least for this evening.

"He could show a little mercy on the rest of us too," one man growled. "I'm out nearly fifty pounds."

"Consider yourself lucky. I'm out eighty," the other one said. "If my wife finds out . . ." He finished with a shudder.

"I'll give you a chance to recoup your losses." Donaldson handled the pasteboard cards with the dexterity of an illusionist.

"Evening, gentlemen, Mrs. Fairchild." Daniel stood lightly on the balls of his feet, a few steps away from his quarry. "Might I have a word with you two?" He pointed to Donaldson and the lady. "In my professional capacity, of course."

He didn't know what he had expected, but certainly not that Donaldson would be the one to panic. He jumped to his feet, flipped the table into the man across from him, sending the poor fellow sprawling backward at Daniel's feet, and bolted for the door.

Unfortunately for him, he chose the door guarded by Sir Bertrand. In a beautiful move, the "drunken" Bertie Thorndike stumbled and stuck his foot out at the precise moment Donaldson passed, tripping the gambler and sending him into a flailing heap on the floor. Artfully, Thorndike "fell" on top of him, pinning him to the carpet, apologizing with slurred words all the way but managing to hold the writhing escapee until Daniel arrived to clamp his hand on the man's collar.

Mrs. Fairchild had risen, but she remained by her chair, her hand pressed to her chest, eyes wide as a child's. "Whatever is happening?"

Two employees of Almack's, big burly men hired to ensure that everyone minded their manners, strode in, ready to toss out those who would disturb the sanctity of the exclusive venue. Daniel kept hold of Donaldson, who tried to swing on him. Grabbing his wrist, Daniel wrenched it up high behind the man's back and nearly bent him double.

"What's the trouble here?" one of the guards asked. "Unhand that man."

"Police." Daniel jerked his head. "I'm arresting the man in conjunction with a murder investigation. And that woman as well." He indicated Mrs. Fairchild, who by this time looked to be regretting that she had not fled through the other door.

Lady Juliette moved closer to her and said something that made the widow's eyes harden. Her entire expression changed from innocent bystander to seasoned con artist. Daniel had seen the look before on criminals he'd placed under arrest.

Sir Bertrand had faded away, and the guards took possession of Mrs. Fairchild.

"Please give my apologies to Miss Victon," Daniel said to Juliette. "Perhaps you and His Grace will look after her?"

"Of course."

Daniel regretted leaving Juliette, but he now had prisoners to escort to Bow Street for interrogation.

A pang hit him as he realized he would probably never see her in a social setting again. Once his guardianship vested, they would be on vastly different paths.

Chapter 8

"I've missed this. I didn't realize it until right this minute, but it's true." Juliette walked with Bertie in Hyde Park two days after her Almack's debut. They ambled, not on the normal path but on a great swath of grass along with dozens of others. Ahead, flags had been strung and a covered platform erected. A circle of carriages defined the competition area.

Bertie carried her equipment, including her shooting jacket, lifting his face to the weak sunshine. "I hope it warms a bit. It seems it's been cold forever. We had one nice day and then back into the frost."

She flexed her fingers to limber them up. "I hope my aim isn't cold. I haven't shot at a target since the last competition at school months ago. I haven't even met any of my clubmates yet, but Mother seemed to think that would not be a problem."

"I believe as long as you pay your dues, the club will not mind. Not with someone of your mother's influence backing you." Bertie gave a wry smile. "The Thorndike name opens doors all over London, including ones to ladies' archery clubs."

The Diana Toxophilite Society banner hung straight with nary a ripple in the now still air, and she turned toward it. Her surname might open doors, but would the people behind the doors be nice because of who she was, or would they pretend to be nice because of *what* she was? They crossed the grass, and Juliette's stomach fluttered.

She reached for her training in deportment and manners. She must do her mother proud.

"The weather is mild enough that the Prince Regent will probably make his promised appearance." Uncle Bertie set her belongings on the grass and held up her shooting jacket, bright-blue with black trim, to help her shrug into it. The long, close-fitting sleeves hugged her upper arms, while the inset undersleeves were loose, allowing for freedom of movement. She nodded her thanks and fastened the crossover closings about her waist.

The belt came next, with its flannel tassel for cleaning arrows, a small box of grease for oiling her glove and brace, and the pouch for holding her arrows. The bow and her selection of arrows resided in a case at the moment, brought home with her from school.

"I should check in with the club secretary. Where will you be?" She put her cloak back on over her uniform. It was too chilly to go without while waiting her turn to compete.

"Oh, you know me. I'll be around." He handed her the bow case. "One must mingle, listen, glean. I'm supposed to meet up with Detective Swann somewhere here this morning. No doubt if I wander about, he'll find me. He is going to deliver the latest on his case, and I have some information to pass along to him."

He shrugged. "You, however, are to remember that you are under orders not to get involved in the Montgomery case. His murder is a matter for the police. We agreed upon that."

A disturbance near the dais caught her attention, and she didn't have to answer. She had no intention of butting in on the investigation, but she also wouldn't shirk helping where she could. "What's going on over there?"

Men strode across the grass, all in rough garb with mufflers about their faces and hats pulled low against the cold. They carried . . . sticks?

"I believe those are picketers. I heard they may demonstrate here today. They must have gotten word that old Prinny was going to attend and want to get his attention."

"Picketers? Protesting what?"

"Hard to say. It's not like there aren't a plethora of social ills to be concerned about. Crop failures and floods have meant food shortages. Industrialization of time-honored skills has led to loss of employment. The severity of the penal code has become ridiculous—men hanged for shooting a rabbit, children deported for stealing bread." He scuffed his boot on the grass. "Pick your cause. Though I feel bad for the blighters, they'll be lucky if they aren't routed out of here before the Regent arrives. The current government does not take kindly to dissent amongst the masses. Their presence is one of the reasons I'm here today. To assess the level of discontent and to report back."

Guilt flicked across Juliette's skin. Bertie was right. There were many in need, many reasons for sections of the population to be disgruntled and dissatisfied. What was she doing to aid them? An archery tournament in Hyde Park seemed to pale in significance compared to the hardship others endured.

"Don't get distracted. You have a job to do. The Thorndikes are working behind the scenes to improve the lot of all Britons." Bertie held her gaze. "If you had not been born into this family, you would not have been in a position to stop a foreign spy from harming this country. Your position was given you by God. Use it. Be charitable and concerned for your fellow man, but don't be ashamed to be an aristocrat. God didn't love Onesimus more than he loved Philemon, though He put them into different situations in life. They were both called to serve, regardless of station. Help where you can, be compassionate, but use your position to better the lives of others."

Such wisdom seemed odd coming from Bertie, who rarely spoke of spiritual things. He rarely spoke of serious things unless they were in the War Room planning a mission. The role of dilettante with a drinking problem came easily to him. The role of sage seemed foreign.

"Check in, compete, and enjoy yourself. I'll be around." He looked over her shoulder. "As will someone else, I see. Good morning, sirs."

She turned. Duke Heinrich von Lowe waited a few paces away. Viscount Coatsworth was with him, and a pang hit Juliette that

Agatha, being in mourning, was not able to attend social functions. However, it was nice to see familiar faces.

"Uncle Bertie, I believe I will call on Agatha later this afternoon, if that meets with your approval? I can tell her about today's festivities and see how she is getting along."

Bertie's eyes narrowed slightly. "Just a social call, right?"

"Of course." If the discussion turned to the investigation of her father's death, that wouldn't be Juliette's fault, would it?

Heinrich and Coatsworth greeted Bertie, and Heinrich turned his attention to Juliette. "You are competing today? I should have guessed you would be an accomplished archeress." His expression and his hand clasp were warm. "You are looking the part." He indicated her uniform peeking from under her cloak. "Very nice."

"Thank you." She returned his smile. "Archery was a favorite activity of mine and Miss Montgomery's at school. The academy we attended had a team, and we were often well placed when we competed." Truth be told, they were first nearly every time, but she did not wish to brag.

His face sobered. "How is Miss Montgomery? I have not seen her since the luncheon after her father's funeral."

Juliette waited for Alonzo to answer, but he stared into the distance, as if he hadn't heard a word, much as he had at Almack's the night before last. Perhaps love was not the cause. Grief touched everyone in a different manner, but she hadn't realized the viscount and Mr. Montgomery had been so close that he would mourn so openly.

Finally Juliette said, "I believe she is faring as well as can be expected. I plan to call upon her later today."

The noise across the way increased, and several of the protestors raised signs.

"It appears this group is agitated about industrial progress. I wonder if Jasper Finch stirred them up." Bertie stroked his chin. "I think I'll toddle over and take a closer look. Juliette, allow these gentlemen to tender you into the care of your club secretary. I'll meet you on this spot after the tournament."

He sauntered away, and Heinrich offered his arm. "May I?" He bent and lifted her case with ease. As they neared the tent, he said, "I shall wait here for you, yes?"

The secretary for the Dianas glanced up from her papers when Juliette approached. A marquee had been erected over the woman's table, and small sandbags stood atop the pages to keep them from fluttering away in the chilled breeze. She took note of Juliette's uniform beneath her half-open cloak. "You must be Lady Juliette Thorndike." Rising, she extended her hand. "I'm Lady Croft."

"A pleasure."

The secretary looked past Juliette at the German duke, and an odd transformation overcame her expression. Her lashes flicked, color tinged her cheeks, and she bobbed a curtsey, calling out, "Your Grace, welcome."

Juliette hid a smile. Fawning was not too strong a word for how Lady Croft comported herself. Heinrich stepped up, shifted Juliette's bow case to his other hand, and took Lady Croft's offered fingers. He clicked his boot heels together as he bent over her knuckles.

Though he released her hand, Lady Croft stood, stupefied, gazing at his face. Juliette cleared her throat, and the woman jumped, as if pulled back to the present.

"Oh yes." She patted her hair and shuffled through some papers. "Since you are new to the club, Lady Juliette, we thought we would start you off in the novice class."

"I see." Novice class. Juliette hadn't competed at that beginner rank in years. Still, it would hurt nothing but her pride—and that only if she allowed it. She would do as she was asked, especially since she was indeed a newcomer. "Thank you. Could you direct me to the portion of the grounds where the novices are gathered?"

"Of course. Or I could show you both?" The secretary addressed her comment to Heinrich.

"I am afraid Viscount Coatsworth and I are expected in the Royal enclosure." He turned to Juliette. "I will be cheering you from the stands. When you win your class, I shall treat you to refreshments to celebrate." He bowed and took the woolgathering viscount away with him.

The secretary watched until he disappeared into the crowd. A sigh worked its way out of her mouth. "He's as nice as he is handsome. I hear he's been invited to just everything this Season. I've seen him across the ballroom, of course, but I've never managed an introduction until now."

It occurred to Juliette that she should be jealous of the attention another woman paid Heinrich, but she was merely amused. And in any case, Lady Croft's assessment was correct. He was as nice as he was handsome.

A contingent of soldiers, resplendent in red coats and brass buttons, marched in perfect alignment, announcing the arrival of the Prince Regent. His carriage gleamed in the sunshine, the glossy horses beautiful with their postilion riders. They drove to the entry to the Royal enclosure, and the soldiers formed two lines, pushing the protestors back.

When the prince was assisted from his carriage with the help of two liveried servants, the shouts of the protestors drowned out any applause that might have occurred.

"He seems to have put on a stone or two every time I see him," Lady Croft said. "Soon they'll have to haul him about with draft horses. Cruikshank's latest depiction of him seems less a caricature and more of a portrait than ever."

Juliette's fingers tightened around the handle of her bow case. She didn't find the Cruikshank's depictions of the royal family humorous. They were cruel and biting indictments that set out to humiliate through magnifying perceived weaknesses. She had never met the prince, and she was aware he had some serious shortcomings, but he was still the nation's ruler, and some deference should be shown, shouldn't it?

"He has his issues, to be sure, but who of us does not? I would not like Mr. Cruikshank's attentions turned upon me, and I am sure you would not either. No one would fare well under the scrutiny of such a mocking man. Why is it that some assume the Prince Regent has no feelings, that they can belittle and sneer and expect him not to be hurt or defensive?" She hitched the case higher. "Where are the novices competing?"

Lady Croft's nostrils flared, and a dull red crept up her neck. Juliette realized she sounded not unlike the Dowager Duchess of Haverly with that little setdown. *Oh my.*

"The novices compete at the farthest point from the stands." Lady Croft's lips were stiff, as were her words. She pointed toward the tree line. "Few people wish to see the beginners. The top grades compete nearer the Royal enclosure."

If she hoped her censure would put Juliette in her place, she failed. It suited Juliette quite well to be away from the spectators.

"I had best get down there, then. I'm sure they will start soon."

Her case bumped lightly against her leg as she walked across the grass. When she reached the far side of the grounds, a kind soul assured her she was in the correct place, and she found her teammates.

"Oh good, our fourth is finally here." Mrs. Carlyle, the wife of the mill owner—and possible amour of Mr. Montgomery?—reached out from the group and took Juliette's arm. "I hope you're a good shot, because the other teams look very skilled for this grade."

Juliette swallowed her astonishment at both the abrupt greeting and her luck at being placed with a suspect. "I think I can hold my own. I hope so, anyway. I'm Lady Juliette Thorndike."

"Mrs. Clarissa Carlyle from Wattleford Hill. This is Miss Anna and Miss Rebecca Bunch."

"We're twins." They announced this simultaneously, though they needn't have pointed it out. They were identical in every way.

"A pleasure to meet you. Are there any rules I should know about? I've competed only in school tournaments before." Juliette clasped her case before her with both hands.

"You can put your case on the table here. We'll shoot four rounds, and the top three scores from each round will count for our total points. There are four novice teams, and the one with the most points at the end of the four rounds wins." Mrs. Carlyle tugged on her shooting glove. "The targets are twenty-five paces for novices. As the team captain, I will shoot last." She smiled and shrugged slightly. "None of us are terribly good, which is why we're in the novice class, but we enjoy the sport and being with the other teams. And the parties are very good at our club."

Juliette adjusted her expectations and tamped down her competitive nature. They would have an enjoyable time. That would be enough, especially for a first outing as a team.

She looked down the range where a paper target had been affixed to a bulging burlap sack. Full of straw, sawdust, or sand? Next to the shooting tables, a matching row of targets had been set up facing the downrange targets. "We all shoot this direction and then go down there and shoot back this way?"

"Yes. It saves on having to retrieve arrows," Miss Anna—at least Juliette thought it was Anna—said. She raised her bow from its case, testing the tightness of the bowstring. "What color are your fletchings? You need to register them with the judge before your turn."

"Blue and white." Juliette set her case on the table and unbuckled the latches. The color scheme had come from her finishing school in Switzerland.

There was no time to practice, for their team was called right away. Juliette was assigned third place in the shooting order, and she stood back, watching the Bunch sisters. After each finished their turn, she understood why they were in the novice division. But they cheered for each other and seemed happy enough with their scores.

When it was Juliette's turn, she donned her shooting glove, walked to the line, nocked her arrow, and took a deep breath.

Center of the target, steady your braced arm, pull back slowly, tighten your grip on the bow, center once more, release.

The small pop of the string impacting her gauntlet sounded at almost the same time the arrow hit the burlap. The vibration of the empty bowstring quivered up her arm.

Hmm. Not a bull. The arrow stood several inches up and to the right of center. She really was rusty.

The Bunch sisters clapped. "Well done." Their simultaneous utterances were a bit eerie, but Juliette smiled her appreciation for their enthusiasm.

Her second arrow found the bull but still toward the right.

"Perhaps you should aim down and left?" Mrs. Carlyle said.

Juliette bit the inside of her cheek. Giving advice to a stranger was bold, especially as Mrs. Carlyle hadn't yet established herself as a good shot.

Her third and fourth were even better, and she flexed her fingers against the slight sting of the bowstring. At one point in her schooling, she'd had distinct calluses from practicing, but with so many weeks off, they had subsided.

Juliette stepped back to allow Mrs. Carlyle to shoot and chided herself for feeling satisfaction that the woman missed the target altogether with her first attempt.

"It must be windy downrange," Mrs. Carlyle excused her error.

Juliette turned away and busied herself with testing her bowstring. Abruptly, she lowered her hands, letting the bow hang at her side.

Daniel Swann stood behind the banner-festooned rope that separated the spectators from the competitors, his head bare, arms crossed.

An odd bump happened beneath her breastbone, and she looked away. She had not seen him since he had removed Mrs. Fairchild and her companion from Almack's on Wednesday evening.

Was he looking for Uncle Bertie? That must be it, for he surely wouldn't seek *her* out.

He uncrossed his arms and tugged on his earlobe. A signal he had a message to pass.

Here, on an open field, where dozens of spectators watched every woman wearing a team uniform, and he wanted to pass her a message? A grin tugged at her lips. She loved a challenge. Finally, another chance to use some of the lessons she had been undergoing with Uncle Bertie in the War Room.

She threaded her arm and head through her bow to let it hang across her chest, and twisted her garnet ring, signaling back that she understood. Though she did not stare or otherwise indicate she had any interest in him, Daniel stood out amongst the spectators along the ropes. He was handsome and tall, and the wind ruffled his dark-brown hair.

"Who is that?" Anna Bunch asked.

"He's quite dashing, isn't he?" Rebecca smoothed her skirt and lowered her chin to look at Daniel through her lashes.

A stab of disquiet slanted through Juliette. She frowned. Why should she be discomfited? Rebecca was correct. Daniel Swann *was* attractive. Why should it bother her that someone noticed and commented upon the fact?

Because now that they had, Juliette couldn't exactly stroll over and get the note without arousing suspicion. Daniel had drawn their attention and foiled the message drop.

"We had better pay heed, ladies. Mrs. Carlyle is nearly finished with her round." It was always wise to keep your wits about you when on the archery range, and she wanted to turn their focus away from Daniel.

"Oh yes. You shot so well that, with Clarissa's score, we might move into the next round." Rebecca shrugged. "They drop the lowest score on each team. I suppose I'll be the one sitting out."

"It's all right," Anna said, hugging her sister's shoulders. "You'll do better next time. And there's always the shopping later to cheer us up."

They finished comfortably in the top four teams, with Clarissa and Juliette tied for points.

"I'll be watching from the sidelines," Rebecca promised. "You'll all do well."

As they waited their turn, Juliette worked over in her mind how to get the message from Daniel without causing a stir. She could do nothing while the rounds continued, so she would have to wait and see what eventuated.

They each shot, and again Juliette and Mrs. Carlyle's scores carried the team into the next round. They were one of the last two teams, but there would be an interlude before the final match.

Anna Bunch linked her arm through Juliette's. "Let's stroll through the vendor booths. Rebecca and I just received our allowance, and we're eager to buy something."

Grateful for their open offer of friendship, Juliette agreed. "I'd love to."

Daniel should be tracking her movements, and if he remembered his training and all the practicing they had done together, passing the note should be smooth and unobserved.

She paused before a fletcher's booth, admiring the tradesman's skill at trimming and inserting the feathers into the arrows. So many beautiful colors from which to choose. Perhaps she should think about getting her arrows re-fletched with the colors of the Thorndike family crest—rose and white.

In the next booth, sparks flew from a grinding wheel as a man sharpened arrow points. Down the way, another man called from behind his table, showing off leather belts and quivers and accessories. Other vendors, unrelated to toxophily, sold food and millinery and bits and bobs. The Bunch sisters squealed and examined and considered everything they could get their hands on, giving a running commentary of opinions. Harmless, uncomplicated fun.

Juliette lagged behind, keeping her hands at her sides. Not many people milled around the booths, it being so early in the day. Crowds would increase later on. With more people about, passing a note would be easier.

Rebecca turned just as Juliette felt something brush her hand. Her fingers closed about a folded piece of paper. Then a thump hit her shoulder, and she staggered. A strong grip prevented her from falling headlong into the grass, but it was a closely run thing. She was hauled up against a sturdy masculine frame, and his arms came around her. One of her hands flattened against the front of a caped cloak while the other fisted around the slip of paper, and she looked up into Daniel's shocked eyes.

Rebecca was by her side in a trice, her mouth gaping. "Lady Juliette, what are you doing?"

She wasn't certain. One moment she had been taking the note—the next she was in Daniel's arms.

"I beg your pardon." He swallowed. "I appear to be most clumsy today." He looked down at her, seemingly unaware that he still held her. "My heel caught on the grass, and I tripped into you."

"Sir, unhand me." Juliette extricated herself from his embrace. She feigned great umbrage while wanting to burst into laughter. She wasn't unaware of the strength of his arms and the solidity of his frame. And he smelled nice. Like soap and cloves. But to be caught embracing on the lawns of Hyde Park would have her reputation in tatters if she didn't watch out. Not to mention what Uncle Bertie would say at their ineptitude at a simple transfer.

The Bunch sisters crossed their arms, eyes narrowed. "I remember you. You were watching us compete. Lady Juliette, check your coin purse. Daddy said there might be pickpockets about today." Anna patted her own pockets as she glared at Daniel.

Daniel bowed, and Juliette smothered a smile at the redness creeping into his cheeks. "I assure you, I am no cutpurse. I merely stumbled on the grass. New boots. My humble apologies." He inclined his head toward Juliette and beat a hasty retreat.

"He may be handsome, but I don't believe he tripped. There's nothing but open ground here. He was practically hugging you." Rebecca stared after Daniel until he disappeared around one of the vendors' booths. "Do you think that was his purpose? Pretending to stumble so he could embrace you?"

"I doubt it very highly. No real harm has been done except he was embarrassed." How she would tease Daniel at the first opportunity. He had demonstrated as much grace as a bull on ice. Juliette kept the note in her palm. "Did you see that display of dresser scarves?"

Thankfully, the girls were easily distracted, and she had a moment to read the paper. It was written in a simple code, and she deciphered it in her head.

Mrs. Carlyle's husband suspect in Montgomery murder. Subtly question her about possible affair with Montgomery.

Juliette had heard the rumor at the reception before the funeral, but she had given it little countenance. Mr. Montgomery, after another man's wife? She couldn't believe that. But Daniel thought Clarissa's husband a murder suspect? Daniel must have his reasons, but how did he expect Juliette to broach such a subject with a woman she had barely met, whilst in the midst of an archery tournament?

If you cannot get the information without betraying your intent, stop trying. Better to live to fight another day.

The instruction from Uncle Bertie came back to her. She would try, but if she couldn't accomplish the task, she would tell Daniel so. Did this qualify as meddling in the investigation? Going contrary to Uncle Bertie's wishes?

When she caught up to the Bunch twins, they had made their purchases—identical silver-backed hairbrushes with matching mirrors. They seemed pleased, though bemoaned having spent an entire month's allowance.

"Let's go find Mrs. Carlyle," Juliette said. "It must be nearly our time to compete again."

"She's probably surrounded by men. She's always surrounded by men." Anna swung a small paper-wrapped bundle by its string ties. "She has more men buzzing around her than a dog has fleas."

"Really, Anna, can you not find a less vulgar description?" Rebecca chided her while hugging her parcel to her chest.

"It's true about Clarissa. You know it is. That's why she didn't come shopping. Too many men to flirt with during the break. I heard she has done more than flirt too." Anna lowered her voice. "I heard she married an old man, and she's tired of him."

"Anna Maria Bunch, you stop that right now. Gossiping is wrong, and Mrs. Carlyle is our friend," Rebecca snapped before quickening her pace.

Chastened, Anna fell a few steps back. Scowling, she stuck her tongue out at the back of her sister's head. Juliette offered her arm to show she understood, and Anna took it with a grateful smile. Gossip or no, Juliette needed to learn all she could about Clarissa Carlyle.

When they found Mrs. Carlyle, her behavior was as Anna predicted. She was surrounded by men laughing and vying for her attention. High color rode her cheeks, and she tapped at one man's hand playfully. Sunlight gleamed off her golden-brown hair and picked out the bachelor-button blue of her eyes.

"See? Like moths to a candle flame," Anna whispered. "It's like she cannot help herself. And she brags about it. Especially when Rebecca and I have never had a suitor between us." Anna gave a forlorn sigh.

Juliette patted her shoulder. Anna's transparent nature and frank speeches made Juliette feel positively ancient. "Your time will come. You are charming and friendly and interesting, and some young man will grasp that truth soon, I'm sure."

Another huge sigh. "That's what my mother says."

Mrs. Carlyle noticed them waiting outside the circle of gentlemen and beckoned. "I wondered where you'd gotten off to. It's nearly our turn. Gentlemen, if you will excuse us, we have a tournament to win." She smiled prettily, fluttering her lashes, and walked past slowly, her hips moving in a way that had all the men looking after her.

Anna elbowed Juliette in the ribs. "See?" she said again.

Juliette did see, but now was not the time to pursue the line of inquiry. Though from the little she had heard and observed, it was not difficult to imagine Mrs. Carlyle playing the coquette. But with Garfield Montgomery?

An hour later, they were admiring the rosettes pinned to their shooting jackets and congratulating one another. Within moments of receiving their awards, however, Clarissa Carlyle had moved into the same circle of men waiting near the ropes.

"I'm happy, but I'm sad too," Rebecca mourned, touching the frill around the red rosette. "Anna and I will remain in the novice class, but you and Clarissa will move up to the next grade for sure."

"Why was Mrs. Carlyle in the novice division? She's clearly a more-than-competent archeress."

Rebecca shrugged and looked away, but Anna spoke up. "The selectors put her into the bottom grade because—" She stopped, her face going red. "Well, there was an altercation between her and the club president. It isn't a secret since everyone knew about it pretty quickly. The club president accused Mrs. Carlyle of having designs on her husband. She didn't say it was an outright affair or that they had a tryst or anything, just that she didn't appreciate Clarissa's flirtatious ways with, and I quote, 'anything in trousers.'"

"Have there been rumors of any others?" Juliette cleaned her last arrow on the tassel at her waist and returned it to her bow case.

"Oh, lots. I don't know names, of course, because we don't move in the same social circles, but the last meeting of the Dianas was rippling with whispers."

"Lady Juliette, I am to return you to your uncle. Are you ready?" Duke Heinrich waited at the ropes. "And congratulations. You are very skilled." He smiled warmly. "It was a pleasure to watch."

"I didn't realize you were a spectator. I thought you were trapped in the Royal enclosure." She buckled the latches on her case and handed it to Heinrich over the ropes.

"I escaped in time to see your final round."

Mrs. Carlyle turned her back on the man to whom she was speaking and hurried to Juliette's side. "Oh, do introduce me. I've heard such wonderful things about this gentleman and have been eager to meet him."

Audacious. Still, the way she clamped on to Juliette's arm told her she wouldn't be denied. It underscored all Juliette had learned of Clarissa Carlyle today. Though she had not been provided an opportunity to ask anything specific, she had enough to tell Daniel that he might find what he was looking for if he pursued this line of inquiry.

"Duke Heinrich von Lowe, may I present Mrs. Carlyle, our team captain. Clarissa, His Grace, Duke Heinrich von Lowe of Brandenburg."

The duke's glance barely skimmed the woman as he bowed. "A pleasure, Frau Carlyle. Congratulations on your win." He motioned to

Juliette, leading her to the opening in the ropes. "Your uncle will meet us at the Stanhope Gate."

As they walked away, Juliette expected to feel triumph, but she didn't. She felt sadness. Mrs. Carlyle was a married woman with a roving eye. Though it was quite common in today's society, Juliette abhorred the notion of being unfaithful to a spouse.

If she ever married, it would be to a man she loved and admired and to whom she would remain faithful.

Daniel made his way around the Royal enclosure to the grounds where costermongers' carts had been placed and barrels and boards set up to create impromptu pubs. Getting away from Lady Juliette and her friends could not happen quickly enough. What a mess he'd made of what should have been a simple note pass.

He had to skirt the protestors, who had been sequestered to an area away from the tournament. That they hadn't been ushered completely out of the park surprised Daniel. Usually such gatherings were broken up and dispersed quickly. Still, they had been pushed far away from where the Prince Regent and his friends could see or hear them.

Sir Bertrand Thorndike stood before one of the makeshift bars, tipping back a mug of ale. Around him, men clapped and cheered, urging him on. With a flourish, he turned the empty cup upside down and slammed it on the board. A quick swipe disappeared the foam clinging to his upper lip, and he gathered the coins the bettors had tossed onto the counter. With a good-natured grin, albeit sloppy, he touched his hat brim and lurched a few steps.

"Whoops. No, no, I'm fine." He gently pushed away the hands that shot out to help him. "I've got important business, gentlemen, but if you're still here when I'm finished, I'll stand a round of drinks for you all."

Again he tipped his tall hat and bowed from the waist, losing his balance and toppling into a pair of ladies purchasing sweets from a nearby cart. They scowled and drew away from him, and he shrugged.

Daniel let him go, following at a distance. They were supposed to meet somewhere in the park, but Daniel would take his cues from Sir Bertrand. He'd made enough gaffes for one day.

Two young men broke off from their compatriots as Sir Bertrand passed and came up one on either side of him as he took the path toward the Stanhope Gate.

Daniel's senses heightened. Pickpockets or robbers? He reached under his cloak for his truncheon and quickened his pace. He needn't have worried. The moment one of the men pulled a knife from his waistband, Sir Bertrand struck with deceptive quickness, all traces of inebriation evaporating. He locked his fist around the man's wrist and wrenched it and the knife high behind the man's back. He grabbed the back of his collar, and with a sweep of Bertrand's right leg, knocked the fellow facedown onto the ground. Sir Bertrand took possession of the weapon before Daniel had crossed half the distance.

The thief's companion assessed the situation and fled. Better a live dog than a dead lion, Daniel supposed, letting him go.

"What is our city coming to that a man cannot amble in a public park without encountering cutpurses?" Sir Bertrand studied the knife while keeping his knee firmly on the back of his captive.

"It's a wicked old world." Daniel tucked his truncheon away.

"Son, I suggest you mend your ways, or you'll find yourself picking oakum in Newgate. You'll have plenty of time to consider your ill-spent youth if you're shipped off to the Antipodes." Sir Bertrand tapped the back of the man's head with the hilt of the knife, just hard enough to sting.

The man grunted and squirmed.

Sir Bertrand rose, lithe and agile, and brushed himself off. The miscreant took the opportunity to push himself up and race after his departing friend.

"It is, as you say, a wicked old world." He adjusted his cravat. "What happened after you left Almack's?" Just like Sir Bertrand to get right to business.

They fell into step, and Daniel recounted the events. "I was able to eliminate Mrs. Fairchild from suspicion in the murder of Mr. Montgomery. She was at a receiver's shop pawning a diamond necklace to pay a gambling debt the morning of the explosion. Her alibi was verified."

Daniel hitched his cloak collar higher as a gust of wind skittered across the path, stirring up last fall's leaves. "It isn't all dire news, however. When we got her into an interview room at Bow Street, she split like a sack of beans, admitting she stole the household money at Montgomery's during the luncheon. She confessed she excused herself and found the office, jimmied the lock, and made off with the money."

He scratched his cheek, remembering. "She would not stop blathering once she started, and she threw in both crying and wheedling. About how she had hoped to marry Mr. Montgomery and solve her financial problems, and how his daughter was being obdurate and not giving her any money or gifts, even though she had put it to her as bluntly as possible. Every time she tried to visit after the funeral, she was told Miss Montgomery was not receiving visitors."

"So you caught a thief but not a killer. Did she admit to the cheating at Almack's?"

"Yes. As I said, everything came gushing out once the sluice gate opened. Mr. Donaldson was fuming when we told him we had all we needed from her to convict him. I turned the pair of them over to an associate, and they'll stand before the magistrate to answer. I plan to visit Miss Montgomery later today to inform her that, while I have apprehended the thief of her household money, none of it was recovered."

"I don't envy you. What is the state of your investigation now?" Sir Bertrand walked with his hands clasped behind his back, his footsteps crunching on the gravel path.

"I had a word with a possible suspect in Wattleford Hill, a competitor of Montgomery's in the milling trade, and now I'm chasing his alibis. The man's wife is here today. In fact, she's a member of your niece's archery club, and she's suspected of having an affair with Montgomery, which fueled her husband's ire enough for him to challenge Montgomery to a duel of honor. I asked Lady Juliette to see what she can find out. See if there is any truth to the rumor that Mrs. Carlyle was being unfaithful to Mr. Carlyle and if that resulted in Carlyle murdering Montgomery. Carlyle swears he challenged him to a duel but that he wouldn't kill him dishonorably, and that he waited for Montgomery on the dueling ground, finally giving up and returning to his mill, thinking Montgomery lost his courage."

Sir Bertrand glanced sideways at Daniel. "So he'd shoot him on the park green, but he wouldn't kill the man in his office during an argument." He frowned. "I cannot say I am enamored of the idea of involving Juliette in your police investigation. I know she is eager and, in fact, has butted in already, but have a care. If she is to be a successful agent, she must keep up an appearance of absolute normality. A socialite with no more thought than what to wear and whom to accompany to the symphony. I have forbidden her to investigate this case. I do not wish her to draw undue attention to herself in any way."

Like being crashed into by a clumsy oaf who had the audacity to embrace her in public? Daniel shrugged and looked away. "I merely asked her to make a few discreet inquiries. I shouldn't think it would draw suspicion to gossip a bit with her teammates. Don't all women love a good natter anyway?"

"They do, but it would be a foolish man who said such things in their hearing." Sir Bertrand dug under his cloak for his watch. "Juliette is too eager to jump headlong into espionage. I often feel like a hen with a duckling, constantly trying to keep her out of the deep end of the pool. I wish her parents would remain on British soil long enough to take over her training, but there you are. When our superiors beckon, we must go."

"Lady Juliette is making good progress, is she not? And eagerness is a good thing?"

"Eagerness is good, but foolhardiness is not. I regret having to involve her so heavily in the mission last month. It's given her an appetite for the job that exceeds her capabilities."

"I've found her to be very capable. There are aspects of the training where she bests me." The passing of messages, for instance. His cheeks still burned at the way he'd bungled that exchange. She'd covered for him well, and he only hoped she had been able to pretend indignation with her friends that would absolve her of any collusion.

"She is gifted in several areas. And soon we may have the opportunity to test a few more. Haverly is hearing rumbles of a possible rally amongst our anarchist friends. He wishes me to attend the rally in disguise and to take Juliette with me, though I think it too soon for her to undertake another mission in disguise. Her last little foray in that direction led to you needing to rescue her from the St. Giles rookery."

"What is the objective?" The thought of Juliette in such a volatile situation didn't rest well with Daniel. "Why does Juliette need to go?"

"Haverly wishes me to ascertain how serious the threat is to public safety. To pinpoint who the principal players are and whether they pose a real danger. Jasper Finch was outspoken earlier this month in a room full of aristocrats, espousing his views on class society and industrial progress. If he would be so bold in that setting, would he be even bolder in front of a crowd of discontented people? Juliette is to accompany me because Haverly thinks she could use the training and because more women have been turning up to events like this. She may glean information from one of them that I could not."

"When is this gathering to take place?"

"It's uncertain yet. Haverly will give us instructions as he learns more. He would also like you to attend in disguise. You will need to have particular care. If it became known the meeting has been infiltrated by Bow Street, you could find yourself in a tight spot. I'll be in communication." They had reached the Stanhope Gate entrance to the park. "I promised to meet Juliette here when the tournament concludes. I left her in the care of Heinrich and Viscount Coatsworth, and they should be here before too long."

Daniel's neck muscles tightened. He liked Heinrich, but he hoped the German would be returning to his homeland soon.

Sir Bertrand stepped off the path. "Have you noticed that Coatsworth seems distracted lately? He was stupefied at Almack's, and whatever is preying upon his mind doesn't seem to have abated." He leaned against a tree, still holding the knife he had taken from the robber. "I tried quizzing him about it when I saw him earlier, but he merely blinked and shuffled away. Have you any idea what might be amiss with him?"

Daniel shook his head. "No. I cannot say that Coatsworth and I are particular chums. He seems to have a bee in his bonnet where I'm concerned."

"He's young, and like many of his class he has been both given more than is good for him and taught that he's better than others because of it." The knife disappeared into the waistband at the back of Sir Bertrand's trousers.

Strange thoughts to hear coming from an aristocrat. "Do you think he'll outgrow his mindset anytime soon?"

Sir Bertrand shrugged. "Some never do. Haverly and I have discussed the matter, especially as we look over possible recruits for the agency. He believes—and I tend to agree with him—that many of Britain's upper-class young men have been shaped and improved by going to war. A tough dose of reality for a lot of naïve snobs. Bullets don't care that your father is a peer. Coatsworth would have profited from some time in uniform."

"I wouldn't have minded serving, but it was a condition of my guardianship that I never enter the military." It was a mandate that had puzzled him more than any other.

"All that will be winding up soon, won't it?"

"Very soon. My birthday is the twentieth of this month. The guardianship ceases then."

The day of his emancipation was a complete question mark in some ways. Would he be able to keep his job? Should he look for new, more affordable lodgings? Should he attempt contact with his mother? Would the identity of his guardian be revealed? Many questions and little hope for answers to the most pressing ones. The solicitors of Coles, Franks & Moody had never given the slightest bit of information or hinted that they even knew any of the answers he sought.

"At least if Sir Michael boots you out of Bow Street, you'll have another job to fall back on." Sir Bertrand straightened away from the tree as applause rang from the spectator area. "I'll let you know when Haverly learns the date, time, and location of the rally. You'd best disappear now. It won't do for us to be noticed together too often. And more than that, for you and Juliette to be seen in company. She has plans to attend Miss Montgomery this afternoon. Perhaps she will find out what is amiss with Coatsworth from Agatha."

He sent Daniel a knowing look and gave a low wave before falling into a slack-jawed, glassy-eyed posture. In a flash, he was the drunken dilettante he wanted everyone to believe he was.

Daniel continued on his way east out of Hyde Park. He'd find a costermonger and purchase a quick lunch, then make his way to Eaton Square. If he timed his journey right, he would encounter Juliette while he was there.

Chapter 9

Daniel waited in the narrow park in front of the Montgomery home, biding his time until Lady Juliette arrived. Her carriage finally rounded the corner onto Eaton Square, and he straightened away from the tree he'd leaned on and made his way across the cobbles to open the carriage door for her.

"I didn't realize you would be here." Lady Juliette alighted with the grace of a ballerina and reached back inside to gather her reticule and a ruffled ribbon. "Though I had hoped to see you soon. I was able to gather some of the information you asked for, but no details." She grinned and poked him in the arm. "You nearly blew the gaffe, staggering all over the park like that. What happened?"

He took her teasing with a rueful smile, knowing he deserved it. "It was as I said. New boots on the long grass. My heel caught just as I gave you the note. We're lucky we didn't both land in a heap on the turf."

"Perhaps you would benefit from some dancing lessons or walking ridgepoles. You need to work on your balance." She smiled smugly. The balance exercises Sir Bertrand put them through always came more easily to her than to him.

Daniel used his truncheon to rap on the Montgomery door, but softly, in deference to all the black crepe draped on the entrance signified.

"What did you learn from questioning Mrs. Carlyle?"

"I wasn't able to question her per se, but I did observe her and hear a few things. She certainly has a reputation, and she demonstrated her skills at flirtation quite openly at the tournament. If the rumors are not true, she is doing nothing to dispel them. I couldn't see a way to get her to admit to me that she'd had a tryst with Mr. Montgomery on such short acquaintance, but from what I saw, she is not enamored of her rather old mill-owning husband and is open to diversions of a romantic nature. I cannot think she would make such a lateral move as to start a romance with another father figure like Garfield Montgomery, no matter how hefty his bank balance."

A liveried footman opened the door. Within minutes they had been whisked into the drawing room where Agatha, still in black mourning dress, hugged Juliette.

"I know it hasn't been that long since I saw you, but it feels ages. I've been shut up here alone, writing letters." She waved to a writing desk covered in black-edged cards. "I feel like a prisoner."

"Have you not had visitors?" Juliette led her to the settee. "I am sorry. I thought you would be besieged by guests and not want any more."

Daniel waited near the door, watching the pair take their seats. Lady Juliette was by far the more beautiful. Or perhaps she was only more beautiful to him. He wished he was her equal in rank. Though he doubted whether she'd give him a second glance even if he were a peer of the realm. She had a German duke pursuing her.

"Yes, I have had many visitors, but not the ones I want. Solicitors, accountants, the vicar, old ladies who want to give me advice."

"What about Alonzo? Has he not been to call?" Juliette frowned.

"I don't know what to think about Alonzo. He's hardly been here, and when he does come, he's so distracted he might as well not have come at all. He does not stay long, and he won't talk to me about whatever is bothering him." She dug for her handkerchief. "He's made no mention at all of our betrothal, and I don't know what to do. I can't ask him if he still means to marry me, can I?"

Maybe Coatsworth was having second . . . or third . . . thoughts, though why, Daniel couldn't fathom. The viscount seemed quite taken with Miss Montgomery only a few days ago, and now she was no longer an heiress to a fortune but the possessor of it outright. What had changed for the man?

"I wish my mother was here to give you some guidance," Juliette said. "She would know just what you should do."

"I've got the dowager." Agatha rolled her red-rimmed eyes. "She's *full* of guidance. Everything from what I should wear, to when I should shift to half mourning, to when I will be allowed to be seen in public."

Daniel could only imagine. The dowager was a woman of definite opinions and, even when she was correct, could make one want to rebel.

The ladies shared a rueful smile, and Agatha turned to Daniel. "I'm sorry, Mr. Swann. Please, do sit down. Are you any closer to finding out who killed my father?"

"The investigation is ongoing." Which was a polite way of saying he had made little progress on the matter. He took the chair opposite, sitting upright on the front edge. "We're making inquiries, and the engineer continues to test the structure for stability. He should have a report for you soon as to whether you can rebuild or if you should raze the mill and start over."

"Did you question that Mr. Carlyle? He and his wife called during the mourning reception, and rumors were flying the entire time. I know people thought I could not hear them, but they were wrong. My father wasn't having assignations with his competitor's wife, and I seriously question whether he was ever involved with Mrs. Fairchild. I haven't heard from her today, so perhaps she has finally understood that I do not wish to have contact with her. She has shown up on my doorstep multiple days, declaring her relationship with my father, how they were nearly engaged to be married and how he intended to lavish her with gifts. I finally told the butler to say I wasn't receiving."

Daniel rubbed his palms on his thighs. "About Mrs. Fairchild. She will not be a nuisance any longer. She is, at this moment, in the women's section of Newgate Prison awaiting her appearance before a magistrate."

Agatha reached out and gripped Juliette's hand. "Prison? What did she do? She didn't kill my father, did she?"

"Er, no. We were able to verify her alibi for the time in question. She was arrested on an unrelated matter. It seems she has quite a gambling problem, not only in quantity but in playing by the rules. She and a partner were caught cheating at cards, and while that in itself is not terribly serious, once we interrogated her she admitted she stole the household funds from your strongbox. When you would not give in to her demands for money, she decided to steal some."

Agatha's jaw dropped. "She came into this house in the midst of mourning visits and stole money?" She sagged back against the upholstery. "The world is full of wicked people, isn't it?"

Daniel nodded. He'd said much the same thing to Sir Bertrand not more than two hours ago. "Mrs. Fairchild will answer for her crimes. I assume your father's secretary will be available to testify if necessary?"

Agatha nodded.

"I'm afraid she has already squandered the money, so there is no hope for recovery. She will be found guilty and sent to debtor's prison."

A tap on the door, and the footman entered. "Your pardon, Miss Montgomery. There is someone here asking for the gentleman." He indicated Daniel. "A Mr. Wilkinson, sir. He says it is urgent."

Irritation clawed up Daniel's spine. He had further questions for Miss Montgomery, but he'd have to answer Owen's summons first.

Owen stood in the housekeeper's sitting room in the half-basement, his hat in his hands.

"What is it?" Daniel could not keep the annoyance from his tone.

"Sir Michael says you're to go to Hammersmith at once. There's been another murder at the blown-up mill." He blurted out the message before Daniel was even properly through the doorway.

"Who? How?" A hundred questions crowded into Daniel's mind, all clamoring to be addressed first. Was it anarchists? Or someone who bore a hefty grudge against Montgomery even after the man was dead?

Owen shrugged and rubbed the heel of his hand against the side of his head. "Guv didn't say. Just said I was to find you and send you out there. I ran all over Hyde Park looking for you, 'cuz that's where you said you'd be. I finally found Sir Bertrand Thorndike, full to the skin with gin." He made a disgusted face. "He said maybe you had come over here to tell Miss Montgomery about who stole her house money. I figured it was worth a try." He seemed to be waiting for Daniel to acknowledge his persistence in the matter.

Daniel shrugged. He didn't need to check in with Owen Wilkinson about his movements and plans. "You've delivered your message. I'll take my leave of Miss Montgomery and be on my way to Hammersmith. You can report to Sir Michael that you found me."

Owen shook his head. "The guv said I was to go with you to the mill."

Gripping the handle of his truncheon tucked into his waistband, Daniel shot up a prayer for patience. Though why he asked, he didn't know. Every time he prayed for patience, God sent something along for Daniel to have to be patient about.

"Very well. Let's go."

He went back to the salon to make his excuses.

Lady Juliette saw them out. "If I learn anything more, I'll let you know," she said. "I'm sorry your duty calls you away. I know you had more you wished to ask Agatha."

"I was going to request that she have her father's personal financial papers made available. Perhaps they will reveal if the motive was power or money."

"I'll ask her on your behalf."

He settled his hat atop his head and bowed. He grabbed Owen's sleeve to direct him out of the house. Once they found a carriage to hire, for Owen admitted he did not know how to ride a horse, the office boy said, "You didn't tell Lady Juliette about the new murder. Nor Miss Montgomery either."

"No, I did not." Daniel closed his eyes, hoping Owen would take the hint and stop talking, but that was too much for which to hope.

"Why? It happened at her mill, didn't it? She does own it now."

Cracking one eye, he glared at the lad. "I will inform Miss Montgomery when I have enough information to do so. I know nothing about the situation, and it would be both foolish and humiliating to put forth a theory and then have to recant it should it turn out to be untrue. Whoever is dead at the mill, there could be another explanation than murder. It may have been an accident, or the person may have fallen ill and died. Assemble facts before you formulate a theory, and certainly before you spread your unformed thoughts to people who have already suffered loss."

Owen crossed his arms and sat back, scowling, and Daniel closed his eyes once more. But his mind did not shut down.

Juliette had ascertained that Mrs. Carlyle was quite flirtatious. But was she carrying on an affair with Mr. Montgomery? Juliette thought it unlikely, but she had not seen as much of the world and human behavior as Daniel. If not Montgomery, then someone else? Perhaps someone who had gotten wind of the rumors of other affairs, suspecting her of cavorting with Montgomery, and in a fit of jealousy sought to eliminate competition for her affections?

And who was this body at the mill? How had he died? Was it related to the Montgomery killing?

As always, Daniel had more questions than answers. His mind raced down several trails, always winding back to who wanted Montgomery dead and why.

The carriage pulled up at the end of the street where Daniel had been knocked over by the blast, and he leapt out, an eerie feeling sweeping over him. He could almost smell the dust and smoke and feel the concussive explosion reverberating up the street. A fence had been erected around the mill property, with placards telling people to keep out. A handful of men huddled at the gate, where another man stood guarding the entrance.

Daniel looked up at the driver. "If you like, you can go up the street to The Dove and wait. I'll find you there when I'm finished." He flipped a coin up to the man, who caught it deftly with a grin.

"I'll do that very thing, guv. Take your time."

Owen shoved his hands into his pockets and sauntered beside Daniel down the lane.

A portion of the roof over the main part of the mill had either collapsed or been taken down since Daniel's last visit. The damage must have been more substantial than first assumed.

Shouldering his way through the townsmen clustered at the gate, he announced his identity to the guard and was shown through. Owen slipped in as well.

"Magistrate and watchman are waiting in the warehouse." The guard jerked his thumb to the right.

A sturdy man of at least fifty summers, who wore spectacles and an air of authority, greeted them. "Mr. Tollar. Magistrate for Hammersmith."

"Sir." Daniel turned to the other man.

This elderly fellow was thin as a grass stem and about as strong. He wavered, a troubled look in his eyes. With small, nervous movements, he picked at his clothes as if he could remove individual dust particles. He didn't speak, so the magistrate introduced him.

"This is Landsem, a night watchman for the town. He found the body."

The watchman shuddered and shook his head, as if he could dispel the memory. Dark smudges hovered under his bloodshot eyes. It was now mid-afternoon. Had he been awake all night and half the day?

"Sir, what did you find?" Daniel asked.

"Better see for yourself." Mr. Tollar jerked his head toward the warehouse entrance and led the way into the smoke-blackened hallway to Mr. Montgomery's office, but he didn't turn in there. He continued into the office of the mill manager, Mr. Coombe.

There, in the center of the floor, sprawled a man on his side, the back of his head a mess of blood. Nearby lay a length of pipe, also blood smeared.

A breeze from the shattered window stirred the air in the room, causing papers to flutter. The explosion had toppled books and files, and the wind had rearranged them several times. Frowning, Daniel toed one of the pages. These shouldn't be here. He'd told Owen to gather the paperwork from the mill. He frowned at the boy, pointing to the mess, then raising his brows. Owen looked away.

Daniel squatted beside the body. A layer of dust, whether dirty flour or just plain dirt, he didn't know, covered the man's clothes, which were of rough cloth. He wore heavy boots and had big, sinewy hands with the large knuckles of a laborer.

"Any idea who he is?"

The magistrate shook his head, remaining by the door. "Never seen him before."

"When was he found?"

Mr. Tollar turned to the hallway and dragged the watchman into the room. "Tell what you know."

Landsem's Adam's apple lurched. "I was making my rounds. The engineer fellow who's been crawling about the place every day asked us to take a look around inside a few times a night because some men had been breaking in and looting. That's why he had us put up that fence." The man's voice, being deep and robust, was at odds with his appearance. "I came through at midnight, and again at half three, but there was no one here. Just as the sun was coming up, I made one more pass through the building, and there he was."

"Did you touch him?"

Landsem looked aghast. "No. It was clear he was dead. Nothing to be done for him."

"Did you disturb anything else in the room?"

"No. I shut the door and got out of here."

"Was the door open when you found him?"

"Yes."

"Did you look through the mill to see if anyone else was lurking?"

"No. I was afraid there might be someone. I didn't want to get a pipe to the back of *my* head. I left and found Pie and put him on the gate, then I roused Mr. Tollar. He had a look, then said we should call for someone from Bow Street."

"I must say"—Mr. Tollar frowned—"it took much longer than I had hoped for you to arrive. Word has spread through the town. There's even a rumor that the Hammersmith Ghost has returned, and he's killing again."

Landsem muttered to himself and looked at the ceiling, his Adam's apple bobbing again in his skinny throat.

"The Hammersmith Ghost?" Owen asked. "What's that?"

Tollar shrugged. "More than ten years ago now it is, but lore said a man from town who took his own life could not rest easily in his grave because he had been buried in the churchyard . . . consecrated ground. He rose at night and wandered Hammersmith, attacking and scaring the life out of people. It was a bad time. People afraid of their own shadows and men patrolling the streets at night. One innocent fellow was shot to death accidentally, and the man who did it was found guilty of murder. He did a year's hard labor, though he's lucky it was only that. He was supposed to hang before the judge altered the sentence. This ghost stirred everyone up, got everyone looking sideways at his neighbor."

He shook his head. "These new murders are doing the same. Hammersmith is a peaceful town. We don't have killings and the like here. You need to find out who did this so we can get back to living our lives without fear."

In half a minute Tollar had gone from storyteller to politician.

"We will find the killer or killers." Daniel jotted in his notebook. Glancing up, he flicked his finger in Owen's direction. "Wilkinson, send one of the men outside to London to fetch Dr. Rosebreen to collect the body."

Mr. Tollar seemed grateful that any responsibility was being taken off his, and thus Hammersmith's, shoulders.

"Now, Mr. Landsem, tell me again what happened."

The watchman went through it again. His story didn't vary, and he finished with a rush. Dabbing his forehead with his handkerchief, he swayed. "Sorry, sir. I'm that tired."

"I apologize for keeping you here. I'll try to be quick so you can get home to your bed. Are you certain you've never seen this man before?"

"No. I've never seen him."

Daniel looked at the magistrate.

"No. He is unfamiliar to me."

"Is it possible he is a mill employee?"

"I don't believe so, but I don't know every man who toiled here." Tollar shook his head. "Can we step out into the hallway? The cacophony of that waterwheel is incessant." He pointed to the gaping windows where the sound of the river rushed in.

Daniel led the way, not stopping in the hall but continuing to the larger, quieter space of the warehouse. "Any of those men gathered outside work here?"

"Yes, most of them."

Owen returned, but Daniel sent him right back out. "Fetch one of the men outside, one who is employed here and would know the other workers."

Without an answer—for once—he departed.

A beefy man with a red nose and cheeks strode inside a few moments later. "Word is there's a dead man in 'ere."

Daniel led him back into the manager's office. "Word is correct. Do you know this man? Was he a mill employee?"

The newcomer's brows came down, and he leaned from the waist to view the man's face. "He don't work 'ere."

"You're certain?" Daniel asked. "And if I could have your name please?"

"Bell's my name. Been working this mill since I was a boy." He tucked his hands beneath his braces. "Know every man on the payroll, and this in't one of 'em."

"Thank you. That's all I needed to know." It wasn't, but it was all the man could probably tell him.

"Who bashed his head in?"

"That's what we're trying to sort out."

"Might have been looters squabbling over something. Been having trouble with folks sneaking in here. That's why we're hanging about outside. Taking turns, as it were, watching over the place. We want the mill up and running again soon, and it won't be if thieves break in to steal the parts and pieces."

"Who patrolled last night? And at what time?" Perhaps, at last, a line of inquiry. Daniel indicated they should return to the warehouse to talk.

When they rejoined Tollar and Landsem, Bell shifted his weight. "We weren't looking after things yet last night. This morning's meeting out there was to get us organized. I know they have the fence, but it wasn't keeping anyone out. I was one of the men that engineer hired to come in yesterday and take off the bits of the roof that were ready to fall." He pointed to the ceiling, as if they could see the roof several floors above. "I could see there were some tools missing and some sacks of flour. I told the boys, and we decided to keep a lookout ourselves. Can't expect the town's watchmen to do everything by themselves."

Mr. Landsem nodded and sent Bell a look of gratitude.

Additional patrol was a good idea, though it was too late for the dead man.

Owen stood in the doorway, and Daniel beckoned him in and handed him the notebook.

"Gentlemen, if you will tell my associate your lodging addresses, I will let you leave. If you think of anything more, please send for me at Bow Street. I would advise you to put those night patrols into action soon." He handed both Bell and the magistrate one of his cards.

Bell nodded, Landsem looked ready to collapse, and Mr. Tollar frowned. "This is bad for our town. I pray you can solve this quickly."

Daniel did too. He returned to the manager's office and the body. When Owen joined him a few minutes later, Daniel glared at him.

"Start gathering all this. Find a crate or box. We're taking it to Bow Street." Daniel examined the body again, turning the man onto his back to go through his pockets. The corpse resembled a plank, no longer supple.

"Paperwork again? Why do you always do this to me?" Owen scowled and grabbed a handful of sheets.

Daniel didn't look up. "You should have done it when you cleared Montgomery's office. And what did I tell you about following the paper?"

"That it's the most important part of the job, that most leads come from correspondence and record keeping." Owen employed a sing-song voice. "But that's just to keep me out of where the real action is. Examining bodies and questioning suspects. You never said to take the paperwork from the manager's office. You said clear out Montgomery's." The office boy shoved some books into a pile. "You want to blame me for everything because you don't think I'm good enough to do this job. You've never liked me, always treating me like a servant, always dressing like a toff and putting on airs and sneering like you're better than the rest of us."

Daniel's temper rose. "Stop acting like a child. How I dress is no concern of yours. If you're looking for someone who has spread dislike from the first moment, perhaps you should look at yourself. You've been insubordinate, rude, with a pointed disregard of doing as you're told. If you expect to rise at Bow Street, I suggest you learn the craft of detection and also how to work as a member of the team. Now, gather that paperwork like you should have done the first time, and get it up the street to the carriage."

Owen turned his back on Daniel, slamming papers and books, his spine rigid.

Daniel rubbed his neck, shaking his head. He'd inserted yet another wedge between them. What kind of leader was he that he couldn't get through to the young man?

Dr. Rosebreen would hopefully give them a more accurate esti-mate of time of death. Sometime between three thirty and sunup was more than three hours. The blood was well dried, and the body was stone cold and stiff.

Was this the result of a squabble between looters? If so, what had they fought over? He saw nothing of value in this office, but if another scavenger had taken something, how would Daniel know? He had little hope of coming upon an answer in the paperwork, but he would hold true to his methods. They would sift through the office parapher-nalia to see if any motives for either murder leapt out.

Chapter 10

Juliette blotted the last page, careful not to smear the ink on the black-edged paper. She had spent time with Agatha over the past two days, helping her with the correspondence surrounding her father's death and filling in time.

"So you'll go with me?" Agatha asked.

"Of course." Juliette was glad to have something to do for her friend, an errand that would get them out of the house this Monday afternoon.

"And you don't mind?"

"No. Now is a perfect time. We can arrive well before they close."

"Thank you. I didn't want to go on my own, but I didn't want to take Mr. Earnshaw. He offered to accompany me, or even go in my stead if I would write a letter of permission. He insisted that, as Father's accountant, he already knows all of Father's business, but what if the bank is holding something personal for my father? It could be anything. Father visited the bank all the time. I think he was there more often than at his club."

Before continuing, Agatha rang for the maid and asked her to fetch their bonnets and cloaks.

"I knew so little about my father that if something personal is in the vault, I don't want to share it with anyone else just yet. Is that odd?"

"I don't think that's odd at all." And she didn't. Her own relationship with her parents was complicated, and she could understand Agatha wanting at least a glimpse into her father's mind and heart. She had felt the same when her parents had gone missing, and she'd been thrown into an entirely different world than what she had thought awaited her after boarding school.

Later, as they neared the Bank of England on Threadneedle Street, Agatha clutched the papers and the key to her father's security vault, as if they might try to escape. "I don't know why this task seems so difficult. Perhaps it is because every time I do something like this, it drives home the point that my father is truly dead. He never would have allowed me, his daughter and a mere woman, access to his personal vault at the Bank of England. But here I am about to invade his privacy, and there is nothing he can do to stop me."

Agatha's maid sat quietly in the corner of the carriage, ignoring them as she had been trained to do. It still seemed wrong to Juliette to behave as if servants were not present, and she wanted to guard her tongue lest she give the woman fodder for gossip. Not that she knew the maid would natter about her mistress to the other servants, but it was always a possibility.

"I don't think your feelings are wrong. Everyone's grief is different. Don't think of this as an invasion of his privacy. Think of it as taking responsibility for the business empire he built."

"I do not think he intended me to take over his business empire. I think he intended me to marry a man who would take over for me."

"Which you will, but it is not wrong for you to have at least some idea of the scope of the inheritance your father left you."

"I will not marry anytime soon if Alonzo continues to act as if he does not wish to be near me." Sorrow thickened Agatha's voice, and she stared out the window at the passing buildings. "He is behaving most peculiarly."

"Perhaps he is processing his own grief. Or he does not wish to burden you with anything and is giving you space to mourn?" Though Juliette wondered if such thoughts were in keeping with Alonzo's nature. Admittedly, she did not know him well, but on their brief acquaintance, he had often seemed more concerned with his own person than with anyone else. She studied her garnet ring, her hand resting on the muff in her lap. Most likely she was doing the poor man an injustice. Agatha cared for Alonzo, and that should be enough to recommend him. She should try harder to like him.

The carriage rocked to a stop outside the Bank of England, and men in suits and hats hurried in and out the massive doors. Juliette was relieved to see ladies as well. They would not stand out as unusual in this bastion of male finance and commerce.

"Wait here. We shall conduct our business and return as soon as possible." Agatha dismissed her maid to wait in the carriage and squared her shoulders, though she looked frail to Juliette.

They walked up the steps of the be-columned center of the kingdom's finance. Inside, tall windows flanked by dark-green curtains let in sunlight. At the far end of the high-ceilinged room, a statue of William III, the founder of the bank, stood in an alcove, staring the length of the space. Juliette dearly would have loved a closer look at the marble image. From this distance he looked more like a Roman Caesar than Good King Billy.

A man in a pink frock coat with crimson vest and black top hat greeted them. "Good afternoon, ladies. I am one of the gatekeepers here. How may I be of assistance?" His voice was barely above a whisper, pitched to be heard below the buzz of business and the echoing footsteps on the marble floor. Along the far wall, men sat behind high counters with barred rails, issuing currency and helping patrons.

A gatekeeper? Did that mean the man was tasked with keeping out the riffraff, or was he a glorified messenger of some sort? Like a footman? His clothing smacked of livery from the last century, but his manner suggested butler.

"I'm here to access a personal vault." Agatha sounded cowed, as if she thought she were somehow bothering the man, and Juliette wanted to put her arm around her friend.

"I see. Allow me to tender you into the care of one of our employees. He will gather your information and assist you in any way he can."

They were led through the large currency issuing room and taken down a white hallway with a rich red carpet. Everywhere Juliette looked, opulence and finery spoke of power and the money behind that power. After many twists and turns, during which time she was thoroughly lost for direction, they entered another vast room with staircases leading up and down and doors marching like soldiers in formation along all the walls. The floor was a massive expanse of black marble with mosaic inlays. The gatekeeper tapped on one of the heavy walnut doors along the perimeter and turned the brass knob without waiting to be admitted.

"Mr. Nighly, this young lady wishes to access a private vault." With a small bow, the pink-coated man gestured for them to enter and closed the door behind them with himself on the other side.

Silly to feel abandoned by someone they had met only moments before, but Juliette wanted to call after him. How were they to find their way back to Threadneedle Street?

"May I help you?" An austere man rose from behind his desk, looking over a pair of half-moon glasses. "You wish to apply for a security box? Do you have an account at this bank?"

Agatha offered the paperwork to him. "I do not have an account at this bank. However, my father had several."

Mr. Nighly perused the papers quickly, then dropped his officious manner. "Miss Montgomery. Of course. I am so sorry for your loss. Word of your father's passing was a blow to many here. He was a valued customer and friend." He handed the papers back to her. "There should be no problem getting access to your father's security vault. There is, however"—he paused—"the small matter of verification of your identity. Have you visited the bank before? Is there someone here who can vouch for you?"

Agatha sent Juliette a half-panicked look. "I have never been here. Are the letters provided by the solicitor and the accountant insufficient?"

The banker paused. "I do apologize, but we've had a recent spate of impostors coming in with papers that appear to be in order but which are in fact forgeries." He held open the door, as if to unceremoniously usher them out.

"I can assure you," Juliette said, "this is Miss Agatha Montgomery, daughter of the late Mr. Garfield Montgomery." She was indignant on behalf of Agatha, who would no more forge documents than dance down Rotten Row in her shift.

"And you are . . ." Again, the stare over the half-moon glasses.

"I am Lady Juliette Thorndike, daughter of the Earl of Thorndike."

His brows rose, but he shook his head. "Anyone can say she is anything. Do you have any connections inside the bank?"

You can say you are a Mr. Nighly, banker here, but how do I know you are not an impostor?

"I have no idea how to answer you. What is it you suggest Miss Montgomery do? She has provided documents, and she has the key to her father's vault. Whom do you suggest she bring with her to prove her bona fides?"

"You have the key, you say?"

Agatha showed him the key, which was stamped with a number and the insignia of the bank.

Mr. Nighly's shoulders relaxed. "Wonderful. If you have the key, that and the papers are enough to establish your identity. If you will come with me?"

They were led down another maze of long corridors with doors on both sides, doors with frosted glass and gold-and-black-lettered names. Mr. Nighly stopped before one labeled *Sir David Button.* "I am in charge of new accounts and security boxes, but Sir David is the member in charge of unlocking boxes for existing customers."

Agatha and Juliette shared a look. These men had such specific duties that did not overlap?

They entered an anteroom occupied by a narrow-nosed secretary with prominent front teeth barely obscured by a rather weedy moustache. "Yes?"

"Miss Montgomery to see Sir David about her father's assets here in the bank."

The secretary leaned over to check a ledger. "I do not have you down on Sir David's appointment schedule. He is a very busy man, you know."

Nighly flinched. "This is the daughter of Mr. Garfield Montgomery, and I am certain Sir David will make room in his schedule to see her. Is he with a client now?"

"No, but—"

"This way." Mr. Nighly brushed by the secretary and opened the door to the inner office.

The palatial room, with rich woods, thick carpets, and bright brasses, smelled of beeswax polish and leather. High windows made the area feel spacious, and a pair of potted palms anchored the corners. Sir David, a gray-haired man with an impressively patterned waistcoat, bent down the corner of his newspaper to peer over the headlines.

Spying Juliette and Agatha, he dropped the paper on the desk and rose with a quick bow.

"Sir David," Mr. Nighly said, "Miss Agatha Montgomery, daughter of Garfield Montgomery. She wishes to access her father's vault here, and she has both paperwork and the key."

Recognition dawned, and deference came over his face. How much money must Mr. Montgomery have banked here that mention of his name caused such an obsequious reaction?

"Please, do come in. Sit. Bardwell," he snapped at the secretary, who'd followed them in, "fetch some tea for the ladies."

The narrow-nosed secretary departed, and Mr. Nighly followed him out. Agatha took one of the elegant chairs before the desk, perching on the edge, her papers in her lap.

"Miss Montgomery, do allow me to express my sincere condolences on the loss of your father. He was a great man of business and philanthropy, as you know." He glanced at Juliette, who took the other chair.

Agatha stirred herself. "Thank you. This is my dear friend Lady Juliette Thorndike. Her father is the Earl of Thorndike. Perhaps you know him? She has come to support me during this difficult time."

"Of course. Lady Juliette. It is a pleasure. Now, what may I do for you today, Miss Montgomery? You wish to obtain access to a vault?"

Agatha produced the paperwork once more. "My father's accountant and his solicitor prepared these."

Sir David perused the letters, his expression grave. When he had examined each page, he set them on his desk.

"Very well. Everything appears to be in order. If you ladies will come with me? Or would you prefer the tea first? It should be here momentarily."

A tap on the door announced the arrival of the tea tray, and though Juliette would have preferred to get on with their business, she wouldn't be rude to the secretary. Agatha looked grateful for the hot beverage, which soon added color to her cheeks.

As they left Sir David's office and started down the long, marble-lined hallway, two men approached, and Juliette couldn't quell her smile. However, she gave no indication that she recognized one of the men, for she did not know if it would be proper under the circumstances.

The Duke of Haverly felt no such restraint. "Lady Juliette. A pleasure."

"Your Grace, it's very nice to see you again. I hope you are well, and your duchess?"

"We are both quite well. Charlotte would be pleased to see you sometime soon if you can spare the time to call." His eyes missed nothing, and his tone was merely pleasant. Then it dropped.

"Miss Montgomery." He took Agatha's hand between both of his, bending a kind look upon her.

"Your Grace." Agatha bobbed a quick curtsey.

Sir David had visibly relaxed. He must have still wondered about the validity of their identities despite Agatha producing both papers and key, but now that they had been recognized by a peer, his doubts were quieted. "I did not realize you were acquainted with His Grace?"

"The duke's mother has been our chaperone to many events this Season. And the duke and duchess have been kind enough to extend to me the friendship they have with my parents." Juliette hid a smile. Marcus Haverly was more than just a family friend. He was her supervisor in the secret agency for which she now worked.

"What brings you to these hallowed halls?" the duke asked.

Agatha sighed. "Tidying up some business of my father's."

He frowned. "You have solicitors for that, surely."

"Yes, but this is a task I wanted to complete myself. I'm checking the contents of his security vault. There may be personal effects."

"I see. Well, I will not keep you. I expressed my condolences and my wife's earlier, but know that you have them once again. If there is anything you need, anything I or my duchess can do for you, please do not hesitate to contact us." He nodded to each of them and continued on his way.

Juliette followed him with her eyes for a moment, feeling again that sense of security whenever the duke was nearby. He was so confident and capable, with perfect manners and an assured quality about him that transferred to those he was with. He wore power easily.

Knowing that he was one of the best spies in the kingdom didn't hurt either.

She hurried to catch up to Sir David and Agatha. The banker escorted them to a wide staircase leading to a lower level and then down another long corridor. The air was cold here, and periodically along the way, iron bars sectioned the corridor. Armed attendants, also in pink coats and red waistcoats, had to unlock the doors to allow them through.

What would they say if they knew Juliette was also armed, with a knife in her half boot and a pistol in a cunning pocket inside her muff?

Sir David stopped before a thick metal door, and at his instruction, the attendant unlocked and opened the heavy barrier, which made no sound as it moved.

Inside, Sir David lit several lamps, and the shadows pushed back to reveal walls full of metal doors, each with a brass keyhole.

"If you will allow me?" Sir David held out his hand, and Agatha put her key into it. He studied it in the lamplight and searched along the right-hand wall until he came to the keyhole he sought. "Here it is." He inserted the key, opened the door, and turned away immediately. "It is our policy to leave the box holder in privacy. When you have finished, please lock the box, and one of the attendants will escort you upstairs. If you need anything, the man outside will assist you. And if I may do anything further, someone will send for me."

He left quickly, and they looked at each other in the lamplight.

"I suppose we should keep our voices down since the guard is just outside." Juliette was grateful the door remained at least partially open. She would not like to be closed into such a fortified place. She had never been comfortable in tight spaces, and the idea of being accidentally locked inside a vault made her skin crawl.

Agatha blew out a long breath. "I feel as if I am on a treasure hunt in an Egyptian catacomb."

"That describes this situation perfectly. I've ridden through the city many times and never once wondered what was *beneath* the Bank of England. There must be fifty rooms down here. Do you think they are all full of valuables and personal effects? I cannot help but wonder what riches are contained in this building, and what other secrets are hidden in London."

Agatha squared her shoulders and pushed her veil farther back on her bonnet. "I suppose I had better look inside the box."

"Do you want to sit at the table, and I can bring you the items? Or would you prefer I wait outside?" Juliette wanted to give Agatha her privacy too.

"Don't go. I can't do this on my own."

Juliette squeezed her friend's shoulder and approached the vault. The opening was about a foot square, and she had no idea how far back it went. She raised one of the lamps and peered inside.

Several blocky shapes, some books, some folders. She removed boxes, noting the jeweler's marks.

"Those were my mother's. Father said he hoped to present them to me as a wedding gift." Agatha blinked and sniffed. "She had several pieces, and I believe even a tiara."

"Do you want to take them with you now?"

"No. They should stay safely here. I can't wear them yet as a debutante. There will be time later to take them to the house. What else is inside?"

Juliette removed the folders, a stack about an inch thick. "Personal papers?"

"His will and deeds and other legal documents are supposed to be here. The solicitor said to bring them all with me."

"What about these ledgers?" Juliette removed two large, leather-bound books and a smaller one with a buckle closure.

"I wouldn't know the first thing about ledgers. Something for Mr. Earnshaw to look into. I suppose we should take them with us, and he can sort them out."

"What's in the smaller book?"

Agatha picked up the slim volume and held it toward the light. "It almost looks like a diary." The words came out on a whisper. "I can't look."

"Do you want me to put it back?" How could she not look? Juliette would have devoured anything left by her father. Just last month he had left her an encoded message in a book, and she had wrestled with the puzzle for hours until she'd broken it and read the letter that had changed her entire life.

"No. You look at it for me. Tell me what it is, and if you think I should read it or leave it here. If it is merely more business, we'll add it to the pile to take with us."

"Are you certain? If it is a diary, your father would not have envisioned my reading something so personal." She hesitated. Who wouldn't want at least a glimpse under these circumstances?

"My father would not have envisioned being shot to death in his own gristmill either." Agatha's voice was grim, made all the more grave by the flickering lamplight and the cave-like surroundings.

Juliette unbuckled the latch and opened the book. She tilted the volume toward the nearest lamp. The first page was dated January 1 of this year. "It's new."

Agatha is coming home. I long for it and I dread it too. How am I to navigate bringing a daughter out in society without the help of a wife?

She stopped reading. "Agatha, it is a diary of sorts. And it mentions you right away. He was worried about giving you a proper debut Season."

Agatha choked out a sob, pressing the back of her hand to her lips.

Juliette leafed through the pages. Only about a dozen entries, but the last one, dated the end of last month, caught her eye.

Must look into the matter. Something is off. After all I've done, can this betrayal be true? I shall have to take care. I wouldn't want to be wrong.

She frowned, flipping back to the previous entry for context, but it was merely a quick notation that his stolen painting had been returned by the police and that he had given a reward to the officer, Swann, in gratitude, acknowledging his competence in the matter.

Had Mr. Montgomery suspected the truth behind the theft of the painting? That it was in fact Uncle Bertie who had taken it for a short time to find the bit of code hidden inside the frame? Was that the betrayal spoken of in the last entry? If so, how had he stumbled upon the truth?

Or was it another matter entirely? Something he had discovered that led to his murder?

"I think you should take it with you, and perhaps you should let Detective Swann look at it. It might help him find whoever killed your father. The ledgers and the diary." Daniel should know that Mr. Montgomery was suspicious of something at the end of his life.

"Did you find anything important?" Agatha sat up straighter, her eyes wide and questioning.

"I don't know if it is important or not, but I have heard Mr. Swann say that clues are often found in paperwork." She showed the last entry to Agatha. "What do you think this means?"

Agatha read the page, her finger trailing over the ink. "I've no idea. It could be something sinister, and it could be something completely harmless. If you had asked me ten minutes ago if my father kept a diary, I would have said a resounding no. I'm beginning to wonder if I knew him at all."

Juliette could sympathize. Her parents had divulged a few of their secrets since she came home from Switzerland, but she was certain there were many more she would never know.

"If you think it best, we'll take the diary to Mr. Swann." Agatha pushed herself up from the table. "I cannot seem to order my thoughts at the moment, nor do I wish to trust these things to a messenger or servant. Would you take them to Bow Street for me?"

Juliette agreed, and they gathered up what they were removing and returned the jewelry to the vault.

She felt as if she'd been freed from a prison when they entered the expansive currency room, and Juliette could feel the sunlight on her face.

Once out on the street, she urged Agatha to take the carriage home. "I'll hire a cab to take me to Bow Street."

"If you are certain? You will have no maid or chaperone."

"I am certain, and don't worry about the maid. It won't take long, and nothing will happen to me on such a short errand. You go home, have some tea, and try to get some rest." She set the folders in Agatha's lap. "Take these with you so the solicitors can deal with them."

"You're a good friend." Agatha squeezed her hand and sat back as the coachman closed the door.

A bank attendant stood behind Juliette, holding the ledgers and the diary. When she nodded to him, he stepped to the curb and hailed a hack parked across Threadneedle Street. She climbed into the carriage and pressed her hand to the stack of books beside her on the seat as the horses lurched into motion.

What would Daniel think about her turning up at his place of work? What would Uncle Bertie think? He'd told her to stay away from the Montgomery murder investigation, but she couldn't ignore Agatha's need for help, could she? While she respected Uncle Bertie's caution about drawing attention to herself and possibly causing those watching to ask questions, wouldn't they think it odder if she didn't help her friend?

Once on Bow Street, before paying the jarvey, she glanced at the

Opera House with its impressive columns and wide steps. The much less imposing Bow Street Magistrate's Court stood opposite, and she gathered up the ledgers and the diary and made for the door.

A utilitarian foyer, with a wide staircase leading upward, greeted her, seeming especially bland after having been at the opulent Bank of England. She noted the signs on the wall indicating the magistrate's office and courtroom were located upstairs, while the investigators' offices were down the hall.

She'd hardly gone half a dozen steps when a door opened and young Mr. Wilkinson emerged carrying a tea tray. His brows shot up his forehead, and the tray wobbled.

"Milady, what are you doing here?"

"I'd like to see Detective Swann, please." She raised the ledgers an inch or two. "I have some things for him."

Mr. Wilkinson set the tea tray on a table and came toward her. "He's in the common room right now. I can take those to him." He reached for the books, but she stepped back.

"I would prefer to deliver them myself. They are of a . . . sensitive nature." She had not received permission from Agatha to show her father's property to anyone but Daniel.

A scowl flattened the young man's mouth, and he shrugged and lifted the tea tray. "This way, then." He walked with an insouciant swagger. No wonder Daniel often seemed exasperated by young Mr. Wilkinson.

He backed into a doorway, using his posterior to push open the door, and his arrival was greeted with a cheer. Juliette followed him into the room. Several desks filled the space, pushed together in pairs. Every desk had an occupant. One man leaned back in his chair, his boots on the desktop, and at sight of Juliette he catapulted himself upright. A book teetered out of his hands and smacked the floor as the other men in the room rose to their feet.

The first man, whose waistcoat strained over his middle, had a pipe dangling from his lips that looked certain to follow the book. Another man rounded a desk that was the epitome of organization. Neat stacks of paper, quill resting precisely in its tray beside an inkwell, and a letter opener aligned exactly with the edge of his blotter.

"Greetings." A tall, thin man shot her a wide smile. "And who might you be?"

Before she could answer, her eyes found Daniel in the back corner, farthest from the windows and the fireplace. He crossed the room and relieved her of the heavy books. "This is a surprise."

"I apologize for arriving unannounced," she whispered while looking around him at the other investigators. "I have some items of Mr. Montgomery's you should see."

"This lovely lady belong to you, Swann? Be sporting and introduce us." The first man elbowed his way close, still grinning.

Daniel winced and sent an apologetic look Juliette's way. "Lady Juliette Thorndike, this is Andrew Jamison."

Mr. Jamison boggled and raised his shoulders. "Apologies for my crass manners, milady."

"Mr. Thomas Fyfe." Daniel indicated the man with the impressive waistcoat and pipe.

"Mr. Matthias Tollivar." He of the immaculate desk.

"Mr. Edgar Piggott." A small man with a moustache that swallowed half his face.

"And you've met Mr. Edward Beck. He's newly returned from a case that took him out of London." Daniel offered his arm. "Perhaps we should speak in private?"

"Here now, you don't mean to rush her off without a cup of tea, do you? It's that cold outside, and she must be chilled." Mr. Jamison all but blocked their path.

"Thank you, but no. I must be about my business and cannot linger." She spoke firmly. He certainly was a brash fellow, brimming with confidence even after being set back by finding she was a lady.

Crestfallen, he stepped aside, and Mr. Piggott gargled a noise that sounded suspiciously like a strangled laugh.

Owen Wilkinson busied himself pouring tea and passing around mugs, and he thoroughly ignored Daniel and Juliette as they passed him into the hall.

"What has him so dyspeptic?" she asked once they were on the other side of the door.

Daniel shrugged. "He's like that most days. Today, however, his displeasure is directed at me because I set him several important tasks that he considers either too boring or beneath him. Never mind." He made a sweeping gesture. "I do not wish to waste time talking of the office boy." He indicated the books under his arm. "Let us retire to the incident room, and you can share with me what you've brought."

At the far end of the hallway, on the right, he opened a door and allowed her to enter first. It was dim inside the room, with the windows looking out directly on the building next door, and he fetched a taper to light the wall sconces. A table took up much of the space. Stacks of papers covered the table, and pages were pinned to the walls. A dank, smoky smell hovered over everything.

"I apologize. Many of these items came from the mill. Some were singed, some were doused, and all were tossed about in the explosion. We're trying to make sense of them, to get a better feel for Montgomery's business and wealth. The task of sorting and organizing them has Wilkinson most put out with me."

"Perhaps what I brought you will help. Agatha and I went to the Bank of England, where her father kept a security vault. Those ledgers and a diary were in the box."

He set them on the table. "Thank you. Will Miss Montgomery mind if we keep these until the investigation is concluded? Things have gotten very complicated over the last day or so. When Wilkinson fetched me from Eaton Square Friday, it was to go to Hammersmith to examine the body of another murder victim at the Montgomery Mill."

Her mouth opened, and an odd sensation feathered across her skin. "Was it someone killed in the blast but just discovered?"

"No. There has been some looting of the property, and at this point it is speculated that two trespassers fought over the same object, and one killed the other. As of now, we have no identification of the dead man. The coroner, Dr. Rosebreen, has examined the body and found no identifying marks or scars. Local men are asking around the village, but so far, nothing. I'm waiting for the engineer to let me know his findings. He's supposed to arrive momentarily."

"I do not believe I will inform Agatha that there has been another murder. She's bearing up well, but this might be too much for her." Juliette fingered the ribbon on her bonnet, suddenly aware that she and Daniel were alone in a room, though the door remained open. She should cut this visit short and get back to Berkley Square.

"Swann, what is your progress? Why do you never check in with me? I refuse to chase you about for a report." A well-dressed man, with sharp dark eyes, strode into the room, halting when he saw Daniel was not alone.

"Lady Juliette Thorndike, may I present my supervisor, Sir Michael Biddle?"

She held out her hand. This was the man Uncle Bertie had told her wanted Daniel's position for a family member and was looking for any excuse to release him from service at Bow Street.

"Lady Juliette, what brings you to Bow Street? Not trouble, I hope? Allow me to escort you to the main office room, where I will assign a different inspector to help you. Mr. Swann is busy with other cases, and I'm sure you would prefer someone else." He offered his arm with a frosty smile.

"Thank you, but no. I came specifically to see Mr. Swann on behalf of Miss Montgomery. I am certain he is the only man I need." The words were out before she thought of how they might be interpreted, and heat rushed to her face. "That is . . . the Montgomery case is his, so it seems right that I deal with him . . . after all." She stumbled to a stop, wishing she could evaporate.

Daniel's eyes held amusement, his brows raised slightly. She looked longingly at the door, but thankfully, Sir Michael seemed not to comprehend any gaffe on her part. Still, what a ninnyhammer. She wished someone would say something, change the subject to anything else.

"Someone else to see you, Swann. I ain't your social secretary." Owen barged into the room with a man on his heels, saw Sir Michael, and skidded to a halt, wincing. "That is, Inspector Swann, there is a gentleman to see you." He bowed to Sir Michael and edged aside, allowing the visitor admittance to the small room.

"Mr. Hoffman, I've been expecting you. If you will give us a moment, I will meet with you shortly. Owen, would you see that Mr. Hoffman has coffee or tea while I tend to Lady Juliette's concerns?"

"That won't be necessary, Mr. Swann." Juliette patted the stack of books. "I will leave these documents in your care, and I trust you will return them to Miss Montgomery if they are not germane to the issue. I will see myself out. Good day, gentlemen."

She was entering the hackney on Bow Street when she remembered her intention to point out Mr. Montgomery's last diary entry. Should she go back inside? Daniel had another visitor at the moment, the diary had only a few notes, and he was sure to see it when he flipped through the pages.

Daniel hated that Lady Juliette fled, but he was in no position to stop her. Sir Michael glared at him, eyeing the ephemera littering the room, his piercing gaze lingering on the pages tacked into the plaster walls. He'd scolded Daniel for marring the walls on the last investigation, but Daniel had dutifully had the holes repaired and the room repainted. He'd do the same again. Though if he was permitted to keep his job after his guardianship ended, he would also see to getting a pinboard affixed to the wall.

"Mr. Hoffman, let us return to the main office. I would like my partner, Mr. Beck, to hear what you have to say. He's recently returned from another case and will be assisting me from this point on. If you will excuse us, Sir Michael?" Daniel rounded the table, nudging the Montgomery ledgers on his way, having to rescue them from falling to the floor in a cascade of paper. As he passed Owen, he said, "When you've seen to your other duties, spend some time in here organizing the rest of this evidence."

Owen couldn't answer with some tart retort, not with Sir Michael in the room, but if looks were murderous, the office boy would be facing charges in the courtroom upstairs.

"Now, Mr. Hoffman," Daniel said as they took seats around his and Ed's desks in the common room, "what are your findings?"

The man carefully untied the ribbons on a folder and laid it open on Daniel's desk. "First, the structure is now sound. I understand you were at the mill again Friday. Such an unfortunate occurrence, another dead body." He shook his head. "As you will have seen, I called in some workers to remove part of the roof damaged in the explosion. It will need to be replaced in any case, and better to take it down intentionally than to have it come down and possibly injure someone."

"Yes. Good thinking."

"I hope Miss Montgomery will not mind my taking the initiative. Mr. Earnshaw, the business accountant for the family, was at the mill, and he authorized the expenditure."

"Earnshaw was there? To what purpose?" Daniel asked.

Hoffman shook his head. "He said he was seeking a status update on when rebuilding could begin, and he needed some papers from the office in order to give a full accounting to his mistress. He was cross to find the offices had been cleared out. He went on for some time about how difficult it was for him to properly do his job for Miss Montgomery if he didn't have the documents he needed."

That would agitate a man, but the investigation had to take priority over all else. Daniel would return the papers as soon as he was able. "We've got many of the papers from both the manager's office and that of Mr. Montgomery here. I did not think about Earnshaw's need to have them. Have you determined a cause of the explosion?"

"That is where I hope you are available to go to the mill. I have a theory, but I have arranged to meet the scientist I mentioned to you to explain it. If we leave now, we can be there when he arrives.

I have a carriage, but you will need your own transport to return to London."

As Daniel and Ed bowled along to Hammersmith in Cadogan's hack, he acquainted Ed with the details of the two murders being treated as one case.

"I've ruled out the widow with the sticky fingers, and it's not looking likely that the milling rival had anything to do with Montgomery's murder either. I haven't managed to pin down just who Carlyle's wife was stepping out with, but I can't see a way to tie either her or any lover to the killing."

"Which leaves you with who?" Ed asked.

"Someone from the mill? A disgruntled employee? I would very much like to question the mill manager, Mr. Coombe, but he has not awakened from his injuries and remains in hospital at St. Bart's. Did he have a reason to shoot his employer? There's been talk of some tension between him and Montgomery over the proposed changes to the mill. Or did he know anyone who had a reason?"

Daniel felt as he always did during the information-gathering phase of a case, as if he had far too many questions and not enough answers . . . with a niggling doubt that he wasn't asking the right questions, or at least not to the correct individuals.

Perhaps today's trip to Hammersmith would drop that perfect question into his mind, and the entire mystery would be unlocked.

Or perhaps he would have to keep searching. One thing he knew. It was not in his nature to give up on a puzzle until he'd solved it.

"You've been busy while I was away." Ed stretched out, propping his boots on the bench beside Daniel. "It was good to get home. I had about forgotten what my wife and kids look like."

Sometimes it was easy for Daniel to forget Ed was a family man. His wife's name was Polly, and they had two—or was it three?—children. Daniel had not met them, but he believed the eldest was a boy of about ten years, named after his father but called Teddy, and there was at least one girl a couple years younger. Odd that he and Ed spent so much time together yet did not socialize out of work.

The mill looked the same as it had Friday, with the fence, the unemployed workers milling about, and half the roof open to the sky. As they walked up the narrow lane, Ed appraised the building and surroundings while Daniel described what it had been like to be so near the explosion when it happened.

"Glad you weren't in the building, lad." Ed's voice was gruff, and he clapped Daniel on the shoulder.

Mr. Hoffman had already arrived, and with him stood a young man—younger even than Daniel. He shifted his weight, tapping his thigh with his fingertips as if playing a tune. He bobbed his head, blinking quickly.

"Are you ready?" he asked. "You are the investigators, are you not?" The words were fast and clipped, and he turned his eyes on Daniel. Remarkable eyes, pale blue with dark rings around the iris, but the color wasn't the most striking feature. It was the undeniable intelligence gleaming there.

"We are. Swann and Beck. And you are?"

He was already walking toward the gate and spoke over his shoulder. "You can call me Rhynwick. This should not take long . . ."

Mr. Hoffman's lips twitched as the young man disappeared into the warehouse. "His name is Rhynwick Davies. Forgive his manners and mannerisms. His mind races at top speed, and the rest of the world must keep up or be left behind. But he's the best man for this job."

"Are you certain he has the experience?" Daniel asked as they followed in Rhynwick's wake.

"Why don't you try him and see? I can find someone older, but no one better to walk you through what we believe happened." Hoffman nodded to the guard at the gate and slipped through.

Ed shoved his hands into his pockets, and Daniel took out his notebook and pencil. They went into the warehouse and found Rhynwick with his nose almost against a wall. He sniffed, rubbed his finger through the soot, and stood back to examine it in the light streaming through the doorway. He rubbed the soot between his fingers, then smelled it again.

Daniel quirked his eyebrow at Ed, who shrugged.

The young man worked his way quickly down the hallway toward the offices, studying the floor and ceiling, stretching his arms out to measure the width of the passage. He paused at the mangled cart—the place where the two millworkers had died—stepped into Montgomery's office, and half closed the door. In a trice he bounded out into the hallway once more and strode into the working area of the mill. In there he moved from place to place, climbing on the machinery, poking into the gears, and yanking on various levers and pipes. Soot and damp covered everything, but the young man was not deterred.

"What is he looking for?" Daniel asked the engineer.

Hoffman shook his head, spreading his hands. "His methods are his own. He will explain everything once he is finished, and not a moment before."

"I say, who are you?" Rhynwick asked from around the corner.

"I could demand the same information from you. Get out of here."

Rhynwick backed into view, an angry man poking him in the chest at each step.

"Mr. Earnshaw." Daniel recognized the accountant. His bandage had been removed, and his bruises had healed to the point of being yellowish green. "I'm pleased you are here. You may be able to assist the investigation. These gentlemen are with me. Go about your work, Mr. Davies."

Earnshaw frowned as Rhynwick climbed over a stack of toppled bins, his coattails flying out. "What are you doing, Inspector Swann? Who are these men?"

This fellow blustered like they were trespassing and he was the owner. "Mr. Earnshaw, this is Inspector Beck from Bow Street. I believe you've met Mr. Hoffman, the engineer who has been checking the building for safety, and this is Mr. Davies."

"He's a scientist who is going to tell us where the explosion originated and its cause," Hoffman said.

"How can he know that? The place nearly perished in a fire."

Earnshaw made shooing motions, as if he could rid the mill of the scientist's presence.

Rhynwick spoke from the far side of a large chute. "I assure you, sir, I have already determined the origin of the blast." He went back to poking, in perpetual motion.

"Would you care to enlighten us?" Hoffman asked.

"The hallway between the warehouse and the mill itself. The blast originated outside the offices." Again his voice came as if disembodied, for he was out of sight.

"How could you know that? You were not here," Earnshaw said.

Rhynwick poked his head up. A streak of soot decorated his cheek, but his eyes were as bright as polished silver. "It's quite obvious for anyone who will look."

"Who is this child? And why should we consider what he thinks? The explosion was the work of anarchists, rousing the workers to shut down the mill before the improvements could be made. Those responsible are probably gathered at the gate outside this very minute." Earnshaw pointed to the eastern wall. "There have been rumblings for weeks that they planned some action. Mr. Coombe worried there would be trouble, and trouble there was."

"No."

"I beg your pardon." Earnshaw turned to Rhynwick.

"I said no. Your assumptions about the explosion are incorrect." The scientist passed by them without looking, and they followed in his wake.

"Why don't you tell us what you've deduced, Rhyn?" Hoffman asked.

"The blast originated here. In this passage, traveling into both the warehouse, where it dissipated quickly by blowing the wagon doors open, and into the working floor of the mill, where it expended energy upward."

"Preposterous," Earnshaw said. "I was here when it happened, and the blast came from the milling room."

Rhynwick's eyes swiveled toward the accountant, but they did not linger. "It is quite obvious. Look at the blast patterns. They travel in both directions from this point." He raised a slender, soot-covered finger, tracing the lines that radiated outward from the wall opposite Mr. Montgomery's office door.

"That's where two men were shoveling up a flour spill. They had toppled a load they were trundling to the warehouse." Daniel toed a twisted bit of metal. "They were thrown against the wall here. This is all that is left of their cart."

"Yes, yes, that explains it." Rhynwick snapped his fingers. "Shoveling spilled flour."

"What are you on about?" Earnshaw snapped. "Are you saying the two men who died in this hallway killed themselves? Were they bombers? Did their bomb go off prematurely?"

"What bomb? Where are your eyes, man? There was no bomb. At least not the type of which you are thinking. If this were a black powder explosion, there would be remnants of the kegs that held the powder. There would be at the very least a hole in the floor and in the ceiling as well." Rhynwick pointed down and then up before poking once again through the mangled cart and twisted shovel blades.

"If there was no bomb, what caused the blast?" Daniel asked.

"Dust."

Daniel looked at Ed and then the engineer. "Dust?"

"Yes. The conditions were perfect." Striding down the hallway, then spinning on his heel and returning, the young man's eyes measured the space. "Didn't you know flour dust was more combustible than black powder?"

As a point of fact, Daniel hadn't.

Rhynwick's shoulders slumped at their blank expressions. He rubbed his forehead, leaving a black smudge behind. When he looked up, his face had fallen into patient lines.

"Flour is a starch. Which means it burns easily. Any starch, when in powder form, exposes far more surface area to the oxygen in the air than it does when piled or sacked or stored in a barrel."

"Oxy-gen? What's that?" Earnshaw asked, suspicious.

"It's a gas in the air you breathe. Discovered in 1774 by Joseph

Priestley. Necessary to support your life, and also, in a pure form, combustible."

Daniel remembered why he'd studied art and history at university and not science.

"If you do not have oxygen, a fire cannot burn. It's why when you put a jar over a candle, the flame goes out." Rhynwick spread his hands, as if asking them to come along this simple journey of logic with him.

"I've heard of mills exploding before, but I thought machinery caused it. Something catching fire in the works," Ed said.

"Though machinery can catch fire, explosions in mills are almost always caused by flour dust in the air igniting. It only takes a pinch of flour per cubic foot of air to combust. A particle of flour burns instantly, igniting the ones around it, flashing quickly. That's why this fire did not burn long. There cannot have been too much flour in the air, because the blast was fairly contained. It went outward from here, fast and hard enough to kill the two men who caused it, though they wouldn't have known it. The men were shoveling, which stirred flour into the air. A single spark from a shovel hitting the stone wall would have been enough to set things in motion."

Removing a handkerchief from his pocket, Rhynwick wiped his hands, the inquisitive light dimming in his eyes, as if, now that he'd solved the puzzle, he was no longer interested.

"So it was an accident?" Earnshaw asked. "What about the threats from the Luddite anarchists? Anyway, there is adequate ventilation in the mill to avoid such explosions."

"That may be so, but there are no windows in this passageway, and that is where the flour was stirred into the air. The doors to the offices were closed when the blast occurred."

"How do you know that?" Daniel asked. Not that he doubted the young man, just that he wanted to know.

"The glass in the door. If the door had been open, the blast would have broken the glass, and it would all be lying along the wall. However, the glass is strewn across the room. I'm surprised the latch held when the explosion occurred. Before you ask"—he held up his hands—"if the door had blown open, there would be a gouge in the wall where the knob hit." He inclined his head toward both offices. "I would have expected more paperwork in these rooms." A pair of lines formed between his black brows, and his head lifted like a dog's on a new scent.

"There was. We've removed it for examination."

"I will need all of it back," Earnshaw dictated. "How am I to report the state of her father's affairs to Miss Montgomery if you have removed all the documents? Those belong to Miss Montgomery, and I shall have to insist you return them at once."

Daniel bristled at the autocratic tone. "I have spoken with Miss Montgomery, and the documents will be returned to her when the investigation concludes. I appreciate that you have a job to do, but so do I. We'll go over the financials and correspondence as quickly as we can, but it will take some time."

He turned away from the fussy accountant and addressed the scientist, who continued to hop from place to place like a flea. "Are you certain the explosion was an accident, not executed to cover up Mr. Montgomery's murder? That the timing was a coincidence?" Daniel rubbed his hand on the back of his neck.

"If it was done to cover up the murder, it was singularly unsuccessful, wasn't it? You were able to identify the owner as having been killed by something other than the blast, were you not?" Rhynwick asked, as if Daniel were as simple as a pudding.

"He was shot through the head."

"I wish I had been able to examine the body in situ." He traveled the length of the hallway again, hands clasped behind his back, his shoes coating with ash and his trouser cuffs stirring the dust. "I might have been able to tell you more." He shrugged. "As it is, I shall take my leave. I have some experiments brewing that need tending. I shall be in touch, Mr. Hoffman."

"Wait! Do you have a card?" Daniel asked. Such a bright young mind could be useful in future cases.

"Hoffman knows where to find me." And like a linnet, he was away. Daniel almost imagined he could hear the flutter of wings.

"A most interesting fellow," Ed commented, a bemused look on his face. Mostly he had stood back and observed, and Daniel looked forward to hearing his thoughts.

"A child, that's what." Mr. Earnshaw wrung his hands. "We've never had a flour dust explosion here. That should prove him wrong. If this place was prone to such a thing, wouldn't it have gone up before now? It was the work of someone who did not wish Mr. Montgomery to proceed with his plans for the mill. They shot him and set fire to the mill on purpose to stop the changes.

"Mr. Montgomery was afraid something like this would happen when he started receiving those threatening letters, and it finally did. I only wish I could have prevented it." He touched the still-healing wound at his hairline. "It's only the grace of God that I wasn't killed too."

"Have you managed to find those letters? You mentioned them once before and said you would bring them to Bow Street." Daniel moved Montgomery's office door, which had been sprung on the hinges and dragged on the floor with a wince-inducing squeal. "We've taken a cursory glance through most of Montgomery's papers salvaged from here, and we've found no indication of a threat."

Earnshaw opened his mouth, shut it, and hung his head. "I beg your pardon. I have been remiss. I was able to locate them in Mr. Montgomery's office at his house, and I will bring them to Bow Street directly. It's just that with the explosion, and my injury, and poor Mr. Montgomery, and then the solicitors after me to provide all the accounting so they could begin to settle Miss Montgomery's affairs, I've been chasing my own tail lately." He touched his bruised forehead. "I will get the letters to you as soon as possible. When you read them, you'll see. The threats were real, and someone acted upon them."

Hoffman cleared his throat and offered his hand to Daniel. "You have my report. The building is now safe for occupation, and the repairs can begin straightaway. I shall inform Miss Montgomery of the fact, and she can decide what she wishes to do."

Daniel shook Hoffman's hand, and the engineer and the accountant took themselves off.

"What do you think?" he asked Ed.

"I think many people have opinions, but the lad made sense. The explosion and the murder are two separate events. *Something* sparked the flour dust. *Someone* shot Mr. Montgomery."

"Do you believe we can rule out anarchists and Luddites?"

Ed shrugged. "A disgruntled worker could have shot him. How much do you know about anarchists? I'll confess, I don't believe I've ever met one."

Daniel held his own counsel. He'd met one, sat beside him at a meal and listened to him spout his views. And soon, when Sir Bertrand gave the word, he'd be mingling with a whole lot of them.

Chapter 11

"I apologize for the delay in getting you this information. We've been chasing leads and combing through paperwork since I examined the mill Monday." Daniel handed Sir Bertrand the engineer's report and his own notes on the young scientist's conclusions.

Sir Bertrand skimmed the pages. "It's only Wednesday. I can forgive your tardiness." He dropped the folder on the desk in the War Room. "The accountant may be correct in one aspect."

Lady Juliette came into the room, and Daniel rose. "In what way, sir?" Daniel asked as he pulled out a chair for her. She seated herself, and he caught that whiff of roses that always accompanied her. Sunshine in an English garden. Did she purchase the scent at an apothecary, or did she have it distilled especially for her?

"Anarchists *are* involved at the mill. The man found dead, from the blow to the head? His name is Pietro Todisco. He's Italian, and he's a known associate of a group called *La Resistenza*. The Resistance. Various sects of the group have caused trouble in Bristol, Leeds, and Manchester. The goal seems to be general mayhem rather than politically motivated, but they are easily influenced by others' agendas. Like Jasper Finch and his ilk, anyone looking for rabble-rousers and malcontents. La Resistenza seems to churn these men out like butter pats."

"How did you identify him?" Daniel asked. In the five days since the body had been found, he'd had no success in discovering the man's name or nationality.

"When the body was in the morgue, Haverly sent someone to sketch the man's features. Then we—and by *we*, I mean one of Haverly's other operatives—made discreet inquiries. It turns out Todisco frequented The Dove in Hammersmith, where Jasper Finch has been known to dominate the conversation, gathering discontented workers around him as he tries to build a consensus to his way of thinking. The publican at the bar identified Todisco."

"What was he doing at the mill in the middle of the night?" Lady Juliette asked.

"That, we do not know. Yet. We found no evidence of tampering or sabotage when we went over the building, which was challenging given the number of people supposedly *guarding* the mill. He was a poor man. He spoke broken English, heavily accented, and he had been out of work for some time. Perhaps he was partaking in a bit of looting."

"The local magistrate said they were having trouble with scavengers. He'd instituted a watch on the place and installed some fencing," Daniel offered. "However, the tie to the Resistenza cannot be ignored. What if Todisco was sent in to finish what the flour-dust explosion started? Blow up the mill and stop the refit from taking place?"

"We'll know more six days hence. It appears, though I have tried to keep my investigation of anarchists and your murder case apart, they have become intertwined. Just as well Haverly wants you to attend the rally. Perhaps it will lead you to the killer."

"Are you certain Lady Juliette should go?" Daniel asked. "It hardly seems the place for any female, much less one like her."

Sir Bertrand shrugged, spreading his hands. "Haverly says to take her along. She will be heavily disguised. I assure you, when I'm finished with my niece, you won't recognize her."

"Pardon me, but I do not care to be discussed as if I am not here or cannot think or speak for myself." Lady Juliette's back straightened, and her dark eyes narrowed.

Daniel still didn't like the idea, but he had no control over Lady Juliette. This wasn't a police matter where he had some authority. This was an agency matter, where Sir Bertrand, and ultimately the Duke of Haverly, held sway.

A tap sounded on the secret door, and from somewhere Sir Bertrand produced a small pistol, aiming it at the center of the top door panel.

"Sir Bertrand."

The gentleman relaxed, lowering his pistol. "Come in, Pultney."

The Thorndike butler opened the door a crack. "I beg your pardon, sirs, milady. Miss Montgomery is downstairs, most distressed. She says she must see Lady Juliette, and though I told her the lady was not receiving, she insisted. She claims she will wait all night if need be. Short of throwing her out on the street, there was little I could do. Mrs. Dunstan has prepared a tea tray, and I've put Miss Montgomery in the morning room."

Lady Juliette was already on her feet and moving toward the door. "Perhaps you should come too, Mr. Swann. She may have some information related to her father's murder."

Daniel looked to Sir Bertrand, who waved toward the door. "Go. I will see you at the rally."

He remained behind as Daniel gathered the report on the latest victim and followed Juliette down the dark, secret staircase to the hallway on the second floor.

"How will you explain my presence in your house?" he asked as they reached the entrance hall.

She stopped, her eyes widening but her mind clearly working behind them. "I will say I left my gloves at your office in Bow Street and you were returning them to me since you were in the area on another matter."

He didn't know whether to admire or regret her ability to come up with a lie on the spot.

They entered the morning room and found Agatha Montgomery in a puddle of tears. Juliette immediately went to her, drawing her away from the window to the settee, keeping her arm around her friend.

"What is it, dear?" Juliette looked at Daniel as she spoke, her dark-brown eyes bewildered.

Daniel rounded a high-backed chair and rested his arms across the back. This level of distress in a woman made him feel powerless. He wanted to do something to alleviate her emotional discomfort, but he had no idea what. And he feared doing or saying the wrong thing and making the situation worse.

"It's Alonzo." Agatha choked out the name. "He's gone. I cannot find him."

"Perhaps he is only very busy?" Juliette asked. "He is overseeing his grandfather's business dealings now, is he not?"

"Yes, he was, but no one has seen him for several days. When he did not call at my home for an expected meeting, I'm afraid I did a brash thing." Agatha held her handkerchief over her face, a sob fluttering the fabric.

"What did you do?"

"I went to his place of lodging. He has rooms in Lambeth, across the river."

A brash thing indeed for a lady to pursue a man to his boardinghouse. "His family does not have a house in London?" Daniel asked.

She shook her red head. "They do, in Westminster, but the entire house is under renovation. Alonzo took rooms in Lambeth to be near the office where the family's interests are overseen."

"What happened at his lodgings?"

Agatha didn't answer right away, as the housekeeper had entered with a tea tray.

A twist hit Daniel's gut. The same one he felt every time he thought of the Thorndike housekeeper.

His estranged mother.

Estranged through her own choice, and after many years, Daniel's. When Mrs. Dunstan had removed herself, Juliette poured three cups.

"He's gone. His belongings are removed, his bill paid, and the rooms empty." Agatha's cup rattled in the saucer as she received it.

"Perhaps he's moved back to the family townhome?" Daniel said, taking a teacup from Juliette. Agatha had not asked why he was at the

Thorndike townhouse. If she required no explanation, he would tell no falsehoods.

"No. I went next to his business office, and no one there would tell me anything. They said the viscount's affairs were his own, and they could not speculate on where he had gone nor how long he would remain away. Which tells me he *has* gone away, but why wouldn't he let me know himself?"

Juliette patted her hand. "Perhaps he's gone once more to his family's estate in Kent? It's only a half day's ride from the city. Alonzo made a visit there recently. Perhaps he was called there again to see his grandfather and was delayed on his return."

Hope lit Agatha's reddened eyes. "Do you think so? If there was a crisis, perhaps he had no time to notify me. But why would he clear out his rooms?"

Daniel shrugged. "If he was preparing to return to the renovated townhouse, he may have sent his belongings on while he made a quick trip to the country."

Juliette nodded. "Something *has* been troubling him since your father died. He's been . . . distracted, for want of a better word."

"Yes, I have been so concerned. He was so sweet and ardent right after, and through the funeral, always by my side, reassuring me. But then he became remote, distracted, and he's all but neglected me over the past week."

Daniel considered the situation. A young man close to the victim changed his behavior, avoided the woman he loved, and disappeared a week after the murder with no explanation. Was there something there?

Everyone was hiding something, from their families, from their friends, most often from themselves.

What was Alonzo Darby hiding?

He set his cup back on the tray. "I could travel to the family estate and make inquiries if you like. If the earl is ailing and Alonzo was called home, I will let him know his manners in not corresponding with you were poor. And I shall report back his whereabouts."

And I can judge for myself if there is *some connection between the viscount's disappearance and Montgomery's death.*

"Would you? I would be most grateful."

Agatha's smile was like sun through rain . . . a bit watery still, but encouraging.

No doubt that smile would disappear for a long time to come should he discover Alonzo's secrets had anything to do with Montgomery's murder.

"I'll leave on the morrow."

<hr />

At least Daniel had a lively mount for the journey. The bold chestnut he had taken out on livery snorted and tossed his head, his long strides eating up the road. And a nice road it was, better than most, with a fairly even surface and trees well back along the verge once he'd left the city.

He still kept a pistol tucked into the waistband of his trousers, for highwaymen could lie in wait anywhere, even in this beautiful countryside.

Kent. England's garden. Spring was advancing well here, with green leaves budding out on the trees. In a month or so, the many apple orchards he passed would burst into bloom. Shepherds worked in their paddocks, and new lambs stayed close to their mothers. Dairy cattle grazed the fields, and the sun rose fully above the horizon.

He inhaled deeply of the chilled air. It was good to get out of the city and blow away some of the soot and grime and frosty fog. The country air reminded him of his boyhood.

He'd been so miserable all those years ago when he had been yanked from his agrarian life as a servant on an estate and shipped off to boarding school. The location of the school had been rural, but the boys were not allowed to roam the countryside. They were kept within the confines of the school grounds, surrounded by a high wall.

Almost like Newgate Prison.

And then he'd gone to Oxford. It was the first time Daniel had lived in a town that size, full of people and commerce and street after street. At first he felt suffocated, pressed in, and at the end of every day, exhausted. Gradually, he had acclimated, but on days like today, when he got out of London, the busiest metropolis in the world, he realized how much he missed the countryside and the pace of life it afforded.

He approached a wagon laden with bulging burlap sacks heading toward town. Potatoes? Apples? Too lumpy to be grain sacks. The driver, a stout man with a florid face, touched the brim of his hat and raised his whip as Daniel passed. At the rate the wagon was traveling, he wouldn't see London before midnight.

The chestnut snorted and leaned into the bit, eager for a gallop, still fresh though they had been on the road since first light.

"You have bags of stamina, my boy, but are you fast?"

The stable lad who'd saddled the gelding at dawn had warned that he was headstrong and not an easy ride, but Daniel loved a challenge, and with a long, straight bit of road before him, he anchored his hat and loosened the reins. The horse leapt forward, his hooves beating out a quickening tempo. Daniel rose in the stirrups, placing his weight over the chestnut's withers, the cold air slicing across his face, some of the irritations and shortcomings of the current investigation falling away for the moment.

He'd spent hours on horseback as a youngster, exercising the master's hunters once he'd proven he could handle them, but since coming to London, his opportunities to ride were few. Most often at the behest of his mysterious patron, who delivered messages through the offices of Coles, Franks & Moody.

All that would end soon. His pay as a Bow Street investigator would not run to keeping a horse of his own. And he had no idea how much longer he might be employed there. Even now he should be searching for new lodgings less expensive than the rooms provided by his patron, but where was he to find the time?

Easing the gelding back in stages to a walk, he settled into the saddle once more. The horse puffed a bit, but then again, so did Daniel. He used the end of his scarf to dry the wind-tears from his eyes.

Within the hour, he approached the gates of Lockewood Hall, seat of the Earls of Rotherhide. The current earl, Viscount Coatsworth's grandfather, resided here. According to Agatha Montgomery, the earl had not come to London this Season, preferring his country estate. Coatsworth had reported that he was frail and infirm, being of an advanced age, and had been unwell during the fall and winter.

The hall's gates of iron, with massive curls and bars held up by brick pillars, stood open. Beyond, a drive of pale rock, precisely raked, curved toward a massive, symmetrical house. Twin towers anchored the corners, and what seemed like dozens of windows ranked one above the other in the red brick.

A black carriage stood before the front door, a pair of grays waiting patiently in the traces. A servant clipped box hedges near the entrance, and Daniel pulled up nearby and leapt to the ground.

"Good day. My name is Mr. Swann. I've come from the Bow Street Magistrate's Court to see the earl."

The man continued to snip without looking up. "No visitors." He cleared his throat and spit into the bushes. "His lordship in't receiving."

Daniel waved toward the carriage. "Clearly, someone is here. I've come a long way, and it is a matter of some urgency."

"That in't a visitor—that's the doctor." The gardener shrugged and spit again, his blades never stopping. "You can ask at the house, but the answer will be the same. He han't had no visitors since his grandson came by last week. And left right smart, he did. Din't even stay the night."

Coatsworth was not here. Poor Agatha. The easy answer had proven wrong.

"And he left quickly?"

"S'wat I said. Came, marched inside, came out, and left." The man shrugged and nodded, *clip, clip, clip.*

"Where are the stables? I'd like to tend my horse."

"Round back on t' left, but you won't be here long enough to need that. You could just tie up right here. If Hillman lets you in to see the earl, his lordship'll probably send you away quicker than he did his own grandson. He's cross-grained always, but more so now that he's ailing."

Daniel wasn't one to give up without trying, so he left the pessimistic gardener and led his mount around the house. Not exactly a hospitable welcome. Still, his horse needed a rest and some water. A bit of grain or hay wouldn't go amiss either.

The stables were magnificent, with a clock tower and a graceful brick arch opening into a quadrangle of stalls. A well sat in the center of the courtyard, handy for the grooms.

Less than a fourth of the stalls held occupants, and the yard had a bit of a neglected air, with weeds growing in some cracks and bits of straw tumbling across the cobbles in the breeze. Clearly the earl hadn't visited his stables in some time.

A skinny, weathered old man emerged from one of the stalls, closing the bottom half of the door behind him. A long bay head thrust over the door and whickered, and the old man caressed the horse's nose. Daniel instantly felt a rapport with the man, for he reminded him of the stable master at his childhood home. Mr. Farley had loved his charges like children and treated them with affection.

"Good day, sir. Might I trouble you for some water and feed for my horse?"

A cold clay pipe dangled from the man's lips, and he removed it, using the stem to scratch the gray stubble over his ear. "Of a certainty. Always feed and water for a horse in need. That's a fine-looking animal ye have. Are ye on yer way to the coast?"

"No, I've come from London to visit the earl on a matter of business. It should not take me long, but this fellow has brought me at a fair pace and could use a bit of a rest." As he spoke, Daniel loosened the girth to make the chestnut more comfortable.

The old man nodded. "Don't know as you'll get in to see his lordship. He in't feeling well. Laid up in bed and wastin' away. If you'd have come a year ago, you could have heard him bellerin' all through the house, striding his land like a giant. Nothing missed his attention, and he kept a tight fist on everything. Knew his property down to the last lamb and apple blossom, he did." The man shook his head, as if he actually missed being shouted at by his employer.

A cantankerous man, the earl, it seemed. That might explain some of the viscount's behavior. Daniel braced himself for an unpleasant encounter. Only the fact that he had given his word to Miss Montgomery to make inquiries into her erstwhile beau's whereabouts kept him from turning around and going back to the city.

He rounded the house again to knock on the front door. Under no circumstances would he present himself at the back door and give a servant the chance to shoo him away like some pesky gnat. If they were going to toss him out on his ear, they would have to do it on the front steps.

The door opened partway before he could employ the brass knocker. A man of about his own age stood there, not dressed in footman's livery but in the dark garb of a butler. A shock of yellow hair fell onto his forehead, giving him an even more youthful appearance. "Don't knock. It'll disturb his lordship."

Daniel gave his name and employer. "I need to speak with the earl, please."

The young man's eyes widened even as his brows came down. "His lordship isn't receiving today."

"I've come all the way from London on a matter of some urgency."

He shook his head, the blond forelock swaying. "He's not to be disturbed. He hasn't been well."

"I'm investigating a murder. I must see him."

"A murder? Who got killed?" He continued to peek around the door. "His lordship can't have done it. He's been here in bed for ages."

Was the young man quizzing him with his simplicity? "Be that as it may, he might have information that would be helpful to our case. Please give him my card and tell him I request an audience." Daniel removed his card from his pocket with a flip that drew a gleam of admiration from the young man. Daniel had seen Ed Beck perform the maneuver and had practiced it until he could accomplish it with panache.

"You can wait inside. I'm Hillman, butler here at the Hall." He stood back and opened the door. As Daniel entered, he looked up at the stone-carved coat of arms over the lintel, a scroll beneath spelling out the name of the place, Lockewood Hall.

Inside, a black-and-white-chessboard marble floor covered what looked like acres. Large paintings hung on every wall. Above them, an oval-shaped gallery on the next floor surrounded by a white marble banister was open to the skylights two stories above.

To Daniel's left, an archway led to a stairwell, carpeted in rich red, with carved panels in each section of the railing. A man in a fine suit and intricately tied cravat descended the steps, a black bag in one hand.

"Dr. Plimpton." The butler jumped to retrieve a top hat and cloak from the hall tree beside the door. "How is his lordship today? Are there any instructions?"

The doctor set his bag down and allowed the nervous young butler to assist him with his garments. "He is much the same, and I gave instructions to his valet. I shall return at the beginning of next week, but you may always send for me if there are new developments."

Daniel returned the physician's inquiring look but said nothing.

"This gentleman has come from London to see the earl." Hillman handed Dr. Plimpton his hat and walking stick and picked up the bag. When the doctor had taken his belongings, Hillman handed him Daniel's card.

The doctor's brows rose, and he gave a rueful chuckle. "I wish you well of your endeavor, sir. And I do hope your visit will be brief. The earl is declining, his mind is not as stable as he might wish, and his temper is . . . variable."

"I will not take much of his time." His mind wasn't stable? Daniel lowered his already minuscule expectations. At this point, seeing the earl felt more like a formality than anything that might prove profitable.

"I would also suggest," the doctor said, tucking the card into his breast pocket before pulling on his gloves, "that you not ask for permission. Hillman, take this good gentleman right into the room and do not give his lordship the opportunity to refuse. He will take the arrival much better without forewarning."

The doctor nodded to Daniel, then left.

Everywhere they went in the house, more opulence greeted Daniel. Paintings, urns, statues, gilt work, carvings, plasterwork. But a rime of dust covered many objects, similar to the condition of the stables. As if the bare minimum was being done to keep the place up, the master none the wiser.

Hillman paused before a set of double doors on the second floor, as if bracing himself. Though he grabbed both doorknobs as if to sweep them open, he eased only one aside, poking his head around the edge much as he had done at the front door. Daniel had never encountered such a timid butler. Those few he had met had seemed lordly and more in charge of the houses than the owners.

The room lay in dimness. Daniel could pick out a massive bed with huge posts from which hung thick drapes in red and gold. Beside the bed, a lamp burned, casting a circle of yellow in an arc that encompassed a sallow, thin old man reclining against a bank of pillows.

"Milord, someone to see you."

The earl jerked as if he had been sleeping, though his eyes were open. "A visitor?"

"Yes, milord." Hillman motioned Daniel closer.

Another man, this one nearly as old as the earl, appeared through a connecting door, carrying a porcelain pitcher with a cloth over his arm. He tottered to the bedside table and set the pitcher near the lamp.

"Cooper?" the earl asked.

"Yes, milord," the old servant, whom Daniel assumed to be the valet, answered.

"Are there people here?" The old man's rheumy eyes looked from Mr. Cooper to Daniel and Hillman and back again.

"Yes, milord. There is someone here to see you."

Hillman scuttled away, leaving Daniel holding his hat, still wearing his cloak, standing at the foot of the bed.

"I pray you will not be long. The doctor's visits tire him." Mr. Cooper dipped the cloth into the pitcher, wiped the earl's face with it, and dried his cheeks. He checked that the nightshirt's laces were secure, prodded the pillows at the old man's back, and took up station in a chair on the far side of the bed.

"Lord Rotherhide, I am an investigator for the Bow Street Magistrate's Court in London. Dan—"

"Where is the doctor? I thought the doctor was here?" The old man spoke to his valet as if Daniel wasn't in the room.

"Milord, may we talk about your grandson?"

This got a response. He blinked. "So many regrets, but what could I do? I had to tell him." His voice wavered, and his skeletal hands picked at the down comforter across his lap. A tiny bit of spittle appeared at the corner of his mouth, and small tremors altered his expression from one moment to the next as his lips quivered. "It will all come out after I am dead, but it did not seem right for the boy to find out that way."

"What will come out? By *the boy*, I assume you mean Alonzo Darby, Viscount Coatsworth?"

"He's gone."

"Do you know where, sir? I've been sent to make inquiries."

"He's strong. Not like my son. Alfred was *soft*." The earl said it as if this was the worst condemnation possible. "Always acting with his tender heart and not his head. He would have ruined this estate. Given the servants too much leeway. Let them take advantage of him. Never acting like an aristocrat. I had to stop him. He had no backbone."

Daniel said nothing, looking to the valet, who stared at the far wall.

"I killed him, you know. I killed Alfred."

"Sir?" Daniel tensed, stepping closer. Was he confessing to murdering his son?

"I forced him to choose. Demanded it." His voice was thready, breathy, but determined. Daniel could not have stemmed the tide of words short of clamping his hand over the man's mouth. "Threatened to disinherit him. I couldn't keep him from getting the title, but I threatened to leave every last shilling it takes to run this estate to someone else. He would be an earl, and he would have Lockewood, but he would be penniless."

His head wobbled, but he pressed on. "So he obeyed. He did what I demanded. And it killed him. He died of a broken heart. Then I find out he didn't really obey at all. Just pretended to." A weak cackle came from his nearly toothless mouth. "Showed a spark of rebellion, though even in that he was a coward. I wish he had stood up to me, just once. Really stood up to me and told me to go to the devil. Lord knows I told him to enough times."

A coughing fit racked his narrow chest, and Daniel reached to help him sit up while the valet found the cloth and covered the old man's mouth. Gasping, the earl lay back and accepted, from the smell of it, a sip of brandy.

"I hated my son for having all the fortitude of a blancmange. I bullied him and pushed him, and he finally couldn't take it any longer. He never knew about the other one. I never told him, and she never told him. But he got his revenge in the end. Now it's all a mess. I've tried to keep it quiet, but it will come out when I'm dead. Do you think God will forgive me?"

From one moment to the next, the earl was awake and then asleep. It happened so suddenly Daniel grew alarmed that the earl had passed away.

The valet, with what must be a well-practiced maneuver, eased the man down and drew the coverlet up. A rattling breath moved the earl's chest, and Daniel drew in his own.

"Sir," the valet whispered, "if you will wait in the hall, perhaps I can answer some of your inquiries."

Daniel went, frustrated that the earl's mind was so far gone he could only ramble about things that happened such a long time ago. Daniel hadn't gotten a single question answered.

The valet emerged, leaving the door to the bedchamber open so he could hear if the old earl needed him. "Sir, you asked about the young viscount."

"Yes. He's gone missing from his London residence, and his . . ."

How could he frame this? Did his family know about the betrothal— or his near-betrothal? "His friends are concerned."

"The viscount visited his grandfather last week, and the earl told him something the young man did not like. There was shouting, but I had been sent from the room, so I could not make out what they were saying. It was all over rather quickly, and the viscount stormed out. The last thing he shouted back over his shoulder was that he would not stand for it and would see the solicitors." Sad wrinkles lined the man's face. "Not long after that, the earl took a turn for the worse. He's failing rapidly. The doctor says his heart is giving out. A few more days, a week at the most?"

"And you've no idea what they argued over? Or where the viscount may have gone?"

The valet shook his head, staring at the wall behind Daniel's shoulder. "I do not know what they argued over, but I believe the viscount may have left the country. His lordship was rambling in the days after the argument, and he said to me, 'The boy will be all right. I've given him the place in Jamaica.' I think the viscount may have gone there."

"If the earl was rambling, can you be certain he was speaking of his grandson?"

A shrug. "He's always referred to him as *the boy*."

"How long have you been in the earl's employ?"

"Since I was a lad. I was born on this estate."

"What about his claim that he killed his son? Is there any truth to that?"

"Guilt does strange things to a man's mind when he's old and frail. The earl despised his son for not being tough, and he was very strict with him, very hard with his expectations. Alfred Darby, then Viscount Coatsworth, died more than a dozen years ago in an accident. His widow, the current viscount's mother, now lives in Hove, on the sea. She left within days of her husband's funeral and has not been back. The boy was at school, Eton, and then Cambridge."

He paused. "He seemed to get on well with the earl. Their discussions had always been lively, but never ending in animosity. I know it preys upon the earl's mind, and I wish his grandson was here in his last days. Such a shame."

So no murder, just family drama.

"You believe the viscount has gone to the Caribbean, then?"

"I do."

"I can check at the docks to confirm he took passage on a ship. I will also inquire at the solicitors to see if he did indeed call upon them. Do you know the law offices they frequented?"

"Yes, as I often delivered messages there when his lordship was in the city. It's the firm of Coles, Franks & Moody."

Daniel almost laughed. At least he wouldn't have to ask where they were located.

Chapter 12

Juliette's nerves tingled as they made their way to the rally. She followed Uncle Bertie through the darkness on the winding lane somewhere downstream of the Tower of London, though she had lost her sense of direction. Her rough woolen cloak swung around her, feeling heavier than it actually was as her muscles tightened with each step and her breath came faster. Another evening in disguise, another mission. A plain black bonnet hid her hair and shielded her face. Uncle Bertie had taken his time with the pots of paint, darkening and filling out her brows, rouging her cheeks, and coloring her lips to make them appear fuller. When she viewed herself in the mirror in the War Room, she hardly recognized herself.

Bertie, in his homespun clothes and hobnailed boots, could have been any stevedore or laborer as he hurried along ahead of her. He moved so differently than when in his society clothes, it was as if he had become a different person. How long before she could change personas with a change of outfit?

Her shoulders ached, and she tried to relax, flexing her fingers and swinging her arms as they made their way toward their destination. She was unsure how Bertie had come across what was supposed to be a secret location, but she had ceased to be amazed at his knowledge. Between Uncle Bertie and the Duke of Haverly, she wondered if anything happened in London of which they were unaware.

Like ants returning to the nest, lines of men trickled in the same direction. No one spoke, barely looking at one another. Juliette kept her eye out for other women, hoping she wouldn't be the only one. What they were doing was illegal, this massing together to foment reform . . . or outright rebellion, depending upon whom you asked. If the authorities got wind of the rally, they would scatter the participants and arrest whomever they could.

Their meeting place, a warehouse that abutted the river, stank of mold and mud and rotting wood. Wool, unwashed humans, and the dankness of the nearby Thames clogged Juliette's nose. She withdrew her handkerchief from her sleeve and held it to her face, inhaling the scent of the rose-petal sachets Agatha had given her as a graduation gift.

She jerked and squashed the linen square into her palm. If someone noticed its quality, they would realize it was out of keeping with the rest of her attire. It was even monogrammed with her initials. She should have replaced the lacy accessory with one of a more plebian origin, but she'd forgotten. Such a lapse would draw Bertie's attention if he happened to see it. Grimacing at stench she could no longer mask with roses, she jammed the handkerchief back up her sleeve.

The crowd grew, and as they passed deeper into the interior of the warehouse, torches were lit and placed in holders around the walls. Juliette kept her head lowered, but she peered through her lashes at the faces near her. Some streaked with dirt, some lined with age, some fresh and eager. Breath misted in the cold night air. Bertie found a place near one of the side walls, close to a door that appeared about to fall off its hinges, and she slipped in beside him.

He bent his head. "You will be tempted to watch the speaker, but I want you to watch the faces in the crowd. Notice who is with whom, who seems particularly interested. Notice if someone is acting strangely. Do not be obtrusive, for I suspect there are others here who will be watching too." Bertie kept his face close to hers. "Mr. Swann will be about somewhere. If you should meet, you do not know each other, understood?"

She nodded, gathering her cloak about her, subservient as instructed.

As she'd been taught, she had created a story about who she was. Tonight she was a downtrodden cook at a boardinghouse full of iron-workers, afraid that if they lost their jobs, she would lose hers. She had come to see if anything could be done since the men had complained about changes at the factory, and one had let slip about the meeting.

For a long moment she considered that there would be no barrier to someone like Daniel Swann pursuing her if she really had been the character she created. But if she were a boardinghouse cook, she would not be an agent, not be in her current position to aid and protect the kingdom. As Bertie had said, God didn't make a mistake when He placed her into her aristocratic family.

So why did she feel this odd yearning for something she couldn't have?

"Trouble may come from these workers." Bertie pressed his shoulder into hers. "Or it may come from those who want to suppress these sorts of gatherings. If we get separated, or if things here get unruly, I want you to head to Hawk's house. It's closer than ours. I'll come for you there."

Hawk. The Duke of Haverly's code name, the one he had used when he was an operative, before he was promoted to supervisor of agents. She had yet to see him in any other persona but his usual handsome, assured, capable self, the duke all of society knew. But from the brief glimpses of Hawk he had portrayed in their meetings in the War Room, she sensed he had been an excellent agent and could be relied upon when required. It brought Juliette comfort to know his house could provide a refuge if she should need it.

"Will he be here tonight?" she whispered.

Uncle Bertie frowned, covering his words with an impolite scratching of his ribs and rubbing the heel of his hand under his nose. His expression reminded her she had been instructed not to speak. He shrugged. "Hawk may be here somewhere, but again, if you see him, you do not know him. Watch, learn, and keep your head down. If trouble starts, go through this doorway, up the stairs, and to Hawk's home."

His fierce stare demanded she acknowledge his command, and she nodded. Keep her mouth shut, watch, and get out if trouble started.

But what trouble? It was a meeting, wasn't it? With a few speeches, possibly some airing of grievances? And then what? Everyone here would go their separate ways, back to their jobs, their homes. At the worst, there would be some shouting, possibly some shoving.

She would have preferred to be nearer the way they had come in, but there was the door behind them. Hopefully, it led outside as Uncle Bertie had said.

As more people arrived, anticipation mounted. Though voices were kept low, Juliette picked up on the discontented tones of the men who milled about. A few women, Juliette was relieved to see, also stood waiting. They whispered together, but none raised her voice. Finally, from somewhere near the back, movement started—people making way for a group of men coming through.

At last the crowd parted, and she saw four men. Three were strangers, but one she recognized.

Jasper Finch. His eyes were intense, fervent, as if he was on the cusp of something of great moment. People patted him on the shoulder as he came by, reaching to clasp his hand, murmuring. As he passed, she turned away and allowed her bonnet to block her profile, praying that Uncle Bertie's efforts with the face paints would fool the man. He had been a guest in her parents' home, after all.

He neared the front of the cavernous room, and someone dragged a wooden crate forward, the scraping noise grating on her ears. Finch leapt atop the crate and faced the gathering. More torches were lit, bringing a fanatical flickering to his face.

Though the vast warehouse had grown quiet, he held up his hands as if to quell cheers.

"My friends." His voice was pitched low, and yet it carried to every corner. "It is a travesty that we must meet in secret. That we are not free to exchange ideas or to bring our so-called *betters* to account for their treatment of us. They may try to muzzle us, but we will not be silenced for long. We will prevail. We will force change. We will be heard."

She could not look away. Though she had been given a peek at his passionate personality at the Venetian breakfast, that Jasper Finch seemed a pale imitation compared to the activist who stood before her.

"We must rally. We must act as one. We must be willing to risk everything to be our own men. Our children starve, our wives go hungry, our jobs are stolen from us, and all the while the rich get richer." His voice rose with each sentence.

You're supposed to be watching the crowd. Juliette forced herself to turn slightly, observing. She tried not to move so boldly that anyone would notice or comment upon her behavior, but she had to stop looking at Mr. Finch in order to break the hold his ardent words engendered. All around her, faces, ghostly in the torchlight, gazed up at him as if he were John Wesley at a revival meeting. They must feel the pull too.

"The toffs in the House of Lords, they don't care about our plight. They make their money off the sweat of our brows and the muscles of our backs, and we are expected to say, 'Yes, milord. Thank you, milord' when they bother to throw a crust or two our way. They and those like them sweep our concerns aside, treat our lives with all the care of a fistful of spillikins, and can end our ability to earn on a whim. As long as their pockets are lined, that's all that matters to them. And a man doesn't have to be titled. He can be wealthy enough to do as he likes, and if what he likes is to cause us misery, what choice do we have? They are far removed from the labor, removed from the struggle to put food in their children's mouths.

"They make decisions that affect many, and not for the good, but only concern themselves with themselves. How can they increase their wealth and their grip on the people who labor for them? It all comes down to brass, and those who would grasp it, connive for it, and harm others to acquire it."

Heads nodded, and a murmur went through the people. Juliette shivered. With Finch's broad-sweeping generalities, he lumped every aristocrat together and painted them all as evil. In his mind there was no difference between the men he described and her father. Any man who had a title, a seat in Lords, or had enough money to employ someone else must be by nature greedy and granite hearted. If a man was prosperous and tried to be broad minded and progressive in the approach to business and industry, he was the enemy. Finch was making wild assumptions that because men were wealthy, they must not care about their workers at all.

Did not these men, by their very wealth and businesses, provide employment, food, shelter, and more for the men they hired?

What about noblesse oblige?

Another shiver racked her spine. What would this crowd say if they knew who she really was?

"It is time to put a stop to this abuse. If they won't listen to reason, maybe they will listen to something more forceful." Finch swung his fist in the air, and a small cheer went up. "They want to ruin our way of life? I say we ruin theirs. Mill owners who want to bring in new equipment and reduce the workforce? They should beware. We will not be silent. We will take action. You heard what happened in Hammersmith. Let that be a warning to all.

"Here in London we must continue the work of our brave compatriots in the north. We will not let our workshops, our skills, our way of life be supplanted by machinery. Weavers, thread makers, brewers, rope workers, miners, smelters . . . we are in danger of losing everything for which we have labored!"

He went on, and it seemed with each word the crowd grew more tense. In glimpses, Juliette caught sight of Finch, whose face, in spite of the cold, gleamed with sweat. He swayed, arms raised, imploring the people with impassioned pleas.

And they responded. As he continued, they packed closer and closer, and she remembered the way he had held forth at her parents' breakfast more than a fortnight ago, expounding his views and drawing every eye in the room.

He had the same power over a crowded warehouse, but it seemed magnified here. These people were afraid, and he stirred those fears. These people were angry, and he fanned the flames of their anger. These people were ready to act, and he put himself in a position to lead them.

Bertie shifted, his fingers opening and closing. A furrow marked his brow, and he pulled his hat lower. Glancing from side to side, he moved away from her, but when she went to follow, he waved her to stay. Her eyes followed him as he crossed in front of her and made his way toward where they had come in. No one else seemed to notice, being fixated on the speaker.

To her right, a pair of men spoke beneath the tenor of Mr. Finch. "Do you think he done it? Or had someone do it? He was that mad, calling for someone to take care of Montgomery before he destroyed the lives of the workers. Do you think Finch killed him?"

"Dunno, but it served Montgomery right, getting killed. He was about to throw half his workers out on the cobbles without so much as a fare-thee-well. Why do they want to change things? We spend our whole lives learning a trade, and some rich toff can wipe it away on a whim? I say we stop them. And if it takes putting a few of them in the dirt, so be it. Better them quick than us slow and starving."

One elbowed the other, and they stopped talking, but Juliette was aghast. They thought Mr. Montgomery deserved murder? And they were ready to answer the call if more violence was asked? They even suspected Mr. Finch of killing Agatha's father.

Uncle Bertie had shown her the report on the explosion, which was thought to have been caused by the ignition of flour dust rather than an anarchist's bomb, but Mr. Montgomery had been shot before the blast.

Had Finch killed him, or had him killed, to stop the renovations and improvements to the mill? Before tonight she would not have thought anyone would kill over industrial progress, but looking at Jasper Finch right now, urging this crowd to become a lawless mob, she believed him capable of anything.

"We cannot be silent. If we are to act, I say we act now, boldly, as one. Decisively, so there is no mistaking our intentions." Men surged around him, raising their fists as he called to them. "Who is with me, to save our livelihoods? To save our families? To force change? If they will not hear our pleas, we must cease trying to reason with them. We must act!"

A cheer went up, and Finch was lifted from the crate to men's shoulders. Juliette stood on tiptoe, searching for Uncle Bertie. Her heart hammered in her ears, and a jolt shot up her spine. What did these people intend? To sweep down the road to Whitehall and attack men as they entered Parliament? Did they mean to kill someone? Or destroy a factory or mill? The power as they jostled frightened her. Where had the silent streams of downtrodden workers gone? In their place, a pulsing, angry mob had taken over.

Someone grabbed one of the torches and shouted, "Let's go! I know the first place." Several others shouted their approval, and as a mass they surged toward the doors.

"Wait! We must organize! We must strategize! We cannot—" Jasper Finch's protests and commands were drowned out by the shouts, the pounding feet, the tide of anger his speech had provoked.

A hard shoulder hit Juliette in the chest, propelling her backward into the wall, where her head struck the bricks. Stars shot across her vision. She reeled, her knees turning to water and her eyes blurring with tears. The floor seemed to rise up, and she was helpless to stop herself from falling. Her cheek impacted the dirty, damp floor. Boots scuffled, buffeting her, and she put her hands over her head both to protect it and to try to mute the throbbing.

Where was Uncle Bertie? Another heavy boot hit her thigh. Pain arched up her leg. She tried to roll over, to brace herself to rise, but weakness overwhelmed her.

Strong hands clamped onto her waist, hauling her up and into a solid form. Panic gave her strength, and she writhed, hitting out against whoever was holding her in such a viselike grip.

"Stop. You're safe now. Come with me. We have to get out of here."

The words shot through her terrified fog, the voice penetrating her senses.

Where was this infernal meeting, anyway? Haverly's message, retrieved from a dead drop near his boardinghouse, had only said Daniel must be at a certain address at ten, dress as a laborer, and gather what information he could from an anarchist rally.

The message had been his first real dead-drop retrieval. He'd practiced the maneuver many times, both in the Thorndike's War Room and in Hyde Park, but this time he'd sweated, sure that everyone who saw him knew he was up to something clandestine. The prearranged signal that a message was waiting, which he had nearly missed in his haste to get to work at Bow Street, had all but leapt out at him once he recognized it.

The chalk mark on the newel post of his rooming house had been easy enough to remove as he passed. Then it was a matter of buying a copy of a morning paper, taking it to the pie seller on the corner, setting the paper on the man's cart while Daniel purchased a mince pie for breakfast, and retrieving the note stuck into a crevice on the underside of the cart beneath the concealing paper.

The fact that he'd managed it perfectly both gratified and grated on him. The last time he had been called upon to use some of his new spy craft, he'd fallen over his own feet in front of Lady Juliette. The archery tournament exchange had not exactly been a rousing success, and his cheeks burned each time he thought of it . . . even as he remembered the feel of her in his arms, the scent of roses, the racing of his heart.

As he made his way down a flight of steps, slick with the damp night air, other dark shadows also moved toward his destination. Men in heavy coats, a few women in cloaks and bonnets. Silent mouths, careful footsteps, furtive glances.

Daniel's conscience nudged him hard. This gathering was illegal. Assembling together to plot the overthrow of the government, the economy, the orderly structure of daily life was contrary to the laws of the nation. While he sympathized with the workers' plight, violence was an extreme response, and in this case, he felt, unjustified. Certainly murder was always outside the pale.

Jasper Finch, though impassioned and erudite when speaking at a social gathering, had been stretching to justify violence as a response. Surely if he could amass a large enough body of workers who all agreed on a peaceful course of action, those who employed them would have no choice but to listen and change. But Finch did not seem interested in peace. He fomented disorder instead.

Men slipped through the half-opened door of a large brick warehouse, and Daniel joined them, hands deep in his pockets, hat pulled low. He'd added a streak of coal dust to his cheek and had spilled a touch of ale on his lapel, giving the impression that he was a collier who, before attending the meeting, had stopped off at a pub after his last delivery.

The place stank of the mudflats left behind when the tide went out and the river went down. Broken roof tiles, rotted wood, crumbling brick. How long since the warehouse had been in use? It was the perfect place for a clandestine meeting, with the windows boarded up and darkness shrouding the area. There were no braziers or streetlamps for blocks, and the night watchmen would give the place a wide berth since there was nothing here worth protecting.

Already a sizable group had formed, and as they filed into an inner area, someone lit torches. The flare of flames illuminated the place with eerie, dancing light and sneaking shadows.

There must be nearly a hundred people gathered, with more filtering in. Footfalls scraped on the cobbles, and a rat scurried along the wall. Daniel grimaced. He hated rats.

"What do you suppose will happen tonight?" one man asked.

Daniel jumped, trying to formulate a plausible answer, then relaxed as he realized the man spoke to his companion.

"Dunno, but something has to change. You know what happened at the docks? They are building a steam crane to move cargo onto and off the ships. How many workers will lose their jobs? They say one of those cranes will do the work of ten men. And if they bring in one, they'll bring in more. Soon you won't need more than a handful of men to shift cargo for the whole of the East India Company."

"Wait until I tell you what happened to me."

Others crowded around, sharing their stories. The tales were different, but they all carried the same thread—industry moving quickly and leaving many behind. Fear of change, fear of not being able to support their families, fear of not having any control over their lives.

Fear was a powerful motivator.

And anger. Their anger seemed directed at the upper classes and at the House of Lords specifically.

Daniel found a place in the back. Observe, his orders were, but observe what? In his mind, he began forming his report. The number of people, the snippets of conversation he overheard, the feeling of unrest that spread through the crowd like a malevolent fever. He wasn't surprised when the leader arrived and was revealed to be Mr. Jasper Finch. As he passed, Daniel ducked his chin into his collar.

He'd encountered Mr. Finch at the Thorndike house, had heard his views, and thought him quite off the beam. Long before tonight the agency had been watching Finch, keeping an eye on his movements and drawing out some of his ideas to hopefully anticipate his next move.

Perhaps he was ready to make it tonight.

As the anarchist began to speak, a strong ripple wove through the crowd, as if it were a shock transferring from one man to the next. The listeners tensed, leaning forward, and Daniel himself felt the pull of the speaker's charisma. Uneasiness fluttered along his skin as the rhetoric increased in tone and tempo. Anger flowed through the crowd, fed by Finch's inflammatory language.

Daniel's ears perked at the mention of the killing of a mill owner, and his gut tightened as Finch appeared to not only condone the murder of a business owner but to encourage a repetition of the act. *You heard what happened in Hammersmith*, he'd said. *Let that be a warning to all.*

Had Finch played a hand in Montgomery's death? Had he known about it? The explosion wasn't caused by an anarchist, but the killing could have been carried out by one. *If they will not hear our pleas*, Finch had continued, *we must cease trying to reason with them. We must act!*

This would get out of hand if someone didn't put a stop to it.

A man to Daniel's left grabbed a torch. "Let's go! I know the first place!"

In a flash, the crowd changed from discontented gathering to angry mob, rushing past him toward the door. As he was situated at the back, near the way out, he was nearly trampled before he managed to leap out of harm's way along one of the side walls.

Then he saw her.

Lady Juliette. Her delicate patrician features, caught in the flickering torchlight, those dark-as-night eyes with their heavy fringe of lashes. She wore rough clothing, and a heavy bonnet, and she'd done something to her face . . . paint, perhaps? But though Bertie had claimed he wouldn't recognize her in disguise, Daniel would know her anywhere.

Bodies passed between them, and he rose on tiptoe to catch sight of her again. She had managed to avoid the worst of the crush . . .

Then she was fallen, struck by a man twice her size as he thrust forward, sending her back into the wall. She collapsed like a sail in a sudden doldrum. Rushing people cut off his view, and he struggled against the flow, fighting to get to her before she was trampled.

His chest tightened, and he was not gentle as he tossed men out of his way, using elbows, knees, shoulders, anything he could. When he reached her, she had pressed her hands into the cobbles, but she was unable to rise. Without thought to propriety, he spanned her waist, hauling her up and into the shelter of his embrace as he turned away from the onrushing mob. He tucked her head into his neck and took the buffeting against his back and shoulders.

But rather than gratitude at his rescue, she tried to kill him. His shins, ribs, and the side of his head received a mauling as she fought him.

"Stop. You're safe now. Come with me. We have to get out of here."

She clouted him again.

"Juliette, stop. It's me." He grabbed her wrists, stemming the struggle and twisting her arms behind her, bringing her up tight against his chest to protect both of them. Their breaths mingled as her eyes, foggy from her head's impact with the wall, began to clear.

She blinked, and he relaxed a fraction.

A popping sound came from outside, followed by another and another. Gunshots.

"It's the police!" The shout ricocheted through the room, drowning out the running feet. Some froze in panic. Others took flight, and the trampling, shoving, and shouting increased.

Though it seemed like years, from the beginning of the riot to the arrival of the first constable must have been less than a minute.

There was no time to tarry. Lady Juliette could not be apprehended at an anarchist's rally, dressed in a disguise. And it wouldn't do Daniel any favors either, though he could probably talk his way out of trouble by claiming he was investigating a rumor of a gathering.

With the entryway clogged with fleeing workers, Daniel sought another avenue of escape.

"This way." Juliette pulled from his embrace, only to stagger and put her hand to her head, wincing.

"Let me help you." He put his arm around her waist once more. "Lean on me. Do you know another way out?" With the torches being doused, the room was quickly falling into darkness, welcome in hiding identities but a hindrance to finding one's way out.

"Along this wall. There's a door. I need to get to Uncle Bertie."

"There's no time to find him. We must get you out of here."

He switched her to his right side and felt along the wall with his left hand until the bricks turned to damp wood. Unable to find a handle or knob, he set Juliette away from him and rammed his shoulder into the center of the panel.

Pain shot through his side, but the door gave way, forcing him to stagger to keep his feet. Regaining his balance, he gathered her close again and edged his way through the door. It was black as pitch, but he could feel a brick wall to his left.

A few paces in and he banged his toe on a step. Searching with his foot, he encountered another step, and another. "Come. We have to climb to the street above." He caught a glimpse of light ahead of him. Moonlight, perhaps? There must be an opening up there somewhere.

He helped Juliette ascend the long flight, keeping his hold on her lest she slip on the wet stairs. It gratified him that she accepted his help, even putting her arm about his waist and holding firmly. Her bonnet had been knocked askew, and as they stepped from the doorway, her hair loosened from the knot at the nape of her neck to tumble in tangles down her back.

Daniel swallowed hard as her hair brushed his hand. Such an intimate thing, touching a woman's hair. Was she even aware?

Her cheek rested against his shoulder, giving her a vulnerability that called all his protectiveness to the fore once more. What was she doing, performing such dangerous work? Where was her uncle when she needed him? Anger flared through his chest. What was her family thinking? She could have been seriously injured, and if he hadn't gotten to her in time, she could have been killed.

They paused in the narrow alleyway, shouts and the pounding of running feet heading away from their location. This close to the river, where the streets were a warren of alleys and lanes, it would be difficult to find a hackney. They might be in for a long walk. But first they would have to wait for the area to clear, for the fleeing mob and pursuing constables to move away. It wouldn't do for them to blunder into a night watchman by mistake.

He would have a better vantage point if he could get to the crossroad ahead. No streetlamps or braziers lit the way, but there was a lighter opening between the buildings, and in the distance he could make out the crenellations of the Tower of London against the night sky.

He kept his arm about Juliette, steadying her. She leaned into him, making his chest feel oddly empty and full at the same time.

"Where are we going?" she asked. Her face turned up toward his, and her whisper feathered across his skin.

With a hard swallow, he answered in a rough-edged voice that barely resembled his own. "I want to make sure the way is clear before we venture too far. That corner should provide a good vantage point to see if there are still watchmen about."

"We need to go to Haverly House. I promised Uncle Bertie I would go there if anything ill happened. Cavendish Square."

"We're a long way from Cavendish Square. Did you happen to arrive by carriage?"

"We walked to get far from our house, then hired a carriage. Uncle Bertie had the driver let us out about a mile away so no one could identify where we were going, and we arrived at the warehouse on foot."

"Where is he? Why did he leave you on your own?" He stopped walking, wanting to stay in the shadows until he had more information.

"I don't know. He moved away from me while Mr. Finch was roiling up the crowd, and I lost sight of him."

"You will be reunited with your uncle as soon as I can manage it," he promised. "Wait here."

He stepped to the corner, peering around the edge of the building. Listening hard, he held his breath. Nothing. No movement in the shadows, no sound of footsteps. Though it had only been a few minutes since they had climbed the dark stairway, it appeared the area had cleared.

Quietly, he returned to her side, took her hand, and led her to the cross street. They rounded the corner of the building, which turned out to be a chandler's shop, and she stiffened.

A man had appeared opposite them, carrying a bullseye lantern and raising it high. In his other hand, he carried a truncheon. The lamplight gleamed off the brass fitments.

Recognition hit Daniel like a punch. Ed Beck. Here. Sir Michael must have sent him with the other constables to break up the meeting. He would know Daniel hadn't been assigned with them, for Daniel had been given the night off.

He had to do something to avoid discovery. Ed would pass by any second.

Daniel grabbed Juliette and pulled her into his embrace, ducking into the chandler's recessed doorway. She squeaked at the sudden movement, and before she could protest, he did the first thing that came to his mind.

He kissed her.

It really *was* to protect their identities. In the shadows here, in a tight embrace, no one could see their faces, nor would they be interrupted.

It was the last sane thought he had for quite some time.

Even in her disguise, she smelled of roses. Somehow, his fingers were in her hair, dislodging her bonnet further, his thumbs skimming her cheekbones. So soft, everywhere. She was so soft.

Her lips were warm, and he caught the intake of her breath.

His heart thundered in his ears, and his eyes closed even tighter. The side of his nose brushed hers.

Smooth skin, feminine mystery. She seemed to come unfrozen, and to his delight she returned the pressure of his lips, only slightly, but then with a touch more ardor, which fired his blood. Without meaning to, he tilted his head and deepened the kiss, a low growl escaping his throat.

He heard Ed's chuckle as he passed and the ring of boots on the cobbles, fading away.

Daniel slowly broke the kiss, feeling dazed. He had never kissed a woman before and had always suspected that the bragging of his university mates had highly exaggerated the experience.

He had been wrong.

Juliette's hands rested lightly on his shoulders, and her eyes were wide, dark pools of surprise.

He swallowed and pressed his lips together, remembering the feel of hers under his.

She cleared her throat and eased back, dropping her hands limply, edging away until her shoulders touched the door of the chandler's shop.

Heat pooled in his neck and traveled to his face. He hoped the darkness hid the flush.

What temerity. Utter madness.

He had kissed Lady Juliette Thorndike.

And he wanted to kiss her again.

What must she think of him? She should probably slap his face, or possibly draw whatever weapon she carried on her person and defend herself from his bold advances.

To his amazement, she did neither. Instead, she put her hands on his shoulders again, stood on tiptoe to peek past his ear, and whispered, "I think he's gone."

She sounded quite normal. Had the kiss not affected her the same way?

Of course not, you muttonhead. Why should a kiss from a Bow Street detective, a man she knew was a by-blow, who didn't even know who fathered him, thrill her in any way? She had to know, to believe, the kiss had only been part of their cover, to avoid detection, and she'd handled it in a professional way. He was the idiot who still felt wobbly about the knee joints.

Had Heinrich von Lowe kissed her? Had she welcomed his kiss with romantic thoughts of falling in love with the German duke?

That notion was like a bucket of cold water in his face.

"Hsst."

Juliette grimaced, and he slowly turned away from her to face the street. Had Ed returned?

"If you two are finished hiding in doorways, it's best we get away. The area is crawling with constables and watchmen."

Chapter 13

"How can all of them so far have alibis for the murder?" Daniel asked. He had raced home after parting from Sir Bertrand and Lady Juliette, changed his clothes, and feigned surprise when one of the office boys knocked on his door to tell him Sir Michael had ordered him to report to the magistrate's court.

Ed shrugged, yawning. Dawn was still a couple of hours away, and no one at Bow Street had gotten any sleep. The interrogation rooms were full, the corridor packed with custodies chased down and brought in last night.

Owen entered with a tea tray. He wove his way around the desks, as nimble as an acrobat, arriving at Daniel's desk in the corner and setting the tray down with panache. "It's a proper crush in here. Never saw the place so busy." He sported a black eye, worn proudly, as he had been called upon to help apprehend the rallygoers last night.

"The gathering wasn't even in our jurisdiction. Why are they all here?" Daniel asked.

"Seemed the easiest to bring everyone here, since we had been called in to lead the arrests. Not certain where the orders came from, but Sir Michael sent all of us who were here to the warehouse district." Ed didn't wait for the office boy to pour, grabbing the pot and sloshing tea into a cup. "He wasn't best pleased that he couldn't find you. I told him he had given you the night off, but that didn't mollify him. I told him it was likely you were chasing down a lead or two on the

Montgomery case, but he's fuming that you haven't put that to bed yet either."

"What have we learned from questioning the detainees?" Daniel asked. There was no point in discussing Sir Michael or his attitude toward Daniel. He could solve fifty murders in a single day and Sir Michael Biddle would still find fault. "Have the leaders been captured?"

He could not let on that he knew who at least one of the leaders was, for no one could know he was at the rally. It was the first time his two lives had intersected and clashed like this. The police detective in him wanted to march upstairs and apply to a magistrate for a warrant for Jasper Finch's arrest, but the secret agent in him knew he must not reveal knowledge he wasn't supposed to have. That would endanger not only himself but others, including Lady Juliette.

Which again brought that devastating kiss to mind.

No, he couldn't think about that now. He had work to do. For the thousandth time, he pushed the memory of the kiss out of his head.

Ed shook his head. "Most of the men we captured don't know much. They heard about the gathering in different ways, word spreading through their workplaces, some overhearing in a pub or being invited by a friend."

"Mr. Fyfe might be onto something down the hall." Owen lifted the lid of the teapot. "He asked that you two gentlemen come help him with the questioning."

"Why didn't you tell us right away?" Daniel stood, his chair sliding back to hit the wall. "Why must we always wait for you to dispense important news?"

"Mr. Fyfe said to let you have your tea first." Owen looked innocent and hurt. "He wanted to let the man stew a bit before going back into the room."

Chagrined to have once more spoken out of turn to the young man, Daniel forced himself to do the right thing. "My apologies. I should not have chastised you. Thank you for the tea. Do you know when the magistrates will begin the arraignments?"

"Word has been sent about tonight's doings, and the magistrates should be arriving soon. Once they're here, we'll begin taking prisoners upstairs to the courtroom."

"Very good." Ed clapped Owen on the shoulder. "We'll make an inspector of you yet."

Owen beamed at the praise, and Daniel chided himself once more. It would cost him nothing to be nicer to the young man, to encourage him in his pursuit of becoming a Bow Street officer. From what Ed had said, Owen had acquitted himself well during the raid on the rally.

Thomas Fyfe met them outside the interrogation room, his waistcoat straining over his substantial middle and his pipe clamped firmly between his lips even at this early hour of the morning. The bowl of meerschaum, now yellowed with age and use, had been carved into the likeness of Admiral Lord Nelson and was Fyfe's pride.

"You have something interesting?" Daniel kept his voice low since they were directly outside Sir Michael's office. He hated feeling as if he had to slink around out of sight of his superior, but at the moment he wasn't up for another confrontation.

"Fellow says he has plenty of information, and he'll spill it if we'll tell the magistrate he helped out." Fyfe had no such reservations about not lowering his voice, and Daniel winced.

"Let's see what he has to say, then."

An hour later Daniel wanted to pound the walls with frustration. The suspect had led them a merry dance, hinting and retreating, afraid or clinging to loyalty or just buying time to come up with more lies.

"Let's go over this again. Mr. Finch had you recruiting workers at your place of business, gathering men to the cause?" Fyfe blew out a billow of smoke.

Daniel blinked, wishing for a window he could open. The room was stale with smoke, the dregs of their teacups, and the smell of an unwashed, nervous male.

"That's right." The man, one Ulrich Reading, turned his empty teacup on the table. "It was all Finch's idea."

The moment Reading had named Finch, Ed had gone upstairs for a warrant. At least they had made that much progress.

"What about the morning of the first? Were you in Hammersmith? Was Finch?" Daniel asked, though they had been over this ground once before. He wanted to pin down the details, to determine if the man was lying.

Because everyone lied, especially to the police.

Reading's face screwed up in noncomprehension. "Hammersmith? I hain't ever been to Hammersmith in my life. And Finch wasn't there that morning either. We was . . . busy elsewhere." His voice tapered off.

"If you were not in Hammersmith, where were you, what were you doing, and who were you with?" Daniel asked. "Enough of this game playing."

"But I already told you what I know."

"I don't believe you."

Fyfe leaned over the table. "If you don't tell us where you were, there will be no good word with the magistrate, and you'll go to Newgate in a fast wagon. You're charged with sedition and inciting a riot, and if we can, we'll pin murder on you as well. Now, spill what you know, or dance at the end of the hangman's rope."

Reading paled, gripping his hands together. For a long moment, Daniel thought he might choose the rope, but then he crumpled like a wadded piece of paper. "We couldn't have killed that mill owner, because we were in the East End planning how to blow up a ropework near the Isle of Dogs." He hung his head. "I can tell you where to find the explosives we was planning to use. Just please tell the judge I co-operated. Tell him not to make me swing."

And with one statement, Daniel's latest theory about the murder evaporated. Once again he had nothing that would help find Mr. Montgomery's killer. Though they would verify Reading's story, he sensed in this instance they had finally gotten to a kernel of truth. Which meant Finch could not have murdered Montgomery the morning of the mill explosion, for he had been planning mayhem elsewhere at the time.

A tap on the door, and Owen stuck his head inside. "Message

arrived for you." He handed an envelope to Daniel. "Before you ask, I dunno who sent it. A street urchin brought it. I gave him a penny for his trouble."

"Reimburse yourself out of petty cash." Daniel tore open the plain wax seal. "And thank you."

"I already did." Owen gave a cheeky grin. "And you're welcome."

"I'll take Mr. Reading here upstairs to the court, and then I'll see about finding those explosives. Do you want to accompany me?" Fyfe knocked the dottle out of his pipe into his teacup and reached for his tobacco pouch.

Daniel barely heard his fellow detective.

Come to the mill at dawn. I've some new information. Rhynwick.

The young scientist. What could he have discovered? Hopefully, something that would aid in the case?

"I say, are you coming with us?" Fyfe asked again as he applied the manacles to Reading's wrists and hoisted him from his chair.

"I cannot." Daniel raised the paper. "I must go on an errand. But take Wilkinson with you. He's useful and wants to learn."

Daniel's ride to Hammersmith in Cadogan's carriage was the first time he'd had to himself since arriving at Bow Street late last night. The moment Sir Bertrand had spoken out of the darkness, Daniel's heart had nearly stopped. Had he seen Daniel kissing his niece? No censure had come, not from Sir Bertrand, nor from Lady Juliette.

Once more his face heated. She had behaved as if nothing untoward or momentous had occurred, while he had been at complete sixes and sevens.

The carriage rocked through the predawn darkness. Sunrise was an hour away, and the heavy overcast bore no promise of brightening the streets of London with much cheer.

He closed his eyes, weariness and lack of sleep catching him up. Perhaps he could snatch a few minutes' rest before they arrived.

The jolt of the carriage stopping brought Daniel upright, and he blinked, rubbing at his scratchy eyes with the heels of his hands. The brief nap hadn't alleviated his tiredness, and he felt dull and stupid.

Cadogan opened the door. "Close as I can get, guv. Should I wait here for you?"

"Yes, thank you." Daniel stirred himself, jumping to the ground and stretching. "Been a long night. Hopefully, I shall return soon." He dug in his pocket and gave the jarvey a coin. "Find yourself some breakfast. There's bound to be a bakery nearby."

Yawning hard enough to crack his jaw, Daniel made his way down the narrow street toward the temporary barrier surrounding the mill. No watchman stood at the opening. Had they discontinued the nightly patrols? Or was the watchman inside the mill with Rhynwick?

Fog hung over the sluggish river in heavy pewter scarves, and Daniel shivered. Flexing his fingers, he tried to work some warmth into them. He entered the mill through the warehouse doors. The smell of smoke still lingered, but fainter. The clearing away of the wreckage had begun, and the warehouse floor had been swept clean and sacks and barrels restacked along the walls.

The first indication of sunrise filtered in through the high windows on the east side of the warehouse, and Daniel made his way down the hallway toward Montgomery's office.

Both office doors stood open, but the rooms were empty. The absence of paperwork reminded Daniel that he had yet to sort everything taken to Bow Street. Owen had begun the process, but other duties had intervened.

The milling floor was silent and empty. Broken equipment had been heaped on one side, and Daniel could see where repairs had begun. Perhaps Miss Montgomery had given permission for the work to start in anticipation of either selling the property or reopening the mill herself.

She would have to do it without the aid of Viscount Coatsworth. Daniel had confirmed that the man had indeed gotten on a ship bound for the Caribbean.

His visit with Miss Montgomery upon his return had gone oddly well. She'd received the news about Coatsworth's sudden trip to Jamaica calmly. "He will return. It must have been urgent business for him to leave so quickly. I am certain he regrets not informing me, but there must have been no time."

Daniel wasn't nearly as certain as she, but what could he say? He had done his part in going to Kent and following up at the docks. In the end, he had not visited the solicitors. They had been particularly closed-mouthed in his every dealing with them, and he doubted they would have told him anything about the Rotherhide's business. There was nothing else he could do.

He listened for voices or footfalls inside the mill but heard none. No watchman, no Rhynwick. The only sound was the splashing of the waterwheel outside. Perhaps the young scientist had not yet arrived.

Shrugging, fighting the weariness that pulled at his limbs and deadened his thoughts, Daniel went back through the hallway to the warehouse and out the smaller door to the walkway that gave access to the waterwheel. Though he understood the shaft had been disconnected from the gear system that turned the grinding stones, the wheel itself continued to rotate, water tipping and gurgling busily on the overshot system.

There was something soothing and fascinating about the sound of moving water, and despite his distaste for heights, Daniel leaned on the railing, closing his eyes. His bed beckoned, but he knew he would not see it before nightfall. He had too much to do today, too many leads to chase.

He should report to Sir Bertrand about Ulrich Reading's confession and the warrant out for Jasper Finch, and he should wade through the paperwork taken from the offices here and those provided by Mifflin, Mr. Montgomery's personal secretary.

Something tickled his brain, some shred of a reminder of something he had forgotten. It had to do with the paperwork, but what was it?

As he straightened, something hit him hard between the shoulder blades. He reached for the railing, but it was too late. His torso shot out into space, overbalancing and tipping him over the rail. He fell the ten feet to the wheel and tumbled into the churning water beneath.

Chapter 14

"YOU'RE UP EARLIER THAN I thought, given last night's activities." Uncle Bertie half rose from his chair in the breakfast room when Juliette entered.

She shrugged. "I couldn't sleep." Not only was her mind too busy, but her body ached from the pummeling she'd taken under the boots of the mob. A dull headache had stalked her in the wee hours, but thankfully that had abated. Hunger finally drove her to dress and go downstairs.

You're lying to yourself if you blame the rally for keeping you awake. No, it was reliving Daniel Swann's kiss that robbed you of slumber.

Mrs. Dunstan entered with a tray and set it beside Juliette. "Shall I pour?"

"I will do it. Thank you."

The housekeeper left the room, and Juliette took the small silver pot and poured a cup of chocolate for herself.

Bertie grimaced and raised his own cup of tea. "I cannot think how you can enjoy such a concoction so early in the morning. Too sweet by half for me."

"I like it. Have you heard anything?" She could not ascertain whether he knew about the kiss or not. His face had given nothing away—not last night, nor this morning.

That kiss. Her first ever. She resisted touching her lips.

Daniel Swann had kissed her.

And she had kissed him right back.

Oh, she knew he had only been thinking of avoiding detection by Mr. Beck. There had been nothing but professional expediency behind the kiss, and yet . . .

Even now her pulse fluttered and her skin felt too tight. She could not stop thinking about the warmth of his breath on her cheek, the slight rasp of his skin where his beard came through, the feel of his hands in her hair. He had been solid and shielding and strong, his arms sheltering her, his body protecting her. Though she had taken a knock to the head, it was his nearness—and the wonderfulness of his kiss—that had made her knees turn to putty and her wits fly away.

"You haven't heard a word I've said." Bertie tapped the folded newspaper beside his plate.

She stirred, chocolate tipping over the edge of her cup onto her saucer. "My apologies. I was woolgathering. As you say, it was a late night."

"You asked if there was news, and there is indeed, if you are ready to pay attention." A dent formed between his brows as he studied her, and she straightened her shoulders and tried to appear bright and attentive.

"The raid on the warehouse made the papers. What hasn't hit the presses yet is that there is a warrant out for Jasper Finch's arrest, and word has it that a cache of explosives and a plot to blow up another factory have been uncovered."

"How do you know all this? It's barely past sunup."

"Our network never sleeps. Haverly has been keeping his eye on developments and apprising me of what I need to know. He'll be expecting your report later today when he calls by."

A report. What should she say? She could give her impressions of the event, the way Mr. Finch had roused the crowd to a fever pitch. And she would have to explain how she escaped the building.

But she wouldn't have to mention the kiss, would she?

"There is also a missive from your parents. They will be home soon, perhaps by the end of the month." He tossed a folded paper her way. "The Prince Regent is a fickle fellow, as always. Send them out, drag them back. He wants them to attend him when he goes to Brighton after the Easter holiday. Forget that he sent them on a diplomatic mission. He wants them in his entourage on the coast." Bertie shrugged. "I fear he will be no less unstable when he becomes king."

Joy flashed through her at the thought of her parents returning. "Will I be able to accompany them to Brighton?" Pray it was so. She had been given so little time with them since returning home. She read the letter, confirming all that Bertie had said. Home at the end of the month and then time spent in Brighton.

Mr. Pultney entered the breakfast room, a silver tray in his hand. "A caller for Lady Juliette." He offered the tray, and she took the card.

A caller, at this hour?

She looked at Uncle Bertie, then back at the card. "It's Duke Heinrich."

Surprise hit his features. "Is something amiss? Why would he call upon you? And at daybreak?"

"I've no idea."

"Should I tell him milady is not receiving?" Mr. Pultney asked.

Her abdominal muscles tightened. Something must be very wrong for him to come at this hour. Juliette looked at Uncle Bertie. "Will you join me?"

"I have to attend to a small matter first. Go ahead and see him. Leave the door to the drawing room open. That will be chaperone enough until I greet the duke."

She supposed no harm would come to her reputation by spending a few moments alone with Heinrich. She had spent far more time alone with Daniel.

Daniel. Just the thought of his name brought forth the memory of his kiss, of his protectiveness, of *him*.

How did she feel about him? He was handsome, kind, brave, competent, intelligent . . . Every time they were together, she felt . . . alive. Colors seemed brighter, sounds sharper. When she was with him, she was more aware of him—and of herself—than when with any other person.

She must stop thinking of Daniel Swann. It would be impolite to Heinrich to be daydreaming when she greeted him.

Heinrich waited in a chair before the fireplace and rose smartly when she entered. His hair was crisply combed and his uniform scrupulously clean. The gleam off his boots could blind someone. But rather than looking into her eyes with his customary friendly smile, he stared over her shoulder.

"*Guten Morgen*, Lady Juliette." He bowed with military precision. "Forgive my early call, and *danke sehr* for agreeing to meet with me. You are looking lovely today."

That he had used two phrases from his native tongue surprised her. He had striven to always speak English. How did he know she looked lovely? He had yet to turn his eyes fully upon her. A nervous shiver went up her spine.

He wiped his hands on his trousers and beckoned her to take a seat. What had happened? Duke Heinrich always behaved with perfect aplomb, and she'd never seen him uncertain, but he appeared almost timid.

"I thought you must have some important news. My uncle will join us shortly, if you would prefer to wait for him. May I ring for tea, or do you prefer coffee? If you have not broken your fast, you are welcome to join us in the breakfast room." She was speaking too fast, trying to forestall learning whatever had upset him.

"*Nein*, I could not eat. Please, will you sit?" He clasped his hands behind his back, his feet braced apart.

She sat on the edge of the seat, twisting her garnet ring, searching her mind for what could have brought him here. Had someone they both knew seen her at the rally and told him?

How would she explain herself? What plausible story could she tell? Where was Uncle Bertie? A pit opened at the base of her stomach, and her insides trickled into it.

"You must know, over the past weeks I have come to have a high regard for you and your family." He sounded as if he were speaking from a script. "Word has come through my government that my time in England is coming to an end. I am being called home in less than a fortnight."

"Oh, I am sorry, for I have enjoyed your company." She relaxed her spine a fraction and lowered her shoulders. This was merely a call to say goodbye.

"I am pleased to hear you say that, for I hope that our separation will not be for long. I would wish your parents were present, for I would like to speak to your father at this time regarding your future."

Her future? The pit in her stomach reopened. *No, please don't.*

"I cannot make a formal declaration nor a formal request at this time, for I must first speak both to your father and to my own family. But I also could not leave these shores without at the very least telling you how I have come to care for you. It is my intention to return to my homeland, consult with my family, and make all haste to come back here to you."

This time his blue eyes met hers, and in them she read his firm resolve. And his regard.

At this juncture, when she was scrambling for something to say, something to answer the hope in his expression, Uncle Bertie strolled in.

"Good morning to you, Duke Heinrich. What brings you to our humble home on such a fresh day?" He sprawled into a chair. "Do sit down. Why haven't you rung for tea, Jules?"

"Good morning, Sir Bertrand." Heinrich looked pained, but he took the seat opposite Bertie. "I have come to inform you . . . and your niece . . . of my soon departure. I am being recalled to my home at the end of the month."

"Work with the diplomatic corps winding up, eh? I could never be a diplomat. I cannot imagine the secrets you must keep, always looking beneath the surface, wondering what the other side is really up to." Bertie took out his watch, then removed his handkerchief and polished the glass. "Good show."

Juliette stifled a laugh. Bertie kept ten secrets before breakfast, and he was always looking for clues as to what the enemies of Britain were really up to.

"*Danke.* I wish I could stay longer, but duty must come first. However, it is my desire to return to England by midsummer to renew my acquaintances."

"We look forward to having you back, don't we, Juliette?"

She paused. "Yes, of course. I wish you safe travels."

Heinrich beamed. "I shall think of you all often, and I shall tell my family about the warm welcome I was given. It is my highest hope that I will be able to return the favor at a time when your family can visit mine in Brandenburg. My mother is going to love you."

He stared at Juliette, and her skin grew uncomfortably warm. Heinrich was making assumptions that she could not, and would not, answer in front of her uncle. The duke had not exactly declared himself, nor had he formally asked for her hand in marriage, but he had ridden right up to the precipice.

What could she do? Why weren't her parents there? If Heinrich had requested permission to propose from her father, she would have had some warning.

Daniel crashed onto the waterwheel, smashing into the angled buckets that filled with water from the sluice of the overshot system. His cloak caught on the shroud plate, yanking him by the neck and cutting off his air. The frog closure bit into his throat as the wheel turned without mercy, dragging him beneath the water. He struggled with the cloak as it tangled around him, pinning his arms to his sides.

Water closed over his head, filling his ears, his eyes, his nose. A rushing, thumping sound roared around him, and his shoulder hit something hard, scraping and dragging along the bottom of the water race.

Uneven stone ground against his side while the waterwheel rotated inexorably. He was scudded along the bottom of the race, all the while struggling to free himself from the strangling cloak.

He began to see stars, but at last his head broke the surface. He opened his mouth to draw in a huge breath, but the tangled cloak cut off his ability to grab air. As the wheel lifted him, he arched his back, kicking to find purchase with his feet to push himself up and bring a little air into his lungs.

At the top of the turn, the full force of the water rushing through the sluice hit him in the face, blinding him, pushing his head back into the sodden wood. He was being dragged over the top of the wheel and down the far side, headfirst.

Once more he plunged beneath the icy water. Dragged over the rough stones, pinned between the wheel and the raceway. His lungs screamed to be filled, pain arcing through him, inside and out.

He must get air. He must break the metal closure on the cape. He would not survive much longer.

Were these to be his last moments on earth? Regret took hold. There was so much more he wanted to do . . .

He had intended to find Montgomery's killer.

He had intended to prove himself a worthy detective.

He had intended to kiss Lady Juliette Thorndike again.

The wheel hauled him up, and he managed to free one hand to dig under the cloak wound so tightly about his neck. He forced open a bare inch of space at his throat and draw in a ragged breath before the sluice doused him once more.

God, please. Don't let me die like this.

Someone shouted, faint above the roaring of the water and the roaring in his ears.

This time when the waterwheel sent him downward, he managed to flip himself to go feet first, but the force of the wheel doubled him over to tug him along the stony race. Another plunge beneath the surface, another grating, pounding, pummeling trip over the rocks.

And this time the cloak caught on something else, the force ripping the fabric away from him and sending him shooting into the wall of the dam behind the wheel. Struggling to stay above the water, he drew in great whooping breaths, coughing, spitting, drawing in river water and choking it out again.

He was pinned in the small space behind the wheel, roiling water cascading around him. There was no room along the sides to escape downriver. The walls of the dam and chase were slick with mossy slime. His hands were frozen from the frigid water and the beating they had taken.

He was trapped.

Another shout, and Cadogan's head appeared over the edge of the walkway above. "Swann! Are you all right, sir?"

Do I look all right? I'm about to drown down here!

Daniel couldn't get the words out. He hadn't the breath. It was all he could do to keep his nose above the water and avoid getting whacked by the waterwheel. His fingers scrabbled for any purchase. Free of the heavy cloak he might be, but his boots were full of water, dragging him under time and again. The backwash from the wheel doused his face continually.

"Take hold of the wheel!" Cadogan shouted. "Let it hoist you up. I'll grab you!"

The man was brilliant. Daniel would have to tell him so once he was on dry land.

Twice, Daniel's fingers closed over the edge of one of the paddles, only to have the wet wood jerked from his hand. The third time, he rode the massive wheel up halfway before losing his grip and plunging into the water below once more, banging off the stone wall, the wheel, and who knew what else on the way down.

Gasping, his strength gone, he tried once more.

You are not going to die this way. You are not going to be killed in such a ridiculous manner without even knowing who tried to murder you.

He gripped the edge of the wood, this time his sodden boot toe finding a hold on a lower paddle.

Don't let me fall, God. If You are listening at all . . .

He rose, clinging desperately, feeling his weight shift as the wheel carried him higher. Cadogan leaned out over the wheel much too far for his own safety, stretching to reach Daniel before he fell again. A fist closed around Daniel's collar at the same moment his fingers slipped off the wheel, and for an eternity he hung suspended by his shirt. He kicked against the wheel, and the force of the turn raised him a bit more, where Cadogan, with a surprising show of strength and little regard for his own well-being, let go of the railing to grab Daniel with two hands, hauling him up and dragging him across the walkway.

Trembling—from cold or weakness or his near death, possibly all three—began in Daniel's core and radiated outward to his limbs. He shivered and shuddered, dragging in great whooping breaths and coughing out water.

Cadogan sprawled beside him, still holding on to his collar, as if afraid he would slip over the edge again.

Daniel was grateful, for he had no control over his body.

"How did you know?" he rasped out when he could speak.

The jarvey let go of Daniel and pushed himself upright. He'd lost his cap somewhere, and his hair stuck out in odd directions.

"Was coming back from the bakery with my breakfast when I saw this fellow running out of the side door of the mill like his coattails were on fire. Looked odd, so I thought I'd have a nose around, see what was up. I couldn't find you anywhere, and I dunno what possessed me to come out here, but bless me, I'm glad I did. There you were, lashed to the wheel like some torture device from the Spanish Inquisition. I thought you were a dead man for sure."

"So did I." With arms as steady as aspic jelly, Daniel pushed against the walkway, forcing himself into a sitting position. "I want to get inside, away from this wheel."

Cadogan helped him to his feet, keeping a firm grip on Daniel's arm as he tottered like an old man toward the safety of the mill.

He couldn't stop shivering, crossing his arms at his waist and hunching his shoulders. Cadogan hurried him to the carriage, and when he had Daniel inside, he rummaged around in the back, tossing a horse blanket inside.

"I think we should take you to the nearest inn where you can get a hot drink and some dry clothes. Or to a doctor. You must have swallowed half the Thames."

"No, I need to get back to London."

"But, guv, you're near frozen and drowned."

In spite of the blanket, the shaking continued, and Daniel realized it was as much the shock of knowing someone had tried to murder him as it was the cold.

"Get me back to the city. I have a killer to find."

Chapter 15

"Keep the blanket till I see you again. I still think you should see a doctor. You came within a tiny cat's whisker of meeting your Maker this morning." Cadogan held the carriage door, his face creased with concern.

Daniel eased out of the carriage in front of his boardinghouse. There was nothing like being pummeled by a waterwheel for making a man feel as if he had been pummeled by a waterwheel. Every bone ached, and the cold inactivity of the ride from Hammersmith had stiffened his muscles.

A long hot soak in a tub would work wonders, but in his current sodden state, the thought of water abhorred him. He might only take basin baths for the rest of his life after this morning's dousing.

Hot breakfast smells came from the kitchen and dining room, where his landlady reigned supreme. But Daniel didn't take his meals there. His schedule was so unpredictable, he had opted not to include board with his rooms and took his meals where he could find them. There were some good vendors operating carts in the neighborhood. Once he was changed and warmed, he would scare up a bit of breakfast before returning to Bow Street.

He made it to his second-story rooms without encountering another boarder, and once inside, closed the door and leaned back against it, eyes shut.

Someone had tried to kill him. Someone had lured him to the mill with the intent of murdering him.

Which meant he must be close to finding out the answers to his case, and that person was getting nervous.

What had the killer hoped to accomplish by ending Daniel's life? Ed knew about the note. If Daniel had indeed perished on the waterwheel, it would not have been considered an accident. Too bad Cadogan hadn't been able to give a better description of the man he'd seen running away from the mill. Average in height and build, dark jacket, dark hat.

But this particular killer didn't seem concerned about concealing his actions. Montgomery had been shot in the head. There had been no attempt to hide the body or make it appear accidental or even a suicide. The weapon was missing, and Montgomery had been shot from a distance.

The second murder, the anarchist Pietro Todisco, had occurred in the mill as well, in the manager's office, but this time the murder weapon lay beside the body.

Daniel straightened, letting the blanket drop from his shoulders onto the floor. If it had not been for Cadogan, he would have perished, trapped in the wash behind the mighty wheel.

For a long moment he considered whether the cab driver might have been the one to push him, but he discarded the notion. If Cadogan had wanted him dead, he had only to leave him where he was a few more moments. Daniel would not have had the strength to haul himself to the walkway alone, nor in his battered state would he have survived long if he had been able to ride the wheel all the way over to be deposited into the river. Cadogan had risked falling into the water himself and suffering the same fate as Daniel.

When all this was over, Daniel would have to find a way of expressing his thanks. And perhaps he'd take a closer look into Cadogan's life. Who was he, how had he come to be a cab driver in London, and why was he always to hand when needed? If a man saved your life, it behooved you to find out more about him, didn't it?

Peeling off his wet garments, he winced with every movement. His shirt was shredded. He threw it aside. Standing before the mirror hanging over his bureau, he examined the reddening marks on his shoulders and chest. When he turned to look over his shoulder, he grimaced. His left side had taken the brunt of the scraping and bouncing along the water race. Had they paved it with jagged boulders?

Once toweled off and wearing clean clothes, he combed his hair and returned his personal items to his pockets. Except his watch, which had stopped working at precisely 6:21 this morning. Could it be salvaged if he took it to a watchmaker? A large dent marred the case, and the crystal bore a spider's web of cracks. He tossed it onto the bureau to think about later. For now, he needed to get to Bow Street. To go back to the beginning and examine the evidence.

As he reached for the knob, he glanced at the calendar hanging beside the door.

The twentieth. Of March.

March twentieth?

His birthday.

Today he was twenty-five years old. This was it. His release day. The day his patronage stopped and he was finally his own man.

Which also meant he had an appointment at the solicitors' office. What time was it?

In spite of the soreness, he hurried down the stairs to check the case clock in the hall. Half-eight. He still had time. How could he have forgotten? He'd received the summons days ago and had circled it in his mind for much longer.

His sore muscles and the state of his murder investigation aside, his spirit lightened. Perhaps today he would get some long-sought answers, and even if not, he would be his own man by day's end.

Breakfast was a hurried cup of coffee and a hot meat pie from the cart on the corner. Then he hailed a cab. Too bad Cadogan wasn't here this time.

"Hurry," he told the driver as he took a seat. The appointment was set for nine o'clock.

Surprisingly, after waiting for this day for thirteen long years, he felt calm. Perhaps it was the lack of sleep and the strain of the early hours, but his mind was at peace.

The offices of Coles, Franks & Moody were unobtrusive from the outside, a redbrick building in a forest of redbrick buildings, but once inside, the opulent furnishings told the true tale.

The clerk knew and expected Daniel, taking his hat and gloves and leading him into Mr. Coles's office.

Daniel stopped on the threshold. The clerk had made a mistake. Mr. Coles was not alone.

"I beg your pardon. I will wait in the front room." He started to back out, but Mr. Coles rose.

"No, no. Come in. We've been waiting for you."

The Duke of Haverly nodded from his chair. "Good morning, Mr. Swann."

"Your Grace." Why was he here? Was it a coincidence? Or did he know something about Daniel's guardianship? Surely the duke could not be his mysterious patron, could he? Daniel had wondered over the past few weeks, but each time had discarded the notion.

"I wish you birthday greetings." The duke waved him to the other chair while Mr. Coles resumed his seat.

Daniel took his time lowering himself into the chair, stifling a wince as his muscles protested.

Coles wore a pair of spectacles with squarish frames, and his grizzled hair defied whatever pomade had been applied. He scooted together a few papers and tapped them into a neat pile in the center of the blotter.

"Yes, yes, birthday felicitations. Twenty-five now." He pursed his lips and narrowed his eyes, assessing Daniel. "Have you had an altercation? The side of your jaw is bruised."

"Thank you. No. At least not with a person. I did have a bit of a mishap while investigating a case, but it's nothing to worry about. I'll be more careful next time."

The solicitor seemed satisfied with the explanation, but Daniel could feel the duke's eyes on him.

"Hmm. Now, let's see about winding up this patronage, shall we? I was instructed by your patron to find a respected nobleman who could assist and advise you once the patronage ended, and when I asked His Grace if he knew of someone, the duke was generous enough to volunteer his services."

Daniel glanced at Haverly. A tidy enough offer, since the man was now his supervisor in the agency.

"First, the final installment of your allowance has been paid. And it is a generous one. Five thousand pounds, deposited in an account at the Bank of England for you."

Five thousand pounds? That was many times his quarterly allotment.

Haverly stifled a noise, putting the side of his finger across his lips as if trying to hide a smile, and Daniel realized his mouth was open like a bream's.

Coles read on. "There will be one final delivery of clothing, and the accounts opened for you at the various vendors will be closed. If you wish to continue having your garments made at these establishments, you will need to open new accounts for yourself. After today all receipts received at these offices will be payable by you."

Fair enough.

"The lease for your lodgings is paid through the end of the month."

He would have to find a new place, though with five thousand pounds in the bank, he could perhaps take a bit more time.

"Finally, your patron insists that you do nothing to attempt to discover his identity. Should you do so, you will be in violation of the original agreement, and every expense that has been paid by your patron on your behalf for the last thirteen years will be placed upon your mother and yourself for repayment."

Daniel sat up straight, pain from his injuries shooting through him. "That was never a stipulation in the arrangement."

"I'm afraid it was, though it was not revealed to you until now. Your mother was made aware of this clause at the outset, and she agreed to it."

So any plan to find out the identity of the man once the patronage ended flew out the window.

"What about the restriction of contacting my mother or speaking to her? Is that still in place?" And if it was lifted, what would he do about it? Resentment still burned at the way she had cut him out of her life. For all he knew, the clause about having no contact with her had been initiated at her request.

"It will be at her discretion whether she speaks with you."

"She must know who my so-called benefactor is, mustn't she?"

"I am not permitted to speak of who knows and who does not."

"Are you aware of his identity, Your Grace?"

Haverly leaned forward. "Daniel, I will ask you to have patience. In time, the truth will come out, I am certain. Your patron has chosen not to reveal himself, and he has forbidden anyone to search for him. At any rate, what difference does it make now? You have all kept your parts of the bargain. He has completed your education and set you up in the vocation of your choice. Your mother turned over all responsibility for your upbringing into the hands of your benefactor, you have matriculated, and you have been a model ward."

Daniel sat back in the leather chair, gripping the arms. How could he resign himself to not knowing? The detective in him wanted to solve the mystery, the agent in him wanted to break into Coles, Franks & Moody in the dead of night and go through their files, and the man in him wanted to know who had plucked him from his home, and moreover, who had fathered him.

Could he force his mother to tell him? No, because to do so would be to assume the entire debt for his education and provision for the past thirteen years. He could not begin to ascertain how much his education and outfitting had cost.

Haverly said the truth would come out eventually, but what if it never did? Could he be content with never knowing?

This meeting had been unsatisfactory, to his way of thinking. He had no answers, and he was still both fatherless and for all practical intents, motherless.

Wasn't there a Bible verse about God being a father to the fatherless? That hadn't been Daniel's experience. He'd been different since the moment he was born, somebody's natural son, unclaimed and unknown by his father. He'd been abandoned by his mother, forced out of her life by someone he didn't even know. That didn't seem to add up to a loving heavenly Father who had stepped into the gaps left in his life.

Mr. Coles again tapped the papers on his desk together. "You have been greatly blessed to have such a patron. If you had not, imagine where you would be now. A farm servant perhaps, or a groom in a stable? You certainly wouldn't have the education or the finances you have now. With five thousand in the bank, you could leave Bow Street and invest in a new business for yourself. Yes, blessed indeed."

Yes, the lawyer might consider Daniel had several debits on that side of the ledger, but what Daniel didn't have was love. Advantages such as an Oxford degree or a wardrobe of fine clothes or an address in a genteel part of London were no substitute for the love of a family.

Daniel dragged himself up the stairs to his rooms as the lamplighters were going about their business. What a ridiculously long day. He'd called in at Bow Street and had a quick word with Ed before tracking down Rhynwick Davies through Mr. Hoffman. The young scientist had been bewildered by the message that had been sent in his name.

The night watchman at the mill had been run to earth, and the reason for his absence was explained the moment Daniel called at his house. A harried woman with a stained apron opened the door a crack.

"He's sleeping."

"I must see him."

"Won't do you no good. He's passed out. Got drunk as a lord last night, he did."

"When last night? He was supposed to be on watch at the Montgomery Mill."

"I dunno. He's got a terrible thirst for gin, and someone left two bottles of the stuff inside the mill with his name on it. He drank most of one at the mill, then staggered home with the other. It were gone by sunup, and he's been laid on the bed snorin' ever since. Won't be hisself for hours, and then he'll be that mad and sick. I think I'll go to Mother's for a few days. He's a terrible one when he's been drinking."

"Who knew your husband liked to drink?" Someone had baited their trap effectively.

She shrugged her narrow shoulders. "Who didn't? Night watchman was the only job he could get, and now he won't even have that. The magistrate said if he drank on the job again, he'd be out of work before he could draw another cork. Dunno what we'll do now." Her eyes were resigned, as if she'd seen too much, endured too much, to have hope any longer.

Now Daniel entered his lodgings and went straight to the bedroom. He'd like nothing more than to burrow into the bed and fall into a deep sleep, but as sore as he was, he eased down atop the coverlet fully clothed, trying to find a place to lie that wouldn't hurt.

His mind was abuzz even as his body cried out for rest.

Five thousand pounds.

Someone tried to kill me.

No more patronage.

If Cadogan hadn't come when he did, I would be dead.

I am free to speak to my mother if she so desires, but she cannot tell me what I want to know.

How am I going to find the killer?

The kiss . . .

Sleep closed in, and his body relaxed.

Until a knock sounded at the door.

He jolted, jarring his aching muscles. With a groan he pushed himself up and tottered through to the sitting room.

Duke Heinrich von Lowe stood on the sill. His smile faded as he took in Daniel's bruised face.

"Vat has happened to you?" His accent thickened as his brows came down.

"It's nothing. A bit of an argument with a piece of equipment. I'm quite fine." He opened the door wider. "Do come in."

The duke had never visited Daniel's lodgings before. He put his hands behind his back, surveying the room. A pair of black leather chairs flanked a fireplace, and a thick rug covered the floor. Heavy drapes bracketed a pair of tall windows, and the woodwork gleamed with beeswax and polishing. Daniel's small library of treasured books graced one bookshelf, with an inlaid tea table close to hand.

"Very nice. Have you lived here long?"

"Three years. I moved in after I finished university. It is a few minutes' walk to work." He beckoned the duke to sit.

"*Danke*, no. I only wanted to come tell you that I have been called back to my homeland and will be leaving at the end of this month. You have been a good friend to me, and I am thankful. This is my first diplomatic mission for my country, and I was warned again and again that I must not trust anyone. Everyone would have their own . . . agenda? Is that the word? And they would conceal it from me if they could. I was to watch and observe and gather information while my superiors performed the actual negotiations."

Not unlike the work Daniel had undertaken for Haverly, watching and gathering information. "Tiring work, I imagine, suspecting that everyone is hiding things from you for their own reasons."

"Yes. Much like being a detective, do you not think? But I never felt that with you. You have been open and honest with me, and I wish to be the same with you." He went to stand before one window, looking out on the street below. "I have wondered for some time whether you had feelings for Lady Juliette. I know you are from far different classes and that a future between you is not possible, but that does not stop the heart from wanting to bridge that gap."

Daniel's collar tightened, and his breath caught short. He did not have feelings for Juliette. He had regard, respect, and a certain rapport, but nothing deeper.

Liar.

"It is because of this . . . *tendre* . . . I have sensed and the friendship we have that I felt it only right that I tell you I have made my intentions known to Lady Juliette. I, too, harbor strong feelings for the lady, and while I cannot formally ask for her hand with her parents away, I did inform her of my intention to propose once the formalities have been observed. I will travel home, but at the first opportunity I will return to England, hopefully with my family, to make official my proposal of marriage."

Daniel felt as if he were back on the waterwheel, turning and churning.

Everything was slipping away. His patronage, that he hadn't even wanted but had grown accustomed to living with, had now ended. If he couldn't solve Montgomery's murder, and without his patron's backing, Sir Michael would terminate his employment, most likely at the end of the month.

And now Juliette. She would marry Heinrich and move to his homeland, and he would never see her again.

Heinrich had been correct. Daniel had been harboring feelings for Juliette, else why would the thought of her leaving cause him to be so bereft? The pain in his chest was greater than the aches and bruises in his body.

"I wish you every happiness. You will make a fine husband for Lady Juliette." He said the right words, with the right inflection, but they were all wrong.

Heinrich held out his hand, and Daniel shook it. "You are a good man, Herr Swann. I hope to meet you again."

The duke took his leave, and Daniel sank into one of the chairs, putting his head in his hands.

Another knock on the door. Had Heinrich returned?

Ed Beck stood in the hallway. Vauxhall Gardens had less traffic on a Saturday night.

"Come in." Daniel held the door open. "What's wrong?"

"Thought I would call in on my way home. There have been some developments. A messenger from St. Bart's came to Bow Street. The doctor sent round that a prowler was chased off the property not an hour ago. A nurse spotted him creeping down the hall toward the ward where our mill manager, Mr. Coombe, is being cared for, and she raised the alarm. The prowler eluded the night watchman."

Daniel was fully awake and focused. "Do you think he was after Mr. Coombe? To finish off what the mill explosion couldn't?"

"It's possible, and if that is the case, then the killer must fear Mr. Coombe can identify him. Otherwise, why bother trying to kill a man who most likely will not survive? The doctor thinks it is a miracle he's hung on this long."

"Our killer has proven he will take risks. He shot Mr. Montgomery at his place of business with workers about. He killed the anarchist Pietro Todisco, probably to avoid being discovered in the mill at night—though what our killer was looking for, I cannot imagine. Did the anarchist know something, or was he in the wrong place at the wrong time? And the killer lured me to the mill to try to murder me and nearly accomplished the job."

Daniel probed his sore jaw with a careful finger. Ed was the only one he had told about his near demise. "Desperate men do desperate things. I have to wonder what the motive is, what secret he is willing to kill for to protect."

"At the moment, our greater concern should be to guard Mr. Coombe. I think we should set our own watch rather than rely on the hospital personnel to guard him."

"Agreed. And I know just the man for the task."

Ed accompanied him to Owen Wilkinson's residence. Daniel had not known where Owen lived, but the closer they rode to his home, the worse Daniel felt. Ed had hailed a carriage, and they had ridden across the river to the south side and into a cramped, crowded, poor neighborhood. When the vehicle stopped, they were still several blocks from their destination, but the driver refused to go any farther.

"How does Owen get to work each day?" Daniel asked. They were miles from Bow Street.

"Walks. And he's the first to arrive and often the last to go home."

Daniel's spirits sank lower. He had rarely had a kind word for the office boy, responding in kind to the sarcasm and resentment that came his way.

Thankful that Ed carried a lantern, Daniel followed down a narrow path that opened onto a small square. A well stood in the middle of the square, and small houses stood cheek by jowl around it.

"This is the one." Ed knocked on a water-warped door.

Owen opened it cautiously, and his eyes widened. "Mr. Beck. Is something wrong?"

"Nay, lad. Might we come inside for a bit?"

Slowly, as if he would have preferred them not to have come, Owen opened the door wide enough for them to enter the single small room. The flue must not draw properly, because a smoky haze hung in the room. The fire barely warmed one corner.

A woman sat in a creaking rocker, a child of perhaps two years in her lap, another leaning against her side, his head coming to about her shoulder. A girl of about six or seven huddled on a pallet, a shawl drawn over her head, and a boy of ten or so sat beside her. A table took up the center of the room, and a small shelf of crockery was all the kitchen the abode could boast. Two pallets on the floor and a rope-strung bed in one corner. And just the one chair.

Shame licked at Daniel. And a feeling of kinship. The lodgings he had shared with his mother when he was small had resembled this level of poverty.

Owen stared at him, defiance in his stance, daring him to say something. "This is my mother. Mum, these are two of the men I work with at Bow Street. Mr. Beck and Mr. Swann."

A single room, five children, one woman. No father?

"We've got a job for you. It pays extra since it's outside your normal duties." Daniel decided then and there he would pay the boy out of his own pocket if need be. "We need a guard for a patient at St. Bart's. It would mean working through the night. I'll make it right with Sir Michael, but the man needs a guard."

Owen reached for his coat. "Do I start tonight?"

Chapter 16

"SURELY ALONZO WILL RETURN NOW. If the urgency remains at their property in the Caribbean, he can hire a manager to take care of it. He's been gone a week, and it seems forever." Agatha linked her arm through Juliette's as they strolled through Hyde Park. Behind them, Agatha's maid walked at a discreet distance, providing proper chaperonage.

It was too early for much activity in the park, with the peak time of five in the afternoon still hours ahead. For now, they had the gravel path mostly to themselves, only occasionally passing a nurse taking an infant for an outing to get some air, or a lady's maid hurrying through the park on some errand for her mistress.

Crisp sunny air streamed through the branches of the trees, where tight buds formed pale-green knots on the limbs. Flowers pushed brave tendrils up through the earth along the path. Hopefully, no frost would kill the plants before the cheerful yellow blooms appeared.

"If he's somewhere in the middle of the Atlantic, he will not know what has happened until he makes landfall, and then not until another ship has followed with the news. It will be weeks, at best, before he can return." Juliette hated to dash her friend's hopes, but a swift return of her fiancé seemed unlikely.

Agatha sighed. "I suppose you're right, but I still cannot fathom why Alonzo sent no word that he was leaving. It must have been something frightfully urgent that took him away. His grandfather no doubt had a duty for him to perform that could not wait. I still don't know why he didn't come to see me first, or at least send along a letter. He must know I would be fretting."

"I don't know why he did not leave word. As you say, it must have been an urgent errand for him to leave so abruptly. And now . . ."

"This will be such a sorrowful blow to poor Alonzo. He cared a great deal for his grandfather, in spite of the old earl being so difficult to get on with." Agatha blinked. "He will feel such sorrow that he wasn't there at the end, and he will not be at the burial services. Still, perhaps when Alonzo arrives back in England and we are reunited, our mutual sorrow will draw us closer together."

"Are you certain he means to return?" Juliette put the question gently.

"Of course." Agatha was undaunted. "He's the new Earl of Rotherhide. He has responsibilities here now. And he has a responsibility to me. He will honor his promise to marry me, I will become his countess, and that will be the end of it."

Agatha seemed so certain of Alonzo's continued affection for her and his follow-through on the promise he had made to her. A promise that had not been publicly announced but enough people knew about to make it binding. Yet he had left England without so much as a word to Agatha about his departure or the length of his time away.

What if he'd left in order to get out of his promise? What if he never meant to return? How would Agatha cope? Would it damage her reputation? Juliette had heard of some girls, with their engagements broken, who could not find another suitor. Gentlemen wondered what was wrong with them that their first fiancés had broken things off. Agatha's self-confidence had always been a fragile thing, but under Alonzo's attention, she had blossomed. Would she suffer a setback if Alonzo proved faithless? Would Agatha have to sue for breach of promise to salvage her reputation? Juliette's heart ached for her friend's predicament, and she didn't know how best to help her.

"I had my own bit of romantic entanglement." Juliette felt she had to tell someone, and with her parents not due to return until the end of the month, she needed to confide in her best friend. Perhaps the subject would also distract Agatha for a time. "I had a visit from Duke Heinrich."

Agatha stopped, her eyes widening. Since their arms were linked, Juliette had to stop too.

"You didn't."

Juliette tried to keep her voice nonchalant. "Yes, he came round yesterday morning very early. We were still at the breakfast table when he called."

"What did he want at that hour?"

"He is being summoned back to his home very soon, and he did not want to leave London without telling me his plans. He did not want me to hear the news from someone else. Also, he intends to make his trip to the Continent short, return to England at the first opportunity, and speak with my father. He intends to make a formal proposal of marriage to me at that time."

Agatha gripped Juliette's arm. "That's practically a declaration right there. Are you overjoyed? He is the catch of the Season. Oh, this is wonderful news. Tell me you are overjoyed."

"Overjoyed?" No, she could not say that. She did feel regard for Heinrich, but was that enough? Not to mention . . . "I am not certain how I feel about it. It is an honor, and more than one young lady has had her eye on him this Season."

"Wait. If you marry him, does that mean you will live in Brandenburg?" Agatha's face fell. "Of course it does. When will I see you? Will you return to England for visits? Oh, I want to be happy for you, but I don't want you to leave me."

"You're getting well ahead of things. He has not formally requested my hand, my father has not given his permission, nor have I accepted his proposal. He merely made his intentions known because he must leave so soon."

"But he will return. And of course you will accept his offer, and you will have a sensational wedding. Everyone who is anyone will attend, and it will be the talk of the year." Agatha's eyes brightened. "Think of the wedding breakfast and the gifts, and your trousseau. How much fun we will have shopping for things for your new house. You will be a beautiful bride."

It was almost like they were little girls once more, sharing a room at the academy, lying awake at night dreaming about what their lives would be when they grew up, the people they would meet, the parties they would attend, the men with whom they would fall in love. But they were no longer little girls. As adults, they both knew that relationships were not as tidy as their adolescent dreams. Real emotions were far more complicated.

You do not love Heinrich. You like and admire him, but there is another who is dangerously close to having your heart.

She must keep a level head. She must not make any hasty decisions. "Time will tell. A lot can happen between now and his return to England. What if his family has another bride chosen for him, one from his own country? What if I find someone else in the meantime?"

Though she had shared about Heinrich to Agatha, she could not bear to share what had passed between her and Daniel. The kiss that had dominated her mind and heart since the instant it happened. That moment was too precious, too tender, too important to share. She held it close, cherishing it, puzzling over it, and reliving it.

The feelings she had discovered for Daniel Swann made anything she might feel for Heinrich pale into insignificance. Under those conditions, she could not possibly marry the German duke, could she?

How she wished her parents would return quickly. She would appreciate their guidance. While marriage to Daniel Swann was outside the realm of possibility, if she loved him, marriage to anyone else would be untenable.

She walked on, and Agatha kept step. "I pray you are right and that Alonzo returns quickly to take up his title and to marry you. You are very loyal, and I hope your loyalty is rewarded. And I am proud of the way you have been so brave in the wake of your father's death."

Agatha nodded her certainty. "I do not feel particularly brave, but I am sure of Alonzo. As for dealing with things concerning my father,

I have had many people helping me. At the urging of my father's accountant, Mr. Earnshaw, I gave the approval to begin repairs on the mill. He says if I have it repaired, I can either continue to run it myself with a new manager, or I can sell it. There is a buyer interested already. Sadly, I am told the former manager, Mr. Coombe, is still in hospital, and though he is showing signs of awakening, there is little chance of a full recovery or his being able to resume his duties at the mill."

"Perhaps you will make some provision for him and his family?" Juliette asked as they neared the end of the path.

"Oh yes. That is already being taken care of. It was Mr. Earnshaw's suggestion as well. I don't know what I would have done without Mr. Earnshaw. He's helped me understand the extent of my father's holdings, and he's taken on so much, seeing to the bills and making certain employees are paid. He's been so helpful. He tells me not to worry about a thing. He's got it all under control. His only complaint is that so many of my father's papers are still at Bow Street. He's asked several times if I can get them for him."

"I'm sure Mr. Swann will not keep them longer than necessary. And I'm glad you have a professional to aid you. I wouldn't know the first thing about managing my father's holdings. I'm not even certain what they are beyond Heild House and the estate. Though since the title would pass to Uncle Bertie, I wouldn't have to manage any of those things."

A chill breeze scudded the dry grass along the path. A pair of young gentlemen on horseback galloped toward them, slowing their mounts to a walk, grinning and touching their hat brims as they passed. They certainly were not bashful in their bold looks, and Juliette merely inclined her head and walked on. Brash in the extreme. Daniel would never behave in such a manner.

Agatha lowered her chin and walked more quickly, and when the riders were out of earshot, asked, "Have you heard anything more from Mr. Swann?"

"Your pardon?" Juliette hadn't said her comment about Daniel aloud, had she? The thought brought a tinge of heat to her cheeks.

"About the book we found at the bank. Has Mr. Swann read it? Did it help at all in the investigation?"

Relief pushed the air out of Juliette's lungs. "I have not heard anything regarding your father's journal. If I see Mr. Swann anytime soon, I will ask."

"I'd like to have it back. I wasn't ready to read it when we found it, but I think I am now. I feel reading my father's thoughts in his own hand might be comforting. I mentioned the book to Mr. Earnshaw and that we had retrieved it from the bank vault. He was most surprised to find my father kept a journal. No previous volumes were found amongst his papers, so the diary must have been a new habit? Perhaps I will send a note around to Bow Street to see if Mr. Swann has finished with it."

"I could go on your behalf, if you wish. After all, I delivered the book in the first place. I could retrieve it for you. It would be no trouble." And possibly she would see Daniel once more. Her heart thrummed even as her emotions waffled. Would Daniel be businesslike, or would he treat her differently? She both dreaded and anticipated seeing him, and she wanted it over, that first meeting after sharing such an explosive kiss.

And she wanted to explore her newly discovered feelings for him, to see whether they were merely girlish fantasies brought on by a few moments outside a chandler's shop and not real.

Though if they were real, what could she do about them?

⁂

"This is ridiculous." Daniel had barely made it through the Bow Street door when he was handed a summons. "My life is my own. I thought I was finished with such demands."

The envelope bore the mark of Coles, Franks & Moody, and the note—in the strongest terms possible—requested his attendance at their offices at nine o'clock sharp that morning. How was he supposed to investigate a murder when he was forced to spend so much time sitting in a law office?

Thoughts of ignoring the summons flickered through his mind even as he discarded them. He would have to go, for it must have something to do with the patronage, or perhaps with his mother's future.

"Swann." Thomas Fyfe stopped by his desk. "Sir Michael is simmering away at the mess you've made of the interrogation room by his office. Papers and books and the whole thing smelling of charcoal. He wants it cleaned up before day's end, and he wants a report from you on the progress of your investigation into the Montgomery murder. Also, Ed said to tell you he's relieving Wilkinson at St. Bart's for a few hours, but you're going to have to work out some sort of timetable, because they can't keep a guard on indefinitely. Does any of that make sense? I should have written it down. And I'm not a messenger service, so sort out your own communications, right?" He poked the air with the stem of his pipe, but he also winked to show he was in jest.

"Thank you. That makes excellent sense, and I appreciate your acting as the go-between."

Returning to his desk, Daniel rubbed his palm on the back of his neck. A report to Sir Michael. Daniel had nothing to report, except that he'd ruled out every suspect thus far.

Mrs. Fairchild, who had been after Montgomery's money but had been pawning her jewels at the time of the murder.

Mr. Carlyle, who had challenged Montgomery to a duel because he suspected his wife of betraying her marriage vows, had indeed shown up at the agreed-upon dueling ground the following day only to be denied satisfaction because the object of his wrath had already been murdered.

Mr. Finch, who had threatened to blow up the mill but in fact had not because he was plotting another bit of industrial sabotage at the time.

Even Montgomery's soon-to-be son-in-law, Alonzo Darby, who had mysteriously absconded to the West Indies, had nothing sinister in his life to indicate he had been involved in the killing.

Daniel could only imagine how a report filled with such negative results would be received by Sir Michael. Not only would he take control of the investigation away and give it to another detective, as he had wanted to do in the first place, but now, since Daniel's patronage had come to an end, he would toss Daniel out of Bow Street on his soon-to-be-unemployed trousers' seat.

But before all that could happen, Daniel must get to the solicitors' office and wind up whatever this meeting was about.

Cadogan's cab stood at the curb, and before he climbed aboard, Daniel reached up to shake the man's hand. "I don't think I thanked you for saving my life. If you hadn't been there and willing to risk your safety, I'd have drowned."

The jarvey leaned over and clasped Daniel's hand firmly. "Couldn't leave you down there, could I? Wouldn't be the Christian thing to do."

Daniel nodded, lowering his arm and trying not to wince. This morning he was, if anything, even more sore. Additional bruises had developed overnight, and everything ached. He gave Cadogan the destination and climbed aboard like an octogenarian.

He leaned back against the squabs, considering how he might properly thank Cadogan for saving his life. When he had the time, he would have to rectify that situation.

The jarvey had him at the law office with a few minutes to spare, but as Daniel was led down the hallway, the clerk did not stop at any individual solicitor's office. Instead, they went to the far end of the passageway, and he was shown into a large room with a long table. Tall-backed leather chairs flanked the table, and some were occupied.

All three of the partners had seats, as well as the Duke of Haverly, who barely glanced up at Daniel, giving the smallest nod. He wore a grim expression, and Daniel's skin prickled.

Another man sat in a chair along the wall, his hat in his lap. He looked familiar to Daniel, and it took him a moment to put a name to the face. Mr. Cooper, the elderly valet at Lockewood, the Earl of Rotherhide's house.

Odd. Daniel could not think why he had been summoned to a meeting that included a valet and the head of British intelligence.

The old man's mouth opened, and his hand trembled as he raised it to his cheek. He studied Daniel as if he couldn't place him either.

Daniel shrugged and rounded the table to see two women seated in the high-backed chairs. The first one he didn't know, but the second stopped him cold.

Mrs. Dunstan.

Housekeeper to the Thorndikes.

Agent for the Crown.

His estranged mother.

The familiar feelings of aching loneliness and abandonment that he had carried with him since the moment he had been thrown out of her house swamped him, but he thrust it away. He was no longer that scared, helpless little boy. He was a man. A man with means, skills, and a future. He no longer answered to a mysterious patron, nor the lawyers who served him, and he would not be made to feel like a discarded child.

What was she doing here? She glanced up at him, her eyes stricken, before looking away. Why did he feel most in the room knew something he did not?

"Do sit down, Mr. Swann. Now that you're here, we can get started." Mr. Moody flicked his fingers toward an empty chair.

Mr. Franks mopped his brow with a handkerchief, and Mr. Coles nodded to the clerk to close the door.

Daniel took the chair indicated, but he turned it slightly so Mrs. Dunstan would not be in his eye line. His mind raced like a leaf on a breeze, scudding about, flipping and tossing with no ability to control its movement.

What was she doing here? How did it involve Haverly? Was this a mission, and if so, why hold the briefing at a law office? Who was the other woman? An agent? Why was the valet here? Was he also an agent?

Daniel wanted some answers. His hands fisted on his thighs beneath the polished tabletop.

Mr. Moody cleared his throat. "Thank you all for attending. This meeting is for the purpose of reading the last will and testament of John David Darby, Seventh Earl of Rotherhide."

Daniel's gaze flicked to Haverly. Not an assignment for the Crown. But why include Daniel for the reading of a will? He'd met the earl only once, briefly, just over a week ago. He had read of the old man's passing in the newspaper and had idly wondered when his grandson would return, but beyond that he'd given the matter no thought.

"We, the lawyers at Coles, Franks & Moody, have been the legal advisers to the House of Rotherhide for nearly two decades, and as such have held the certified will and testament of the seventh earl since we aided him in drafting it years ago. Over those years he has made provisos and addenda and has completely redrafted the document twice. In the past forty-eight hours, since the earl's passing, we have come into possession of a final codicil to his will that involves each of you here."

Again Daniel was stunned. How could he figure into the will of a stranger, be he earl or beggar?

"Mr. Cooper, long the faithful servant of his lordship, has delivered the codicil, which is, in fact, a deathbed confession of a most serious nature. Mr. Cooper is here to testify that he took down in his own hand the document provided six months ago when his employer first took ill and before his mind began to fade, and that the earl's physician, one Dr. Plimpton, witnessed the document with his own signature."

The old valet nodded, his eyes grieved. Poor old fellow. He'd served the earl a long time. Would the new one have a place for an old retainer like Cooper, or would he be swept out to a pension when the new earl took up residence?

"I shall now read the codicil, which will detail some facts hitherto unknown. Be advised that the information laid out here as facts will have to be thoroughly researched and verified before the earl's wishes can be carried out, but rest assured, they will be investigated and every pain taken to ensure they are true before moving on."

Sounds like they suspected the old earl may have been dotty even a few months ago when he had the codicil written. Daniel relaxed. This clearly had nothing to do with him. He must have been called here as an officer of the magistrate's court. Perhaps he would be asked to investigate whatever claims were in the documents.

Though what this could have to do with his mother was still a puzzle.

"We wish Mr. Alonzo Darby could be here, but we are informed that he is currently out of the country. We've dispatched a courier on a fast ship to apprise him of today's matters and to request he return to England as quickly as possible. His mother, Viscountess Coatsworth, who is also named in the codicil, will stand in as his representative. We would have delayed this meeting if we could, but circumstances made it necessary to continue, even in the absence of the heir presumptive."

Haverly's head came up, and he stared at Mr. Moody. Daniel's senses heightened. What had the lawyer said that caused such a reaction?

"First, the codicil," Moody said.

"'I, John David Darby, Seventh Earl of Rotherhide,'" he read, "'being of sound mind and ailing body, wish to set the record straight, to confess the terrible wrong I have done, and to beg the forgiveness of all those affected and Almighty God.

"'In the year 1790, my son, Alfred Alonzo Darby, then aged twenty, against my express and implied wishes, eloped with one Catherine Swann, scullery maid, aged sixteen years. Though my men gave chase to try to forestall the nuptials, they were not in time to prevent the marriage of my son and our scullery maid over the border in Scotland.'"

Roaring began in Daniel's ears, blocking out any other sound.

Catherine Swann.

Scullery maid.

His mother.

His chair swiveled, and he locked eyes with her.

Those eyes pleaded with him . . . for what? Mercy? Understanding?

Her bottom lip had disappeared, and her fingers gripped each other at her breast.

She had eloped with a viscount? Why had she kept such a thing from him?

"'My men brought the couple back to Lockewood, and there, after I had the maid shut up in her room with a guard on the door, I railed against my son. How dare he defy me like this? I would not have it. A mere maid as his viscountess? We would be laughingstocks. I forbade it. I may have had no choice in his inheriting the title, but I would take every last shilling away from him. I would spend it, give it away, or burn it in my own fireplace before I would see a farthing of it go to a scullery maid. My son, who had always been weak, eventually saw reason. I convinced him to have the marriage annulled. I agreed to find a new place of employment for the girl, and as quickly as possible, Alfred would marry a woman of my choosing.'"

Mr. Moody looked up from the papers before him and made eye contact with the other woman in the room, whose face had gone paste white. Her lips were a bloodless straight line, and cords appeared in her thin neck as her jaw tightened.

The lawyer looked down again, his jowls moving as he swallowed.

"'I contracted with my friend Lord Cutshall that my son would marry his daughter, Miss Lucy Cutshall, with all haste in a very public wedding. Lord Cutshall knew nothing of the first marriage, and my son agreed to keep it from his new bride as well.'"

Daniel's hands hurt, and he glanced down to see he was gripping the arms of his chair until his knuckles turned white.

"Nearly thirteen years after these events, when Alfred had been married and produced an heir, one Alonzo John Darby, my son was thrown from his horse during a hunt. He was brought back to Lockewood, and the doctor said he was not expected to live through the night. At his bedside, I and my valet, Cooper, heard the dying confession of my son, and he revealed his terrible secret.'"

Tension flowed through the listeners, and Daniel's chest tightened until he could barely breathe.

"'My son, who had never shown any initiative beyond that one wild hair to elope with a servant girl, who had never stood up to me before or since that day when he acceded to my wishes to have his first marriage annulled and the woman banished from his life, had been lying to me for thirteen years.

"'He confessed that he had never had his first marriage annulled at all. He had gone to London, found a forger, and had annulment papers drawn up.'"

The air disappeared from the room. Several people, his mother included, gasped.

The viscountess bolted to her feet. "No. That's a lie. There is no truth to any of this." And quick as that, she fainted, sliding to the floor.

Haverly and Daniel reached her first, lifting her to the chair. The lawyers were all on their feet, milling, opening the door, calling for tea, shouting for smelling salts, and generally adding to the hubbub without doing anything constructive.

"Chafe her hands," Haverly ordered. "Ma'am, can you hear me?"

Daniel gently rubbed the woman's fingers between his, noting their icy coldness with detachment. He glanced over his shoulder at his mother, who sat as if made of stone, except for a pair of tears that overflowed her lashes and tumbled down her cheeks.

The viscountess stirred, moaning and flickering her eyes. When she took stock of where she was, she stiffened, jerked her hands away, and declared, "This is all a lie. I will not let you slander my late husband's name."

"Madam, get hold of yourself." The duke gave her a stern look. "We are here to listen, to assess, and then decide upon a plan of action. If you cannot compose yourself, you will be removed from the room, and someone will tell you what was determined."

His bracing tone seemed to grab her attention. Two spots of red suffused her ashy cheeks, and she glared at him. "I will not be shunted away. I demand to hear the rest of it so it may be refuted wholeheartedly."

"Very well." Haverly reached for the cup of tea the clerk had rushed into the room and handed it to the viscountess. "Drink this."

Everyone resumed their seats, and Mr. Moody took a moment to gather his thoughts and find his place once more. Daniel wanted to snatch the papers from the older gentleman's hands and read them himself.

Moody picked up the narrative. "'When my son made his confession, I was in a rage. I knew I must never tell a soul, and I swore Mr. Cooper to secrecy as well. My son left this world that very night, with his conscience purged of his secret, but mine as heavy as lead. For several weeks I did nothing. If I told no one, then the secret would remain buried. My daughter-in-law and her son, Alonzo, would be free of any stain. Alonzo would be my heir.

"'And yet somewhere out there was my son's true wife, treated shamefully by both of us. I had found her a position at the estate of a friend—had, in fact, paid handsomely for him to employ her for at least five years without question.

"'At last I could stand it no longer. I had to know if she was well. I made up my mind to, through my solicitors, ask after her welfare and perhaps provide a little something for her. When they located her, now in a different man's employ on another estate, they brought word that she had a child. A son.'"

A shaft of doubt thrust through Daniel's chest. He locked eyes with his mother, and again hers pleaded for understanding. After she had been rejected by her newlywed husband, she had become pregnant by another man? Or . . .

"Go on," Haverly ordered the lawyer. "Finish it."

"Yes, Your Grace." Moody nodded. "I'm nearly done."

Daniel didn't know if he wanted to hear it.

"'The boy was twelve, and when I demanded to be taken to see him, to observe him without his knowledge from the privacy of my carriage, there was no doubt. He was the image of his father at that age. My son had a son by his legitimate wife.'"

The viscountess made a strangling noise, but she stifled it, gripping the edge of the table as if she would break off a chunk and hit someone with it.

Daniel's mind was blank. At last the greatest mystery of his life had been solved. He knew who his father was. Regret that the man had died so long ago nearly overthrew him.

"I arranged, again through my solicitor, for an agent to approach Catherine Swann and make her an offer. I was not ready to acknowledge the boy as my grandson and heir, for I did not wish to expose my son's memory or my family name to such a scandal. I would provide for the boy, educate, feed, clothe, and house him until his twenty-fifth birthday. He could enter the trade or vocation of his choice, as long as it was not a military career, for I loathe the incompetency of the military. In exchange she was never to tell the boy who his father was, nor to reveal her story to anyone.

"'I thought I had solved the problem. The boy, Daniel, was cared for, much better than he would have been without my stepping in, and Alonzo would continue to be my heir. I followed Daniel's academic career. Occasionally I sent tasks for him through my solicitors, and he performed each one well. Though I was not pleased with his choice of occupation—a detective?—I suppose he was showing the more common side of his pedigree by choosing such a lowly place of employment where he would encounter the squalid and depraved every day, but what could I do? I kept my part of the agreement.

"'However, as I am nearing the end of my life, I question the wisdom of my actions. I know I shall face God soon. Plimpton makes dire predictions each time he visits. Can I meet my Maker with such a thing on my conscience? I will have to inform Alonzo. I would not have him find out after I'm gone. I shall have to choose my time carefully and give him a way of escape before the storm bursts. I have wronged many in this entire affair. My son, my real daughter-in-law, my true heir, my son's wife by a bigamous marriage, and the child they produced.

"'Can God forgive me? Can any of those I have wronged so terribly?

"'For the sake of the procedures that must follow, I hereby renounce Alonzo John Darby as my heir for being the son of a bigamous marriage, and I claim Daniel Swann Darby as my rightful successor.

"'In closing, I appoint Marcus, Duke of Haverly, as the executor of my estate. Haverly has the power and the intelligence to investigate what I have laid out here, as well as to see to the petition to the attorney general.

"'Though I have confessed, I do not feel as if I go to my grave with a clean conscience.'"

Mr. Moody looked up. "It is signed and dated by Lord Rotherhide and witnessed by Mr. Cooper and Dr. Plimpton."

Silence struck the room.

There was so much to say, so much to ask, but no one said a word.

Haverly stirred. "I suggest we adjourn. And I further suggest that no one reveal outside this room anything that has occurred here today. I, along with the solicitors, will begin an investigation. In my limited experience, establishing the legitimacy of Mr. Swann as heir will be difficult at best. No doubt Miss Cutshall and her son will wish to dispute the claim."

"I can assure you, we will." The viscountess's nostrils flared, probably at being called by her maiden name. "I shall begin the process of selecting my own solicitors to fight this, and you have no right to tell me whom I can and cannot speak to about this travesty of justice." She waved her hand over the documents in front of Mr. Moody.

"Madam, if you want to let it be known that there is a cloud of doubt over your son's birth, I cannot stop you. I only wished to safeguard the information presented here until we had better proof one way or the other than that of a sick old man. But if you desire us to move openly with our questioning and these claims, by all means, it will simplify my task considerably." Haverly's expression was innocence itself as he spread his hands.

"Of course I don't wish that. Don't be totty-headed." Even as she snapped the words, she seemed to realize she was addressing a duke of the realm and slumped in her chair.

Daniel felt as if he'd been struck by lightning. What did this mean for him? For his mother? For Alonzo Darby, who was, in fact, his half brother? This must have been Alonzo's reason for fleeing the country. The old earl—their mutual grandfather—must have told him the truth, and rather than stay and face the affair being played out in public, he had run.

As people filed out of the room, Haverly stopped Daniel. "I suggest we meet to begin our application to Sir William Garrow sooner rather than later. This could drag on for years, but if you are the true heir, I will fight to have you recognized as such."

"Thank you, Your Grace. This is all so sudden and unexpected. If you don't mind, I should like a few days to consider things before we move forward. I am in the middle of a murder investigation, after all, and I must give that my full attention."

"Of course, but don't delay too long. I shall begin interviewing witnesses and looking over documentation, as well as speaking with your mother about what she remembers and what she was told. No doubt you will wish to speak with her yourself now that your estrangement is over."

Daniel nodded, but he wondered. Was their estrangement over? Would it ever be?

Chapter 17

DANIEL ESCAPED INTO THE PAPER-CLOGGED interrogation room and shut the door. Boxes and stacks surrounded him, as Owen had begun to organize them, creating new tack holes in the plaster that Daniel would have to repair once the case was over.

The chair made a hideous squeak on the wooden floor when he pulled it away from the table. Dropping into it, he put his head in his hands.

He knew who his father was, and the man had been a coward and a scoundrel. He had married a young girl, gotten her pregnant, then folded like a damp receipt when his father challenged him. But he wasn't even bold enough to abandon his bride completely by giving her an annulment. He'd faked one and knowingly entered a bigamous marriage.

Lie after lie.

Daniel came from a long line of liars, for his grandfather had learned the truth more than a decade ago and had tried to bury it. The old man had salved his conscience here and there, but he had carried on the lie right up to his deathbed and then hoped an eleventh-hour confession would make everything right again.

The door opened, and Ed strode in. He held a mug of tea in one hand and a bun in the other, munching contentedly. When he observed Daniel, he closed the door, set down the food and drink, and asked, "What's wrong? Have you discovered nothing new on the case?"

Daniel had to tell someone. Not the details, but how he was feeling, the anger burning in his chest that had to come out.

"It's not the case, though that's frustrating enough." He puffed out his cheeks and straightened in his chair. "Today I found out who my real father was, and the truth is, my pedigree is littered with liars and scoundrels."

Ed's brows rose, and he pulled out the other chair, turning it around and straddling it, crossing his arms along the back. "I see."

"Do you?" Daniel bounded up to pace the small open area between stacks of ledgers. "Because I don't. I suppose it was a stupid game played by a stupid boy, but I used to make up stories about who my father was. Was he a brave soldier, fighting for king and country, or a dashing highwayman full of daring and grit? Perhaps he was a steady farmer or a sailor or even a minister, but you know what he never was? A coward or a liar.

"What makes a man do such a thing to his family? He never knew I existed, casting my mother away without so much as a by-your-leave. Do you know how many times I've sat through a church service listening to a sermon of how God is a Father to the fatherless, about how He is a good Father, and I've felt nothing? You know why? Because I have no idea what it's like to have a father. Now that I know about mine, I suppose I'm glad I didn't for such a long time." He dropped into the chair again, folding his arms and scowling. "God doesn't care about me any more than my real father did."

Ed remained calm, picking up his tea and sipping. "That's plenty to be going on with."

"I suppose you're going to try to change my mind?" He set his jaw. "Tell me I'm wrong?"

"I could try, but I'd rather ask you some questions first."

"Proceed, but you won't change anything."

"How is your mother? Does she know you are aware of your parentage?"

The question hit him amidships. His mother. He had been so eager to get out of the law offices and begin to work through what he had learned that he hadn't spared her a backward glance. Shame licked at his heart. She owed him an explanation, if nothing else, but he also owed her some courtesy.

"She knows. She was present when I was told, but she is not the focus here. I want to know how you can hold to the idea that I am supposed to believe that God is a good Father when nothing in my experience proves that fathers can be good at all."

"So we are to base truth upon your experiences alone? What about other men's experiences? What about mine? I had a good father, and I am trying my humble best to be a good father to the children God has granted me."

Heat flickered through Daniel's veins. He had forgotten Ed was a father.

"Furthermore, I assert that you have had more than one good father figure in your life, though you may not have recognized them as such. What about the teachers you have mentioned at that fancy boarding school you attended? I know some of your instructors were not kind, but you've remembered one or two to me that had your best interests at heart. And your tutor at university? He seems to have had a positive influence on you. Not to mention my humble self. While I am not quite old enough to be your father, I have tried to lead and guide you. And behind your current circumstances is a patron somewhere who has taken on the role of provider and protector, things a father would do. Through all of that, can you not see the hand of God?

"You were plucked out of a terrible situation, an illegitimate child with no prospects of anything other than a life of drudgery, and you have been gifted a fine education, fine clothes, a warm place to stay, plenty of food. You have the skills to earn income, and you have other opportunities available to you as a result of those blessings. Others in this world—in this very office, in fact—have a far more difficult existence living without a father than you ever had. If you cannot see that, you are at heart a coward and liar yourself."

Daniel jerked as if Ed had slapped him. He was no coward and he was no liar, but the memory of the single, cramped, cold room that housed Owen and his fatherless family rose up and kicked him in the conscience.

"Admit, even if only to yourself, that while you might not have known your father—and now that you do, you are less than enchanted by the reality of who he was—that God has had a hand in your life, that He has been guiding and caring for you, bringing into your life men to mentor, disciple, and train you as a father should have. God is good regardless of your experience because the Bible says He is, and the Bible never lies. We cannot judge Scripture or what we know about God by our own experiences and emotions, because those are changeable and untrustworthy most of the time."

Pondering these words and having to take a hard look at what his friend and mentor was telling him, Daniel leaned forward. Ed had valid points. Daniel had much for which to be grateful, and he had been blessed to have some good men in his life to guide him. His conscience poked him. From the Duke of Haverly to Cadogan . . . But did having such men make up for the losses he'd suffered? How would his life have been different if his parents had stayed together and he had grown up at Lockewood? "I will have to consider what you've said."

"That's all I ask. Don't blame God for the shortcomings of men. It's too easy, and it's an excuse not to be grateful for what He's given us. Now, where are we on the investigation? I've just come from the hospital, and Mr. Coombe has shown further signs of awakening. Owen is with him now, but we'll need to get more men to keep watch if we're going to maintain a guard on him night and day."

"The only thing left is this." Daniel waved at the paperwork. "Sir Michael wants it organized and out of here soon, and he wants a full report by the end of the day. I don't know where to turn now. I've gone over our suspects, ruling each one out, and I don't know where that leaves us."

"Back at the beginning. Like I have always taught you, *follow the paper.*"

They began on one side of the room, where Owen had already

organized some stacks, and slowly sifted through invoices, memoranda, sales numbers, advertisements, and other paraphernalia.

Daniel moved a stack of ledgers and found a slim, leather-bound volume on the corner of the desk. "What's this?" He leafed through the pages, starting at the back. Was it empty? But then he reached the front.

Ed looked up. "What have you found?"

"It appears to be a diary of some sort. Begun this year." He trotted back in his mind. "I think it was brought in by Lady Juliette Thorndike. She and Montgomery's daughter, Agatha, retrieved it from his vault at the Bank of England. I had Owen put it with the other papers to go through later, and I forgot about it." He grimaced. "It's probably nothing, but I should have looked it over and returned it to Miss Montgomery before now."

"I'm sure she won't mind. Give it a quick read, and let's press on with this stuff. I want to get home to the family tonight. It's my eldest son's birthday, and the wife has made a currant cake for the lad."

Daniel barely heard. He skimmed the early entries in the diary, about how proud Montgomery was of his daughter, how he looked forward to her homecoming and bringing her out in society. How he had missed her, how proud her mother would have been if she could see the woman Agatha had become.

It would gratify and perhaps comfort Miss Montgomery to read such nice things. He only hoped Mr. Montgomery had taken the time to express his feelings to her before his death.

Then the entries changed.

Must look into the matter. Something is off. After all I've done, can this betrayal be true? I shall have to take care. I wouldn't want to be wrong.

What did that mean? And why did the entries end there? Daniel flipped through the book, and a flash of ink caught his eye. Montgomery had written on another page, about halfway through the book, as if he'd grabbed the volume at random and spilled his thoughts.

I cannot trust him. His perfidy is the ultimate betrayal. A trusted friend. How could he have done this to me? I made him the man he is, hiring him right out of his apprenticeship and giving him full access. I couldn't believe it at first, and I still find it difficult to swallow. How many thousands has he stolen? I shall have to confront him tomorrow.

The entry was dated the day before Montgomery was killed.

In that moment, Daniel knew who the killer must be.

It was time to lay a trap and see if the right mouse came for the cheese.

———— ✿ ————

"He took the bait, right?" Daniel shrugged into the dressing gown Sir Bertrand held for him. His muscles still protested. Perhaps when this was over he would finally get that long hot soak and a few days off to recover.

"Yes." Lady Juliette studied her reflection, holding up a shaving mirror to the lamplight. A mobcap concealed her glossy brown curls, and a shapeless woolen dress and stained apron disguised her slender form. "I did exactly as you said, and after he left, I checked. The book was gone. He must believe, if he only tidies up this one last loose end, he will get away with all of it."

They stood in a side ward at St. Bart's, and the clock was gone midnight.

Daniel had volunteered to take the guard duty for the night, to watch over Mr. Coombe at the hospital. Owen had been less than pleased when Daniel sent him home, having enjoyed two nights of extra pay. But with Sir Bertrand and Lady Juliette involved, no one from Bow Street, not even Ed or Owen, could take part in tonight's gambit. Just as well no one knew Mr. Coombe had succumbed to his injuries less than half an hour after Owen left the hospital. And just as well that Sir Bertrand had arranged for the ward to be cleared and one of his men to keep hospital workers away from the area.

If Daniel hadn't needed Lady Juliette to pass along information to their quarry, she wouldn't be here now. But, of course, he'd needed to go through Haverly and Sir Bertrand, and Haverly had decided this would be another excellent opportunity for Lady Juliette to gain experience in field work. So here he was, trying to perform his lawful duty as a Bow Street officer and capture a killer while entangled again with agents for the Crown.

His life had been rather simple before he'd met the Thorndikes. Before he'd been recruited by Haverly into the intelligence game himself.

How did Lady Juliette manage to look so different with just a few changes to her appearance? Though he would still know her, for she was written on his heart, she really did have a knack for this sort of work. He had seen her as a glittering debutante gracing the most exclusive ballrooms in London, and as an equestrienne flying fences with panache, and as a toxophilite winning prizes in Hyde Park, and as a boardinghouse maid sneaking into a Luddite rally, and now as a lowly hospital nurse.

How would she look as a duchess to a German duke?

He shook his head, trying to chase that thought away. He must keep his wits about him tonight. If he failed to be vigilant, he could not only lose his quarry but someone could get hurt, possibly killed.

"You are to stay at the far end of the ward. No matter what happens, do not come forward and allow him to see you fully. If he discovers your true identity before we apprehend him in the act, the game will be up." Daniel stared hard at her.

"You've reminded me three times already. I know my responsibility." Juliette looked at him in the mirror, touching her cheek with a smear of dirt. "See that you do yours."

Sir Bertrand lit his bullseye lantern and closed the vents until hardly any light escaped. "I'll be nearby, but stay on your guard. He's killed twice before. He won't hesitate to kill again."

Daniel checked the pocket of the dressing gown, feeling the hard lump of a loaded pistol. His truncheon dangled by a loop from his wrist. "We should get into our places. He could come at any time." He checked the prime on the pistol, keeping his finger away from the trigger. He hoped he would not need it, but in case he did, he must be ready.

Sir Bertrand disappeared through the doorway, and Juliette went to the bed, punching up the pillow and turning back the sheet. "I shall signal if I see him coming."

Daniel climbed into the bed, turning onto his side with his back to the door and pulling the sheet up to his chin. "Will this do?" He put the pistol alongside his leg beneath the blankets, where he could reach it easily.

"Yes. In the darkened room, it's impossible to tell you from Mr. Coombe, especially with that bandage on your head."

There were six beds in the ward. Three were empty and unmade, and two others had pillows lined up under the blankets to appear occupied. Juliette went to the table at the end of the ward opposite the door and slumped into the chair, sprawling her arms across the table and laying her head on the wood.

She took on the appearance of every night nurse Daniel had ever encountered. Nurses were not highly regarded, being mostly poor women with few skills. They were to empty the slops, mop the floors, and keep the fires burning. Hospitals paid very little, and half of their salary was given in ale or gin. Most nurses were drunks with no medical knowledge.

A sleeping night nurse would arouse no suspicion in their quarry.

Silence descended on the room, and Daniel waited. Juliette kept still, and Sir Bertrand, wherever he had hidden himself, made no sound.

With all his clothes and the dressing gown and the sheet, Daniel was warm. Lethargy seeped into his aching limbs, and his lids began to close.

Snapping awake, he chided himself. He was waiting for a killer. How could he fall asleep?

Concentrate, man. Focus.

He bit the inside of his lip and clenched his fingernails into his palms, hoping the pain would keep him alert. He blinked hard and stared into the darkness. Faint light came from the tall windows, and the small candle burning on Juliette's table created a halo of gold that did not penetrate far.

Juliette. He had met her in the War Room this morning, uncertain of his reception. The kiss they had shared hung between them. Would she mention it? Should he?

In the end, neither had. He didn't know if he was disappointed or relieved.

She had accepted his request for help in baiting their trap. What he hadn't anticipated was her involvement tonight. Though he would prefer she keep out of harm's way, he had to admit he liked being with her. If she was indeed going to marry Heinrich and move to his homeland, Daniel would take these last few opportunities to work with Juliette as a gift.

Haverly had cautioned him to say nothing of his possible inheritance just yet, a decision with which Daniel agreed. The viscountess had indicated she intended to dispute any claim against her son's title, and the battle to prove Daniel's pedigree and right to the earldom would most likely be protracted and difficult. Before it became public knowledge, Haverly would be putting together Daniel's case.

Before the duke petitioned the attorney general, Daniel would have to think long and hard about whether he even wanted to pursue the earldom. Precedent said the attorney general would be forced to send the petition to the Select Committee for Privileges for review. At that point the fight could get ugly.

As far as Daniel was concerned, the only reason to pursue this matter was to salvage his mother's reputation. For himself, he was no landowner, no peer, no gentleman. The old earl's assertions as to his parentage and pedigree had felt as if they were about a stranger, not him.

If he fought for the title and won, he would have all the rights and responsibilities of a peer. He would own that big house in Kent, Lockewood Hall. He would have a townhouse in London and a proper fortune.

But he would still be that same abandoned boy at heart. He would still be the youngster who had cleaned stables and blacked boots and carried coal buckets and dug potatoes.

Which brought him to all Ed had said of what God had been doing in his life, even though Daniel hadn't seen it. How Ed believed God had been providing for him, directing his life, and bringing into his path those father figures he craved. Only three days ago Daniel had nearly died, crying out for God to help him, and God had provided Cadogan, who had risked his own life to save Daniel's. Daniel had thanked Cadogan, but he had neglected to thank God.

I must be the worst of Your children. Thank You for preserving my life, and thank You for putting Cadogan in the right place to save me. I'm still struggling with doubts about fathers, but I do thank You.

If Daniel had known his true father, had been brought up by the man, what sort of person would he be now? His father had been a coward and a liar. Would those traits have rubbed off on him? Was it possible that, as difficult as his life had been, he was better off not having been reared by Alfred Darby, heir to the Earl of Rotherhide?

A tiny scratching sound reached his ears. The scrape of a shoe on a stair?

He strained his hearing, holding his breath.

Another small sound, perhaps the brushing of a sleeve against a wall.

Juliette let out an inelegant snore, turning her head on her arms.

Daniel tensed. That was the signal that their quarry had arrived.

As hard as it was, he held still. Because he didn't want to chance being recognized too soon, he had kept his back to the door, but now he was allowing a killer to sneak up behind him. The hairs on his neck stood up, and his heartbeat quickened.

Show no movement. Let him come close. Sir Bertrand, you had better be nearby as you promised.

His hand tightened on the pistol. Another footfall, and he stopped breathing.

"Drop that gun." Sir Bertrand spoke from the shadows, and at the sound of his voice, Daniel rolled over, raising his pistol and pointing it in the killer's startled face. Sir Bertrand opened the vents on the bulls-eye lantern, illuminating the area around the bed.

Hubert Earnshaw, Montgomery's accountant, blinked, the small pistol wavering in his hand. Daniel flung aside the bedcovers, wincing at his sore muscles, and got to his feet, keeping his gun level.

"Do as he says. Put that gun down. You're caught. You're going to pay for your crimes."

Earnshaw's face hardened, and he twisted wildly, trapped between Daniel and Sir Bertrand. Faster than Daniel would have thought possible, Earnshaw fired in Sir Bertrand's direction. Sir Bertrand rocked back, beginning to fall.

Daniel froze in shock at the swift violence of it all, and before he could turn back to cover Earnshaw, the accountant reached for the bed Daniel had just vacated and flipped it straight at Daniel. Dodging the hurtling mattress and bedframe, Daniel tried to aim at the fleeing accountant, but instead of heading back into the stairwell from whence he had come, Earnshaw raced down the ward in Juliette's direction.

The small pistol Earnshaw carried, now useless, clattered to the floor, and as the man reached into his waistband, Daniel's heart vaulted into his throat. Did he have another weapon? Earnshaw was between him and Juliette, and Daniel dared not fire lest he hit her.

Run, Juliette! Get out of the way!

The words ricocheted through Daniel's head as he raced after the killer.

Juliette had risen from her table, but why wasn't she dodging out of the way? What was she doing?

Everything slowed and seemed to take an eternity—except for Earnshaw's pace toward the far end of the ward. At the last moment, when he was close enough to Juliette to run her over, he skidded to a halt.

"Stop, Mr. Earnshaw." Juliette's voice was calm, but her eyes were wide, the faint moonlight from the windows gleaming off the whites. "I cannot let you leave."

Daniel could hardly believe his eyes when the accountant froze, but Daniel did not stop running, cannoning into Earnshaw and tackling him to the ground. The impact hurt, but he ignored the pain. He pressed his knee into the accountant's back, wrenching the man's hands behind him and pinning him to the floor like a trussed chicken. Only then did he look up to see Juliette aiming a pistol at Mr. Earnshaw.

"Where did that come from? I didn't know you were armed." He almost shouted, so scared had he been. "I told you to stay out of it!" Dash it all—he *was* shouting.

"Good thing she didn't, or we might have lost our quarry." Sir Bertrand came up from behind, and Daniel spared him a glance.

"Are you hit?" Juliette asked, rushing to her uncle's side.

"A mere scrape. Fortunately, Mr. Earnshaw's aim tonight was not as steady as when he shot Mr. Montgomery." Sir Bertrand frowned, plucking at his sleeve. "He has managed to ruin a perfectly good jacket, however."

Juliette's face paled, and she wobbled her way to a chair. "You're bleeding."

Daniel clapped the darbies onto Earnshaw's wrists, making them good and tight. "Stay there, or I'll cuff you to a bedframe." He pushed himself upright and went to Sir Bertrand.

"That looks like more than a scrape." Daniel shed the dressing gown and reached for Sir Bertrand's cravat. "You'd best let me wrap that up." Without waiting for permission, he wound Sir Bertrand's upper arm with the neckcloth. "We're in a hospital, after all, but perhaps you would prefer to treat this at home?"

"Absolutely. Juliette, some fortitude, please. I am fine, and you performed creditably. I'm glad you took my advice and did not go out without a weapon."

Daniel shook his head as he retrieved the gun Earnshaw dropped after firing it. "Is this the gun you used to kill Montgomery?" Owen Wilkinson had been correct when he'd surmised the killer had used a muff gun.

Earnshaw said nothing.

Chapter 18

DANIEL STUDIED THE BEAUTIFUL BREAKFAST room in the Thorndike townhouse as he took a seat. The early morning summons had been delivered to Bow Street before dawn, where Daniel had been filling out his reports and winding up his case to present to the magistrate. He had seen some of the opulent rooms of the Thorndike townhouse, of course, but that was before he knew he might own one himself. What might the Darby London abode be like? Newly renovated, he understood. It seemed odd to be keeping this secret, and yet it had been kept a long time from a lot of people. Another little while would do no harm.

He traced the lace pattern on the tablecloth with his thumb. Somewhere in this house his mother was at work as the housekeeper, yet she was a titled woman. Would she be addressed as the Viscountess Coatsworth? Lady Darby? With a jolt, he realized his proper last name was Darby, not Swann. Daniel Darby? Lord Rotherhide? An odd feeling of not belonging to either name swept over him.

Sir Bertrand sat at the head of the table, his left arm cradled in a sling. He tapped a special edition broadsheet beside his plate.

"How are you faring this morning?" Daniel asked.

"Fine. A surgeon with the ability to keep his own counsel was summoned late last night, and according to him the sling is necessary for a few days. I think it gives me a bit of flair, don't you? Perhaps someone will think I've been dueling on the heath over some woman's honor?"

"Or that you were drunk and accidentally shot yourself." Daniel grinned.

"Quite possible." Sir Bertrand did not seem put out at the jest. "The arrest made quite a splash." He pointed to the large headline. *Montgomery Murder Solved.*

"It took most of the night, but he confessed in the end." Daniel stifled a yawn. He had taken Earnshaw directly to Newgate Prison, that edifice being much closer to St. Bart's Hospital than Bow Street. He'd questioned the accountant at length, presenting him with the mounting evidence against him. In the end, Earnshaw had crumbled. The newspapers always had sources at the prison, and they must have been quick to race back to the office to get the word out so rapidly.

Lady Juliette entered the room, and Daniel shot to his feet so fast his chair toppled over. He mumbled a greeting as he righted it.

She smiled brightly, as fresh as if she had not been out of the house for hours last night.

He rounded the table to pull out a chair for her, and as she sat, her perfume—roses—swirled about him. He shook his head. Was she even now carrying a pistol or knife? How could he align the beautiful debutante and the capable agent in one alluring girl?

It was as much a dichotomy as reconciling that he was a baseborn Bow Street detective and also the not-yet-proven-to-be-heir to an earldom.

"Your trap worked perfectly, Mr. Swann." She inclined her head toward her uncle. "Except for the part where Bertie got shot. I do hope you're faring well this morning, Uncle?"

Bertie nodded and poured her a cup of tea.

Daniel returned to his seat. "You must have played your part to perfection yesterday afternoon at Miss Montgomery's. Earnshaw could not resist the opportunity to tie up yet another loose end. He had to believe that by today he would have erased all traces of his involvement, including silencing Mr. Coombe for good, and would escape unpunished. Just as well he didn't discover that Mr. Coombe had already passed away earlier in the day, or he wouldn't have come to kill him, falling into our trap."

Juliette sipped her tea, her brown eyes shining with intelligence and satisfaction. "Mr. Earnshaw was already at Agatha's when I visited yesterday. It was quite easy to allow him to see me returning the diary, talking about how Bow Street had finished with it and found nothing of interest to the case. I also told Agatha that you had mentioned that Mr. Coombe was coming back to himself and you intended to interview him on the morrow."

She shrugged. "Mr. Earnshaw put a stack of papers atop the book, and when he excused himself, he picked up the papers and the book together. It was neatly done, and if I had not been looking for it, I would have missed it. As it was, Agatha suspected nothing. Especially as I had the original in my bag and put it on the table before I left. She will never know of the substitute stolen by Mr. Earnshaw."

Daniel had to admire how far she had come in her spy craft in just a few weeks. It chagrined him to know she was more adept than he at the subtleties of intelligence work.

"You did well with the forgery, for the book Earnshaw took looks identical to the binding of the original. Who wrote the entries?" she asked.

"Owen Wilkinson. It turns out he's a dab hand at copying signatures and writing styles. He does not know why I wanted them, but he was quick about creating them. I came up with some fairly innocuous entries for him to fill the book, and it seems they were innocent enough not to arouse Earnshaw's suspicions."

Sir Bertrand stroked his cheek. "Forgery is a useful ability in our line of work. Perhaps we can use Wilkinson in the future."

Daniel kept his face neutral. He and Owen would most likely always have a scratchy relationship, but since seeing the boy's living situation and the family he provided for, Daniel had more compassion and patience with Owen's rough edges and prickly nature.

"How did you tumble to it being Mr. Earnshaw who killed Mr. Montgomery?" Juliette asked.

The door to the kitchen passage opened, and a footman came in with a laden breakfast tray. He set a plate before each of them before retiring. As he reached the door, Sir Bertrand said, "Please don't disturb us until we ring. And thank Cook for us. This looks splendid."

Daniel waited until they were alone before answering Juliette. "It was the entry in the journal that held several clues, all pointing to one man." He dug out his notebook and consulted it.

"One day, Montgomery wrote, 'Must look into the matter. Something is off. After all I've done, can this betrayal be true? I shall have to take care. I wouldn't want to be wrong.' And on the next day, the day before his murder, he entered this: 'I cannot trust him. His perfidy is the ultimate betrayal. A trusted friend. How could he have done this to me? I made him the man he is, hiring him right out of his apprenticeship and giving him full access. I couldn't believe it at first, and I still find it difficult to swallow. How many thousands has he stolen? I shall have to confront him tomorrow.'

"Montgomery had been betrayed by a trusted friend. The man had been employed by Montgomery for a considerable length of time. The man had been apprenticed in whatever capacity he now held a position in, and Montgomery planned to confront him on the day he died. Who had an appointment with Montgomery on the day he died? Not Carlisle, because he showed up unannounced. Only Earnshaw had a scheduled appointment." Daniel bit into a triangle of toasted bread.

"You rescued him from the walkway over the waterwheel after the explosion." Sir Bertrand poked at the soft-boiled egg on his plate, grimaced, and pushed the whole breakfast away.

Was his arm hurting too much, or had the surgeon given him something for the pain that made his stomach delicate?

"Yes. Earnshaw confessed this morning that he went to the mill, and Montgomery confronted him about stealing the profits not only from the mill but from several other businesses as well. Earnshaw had been keeping two separate sets of books for the Montgomery finances and skimming and dipping for years. Their argument took place while the mill was in full operation, and the noise was deafening. Earnshaw was certain no one could have overheard them, except perhaps Mr.

Coombe, the mill manager. As unlikely as this was with all the noise, Earnshaw couldn't take the chance."

Juliette shook her head. "I still am unclear on the sequence of events that led up to and immediately followed Mr. Montgomery's death."

"Earnshaw was desperate. Montgomery fired him on the spot and told him he was going to the authorities to report the embezzlement. He swore Earnshaw would be in prison by nightfall. Earnshaw stormed out of the mill, went up the street to a receiver's shop, and purchased a muff gun. When he returned to the mill, he couldn't sneak into Mr. Montgomery's office because Mr. Coombe was in the warehouse, the mill workers were in the mill proper, and two workers were cleaning up a flour spill in the passage immediately outside Montgomery's office door. They were creating a cloud of flour dust as they shoveled up the spill. Earnshaw went outside, around the back of the mill, and accessed the walkway over the waterwheel, which also passed by Montgomery's open office window. He leaned in and shot Montgomery in the head."

"But the explosion . . ." Juliette trailed off.

"According to the scientist I consulted, flour dust is more explosive than gunpowder under the right circumstances. It's possible either the striking of one of the shovels against stone in the passageway produced a spark, or the firing of the pistol in that small room set off the explosion. Though the door to the hallway was closed, a transom window over the door was open, letting in enough of the flour dust to ignite when the pistol went off. The blast sent Mr. Earnshaw backward, hard into the railing on the walkway, and stunned him for a time.

"When I found Earnshaw, he was dangerously near to dropping into the water. When questioned, however, he was quick enough to say he had been on the walkway trying to see if Mr. Montgomery was in his office, since they had an appointment that morning and the way was blocked by the men cleaning up the spill. He acted as if he had not yet seen Mr. Montgomery that day."

"What about the anarchist who was killed in the mill later?" Sir Bertrand asked. "Was Earnshaw involved, or are we looking for another killer?"

"The anarchist was an expert in explosives, and we believe he had been sent by Jasper Finch's group to lay the plans for destroying the mill once all the repairs were completed. It was his misfortune to have chosen the very night Earnshaw had sneaked in to look for the murder weapon. The explosion jerked the gun from his hand as he held it through the window, and he was certain it was in the office somewhere. He killed Pietro Todisco with a blow to the head and managed to find the gun not in the office but wedged into a crack between the rail on the walkway and the mill wall."

"Two murders, two mill workers killed, another wounded so badly he later died, and for what?" Juliette asked. "To hide a theft."

And one attempted murder of a nosy policeman. Daniel had wrung that bit of information out of Earnshaw at the end of the interrogation. Earnshaw had lured him to the mill and pushed him over the walkway railing onto the waterwheel. "Not just any theft. Earnshaw admitted that over the years he had managed to bilk the Montgomery estate out of more than fifty thousand pounds."

"Fifty thousand?" Though it was bad form, Sir Bertrand let out a low whistle. "Enough that Earnshaw would be desperate to hide it."

"Enough to kill for, in his estimation."

"What happens next?" Juliette asked.

"Earnshaw will be tried and sentenced, and he'll pay for his crimes. There's a warrant out for Finch, and when he's arrested, he'll also be tried for sedition, violating the Luddite laws, and a few other things besides. The River Police are watching the docks, and we've circulated a likeness of him amongst night watchmen and cab drivers and posted a reward for information as to his whereabouts in the dailies. We'll find him."

A commotion began in the hall, and Sir Bertrand frowned. "I said we were not to be disturbed."

The door burst open, and the Countess of Thorndike entered, a fur-lined cape swinging from her shoulders and her arms outstretched. "Juliette, darling, we're home."

The earl came in next, shedding his outerwear and tossing a leather case onto the table. He took in his brother's bandaged arm, and his brows rose. "What have you been up to while we were away?"

Daniel stood as Lady Juliette embraced her mother, her face shining with happiness. Her father was next, folding her into his arms and rocking her side to side. "We missed you, Jules-girl."

He held her away from him. "I only hope the information we were sent to retrieve was worth the separation." The earl looked at the case. "Still, we did what was asked, and Haverly can take our findings to Whitehall, and they can make what they will of it. I am going to put my foot down. We are staying home. No more missions for a while."

"Really? You mean it?" Juliette launched herself into her father's arms once more. "I'm so glad. I've missed you both terribly."

A stab of envy at their relationship plunged through Daniel, and he gripped the back of his chair. Would a reconciliation with his mother be possible? Was he anywhere near ready for that? The hurt he had worn for years was comfortable, safe. He had built a wall between himself and the mother he had loved so fiercely as a child, and that wall had protected his heart from further pain. If he let the barrier come down, would more pain be his?

He nodded to Sir Bertrand and indicated his intention to leave. Best to allow the Thorndikes their private reunion. He had a report to make to Sir Michael.

In the front hall, he took his hat and cloak from Mr. Pultney. Movement at the back of the hall caught his eye, and he turned. His mother stood in the doorway to the servants' area. They looked at each other for a long time, the only sound the ticking of the tall case clock.

Should he say something? Would she?

Mr. Pultney cleared his throat, holding the front door open, and the moment was broken. Daniel took his leave, not knowing if he was grateful or sorry.

Juliette stood beside her mother at the ball the week after Earnshaw's capture, shaking her head at the incongruities of her double life. One minute she was a debutante, the next she was a hospital night nurse, then an earl's daughter again. Before them, dancing couples performed a reel, and Juliette kept time, tapping her toe on the polished floor.

Not hard enough, however, to dislodge the pistol she'd tucked into her stocking and tied securely with a garter ribbon.

She smiled as Anne Victon and her partner pirouetted gracefully. Mother had asked their hostess if she would invite the young girl to the party as a special favor.

"Everyone seems to be having a wonderful time," her mother remarked, flicking open her silk fan and stirring the air. "Lady Erskine's home is lovely, just made for parties, isn't it?"

"I wish Agatha could be here. And I wish Alonzo hadn't left the country without so much as a fare-thee-well. She's going to miss the lion's share of her debut Season because of being in mourning, but it wouldn't be as terrible if she had the man she loves by her side." Juliette twisted her garnet ring. "She remains convinced he will return soon and keep his promise, but I am of two minds whether I want him to. If he would leave her with no explanation, what is to prevent him from repeating the act at a later date?"

Mother smiled at a man and woman as they passed, and once they were far enough away, she leaned over to whisper behind her fan. "Alonzo will return when he is ready. Things have happened and are in play of which you are not aware. I cannot go into detail, and you must not say a word to Agatha, but you should also stop speaking of the matter in public. Things of a sensitive nature are afoot, and your speculations may reach the wrong ears."

Abashed, Juliette ducked her chin, but Mother used the tip of her closed fan to lift Juliette's face. "Give us a smile. The duke approaches."

Her stomach dropped. Duke Heinrich, resplendent in military dress, handsome and precise, strode across the room. He was the guest of honor tonight, a send-off to conclude his time here in England. He smiled warmly, halting with a measured bow. He never looked away from Juliette, and the ardent affection in his gaze made her want to turn and run.

"Good evening. I was pleased to hear of your parents' return. I have just come from a quiet word with your father."

Her windpipe closed. He'd spoken to her father? But she hadn't had the chance to talk with Father yet about Heinrich's intentions.

"Lady Thorndike, may I have a moment with Lady Juliette?"

Juliette turned her head far enough she hoped the duke could not see and sent a pleading look to her mother. But Mother wasn't looking at Juliette. She smiled, radiant as ever, at the duke and nodded.

"Perhaps a quick turn about the conservatory? I hear Lady Erskine has some lovely roses beginning to bloom."

Heinrich offered his arm, and Juliette placed her hand atop his elbow. Her mind hurtled about in her head. What should she do? What should she say? She was not ready for this.

The conservatory, with a heated floor and several braziers, was warm on this cold March night, and as promised, there were roses. It was a beautiful setting. The time, the place . . . but not the loved one.

"Heinrich," she began, but he stopped her.

"Do not speak yet, please. I must say this." He turned to her, cupping her shoulders with his hands. "Your father has given me wise advice. He reminded me that you are young, that you are barely into your first Season as a debutante, and that he and your mother have had little time with you since your arrival back in England. He has cautioned me to wait. Not to rush you into a decision. Though I am eager to formally propose to you, to marry you, and to take you home with me to my lovely valley near Brandenburg, as your father spoke I could hear the wisdom of his words."

He sighed, his fingers tightening on her arms. "So though it pains me, I will wait. I will return home. But know this—I will come back. Hopefully, by that time you will be ready to accept all I can offer you."

Reprieve. Her father had bought her some time. *Bless you, Father.*

And yet, was that fair to Heinrich?

Daniel. Images of the detective flashed through her mind. The way he had seen to her safety when the mill exploded, then run toward the danger to help others. The clumsy way he had approached her at the archery tournament, and his ability to laugh about it later. His careful handling of Agatha in her grief. His rescue of her when she had been tossed down during the mad rush in the warehouse.

That kiss.

Though their lives were very different—his as a detective, hers as a debutante—Juliette could not deny her feelings for him.

To give Heinrich hope that she would accept his proposal in due time would be wrong when she cherished feelings for another, however unlikely their coming to fruition may be. Her sense of justice would not allow her to let Heinrich leave with false hope in his heart.

"Heinrich, you have done me a great honor, and I appreciate the patience you are granting me, but . . ." She took a deep breath. "I must refuse your generous offer. I regard you as a friend, and you have been kind to me, but I do not love you. I vowed long ago that I would only marry for love, to have the sort of love match my parents share. I cannot settle for less, nor should you. You deserve a woman who will love only you with her whole heart."

His hands fell away, and his expression sobered. "I see. I should have expected as much. Is it that you love another?"

Her cheeks warmed, and confusion writhed in her chest. She lowered her chin to look at her hands.

"That was unfair of me to ask. I beg your forgiveness." His words were stiff, but she sensed only sadness from him, not anger. "I would ask one indulgence before I return you to the party."

She looked up, and he smiled, but his eyes were sad.

Slowly, giving her every chance to refuse, to pull away, he cradled her cheeks in his palms, leaned forward, and kissed her gently.

It was over in a trice, a brief brushing of lips so sweet it brought a welling of emotion to her eyes.

Was she a fool to refuse him? He was everything a debutante should want. Kind, handsome, titled, wealthy.

And yet the kiss he had bestowed on her, while sweet, brought only friendship and sorrow to her mind.

Completely different from the only other kiss she had shared with a man, which had made her feel as if she had been struck by lightning and had lingered in her thoughts for days.

Daniel's heart hit his boots. Through the condensation-streaked glass walls of the conservatory, he saw Heinrich and Juliette. Their conversation seemed quite intimate, and Heinrich had his hands on her shoulders. A wave of jealousy turned the night green.

You're hired to provide extra security, not to gawk at your betters.

Defiance bloomed in his chest. Were they his betters? What if he truly was the new Earl of Rotherhide?

Did that matter? He could be one of the royal dukes, but if Juliette loved Heinrich, accepted his proposal, and went off to live in Germany, there was nothing he could do about it.

Owen Wilkinson, hands thrust into the pockets of his coat and his collar turned up against the night air, strolled by. "Quiet night. Why did Lord and Lady Erskine want protection? Not that I mind the extra pay." They had been tasked with circling the house in opposite directions, watching for any trouble or sight of anyone trying to break into the house.

"They're still twitchy about all the valuables being stolen during social events last month. At least, that's what Sir Michael said when he gave us the assignment." Daniel blew on his hands. Nearly April, and still frosty. Would this winter never end?

"But you caught that fellow. That case was closed a month ago." Owen stomped his feet, his cheeks red and his eyes watery.

And he had, with the help of Juliette, Sir Bertrand, and the Thorndikes.

He stared through the water-streaked window at the blurred images inside, and when Heinrich kissed Juliette, Daniel's nails dug into his palms. He barely felt the pain.

For too long, secrets had been kept, secrets that would have changed his entire life, and in this moment he couldn't bear it. He could not hold this secret a moment longer.

He turned and marched toward the Erskine's front door.

"Where are you going?" Owen called after him. "Aren't we going to do another circuit of the house?"

Daniel ignored the lad, his mind focused. A footman met him at the door.

"What do you want? Is there trouble?"

"I must get inside. I have a message for one of the guests." Which was true.

"Who? I'll take it to him." The footman held out his hand.

"It's not written. I have to deliver it in person."

"I can't let you barge into the ballroom." He stared at Daniel as if he had rocks where his brains should be. "Look at you."

Glancing down, Daniel took in his boots, breeches, and cloak. A truncheon stuck out of his waistband, and though the footman couldn't know it, he also had a knife in his boot and a pistol at the small of his back.

Short of shoving past the man and causing a scene, there was little Daniel could do. "Please, would you bring Lady Juliette Thorndike to a private room where I may deliver my message? Tell her Mr. Daniel Swann would like to speak with her."

The footman frowned, considering the request. "You may wait in the receiving room." He indicated a door to the left. "I will see if the lady is willing to meet you."

The wait was interminable, and he changed his mind about the wisdom of his actions at least a few dozen times, but each time he returned to the desire for the truth to be known. What if she refused to come? What if she was so busy with the duke she didn't care what a simple detective might want?

The door finally opened, and his heart jumped, then tumbled. Sir Bertrand came inside.

Then Lady Juliette followed, and his mouth went dry.

She had a white ribbon threaded through her dark curls, and her brown eyes were wide as a deer's.

He swallowed.

Sir Bertrand closed the door and said, "What is it? Has Haverly sent you?"

"No, sir. This isn't an official call. I . . ." How did he say to her uncle that he wanted to pour out his heart to Lady Juliette before she was married to Duke Heinrich and beyond his reach?

Sir Bertrand's brows rose, and he looked from Daniel to Juliette and back. "I see. I believe I shall wait outside the door. I can give you ten minutes."

Daniel had always appreciated how perspicacious Bertie Thorndike could be.

Once they were alone, Daniel was certain he was making an absolute cake of himself. He should never have come inside. He should have let well enough alone. She must think him an utter fool.

He glanced upward and realized he was still wearing his hat. With a quick jerk, he snatched it off. How awkward could he be?

Juliette fairly glittered in a white gown sewn with little crystals or pearls or some other expensive frippery. The delicacy of her features, that upturned nose that drove him to distraction, and—he inhaled—yes, the scent of roses.

She was an earl's daughter, for the love of mincemeat pies. What was he doing here?

"Daniel, what's wrong?"

"Me. Us," he croaked.

Her arched brows rose, and questions filled her lovely eyes.

He could not believe his stupidity, but he might as well be hung for a sheep as for a lamb. *Just say it.*

"Juliette Thorndike, I love you. I cannot eat. I cannot sleep. I can barely function for thought of you. I know it is probably far too late and that you are most likely betrothed to the duke, but I cannot let you leave England without speaking my heart." He throttled his hat brim, his face burning.

Her pink lips parted, and she blinked.

Shaking his head, he mumbled, "I just wanted you to know." Clapping his hat on his head, he started for the door. What a fool he was.

"Daniel Swann, don't you take another step."

He froze for a long moment, then slowly turned around, removing his hat to throttle the brim once more.

Would she smack his face? Would she blister him for his hubris?

She put her hand on his arm, and a fizzing shock went through him.

"Is that all you have to say? You love me? And then you bolt like a fox with a pack of hounds on his tail?"

"What else is there to say?" The walls seemed to inch closer, all the air being sucked from the already-too-small room.

"You might at least have shown me the courtesy of an opportunity to reply."

He should have, but he dreaded her response. *I'm marrying Heinrich, and you've got a cheek even speaking of such things as love to me.*

"You do not need to say anything. I only wished to express my feelings to you. It was intolerable that you go away without knowing that you inspired such emotions in another."

"And I do not get to express my feelings for you?" Her hand tightened on his arm, giving him a little shake. "You've made several assumptions, and I feel I must set you straight. First, I am not going to marry Duke Heinrich von Lowe. As much as I regard him as a friend, I cannot possibly marry him when I am in love with someone else."

Daniel could not have moved if the room had caught fire. She was not betrothed to Heinrich. And she was in love.

With a parched mouth, he asked, "And who is the recipient of your love, if I may be so bold as to ask?"

"For a detective, you can be particularly obtuse at times." Her smile melted the ice that had sprung up around his heart. "I happen to love one Daniel Swann, Bow Street runner and budding agent for the Crown."

An odd flipping, sinking, soaring sensation gripped him.

"But . . . I'm nobody. You know my beginnings. You know I'm a mere police officer. There can be no future for us together unless I win—" He broke off. He could not talk about the pending petition, on Haverly's orders. And he was loath to in any case. He did not want her to choose him based upon his supposed inheritance and title. If she were to choose him, it must be for the man he was.

Her face softened, a warm light in her dark eyes. "I know you to be kind, intelligent, brave, and caring. Is that not enough for any man to win a girl's heart?"

She closed the few inches between them, and his arms went around her, crushing her to his chest. "Are you certain? My heart is yours for the asking, but what of your family? What of society?"

"I am certain, Daniel. I love you, and we'll sort out my family later."

It was enough for that moment. He bent his head, his lips finding hers. This kiss, given with love and promise, was even better than their first, and he savored every moment. She fit perfectly into his arms, and he dropped his hat to the floor to spread his hands on her back, tightening his embrace.

Chest heaving, he finally broke the kiss, putting his nose into the curls at her temple and inhaling her scent. They had several mountains to climb, but as long as they were together, he felt sure they could accomplish anything. It was time to shed his doubts, doubts about his parentage, his worth, his standing in the eyes of God and man. He had a long way to go to become the man he wished to be, but with Juliette's love, he could conquer any challenge.

A sharp rap on the door jerked him out of the rosy haze.

"I suppose our time is up." He leaned back to look into her beautiful face. Her lips were red from his kisses, and her eyes were North Star bright.

The door opened before he was ready, and they sprang apart. But it wasn't Sir Bertrand who entered.

"There you are, lad." Ed Beck blew on his hands. "Sir Michael sent me to fetch you. We have a new case."

Daniel looked ruefully at Juliette and back to Ed. "I'll come. If you'll wait in the hall?" Where had Bertie gotten off to? Wasn't he supposed to be guarding the door?

Ed seemed to realize he'd intruded on a private moment. "Of course." He bobbed his head and backed out, but not before giving Daniel a questioning, humorous look.

When the door was once again closed, Daniel took Juliette's hands in his, lifting his shoulders in an apologetic shrug. "What do I say?"

She sighed, stood on tiptoe, and kissed his cheek. "You don't need to say anything. Duty calls." A gamine grin lit her face. "I might as well get used to it. Go. Mr. Beck needs you. But be careful. It's a dangerous world out there that needs men like you looking after it."

With a full heart, he retrieved his hat from the floor, paused to take her hand once more, open it palm up, and place a kiss there before folding her fingers to cover it. "I'll think of you every moment."

She laughed and pushed him away playfully. "If you do, you'll be easy prey for whatever villain you're chasing. Keep your mind on business."

He was still laughing when he joined Ed on the steps. "Tell me what you know about the case."

Whatever lay ahead, be it a fight to obtain the title and his inheritance, his job at Bow Street, or a future together with Juliette Thorndike, he was ready.

Author's Note

ONCE AGAIN I MUST BEG the reader's indulgence, as I have accelerated and accentuated the abilities of the Bow Street detectives for the sake of the story, enlarging their parameters beyond the scope of what they would have had at the time the story is set.

I took a fascinating tour, via research books and websites, into the inner workings of gristmills during the Regency. I was also able to tour a gristmill here in Minnesota that was built about forty years after *Millstone of Doubt* takes place, and the docent was able to guide me through the mechanisms and processes of water-powered stone grinding. If you're ever in southeast Minnesota, the Pickwick Mill is worth a look. https://pickwickmill.org.

Hammersmith on the Thames! I decided upon Hammersmith as the setting for the Montgomery gristmill because it met all the qualifications I needed. It is on the river, it is near London, and it even had a legendary ghost. You can read more about the Hammersmith Ghost, the tragedy, and the trial at https://londonist.com/london/features/hammersmith-ghost-story-murder.

The Dove, mentioned in the story, is a real pub, and it's been in Hammersmith since the early eighteenth century. It is rumored that the lyrics for "Rule Britannia" were penned in The Dove in 1740. If you're in Hammersmith, be sure to pop in! https://www.dovehammersmith.co.uk.

Many thanks to author Maria Grace, whose blog *Random Bits of Fascination* was so instructive and informative on the topic of Regency archery. I loved getting to use the word *toxophilite* in this story. https://randombitsoffascination.com/2019/07/16/regency-era-archers/.

Lockewood Hall is a fictional estate in Kent, but the house described in *Millstone of Doubt* is based upon the fabulous Ham House in Richmond, near London. You can learn more about Ham House at https://www.nationaltrust.org.uk/ham-house-and-garden.

As to the succession of titles, I was privileged to take a class given by Isobel Carr on "Inheriting an English Peerage (With a Few Notes on Scottish Ones as Well)" through the Regency Academe at The Beau Monde. If you're a Regency fiction writer, I encourage you to check out The Beau Monde. It's a wonderful resource and community of Regency writers. If you have a research question about the Regency era, someone there will know the answer! https://thebeaumonde.com/main/.

A conspiratorial nod to CJ for the loan of your name for my Italian anarchist and help with a few German words. You were there from the very beginning of this writing journey, and I thank you! And a thank you to Becky Cromwell Cromer for her aid in the Italian translation.

While I'm saying thank you, I'd like to say to Julie Klassen and Michelle Griep. Whether it's your willingness to jump in on whatever my latest harebrained video venture might be, or sharing your vast knowledge of all the history things, or celebrating and commiserating this crazy writing life with me, you are simply the best.

And to all the members of the Inspirational Regency Readers group on Facebook, thank you! Thank you for making the group such a fun place to hang out, for your enthusiastic support of the genre and your favorite authors, and for your encouragement and kind words about our work. www.facebook.com/groups/inspirationalregencyreaders.

Researching the Regency era is fascinating, and there is always something new to learn. Above, I've included just a handful of the websites I've visited in my research, as well as a brief list below of some of the titles I've consulted that might be of interest to you too.

Erica Vetsch
Rochester, Minnesota
2021

Recommended Reading

General Regency History
Laudermilk, Sharon H., and Teresa L. Hamlin. *The Regency Companion.* New York: Garland Publishing Inc., 1989.
Mortimer, Ian. *The Time Traveller's Guide to Regency Britain.* London: The Bodley Head, 2020.
Wilkes, Sue. *A Visitor's Guide to Jane Austen's England.* Barnsley, South Yorkshire: Pen & Sword History, 2014.

Architecture
Girouard, Mark. *A Country House Companion.* New Haven, CT: Yale University Press, 1987.
St. Aubyn, Fiona. *Ackermann's Illustrated London.* Ware, Hertfordshire: Wordsworth Editions, 1985.

Mills and Milling
Macaulay, David. *Mill.* Boston: Houghton Mifflin, 1983.
Yorke, Stan. *Windmills and Waterwheels Explained: Machines That Fed the Nation.* Newbury, Berkshire: Countryside Books, 2006.

Crime and Police
Beattie, J. M. *The First English Detectives: The Bow Street Runners and the Policing of London, 1750–1840.* Oxford: Oxford University Press, 2012.

Fullerton, Susannah. *Jane Austen and Crime.* Madison, WI: Jones Books, 2006.

Hamilton, Joseph. *The Duelling Handbook, 1829.* Mineola, NY: Dover Publications Inc., 2012. First published 1829 by Hatchard & Sons (London).

Richmond [pseud.]. *Richmond: Scenes in the Life of a Bow Street Runner, Drawn up from His Private Memoranda.* With a new introduction by E. F. Bleiler. New York: Dover Publications Inc., 1976. First published 1827 in three volumes by Henry Colburn (London).

Worsley, Lucy. *The Art of the English Murder.* New York: Pegasus Crime, 2014.

THORNDIKE & SWANN
REGENCY MYSTERIES

The
Debutante's
Code

ERICA VETSCH

"Vetsch kicks off her Thorndike and Swann Regency Mysteries with a propulsive tale about a family of spies. . . . [Juliette and Daniel's] slow-burning romance comes together naturally as they navigate the glamorous world of debutantes. Fans of Jen Turano will delight in this pleasing mystery and eagerly await the second installment."

—*Publishers Weekly*

"Carefully crafted Regency mystery. . . . Part of an inherently fascinating new series that combines mystery and suspense with elements of Regency-era elegance, decadence, adventure, and romance."

—*Midwest Book Review*

KREGEL
PUBLICATIONS

Return to Regency England with Erica Vetsch and the Serendipity & Secrets series

"Vetsch's impeccable research and compelling Regency voice have made Serendipity and Secrets one of the strongest offerings in inspirational historical romance in years."

—Rachel McMillan, author of *The London Restoration* and *The Mozart Code*

"I love the way Erica Vetsch creates characters I care about. Get them deep into trouble, and in the end, loyalty, bravery, love, and faith save the day."

—Mary Connealy, author of *Braced for Love*

"Vetsch's rich writing and carefully crafted stories sweep the reader into Regency England with all the delights of this fascinating genre."

—Jan Drexler, award-winning author of *Softly Blows the Bugle*

KREGEL
PUBLICATIONS